MISSING MIDNIGHT

BY REBECCA FOX

The sequel to *Leaping Beauty*

Produced by Softwood Books, Suffolk, UK

Text © Rebecca Fox, 2024

Cover design by Cherie Chapman
Cover images © Shutterstock.com
Illustrations by Sally Parker

First Edition

Paperback ISBN: 978-1-7393561-1-8

www.softwoodbooks.com

www.tinytruths.co.uk

*'What seems to us as bitter trials
are often blessings in disguise.'*

Oscar Wilde

PART I

THE TRAITOR

'There is nothing I would not do for those
who are really my friends.'

Jane Austen

PART I

THE TRAITOR

1

THE BOUNTY HUNTER

For the first time in years, Red Felian had slept without her fists clenched or her mind tight. She'd woken with the shock of someone who has been in the deep well of sleep, acutely aware that they might never get out. She had opened her eyes to find she was no longer in the palace. No longer in her small turret room at Paloma, no longer in the North Realm with Julia purring at the bottom of her bed. No, she was staying at a travellers inn called The Cat's Back. That was it, she remembered now, she was in Alba, the capital city of the East Realm. The princess smiled. *At last*, she thought and, *about time. I'm free, on my own quest! Well, sort of ...* Her ankle was no longer held by the tight clasp of voodoo. Her ankle and the rest of her felt lighter without the vice of teeth. Apart from a polite throb, it seemed to be healing well. Red wanted to go outside, see her horse, and tell some people how good she was feeling. For once in her young life, she *actually* wanted to go to a party rather than leave early pretending she had contracted an extremely contagious form of pox.

She asked the pleasant, beamy room in a clear voice, 'Where is everyone?', eager to see her new friends again. Red sat up and said suddenly, 'I have friends now!'

A curious tap answered at the window, but when she hobbled over to look, there was no one there. The sky appeared in the throes of night – the clock on the mantelpiece said five minutes to midnight. 'The witching hour,' Red whispered dramatically to a portrait of a large pig above the mantelpiece.

How long had she been asleep? The city of Alba was not a view she was accustomed to. Red cautiously opened the window and took a deep breath of smoky, dank air. She gazed at the silver rooftops and the moon and inhaled an exciting cocktail of drains and recently put out fires. She looked down at her feet, enjoying the absence of the cold, dark hex and was relieved to see all her toes were still there. Yawning happily, Red walked back to her bed and stretched. She ached after the strain of the last few days, but it was very warm with the fire and the extra blankets on her bed. Unable to settle, she returned to window and took in another breath of city air. Outside, there were still a few glowing lights in several windows the other side of the alley and beyond them a silver sea of countless twisting chimneys and rooftops. The flags of the citadel fluttered enticingly back at her from the highest point of Alba.

The princess was now wide awake and eager to find out what went on late at night in this Landfelian city. It beckoned her. Red wanted to look around, do a little dance, and generally get down before the sun came up and she had breakfast. Understandable for a young and recently palace-bound princess. Seven years is a long time to look upon only one rose garden and contemplate where the hell her parents had gone. Soon she would have to consider her journey and the least dangerous way to reach her godparents. One of them had to know something of her father or mother's whereabouts. And then she would continue her search. It was clear, from what little Red had seen of the kingdom, that the throne needed someone to sit on it. And she knew her parents were still alive; she could not explain how, but she knew it to be true.

Below the high walled garden of The Cat's Back, Red could see where her valien and Robbie's mare were asleep, leaning against an ancient sycamore like old friends. The sound of a woman's mysterious laughter lilted up from the dark somewhere, alongside some faint folksy music. Landfelians would call the princess' current feeling 'wanderlust', although amongst the peasants, the more common expression was, 'She wants to ride on a white horse'. Either way, Red's boots were back on and she was lacing them up. What harm would it do?

11

There was no one about, only bats and toast-sellers. It would not take long to walk around the old, interesting part of the city. She would wrap herself up, cover her hair, and take in some history. She looked around the room, feeling uncertain. There was a jug on the table next to her bed and beside it a note from the Man of the Road.

Red smiled. She felt something inside her somersault, and then her stomach rumbled hopefully. She drank the milk Robbie had left for her. It was still warm and sweetened with nutmeg and honey. Her father's coat was folded – clean and dry – on a chair near the fireplace, with another note.

Milady,
You may stay as long as you need.
We don't advise you wear this coat until you're out of Alba.
Good luck on the rest of your journey.
It's been an honour to have you.
You have our vote and our help should you ever need it.
Laura and Timothy Dibbles – Keepers of The Cat's Back

Downstairs, Red found Amber asleep by the window, and the inn's large hairy cat on her lap. He opened one eye yawned and flicked his tail lazily at the young woman with the auburn hair stuffed hastily into a Man of the Road's hat.

She stepped quietly towards the door, wrapping herself in a large grey shawl draped over one of the chairs. 'I'll be back before dawn.' Red winked at the cat, whose name was Naps, he blinked slowly at her.

The street outside, Dead End, dripped and shone. Large puddles formed deep pools in the gaps between the cobbles. Red shivered and took a nervous breath. 'Here we go,' she whispered, heading towards the House of Gold. 'I am doing nothing wrong,' she told herself, joyfully unfolding her map. 'Just a quick look at the sights.'

An easy twenty-minute walk from Dead End, by the water's edge, a sign on weathered door read:

MARLENE'S SOUP KITCHEN
OPEN ALL NIGHT
NO ACTORS

The kitchen shack rested on wooden stumps and had a tin roof. Inside, Marlene served the best kind of street food the city of Alba had to offer: greasy parcels of ringed stotties, warm and crunchy with sugar. The tea and coffee were free, the bread was thick and fried, and the eggs runny – although Marlene's regulars mostly went there for the spicy tomato soup and the fish pie. It was the only place in the whole kingdom known to serve brown sauce, and it was delicious with fish pie. Marlene had in fact invented brown sauce by accident in a fierce rage after she'd overheard a foreign merchant comment on the lack of seasoning in her food.

'I'll give you seasoning!' she'd muttered, storming into her tiny steaming kitchen under a tarpaulin supported by four stakes. There, like a witch, she'd thrown a mixture of vinegar, sugar, salt, lea, perrins, tab, asco, raisons, and some other brown things into a mortar and pestled the life out of them. She tipped the sludge into a pot, added a drop of water … and it turned out to be a real winner; Marlene's brown sauce went with everything! The merchant returned to the country of Fronze abashed.

Tonight, her soup kitchen was full. It was Sunday, and every sea-scarred, Landfelian fisherman with the night off sat quietly staring out at the dark water lapping against the bay. Folk came here to eat alone and listen to the murmur of other weather-beaten souls and the slap of the waves.

William English, a mostly-out-of-work actor (trying to hide his face from Marlene behind a ragged, scarlet silk scarf), and Robbie Wylde, an often-homeless Man of the Road, were also looking out at the oily water. The two men were sitting opposite one another at a table next to a fogged-up window and having a man-to-man chat. This was unusual as they had only been introduced a couple of hours prior to this moment. Even more unusual, their first meeting had included rescuing the recently escaped and only remaining heir to the kingdom from an unpleasant case of bewitched voodoo. Not the evening game of cards with a coffee as they might have imagined. Although it had only been a short time, Will now considered Robbie to be one of his greatest friends. Like I said, William was an actor.

'You would have made a great performer, you know, Robin.'

'It's Robbie.'

'You are meant for the stage … So much intensity and silent strength.' Will leant back, regarded at his new friend, and sighed. 'Woman! Another bottle of wine?'

'Bring your own! Filthy actor,' came Marlene's reply.

Robbie stopped tapping his glass and looked distractedly around him as the door banged shut in the wind. It must be close to midnight. Soon he would have to go and meet the son of a lawyer, Daniel Blackwood. He turned back to the table and observed the man before him, marvelling at how he had ended up in such unlikely company. William English wore a blousy frock shirt, and a ratty floor-length velvet coat that flapped pleasingly about him in a strong wind. He wore his collar up and spoke with an unlit pipe hanging from the side of his mouth. He seemed to like the worldly effect it added to his general appearance. Although his general appearance to Robbie was that of a ropey player.

'I think I'll stick to being a Man of the Road.'

'Yes, probably best, you're too tense,' Will went on. 'You see, to live an acting life, one has to bend like the willow.'

'Tense? I'm not tense.' Robbie dropped his shoulders.

'I'm afraid so, Roberto. Too tense to be a professional player like me. Something is clearly on your mind. Tell me; a problem shared and all that.' Will leant forward, his brown eyes twinkling, he took the pipe out of his mouth, and grinned.

'Listen, Winifred, my name is Robbie. If you call me anything else, I will remove that pipe of yours and break your nose, and I suspect noses are quite important in your line of work.'

'But you could do amateur work or panto, no problem.' Will chewed on a crust of bread left on the table and smiled. 'The ladies and children would love you. However, I am in no doubt ...' He dropped his voice to an obvious whisper. 'A certain royal will reward you amply for escorting her away from those terrible pretenders up at Paloma and through this slum of a city to safety.' Will put his hands behind his head and whistled, becoming more punch-able by the second. His right eye was already puffy where Robbie had hit him last. The lovely thing about William English was his belief in the good in everyone even after a beating. 'Robert Wylde. It is a fine name! You can tell a lot from a name. I always wanted something double-barrelled myself, at least one hyphen, but my mentor Sir Rodney insisted. "Truth, Will," he said to me. "Truth is the most powerful thing."'

Robbie had stopped listening. Whoever Sir Rodney was, he needed a good punch too. The faint orange lanterns of fishing boats blinked back at them from far out at sea. The night was cold and damp, the stars sickly through the city smog. It began to drizzle. He wanted to be far away on board one of those boats, heading into uncharted waters. Heading anywhere away from Landfelian, where there would be new mountains to roam, orange winds that smelt of strange spices, and places where he could forget his past. At least, that was all Robbie had wanted for as long as he had been on the road. But in the last week, something had changed. A part of him wanted to stay and see what path Red Felian, the Questing Princess, would take. From the moment Robbie had run into the last heir of Landfelian, his world had turned upside down. And now he only wanted to be a part of her rebellion-blazing trail. Although there was one small problem...

He had agreed to meet Daniel Blackwood, the notoriously corrupt son of a lawyer and handover the secret hideout of the princess. It was a mistake to sign up to the bounty hunt and involve himself with that rat. He would find another way to make his fortune without deceiving the young heir. And there was the arrival of the fog; a fog Robbie had encountered only once before when he was a boy. A fog that had orphaned him, and now, whether he liked it or not, he could not leave Landfelian without finding out who was behind it.

Will was still looking eagerly at him. 'Tell me about them.'

'Who?' Robbie dragged his gaze away from the grimy window and looked at his companion.

'The ladies and gentlemen of great esteem you've helped on the road; the Quest families.'

'There are many, in every realm.'

Will flicked over Robbie's calling card thoughtfully. 'At Your Service, Milady ... It's quite brilliant.' He clapped his hands. 'Soft! I have a crowd-pleasing notion – Amber and I will join you on the road. I will provide sonnets and comedy for these lonesome families you cater for and Amber can sing.

You stick to the cooking and mending. We will make double the gold in tips and brighten up their drawing rooms a bit. What do you think? A travelling company of song, verse, and domestic help, if you will.'

'No,' Robbie said. 'And absolutely no.'

'Don't rush. Take a few days, mull it over.' Will said thoughtfully. 'It will be hard returning to the day job after the last week. By Jove, what adventures!' Will washed glasses and mopped the privy at the Cat's Back Inn when he wasn't acting. His face turned dreamy. 'I will never forget the last week – the ball, the waterfall, the giants, and meeting that courageous young ...'

'There is no gold to be made in Landfelian anymore.' Robbie lay his hands on the table and smiled kindly at Will. 'This little kingdom is breaking apart and ready for a hostile takeover. You would be wise to leave and head north.'

'Do you think so?' Will looked at his empty glass and dropped his voice to a very stagey whisper. 'Yes! Amber and I must get out of this lawless pit.' He looked out at the tired city. 'It's too dangerous for us to stay here now. That son of a lawyer's guards won't look kindly on our part in ...' He looked around cagily. 'You-know-who's escape.'

Robbie stood up quite suddenly at the mention of Daniel Blackwood. 'I must go. What is the time?'

Will frowned. 'What is it, brother? You look a bit peaky. Tell me, we are practically family after all. Have you got a meeting with a voodoo-seller later? What is the rush?

Who can you possibly be seeing this late?' Will fumbled for his pocket watch and lowered his voice. 'It's not far off midnight. I have a notion: buy us both a brandy for the road. Our work for the princess is done; she can go on her merry way. We've got ourselves a good reference and a ruby!'

Will waved at Marlene and pointed meaningfully to his empty glass, which she ignored. 'I wonder where she will go next. Does anyone have the faintest idea? Clever girl keeps it to herself – but she's determined to find the king. I hope she makes a detour to the Lake of Stars. It's the festival in a few days. It would do her the world of good to let go, hang loose, take a ride on a swan boat, eat some mooncakes, samba ...' Will dropped his voice even lower. 'And the guards won't go to Lake Country. They're superstitious about it you know.'

Robbie asked Marlene for the bill and if she could slap Will again.

She sighed, looking down at the actor with her hands on her hips. 'I've told him to stay away, but he keeps showing up.'

'Good woman,' drawled Will with a debonair smile. 'I couldn't do without you or your brown sauce.'

Marlene slapped him with a dirty cloth, and several men jeered. 'If you don't pay me this time, William English, you can stand outside with the menu board and earn your fish pie.'

Will wiped his chin and watched her substantial bottom swing away. 'Strong as a sow.' He fumbled in his flappy coat for some coins, which weren't there. 'Time is time, Robbie

Wylde. What is the urgency? It will pass whether we ask it to or not. Time is a harlot like that. How about a nightcap and a bag of peppermint creams down at the docks? Or is there a lady you must meet at midnight?'

Will looked up and smiled to find Robbie was no longer there. A cold draught whistled passed him as the door slammed shut again. He turned to the window.

'Did anyone see where that Man of the Road went?'

'You're not leaving, English,' Marlene stood in front of the door, her ample shadow eclipsing their table, 'until you find some gold in that grubby coat of yours.'

Outside, something chittered, and Will heard a tap on the dripping window. 'What in the world is that.' He peered out, horrified at the creature he saw hovering. 'Don't fret, Marlene, I will settle up as soon as I have squashed the grotesque flying spider outside your window.' He fumbled around in both pockets. 'What a sinister looking beast. Must have been brought in with the Long Wind. So long, dear lady.' He made a run for the door and bounded out into the cold before anything could be thrown.

Will wove his way back to The Cat's Neck — no, The Cat's Claw — oh, arse it, where did he live? After three hours of washing up dirty dishes at Marlene's, he'd shared a drink with a gentleman who distilled his own gin and had emerged a few hours before daybreak.

He walked in the manner of a man confidently drunk and not about to ask for directions.

'I must return to Amber.' It was uphill all the way to the citadel. A breeze flicked off a piece of parchment that had been shabbily and recently stuck to a wall. It landed on his chest like a stamp. 'Well, hello there, my papery friend. What manner of prose are you? No doubt another advertisement to join Blackwood's Guards.' He passed an unfocused eye over it.

There had been a noticeable recruitment drive recently, with flyers licking every lamppost. They were urging peasants to enlist, boasting new opportunities in somewhere called Mirador, a new kingdom, south of Landfelian, where drum, boots, and a clean record would be provided in return for labour.

Will tried to focus on the poster and fell over. It was not a call to arms for Blackwood's Guards, it was a *Wanted* poster. A *Wanted* poster with a substantial bounty.

'Oh good, I hope it's for Claude,' he said, trying to read the bouncing writing.

Claude was a mime artist known for picking pockets and booing whenever Will performed in his patch of the city. But the poster was not for Claude.

It was for Will and all he held dear.

He studied it closely. There was a drawing of him, Amber, Ophelia, Marilyn, the princess, and the tapestry, standing in height order and looking startled.

'No ...' He looked up and down the wet street. '*I* am a wanted man?' There was no one about. He looked at the unflattering picture again and said, 'I have more hair than that!'

21

But marvellous fame had found him at last. The part Will found difficult to swallow were the words beneath their names, in official-looking ink.

1000 GOLD PIECES EACH
WANTED ALIVE OR INJURED
ANY INFORMANTS WILL BE GRATEFULLY RECEIVED
AND GENEROUSLY REWARDED BY THE HEAD OF
ROYAL SECURITY, DANIEL BLACKWOOD,
AT HIS TEMPORARY RESIDENCE IN
THE HOG'S BREATH CAFE, VIPER STREET.

'Holy hell! One thousand gold pieces! I must tell Amber.' He struggled to get up. 'First, I must tread carefully along these cobbles and find some form of disguise.'

Will found little to help him by the wall where he stood, but it did not deter him from asking a passing rat if he could borrow a hat.

Red took a right turn; there was no left, it was a dead end, and she would have looked stupid if she had persisted left. She made her way past a very narrow alley that ran between The Cat's Back and an old, ruined merchant house. There was a curtain of ivy at the end that concealed the door to the garden where her horse was tethered. Two once-empty whisky barrels blocked the entrance of the alley from the street. The smell suggested they had filled up with putrid water and dead things.

A fire escape – a wooden one – ran up the wall of The Cat's Back to the window of the attic room. Red knew this to be Amber's room where Robbie had taken his bath. This thought made her feel warm and nervous at the same time. She doubted he was inside and frowned, wondering what nocturnal errands a young Man of the Road had to make at this hour. And then she heard him. It came as a shock to suddenly hear the voice of the person she had been imagining in a bath only a few feet away, behind some barrels. Red jumped back, her heart beating hard, and splayed herself against the wall. Robbie spoke again, but not to her.

'How long have you been in the voodoo business?'

'Studying the law opens many doors.' The gentleman with him had a drawling, nasally voice. It sounded so like – Red turned cold. No. It was unmistakable.

'That's an expensive-looking cane. It must pay well,' Robbie answered.

'Do you want your bounty, Mr Wylde, or do you want your throat slit? If you have the princess, I suggest you tell me where. If you refuse, I will show you one of the many uses of my cane.'

Red took such a large breath she nearly sucked in and swallowed a leathery insect treading the air above her head. It chittered unpleasantly. She gasped at it, not hearing Robbie's reply, and ducked behind the barrels. Red swatted at the creature wildly with his hat. It was hard to think, to stay calm, and not pick up the first piece of rotting mouse or ladle of bin

23

juice and hurl it at the deceiving scoundrel's head. The lovely leaping thing that had taken residence inside her stomach during the last few days she'd spent with Robbie Wylde vanished, and Red felt something in her close down. She had forgotten for a brief spell that she was alone in this quest and would continue so.

2

CLOAK AND DAGGER

'The liar. The bounty-hunting, fortune-seeking, jerkin-lending LIAR!' The matter of her high birth did not stop the princess slagging him off to the nearest rat she saw though. She said all this at a whisper – a very upset one – while crouched behind the bins in Robbie's hat.

She told herself to get away from the stinking alley fast. With Daniel Blackwood in the citadel, sightseeing was no longer an option; Alba had turned into another place she had to escape. She crept back along Dead End and hurried into The Cat's Back to wake Amber.

'The snivelling, slug-slimed, bogey-arsed bandit!' Amber said with gusto.

Red realised she could learn a lot from Amber's catalogue of abuse after she'd told her what she'd heard in the alley. They were sitting behind a large mahogany cabinet, out of sight of the windows, having locked the doors. They were whispering urgently.

'Were there any guards with him?' Amber asked.

'I don't think so. There wouldn't have been room for anyone else.'

'It is a very narrow alley.' Amber's face looked pale in the dim light. In all the years she had lived there, Daniel Blackwood had never found Dead End. And now he was here. He must have had help, spies of some sort working for him.

Red watched her carefully. 'Do you know of him?'

Amber pulled a face. 'Monsieur Blackwood? Yes.' Naps crawled onto her lap. 'A long time ago, I fell for the charms of that son of a lawyer.'

'How?' Red was flabbergasted.

'I was young.' She shook her head. 'He wasn't *as* bad then. It's a long devils' spoon of a story and we haven't the time. You must get out of the city while his guards are drunk and the Alba patrol is asleep.' She glanced at the curtains. 'It will be light soon.'

Red felt tired and her ankle ached quietly. 'I should have known not to trust a Man of the Road.' She rubbed her eyes. 'I thought we were friends.'

'It's not like Robbie,' said Amber quietly, squeezing Red's hand. 'Did you see him accept the bounty?'

'No, but he must have led Daniel Blackwood right to The Cat's Back.' Red removed Robbie's hat and gave it to the inn's cat. 'Here Naps, take this and pee on it.' She tried to think sensibly, but it felt like someone had just sat on her childhood den and ripped the map out of her favourite book.

Amber patted her knee and wondered if there was time for tea. 'Robbie loathes Blackwood's guards. He would never voluntarily side with them. Unless he was truly desperate for gold …' She rubbed the mark on her left finger again, and Red wondered what it was. 'Or in some kind of trouble.'

'I'll leave now.' Red looked at the front door. 'I need a disguise and a back door. I need to collect my horse without being seen. He's in the garden.' Her hands shook. 'Waiting for me.' All that mattered was getting to her godparents, finding out what had happened to her parents, and putting at least one of them back on the throne. That was the plan, she reminded herself. *Do not deviate.* If anyone had news of the royal quest, her godparents would. They were the nearest thing she had to family now. Red just hoped they still wanted to see her. In all the years up at Paloma, neither one had come to visit or written a letter. She swallowed and looked at Amber. 'I'm glad I met you.'

The sound of snoring interrupted them. 'Who else is in here?' Red looked around her.

The large, dark room appeared empty. The snoring persisted.

Amber looked relieved. 'Oh, don't worry, it's just Will. He's the most dreadful snorer.'

Will was very close, far closer than they expected, in

27

fact. He was under the grand piano next to the corner dedicated to romance novels. After discovering the *Wanted* poster, he had crawled up to the Cat's Back from the docks and found the fire escape to Amber's window. Discovering she was not in bed; he'd slid quietly down the stairs and come to rest under the piano in the music room.

(The last bottle drunk had been a mistake; the label said *RAM*, not *RUM*, which should have told Will all he needed to know of its quality. But the fake moustache he'd purchased from the hair dealer on Fortune Lane had proved a triumph, and he'd managed to tear down twenty-seven *Wanted* posters on his way home and draw false noses on another eleven.)

The two ladies behind the cabinet ignored him for the moment. 'You're right, the next disguise needs to be a winner or you're toast,' Amber told the princess. Toast torture was not commonplace in Landfelian, although the process of slowly burning things was declared painful and effective. 'But don't worry, there is one woman I know who will help … if she's still in the cloak and dagger business.'

'The fairy godmother?' Red looked into Amber's eyes and smiled with a hopefulness that would break your heart. She had heard there was one about somewhere in Landfelian, although, like Father Christmas, no one truly knew for certain.

'Fran? She retired years ago. No. Better. This lady transformed Will into Blanche du Bon Bon for your ball.' Amber looked at the princess and smiled a smile you would only see on a woman who had recently purchased a pair of bright red bloomers. 'She's the queen of makeovers. Will knows where to find her. She's very secretive about her work.' Amber's eyes shone with excitement.

The actor was now flat on his back and snoring with commitment. Amber stooped over him. The odour coming off Will was eye-watering. She gathered a large bucket of cold water and, with a mighty heave, threw it over his head.

'Man overboard!' he bellowed, sitting up and hitting his head on the piano. 'OUCH BISCUITS!'

There was a sudden duet of female whispering around him.

'Shush! Over here! Quick. We need you!'

It took three seconds for Will to get to Amber's side.

'I love y–'

'Shut up and listen, William.' She sniffed and made a face. 'We are all in a lot of trouble. Sweet daisies, have you been at The Hog's Breath?'

'No, Marlene's first and then the gutter I think. Hello, milady.' He smiled blearily and tried to doff his cap at Red.

'Hello,' Red smiled. She couldn't help but like the actor. He reminded her of a labrador she'd once had called Waggy.

'I had something to tell you. What was it?' He began to rifle around in his long, flappy coat. 'It was right here, I had it. Now, where the devil …? Oh yes, here it is, in my sock, safe as houses.'

It is very difficult to lose something in a sock. Will used them to store all his valuables. He handed Red the *Wanted* poster and tried to put his arm around Amber.

'We're famous, my love!' He grinned. 'At last.'

Amber snatched it and stared at the bounty hunting poster for a moment before saying, 'But I don't have a moustache.'

Will tapped his nose with great cunning. 'You do now, my sweet.'

Amber scowled. Whatever land or time you live in, it is unwise to bring up facial hair with women.

'We need more than a fake moustache to disappear, Will,' she said tartly. 'We need Tall Sal to disguise us so we can get out of here.' Amber waved the poster. 'Do you know where she is?'

'Last I heard, Sal was more into the counterfeit stuff.' He scratched his head. 'You know, fake papers, permits for crossing realm borders, that kind of thing.'

'She bent her rules for the Blanche du Bon Bon disguise …' Amber said.

'True. I believe she's still working out of the old coliseum,' Will whispered.

'Whoever this woman is …' Red was running out of time. She glanced at the window as a shadow passed behind it. 'I need her help getting out of the city.' She tried to look brave. 'There's no time for breakfast now. Can you tell me how to reach her?'

'Certainly not!' They both looked at the princess aghast, and Will smiled. 'We are going with you. Do not fear, milady.

Tall Sal is the best costumier in the land. She could turn you into a bilberry if you found a bush big enough. Let's go!'

Daniel Blackwood stood back and tried to put his finger on what was unusual about the bounty hunter. There were faint alarm bells ringing at the back of his mind, and he didn't know why. They had never met, of course. The son of a lawyer did not have friends, and if he did, he would not have associated himself with a homeless cook of low birth. Yet somehow the man was familiar. Was it the knives? His unkempt hair? No, something Selina Carnal had said, warning him of a marked man. Whatever it was, he could not make a stab at it. This young wanderer did not seem especially marked in any way – other than the fact that he was dirty.

'It is a shame we do not see eye to eye. You could have been rich.' Daniel Blackwood bent over Robbie and blew a worm of putrid smoke in his face. His cane had done the trick, as the young peasant was now unable to stand. 'You must understand, I only want to protect the princess from a worse fate. She would not survive long in this stinking hole.' He gestured at the soot-blackened walls. 'I don't fancy her chances with the citizens of Alba. Not now.'

'I do,' Robbie said through gritted teeth. 'Watch your back, Blackwood. Red Felian is on the loose and she's gathering a rebellion.'

Daniel kicked him in the stomach and lit another cheroot. 'The princess is young and helpless. Nothing but a worm for the witch.'

'Witch?' Robbie winced. 'What witch?' he asked, trying to delay Daniel from continuing his search.

'Yes, a great shadow is spreading.' Daniel sneered. 'A little worm is all the witch needs now.'

Robbie did not know what worms had to do with anything, although he did know a disturbed son of a lawyer when he met one. 'I don't know where the princess is. She slipped away when we were camping in the woods. You can keep your bounty. I want no part of it.'

'Very bold.' Daniel hissed and pressed the point of his cane further into Robbie's chest, which hurt a lot. 'Tell me and I will give you double the gold and the feeling back in your legs.'

'The king will hear of this.' Robbie shook his head and smiled. He was not at all sure the king would, yet in that moment, he hoped so, for Red's sake more than anything. 'And he will return and put you, this witch, and all your guards on the first ship bound for Mosquito Dench.'

Daniel's laugh filled the narrow alley. 'The king, you ill-dressed pock of a man, is lost. If he does return, do you honestly think he would listen to a travelling tick like you? I'll find the princess and leave you here for the rats.'

Daniel vanished from the alley with a stab of his cane and a flick of his cheroot. Just as Red, Will, and a valien squeezed through a hidden back door, he emerged onto Dead End, stopping short next to a rotting ladder. He looked closely at it and picked up a fine thread of red hair hanging there.

Sniffing it, like a man possessed, Daniel smiled up at the wall of a large house as if seeing it for the first time. A sign creaked above the door in the shape of a large black cat arching its back.

'And what have we here?' he said.

He rapped on the door of the sprawling merchant house with his cane. Some men collected umbrellas, Daniel preferred canes. Wonderfully stylish things. His favourite had a spiked point, which could be dipped in a strong opiate and used to temporarily paralyse his victims until they agreed to the terms of his contract. Swords were too obvious and cumbersome. A simple ebony cane could contain a multitude of sins. Daniel's current one had a silver top sculpted into a rat's head.

He rapped on the door again, but there was no answer. The door was locked. He returned to the ladder and began to climb. Behind him, Daniel heard the fold and snap of wings.

'Lidia.' He sighed and turned around to find the strange girl there. 'How lovely to find you here.'

'She's gone,' Lidia hissed. 'You're too late.'

Lidia was in a foul mood; the rain had made her surveillance of Alba difficult, and she had just found one of her swarm squashed flat against the wall by the bins. Every death caused her a tiny pain, a pain felt by every spiderling. The one thing that had not changed in Landfelian was the rain. It was stubborn like that. It came when it darn well wanted to, it was chubby, and everyone enjoyed moaning about it.

'The singer,' she continued. 'The princess was talking to her. That was the last I heard. She'll know something.'

'Amber Morningstar. Excellent.' Daniel's teeth shone in the moonlight. 'This won't take long.' He spun around, a mean glint in his eyes, and started the climb up to the attic room with the yellow curtains …

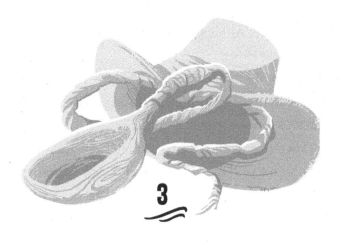

3

ALBA'S COBBLES

Tall Sal's costume shop, Escapade, conducted its business in another rather large attic. The coliseum, like many great houses of culture, had fallen from favour when the queen vanished. For a brief season it opened its doors as a venue for the city's more obscure performing arts, but after a risqué run of a puppet show entitled 'Butch and Julie', the artistic director was banished to Hardplace Prison in an area of Landfelian called the Goby. As a result, the coliseum had not opened its brass doors or lit its flaming torches for seven years. Funding for the arts had run dry. The Half Queen, Caroline, and King Gerald were only interested in throwing extravagant and excessive balls at Paloma Palace. Although now, there was no gold left in the coffers for those either.

Up in the rafters was Sal's home. The top floor had generous ceilings for a lady of height, and generous ceilings were hard to find in most parts of Alba's citadel where concussion due to low lying beams was commonplace. This remarkable lady had begun working at the coliseum as a seamstress when she was fifteen years old and never left. She was the same age as the lost queen and a once upon a time had designed her wedding dress, which went down a storm.

Sal was a naturally solitary woman, as solitary as one can be in a theatre. But like the best solitary people, she was happiest doing what she loved, which, in her case, was sewing feathers onto the sleeves of dancers. Sal had once shared her lodgings with a giantess – a talented performer with a quiet temperament much like her own. The giantess had stayed for only a few months, and then one day a well-tailored man in black arrived and persuaded her to travel with him; apparently, there was an exciting opportunity in the North Realm working for the guardians of the throne. Sal hadn't been able to convince the giantess to stay. In the end, she had wished her luck and waved her away with a sense of foreboding.

'I am not convinced by that gentleman,' Lyndon, the stage door man, had muttered the night the giantess left. He and Sal often shared a pot of coffee and a flapjack in the evenings.

'I agree, Lyndon. Something about his eyes?' she had replied. 'And his smell, it's too metallic.'

The stage door man sniffed. 'A son of a lawyer is a son of a lawyer, no matter which end you look through it. And that one's father was a bad sort.'

Lyndon manned the stage door every night, even though the building was now closed to the public. He had nowhere else to go. He sat behind a little desk, sweeping the stage, brushing down the velvet seats, and enjoying his daily gossip with the tall costumier. Until the coliseum opened its doors once again.

When Blackwood's Guards had arrived in Alba shortly after the king left on his quest, seamstress Sal became a revolutionary overnight. The attic turned into an office for a less lucrative business: counterfeit permits and forgery. Lyndon and Sal helped those in need find a way out of the city without attracting the attention of the corrupt guards. She shared the city's news with her oldest friend Richard Losley, the king's herald, by placing hidden messages in the personals of the *Palace Times*, to which he would reply when able. His calligraphy skills were second to none, and she wished he would leave Paloma and help her with the more intricate parts of her business. So many more Landfelians needed help escaping Alba – and a worrying number of young were disappearing south to be part of some promising new kingdom called Mirador …

Sal refused to leave the coliseum herself unless it was to celebrate the return of the king or in a six-foot-three coffin. Daniel Blackwood soon forgot about the batty costumier living with the pigeons in the rafters of a derelict theatre; his gaze was too focused on the palace of Paloma where Red Felian remained imprisoned. Until nearly a week ago …

It was now Monday night and Sal was painting buttons and enjoying a boiled egg, while across the square, a few streets away, Daniel Blackwood climbed into the window of The Cat's Back.

In a cobbled square, the coliseum left little room for any other buildings. It stood high up on the hill of the citadel, stained by the soot that blew up from the smoking slums below. A thick layer of ash had gathered all around the building, muffling the sound of people's footsteps. Will and Red reached the stage door as dawn light shone upon its boarded windows.

The princess stared up at the opera house in wonder. Beneath the grime lay the softest limestone, semi-precious stones adorned the crowned nymphs that danced around the top of the building. Despite needing a good hosing down and a reason to light the torches, there was an undeniable majesty about the place. The excitement of opening nights had never quite left the square. That and the graceful trunks of lime trees that led up to the front entrance. Red would love to return in happier times and watch a performance – her mother had taken her to see her first orchestra here and she had never forgotten the sound of the musicians tuning up. They left the valien behind an old billboard; Red told Face to lie down and stay hidden. 'I won't be long.' She covered him in old newspapers. 'Just try your best to look old and diseased.'

Amber remained at The Cat's Back to keep guard and hit Robbie over the head with a frying pan if he returned. She put a *CLOSED DUE TO PLAGUE* sign in the window once the princess left, packed a bag, and tried not to worry. Daniel Blackwood could find her in a sewer if his mind was bent on it, but up until now, his mind had been filled with a more royal distraction. As she opened the door of her room to leave, cold air whistled in through the broken window and cheroot smoke choked her scream. Amber knew then she should have gone with Will and the princess when she had the chance.

Red waited nervously behind Will as he knocked three times on the stage door of the coliseum, a less grand entrance tucked on the side of the building. A burly voice bellowed back,

'Who's there?'

'William English.'

'Password!'

'Oh, for goodness sake, Lyndon, you know I never remember.'

'Go on, have a bash at it.'

'Curtains?'

'Nope.'

'Macbeth.'

'Mac who?' The voice grunted. 'Fancy word, three syllables, begins with O.'

'Overture.' Red suggested quietly to Will.

'You're in!' Lyndon shouted, and the door creaked open,

showing a small, portly man with a beaming smile. He was holding a club. 'Clever girl.'

'Allo, princess,' he said gruffly, turning a little pink and bowing his head. 'We heard you were on the loose. It's an honour.' Lyndon stepped out the way and gestured for Red and Will to come inside the dimly lit hall.

'Dear Lyndon, is Tall Sal in?'

'Of course she's in. Follow me.' Lyndon glanced outside before closing and locking the stage door behind them. 'We hoped you'd show up.'

Tall Sal honey coloured hair wafted out of a loose bun, it was beginning to go grey. She had a long, almost sombre face and yet her eyes shone bright and knowing. Red noticed she was wearing gentleman's slippers.

'It's hard to find a shoe big enough.' Sal looked at her feet and then at the princess. 'It's wonderful to have you here, my dear, you are always welcome in this theatre.' She smiled kindly. 'Come, both of you, I've made coffee.'

The attic was lit with candles and covered in colourful drapes and rugs; one false move and the place would go up in smoke. It was miraculous that Sal had survived all these years. 'Some people were just not meant to be burnt alive in attics.' She said reading Red's mind. 'Do you know, once, a long time ago, your mother came up here and together we tried to wrangle a rather stiff, antique wedding dress into something a little more exciting.' Sal smiled at the memory.

'I had no idea.' Red stared around her.

'Yes, yes, she was very like you.' Sal looked kindly at the princess, handing her a cup of creamy coffee.

Red braced herself for the tearful reminder, of how she resembled the lost queen, but the costumier simply said, 'She danced to her own drum your mother, as you are doing right now.'

Red looked up and felt relief, and her shoulders dropped an inch. She took a thankful sip of the steaming cup and sat down on a chaise longue covered in various garments.

'Now.' Sal clapped and perched on a high stool. 'Do excuse the mess. What can I do you two rebels for?'

Will stood up and took the folded up WANTED poster out of his coat pocket. 'Allow me to explain.' He handed it to Sal.

'I see,' the costumier said after a moment, and she blew her hair out of her eyes. 'So, you need to disappear from this city without being seen. Well.' She smiled. 'You've come to the right place.'

Several more cups of coffee later, Tall Sal stood back and admired her handiwork.

'Not bad. I surprise myself sometimes. Amidst all these moth-eaten costumes, there's always something to be found with a bit of razzle dazzle.' She looked at Will. 'I found a whole trunk of the most fabulous tights the other day under an old backcloth for Arabian Nights.'

Sal sucked on the end of a measuring tape that hung around her neck and looked about for her cup. She drank between six and eight cups a day; they lay half-drunk and gathering dust all over her work room.

'Turn around, my dear. How does it all feel?' She looked encouragingly at Red.

Red fiddled nervously with a tassel hanging from her waist. 'I'm not sure. Do you think it's bland enough?'

Will admired the carriage-stopping merchant lady standing in the middle of the room. 'Sal, you are a miracle, a walking wonder. I shall kiss your dusty, slippered feet.'

Sal wrinkled her nose. 'You need a wash, William. Did the do at the palace go well? And the grapefruits work okay? I don't suppose I'll be seeing those again.'

'I'm afraid we lost the citrus fruit and much of the disguise to a spectacular waterfall.' Will had the good grace to look crestfallen. 'But the ball was fantastic.'

'Naturally.' Sal raised an eyebrow. 'Did you meet any giants?'

'A whole village of them, and we saved the giantess Ophelia from a life of confinement. It was marvellous! They sleep in teepees, you know, and have an amphitheatre of godly proportions. No other disguise would have cut it. Blanche du Bon Bon of the South Tequeetahs stormed Paloma, and the half-king was particularly taken. I don't suppose you could create two more ensembles before lunchtime. Amber and I need to disappear for a few months. We are wanted criminals.' He grinned proudly and looked at the poster again.

'I know, your faces are stuck up everywhere. What

did you have in mind?' Sal glided about her workroom, lifting various costumes off pegs and mirrors.

'Something inconspicuous.'

'You mean drab.' Sal collapsed onto an armchair, which released a gentle puff of dust. She crossed her long legs and looked about her attic for inspiration. 'Oh dear. Let me see. It will be hard. Everyone wants drab these days to escape the guards. This is a theatre – the costumes here were not made to be quiet, and both Amber and this young lady are rather eye-catching.' She looked at Will. 'You, less so.'

Will frowned.

'Hang on, I may have something in the clown's trunk.' Sal sucked on her tape measure thoughtfully. Gathering herself up, she cracked like an extending ladder. Stepping behind a folding screen painted with swans, she began hurling wigs and shoes at Will from a large trunk while the princess stared nervously with her braces. Sal couldn't help thinking how young the heir looked and what battles lay ahead of her.

'Right.' She turned around to face Will. 'How about fisherman and fishwife? I have the props for that one – a lobster cage, minnow net, and matching hats.'

Will was pleasantly taken back to his last sojourn in a boat with Amber and wondered if the swan pedalo was still in the bay. 'Anything that does not involve fish and boats would be preferable for my lady.'

Red was dimly aware of the discussion going on around her. She was gazing into a standing mirror, looking at the spice

43

and nut selling merchant reflected back at her. A nut-seller's allure was widespread across the kingdom. They were a long way from the run-of-the-mill farm girl selling potatoes with a muddy bucket balanced on her head. For a time, the nut-sellers had been the one magical thing left in the kingdom that had not shrivelled up and dried on the windowsill of lost hope. When the queen had disappeared, the Age of Romance gasped its final breath, the endless Quest began, but these women had kept their boots high and their presence known. They continued to sail from the Islands of Aquila and kingdoms beyond, where the nut and spice trees grew in abundance, and would sell the bounty of their estates to Landfelians. Their skin glowed clear and golden – natural oils will do that for you – and their hair shone like silk. Even a celibate with an allergy stopped to buy a teasel of sweet almonds, honeyed cashews, and pouches of freshly-grated nutmeg on a fine autumn day when the first ships began to arrive.

The merchant ladies' traditional dress was not a traditional dress at all. They lived, worked, and picked fruit on large farms, and it was work no one wanted to do in a corset and bustle. They wore large, floppy hats – pinning their hair up to keep their necks cool – and white smock-like shirts. Around their necks hung strings of amber or turquoise. Pale cropped trousers held up by braces were teamed with soft leather boots. A rope swung from their waist on which a teasel – a form of wooden scoop – was used to measure out the nuts and spices.

These ladies did not need to ply their trade. With their

own income and a worldly view of the land, trade followed them willingly. Landfelian's women discouraged their sons from buying from the visiting islanders; it only led to trouble. Landfelian's young men ignored this advice and survived solely on a diet of nut-related items in the autumn and the memory of them for the rest of the year.

The princess was a natural; she looked so comfortable, dressed as a merchant. Sal had never had such an easy model to work with.

'You're a chameleon, my dear,' she said, watching Red for a moment. 'Take this riding coat with you too, it is a suitably murky colour, and do try to keep most of that hair hidden under your hat.' She pulled out a wimple and a dog collar from the trunk. 'William, I think I have found the perfect thing for you and Miss Morningstar: travelling holy man and nun.'

Will passed a sage eye over the items. 'Amber may struggle with the wimple.'

'She may not have a choice,' said Sal, folding and tying the clothes into a paper parcel and thrusting it into Will's arms. 'There has been a flurry of runaways in the last month and I'm running out of wardrobe. Unless you want to take the box of fabulous tights?'

They all jumped at a sharp tap on the window. Red stepped quickly behind a coat of arms and held her breath. The noise was followed by a faint chittering. It was coming from the roof.

'Did everyone hear that?' she whispered, ducking down

to the floor.

'Mm.' Sal looked grave and briskly closed the curtains. 'I don't know any pigeons that knock.'

'I heard the same noise on the window of my room at The Cat's Back,' Red said quietly. 'Last night.'

Will looked worried. 'Amber. I must get back; she should be here by now.'

'What creature can fly, hover, and knock on the highest window of the coliseum without stilts or knuckles?' Sal looked at the princess with curious eyes. 'Who else is following you? I don't believe for a second that was a house martin. If I didn't know better, I would say the spiderlings have been awoken.' Her eyes narrowed.

'Spiderlings?' Red had never heard of such a creature.

'On second thoughts, it's highly unlikely.' Sal shook her head. She didn't want to frighten the girl. 'Don't tell me anymore. It's best I don't know where you're going in case the guards use thumb screws or, Heaven forbid, the stretcher.' She loved a touch of cat and mouse, but Sal didn't need to get any taller. 'The spiderlings have been asleep for years and are a long way from here. I very much doubt ... You are thankfully too young to remember the last time.' They all heard the second tap. Sal looked at Red and said, 'Better dash.'

Red nodded, picked up her bag, and whispered, 'Is there a back door?'

'We have one better, duck. This is a theatre. We have a trapdoor. Follow me.'

Underneath a reindeer skin rug, Sal revealed the trap door.

'Follow the steps all the way down four floors to a passageway; it runs under the stage,' Sal urgently explained. 'It will take you to a small door that leads out of the south side of the square. Go carefully. This old theatre is being watched.'

'I understand.' Red tucked her hair further up inside her hat and buttoned up the fawn-coloured coat.

'You will need this if the guards stop you.' Sal held out a roll of official looking paper. 'It's a visitor permit for Alba. And here's one for the South Realm. Apparently, there are check points across the borders of all the realms now.'

Red took them. 'Thank you.' She began to climb down the ladder.

'One more thing.' Sal held firmly onto her hand. 'Try not to strike up a conversation with any of the scrapers on the way.'

'Scrapers?' Red frowned.

'No time to explain. You'll hear them before you see them. If you do, don't stop. Keep going. If the guards find you, tell them you're heading to Half Moon Bay to board the next ship bound for the Islands of Aquila. You've been stranded here due to the fog. Good luck, Your Highness.'

'Thank you.' Red nodded and began hurrying down the ladder. 'I have a map.'

'Wonderful, my dear.' Sal didn't like to say, but a map was about as useful to the princess as an oil painting of some sunflowers. Landfelian was not the same; parts of it were unreachable now. She squeezed her hand and said quietly, 'I hope you find what you're looking for. Landfelian is rooting for you. It has not forgotten.' She threw down a large, soft cloth. 'Put this cape on your horse – it's the best I can do for a valien.'

Red opened her mouth to say more but was cut off.

'Hurry.' Sal smiled, closing the trap door. 'You must hurry now. There'll be time for coffee and cake later. I have no doubt I'll be seeing you again, Red Felian.'

Will gave the sign of the cross and said, 'May only the good and trustworthy gods light your way with rainbows and very clear signs.' He glanced at the window and whispered. 'Will you not allow me to escort you, at least until you are out of the city?'

'No, you'll be safer without me.' Red smiled at Will in the dark stairwell. 'I've put you and Amber in enough danger already ...' She paused. 'And if you see that Man of the Road, hit him hard with your case of holy books.'

'As you wish,' replied Will, bowing before her. 'It has been an honour to serve you, milady.'

Red smiled. 'I hope I see you again, William English.' The trapdoor was closed above her and leaving the warmth of the attic behind, she began to climb down into the bowels of the coliseum. When she reached the last passageway, she raced under the stage, and dimly lit torches lit up doors to dark dressing rooms, armoury, and props-making workshops. She had already begun to miss her new friends. Why was there now a bounty on her head? During her years at the palace, her step-aunt and uncle barely knew she was alive. What was the sudden urgency to capture her? She had to find out what was going on before anyone else got hurt. Red felt nervous; it was Tall Sal's words: the kingdom is rooting for you. The weight of royal responsibility began to settle awkwardly on the princess' shoulders. And for the first time since her escape, it dawned on her that Landfelian's people may be looking for her to rule, to put on a crown, and ... 'I'm not ready,' Red said out loud. She wanted to be back in Celador's library with her books, her wolfhound, and her marbles. She was darned if she was going to let her parents leave with absolutely no handover notes. The thought made her angry. 'This Quest has lasted long enough,' she said to the passageway.

At the sound of Red's whistle, Face trotted out from behind a billboard still advertising Butch and Julie's show. He whinnied when he saw her.

'I sell first grade pistachios, figs, almonds, and spices from the Islands of Aquila, and you, my friend, are my horse, Peanut.' She flung the damask cape over him. 'We'll go cross-country to my godmothers'. According to my map, Tikli Bottom is only three days away and closer than Father Peter's folly. We should make it there in time for tea on Thursday. There may be spies watching, Face, so ride fast and stay alert.' She gazed up at the early morning sky, stroked his long nose, and looked into his trusting eyes.

'It's just you and me now. We must look after one another.' He snorted gently and knelt to allow her onto his back. Quickly they clattered away from the coliseum, turning into Short Street, which took them down a long, gradual hill out of the city.

Short Street turned out to be a joke designed by the city planners. It was the longest street in Alba. It zigzagged out towards the borders of the South Realm and open countryside in the most haphazard fashion. It was the least guarded road because of the rags and scrapers that lived there, although Red had failed to find out what scrapers were. She was quite enjoying being on her own again. Her journey so far had been full of the noise of others, one of whom she could no longer trust and vehemently hated. Robbie Wylde had betrayed her for a bounty of one thousand gold pieces. The princess was livid. She had read enough books to know that true friends did not betray each other for gold. They trotted on, passing houses that tilted forwards and houses that sank in the middle and houses that looked very thin and crumbly.

Face began to trot a little faster when he heard the scraping. His hooves made a very loud *CLIP-CLOP CLIP-CLOP* sound on the road, which was difficult to avoid for he was a horse with shoes. It was now light enough for them to be seen with clarity. The princess was shocked by the state of the buildings and businesses they passed. She was so absorbed in reading the tarnished inscriptions nailed to the boarded-up doors that she did not notice the scraping noise.

GENTLEMAN'S TAILOR: HAWKINS AND WADDLE
– FINE SILK TIES AND WAISTCOATS

CANDLE SCULPTORS: RUBY WAX AND SONS –
EROTIC FIGURES AVAILABLE ON REQUEST
ROMANCE WRITING FOR BEGINNERS: LET REBECCA TEETER HELP
HARPSICHORDS AND HARPS – INQUIRE WITHIN FOR HERNAN RAKER

Underneath the plaques that had not been stolen for smelting were further notices.

50% DISCOUNTS AVAILABLE INSIDE
95% DISCOUNTS
JUST BRING FOOD AND SHOES AND WE'LL
GIVE YOU ANYTHING YOU WANT.

The valien began to canter as lightly and quietly as possible. The scraping on Short Street was now accompanied by an unpleasant chuckling. But Red was still lost in her own thoughts.

'Where are all the trees?' she asked the desolate street. 'And there are cobbles missing, Face. And the stone pineapples from people's porches are gone!'

Alba was known for its ornamental trees and fine quartz cobbles, as well as the decorative front facades of its businesses.

'Have they all been chopped down? And who took all the cobbles?'

The street was full of holes. There was not one tree, hanging basket, or geranium, only the smell of burning wood, which upset the princess, who loved trees. Her horse was more concerned with the scraping sound than the lack of trees, though, and he hurried her on as fast as he could.

Red was finally interrupted from her thoughts by the odour of unwashed human.

'Urgh! What is that terrible smell?' She covered her nose with her sleeve.

She glanced to the sides of the street and saw them. Large mounds of rags, dirty ribbons, patches of quilt, and old copies of the *Palace Times* were balled together and shuffling along the gutters like hunchbacked crabs. She saw a bloated and stained foot poking out from one of the shuffling mounds nearest her.

'Oh my goodness. There are corpses rolling down the street!'

'Who are you calling a corpse?' one of the mounds looked up and shouted at her.

Face reared up in fright.

'You're alive!' cried Red. 'Oh, you poor thing. Here, I've got water and erm … a little bread.' She struggled inside her hemp sack.

The scraping sound stopped and bundle of dirty cloth approached her. A small head protruded out of the rags and snapped at Red, 'I said, who are you calling corpse?'

This corpse was incredibly well-spoken.

'I was mistaken.' Red tried not to look shocked at the sight before her. 'You're alive and erm, well.'

'I'm no corpse, young lady! Hey, everyone! One of those

nut-sellers thinks we're corpsed.'

Coarse cries of indignation came from under the balls of stinking eiderdown, denim, and safety pins that shuffled along the sides of the street.

'Bloody cheek.'

'How about that?'

'I'm sorry. Please don't upset yourselves.' Red was appalled. 'You just, well, don't look in very good health.'

'Corpsed, eh? Not quite.' The nearest rag came closer and smirked up at her, holding out a withered wrist. 'Still got a pulse, see!'

Angry screwed-up faces appeared out of their bundles to wave their limbs at the lady on the big horse. Short Street was crawling with them. Nothing was left of these people but bones, teeth, dirty hair, and toenails. Red was horrified and had no idea what to do. There were so many of them and they were beginning to make quite a racket. Some tried to touch Face.

'I'm sorry. I … I … couldn't see you under your … lovely clothes.' She looked at the yellow, drawn face of something that used to be a woman. 'You must be hungry. Please take what I have, it's not much.' Red untied a parcel of food.

'You couldn't see? Not surprising on a horse that size. Watch your step next time, Teasel, and your manners.' The rag grabbed Red's bundle of supplies greedily.

These were people – good, educated citizens of Alba, Red realised. What had happened to them? 'Forgive me. Pray, what line of work are you and these other people in?'

'We are scrapers. We scrape,' they muttered.

'I see.' Red remembered Sal's warning. They were starving, rotting balls of people living on the streets with not a bath between them, sharing only the smell and the boarded, crumpled-up houses. 'What do you scrape?'

'The cobbles, pineapples, ornate bits, the odd door knocker or brass knob. Then we sell them,' the scraper answered whilst shovelling the princess' modest picnic into her mouth.

They were scraping out the city's beautiful cobbles! A small cart trundled past Red, loaded up high with the chalky white quartz. 'Why? Wherever are you taking them?'

'South somewhere.' A dirty, calloused hand pointed down the hill to the countryside beyond Alba. 'Not a clue, love. It's mainly the Blackwood guards who buy them, then take them towards the Misty mountains. New kingdom there, still building it … Mirador or something.'

'But they belong in Landfelian!' Red was indignant. 'In Alba.'

The rag made a sudden grab for Red's boot. 'Your ruby-coloured hair – is it for sale?' The whole street behind her began to cackle. She heard snipping from across the street.

'Oh, no, it isn't.' Red tried to leave and take her hair with her.

'Ah, go on. You've got enough to spare half.'

She pulled Face away from the rag. 'We must go.'

A hand came out and snatched hold of the valien's mane, while another pulled hard on the princess' boot. 'What

54

about your horse's hair?' they cackled.

'Leave him alone!' Red cried. 'Face!'

The valien whinnied louder and clearer than the silver bells of Celador's tower. He reared up, and the ragged people backed away in terror of his enormous hooves.

Red felt terrible galloping off and leaving those poor, desperate people with only a small picnic. But she had no choice. Her head was filled with a thousand questions. Why were the guards after the foundations of Alba? What was being built in the south and who was giving orders to dismantle the city? She suddenly felt like shouting at her father to come back from his wretched quest. This was not her area, and no one else seemed to be trying to stop it. There was no time to add saving a kingdom to her current workload. Red had her own quest to be getting on with. But even as she clattered away, the princess knew she would not be able to forget what she had seen. Something had to be done.

She quickly forgot about Robbie Wylde and his treachery. She barely gave a glance behind her at the fading capital. Red prayed her godmothers would be at home and that she reached them before any guards discovered her. Nothing dealt with doubt better than godmothers.

'Faster, Face. I'm not going to sit back and let anyone steal our cobbles.'

They thundered on, passing into the east realm's borderlands as night fell.

HOLY MAN TO THE RESCUE

Amber glanced out of her broken window. She could see that Dead End was empty, although she had one of her funny feelings that it wasn't. It felt like dawn was holding its breath. She drew her curtains, blew out the candle, and waited for Will by the fire, sitting on her hands to stop them shaking.

Why didn't she sew? At times like this, didn't sewing help? Humming 'God Save the King' didn't work. She only sounded frightened. She closed her eyes and told herself to get a grip. Amber should have taken that moment to open her eyes and grab something pointy instead.

Napoleon hissed at a shadow as it passed the window downstairs. He clawed at the door, but it was locked, and then he heard chittering from above. Daniel put one gloved hand through the broken pane of Amber's window, opened it, and climbed calmly inside from the entirely useless, wooden fire escape.

She opened her eyes and screamed.

Robbie heard the scream above him from the alley, but he couldn't move. Every part of him from the neck down felt heavy and numb. He couldn't throw a stone. The opiate from Blackwood's cane had sunk its claws deep into him. He struggled to lift himself up into a seated position as Amber's cries went quiet. He tried yelling for help but the voice that came out was broken and hoarse.

Someone has to stop that son of a lawyer, thought Robbie. But he could not get his legs to move.

The Dibbles did not hear Amber or their cat yowling downstairs; they were busy dealing with the most horrifying infestation of spiderlings. Hearing a persistent tapping in the room where the princess was staying, Laura had tentatively opened the door to discover the window wide open and a swarm of the creatures franticly searching the room. The other residents of The Cat's Back were doing all they could to spritz the spiderlings with garlic spray and avoid being chittered at.

'They're looking for her.' Mr Dibble turned pale.

'What are they?' Laura hurled herself at the door to stop the creatures getting into any of the other rooms of the house.

Mr Dibble looked at his wife. 'Spies.'

Amber's scream was cut short before it really had a chance to get going. It was gagged by a black silk handkerchief that absolutely stank of cheroots.

'What lovely curtains.' Blackwood held up the standard sized mid-length blonde wig that had been brought to Paloma for the princess to wear for her escape. 'Darling, I believe this is yours?' Amber had forgotten all about her wig. The night Billy True, the groundsman's boy, had come from the palace to ask for help. Months ago, she had given it to him, a loan for the princess at the request of the herald. She tried to run towards the door, but Daniel Blackwood's cane came down hard and barred the way. His gloved hands dragged her back.

'People always run, even when they know full well the door is locked.' He lit a cheroot and smiled down at her. 'People are inherently hopeful, I find it amusing.' Holding the spiked end of his cane against her arm, he removed the gag and blew a thin line of smoke in her face. 'My dear, we have to talk *through* our problems, not run from them.'

Amber glared up at his flinty eyes. 'What do you want?'

'Your matrimonial welcome needs work.' He pressed the cane further into her skin. 'Where is the princess?'

'A long way from here.'

'Don't be trying. Everyone knows a little of something.' Daniel's eyes hardened.

The years had not softened him. If anything, Amber thought, he was worse, driven by something more than his own idle greed. Something that seemed to possess him. His eyes had an unnatural gleam. If she knew better, she would suspect sorcery.

'Princess Felian did not tell anyone where she was going. And if I knew, I would not tell you.' Amber smiled. 'I would sooner die.' She spat on him.

'Another thing people say, but really, would they?' Daniel wiped his face with his handkerchief and sighed. 'Your actor friend doesn't know about me, does he? Well, there'll be no awkward confessions necessary. He's dead.'

The only thing to hear Amber's next cry was the gag, which returned to her mouth as another tied her hands. 'Come milady, it's time to go home.'

Daniel Blackwood lifted Amber over his shoulder and walked out the door. Lidia was waiting in the street, close to where Robbie lay helpless, bloody, and more than fed up on the ground. There was something familiar about the Man of the Road. Lidia watched him curiously, hidden from view until Blackwood emerged from the inn. An ornate purple and copper barouche stood outside The Cat's Back, with two frostbitten guards at the helm. Soon it was flying down the hill, out of the citadel, and back towards the belching smoke of the Chimmeries as morning broke.

The herald approached The Hog's Breath, tired to the bone and gasping for some coffee. Usually, not even a new calligraphy set would entice him to put one toe inside such a pit of pestilence, such an unrighteous den of disease and foulness.

'Morning, Barry.' This morning was different. Richard knew the Hog's Breath was the place to go for news of Blackwood and his guards. He was also extremely thirsty and tired.

'If it isn't the king's herald! Vacation from the royals? Good for you. Can I tempt you to a bed and slice of gristle pie?' Barry Grub looked up from picking his nose and slapped the herald on the back.

'And a louse-infested pillow?' Richard smiled politely and adjusted his silk neck scarf.

'No, still no pillows,' said Barry. 'Plenty of lice, though.' He grinned.

'Thank you, Barry, but I'm not stopping long. Send my regards to Sarah.'

'Will do. Looks like the weather took the stuffing out of your wheels ...'

Richard Losley's journey to the city had not been a comfortable one. Just then, the final spoke of his Penny Farthing's wheel pinged onto the welcome mat of The Hog's Breath. 'On second thoughts, do you have any coffee?'

Barry scratched his chest, which was thankfully covered by a vest and a stained apron. He looked into the middle distance and thought for a moment. 'Dark stuff; hot, bitter, non-alcoholic?'

'That's it, often accompanied with cream or a little frothed milk and sometimes a thin almond biscuit. Gives you a boost if you have recently slept in a ditch, which regretfully, I have.'

The herald leant wearily on what was left of his transport and wondered how long it would take for it to be stolen. He prayed Tall Sal was still working from the attics of the coliseum. She was only friend he had left in Alba with an endless supply of coffee and clean, well-tailored clothes. His coat and hat were stained and damp from the journey. Nothing upset the herald more than starting the day grubby and unpressed. He wanted to wash, shave, and head straight to The Cat's Back for news of the royal runaway.

'You're in luck!' Barry told him. 'Pair of lovebirds left a pouch of that coffee stuff behind in Room Thirteen. Sarah! Boil up some water – and make it clean for the king's herald.' He snorted and pulled up his trousers.

Richard winced, followed Barry into The Hog's Breath, and hoped no guards would hear. He raised his eyes to the heavens and asked the gods to spare him from typhoid. Inside, he braced himself for the aroma of grease, feet, and foul thinking.

The Long Wind had caught him not long after leaving Paloma. The wheels of his bicycle looked like two steamrolled satsumas, and the little bell now rang of its own accord. He'd had no choice but to take cover in a deep ditch alongside an overgrown trail that led into Waterwood. The noises he had heard from within the wood had kept him awake all night. The herald preferred the ordered gardens of the palace and the civilisation of a city over the call of the wild. In the wild, things tended to be a lot bigger than him.

He sat down gingerly and looked at Barry's dog. 'Still alive, Mitzy?' She snarled at him. 'Never mind.' Despite being the smallest dog in the neighbourhood, Mitzy was the most feared. The herald tried to ignore her and looked around the room, thankful that no guards seemed to be in evidence this early in the day. 'You've done a lot to the place.'

'Yup,' said Barry. 'The chairs were my idea. The flowers and curtains all Sarah's doing.'

A broken bottle of dried nettles was arranged on the table in a simple bouquet, and the curtains, Richard noted, were a string of drying dishcloths and underpants. It did not smell of roses. Although it *was* empty, which was a blessing. The guards must have all left first thing.

'Double up as a washing line,' Barry said, nodding at the curtains and returning with a chipped bowl of boiling water and a leather pouch smelling reassuringly of coffee. He slammed them down without aplomb. 'We don't have any cream, sugar, or milk froth.'

'Ahh, a purist. I prefer my coffee black, anyway. Thank you.'

'One shiny gold piece for you, herald.' Barry grinned.

The enterprising swine. The herald gave Barry a coin. 'Smells like you were busy last night. Any illustrious guests sampling the delights of Sarah's cuisine? Anything interesting happening downtown?' Richard tried, hoping to gain some information on the comings and goings of Alba.

Barry looked blank. His mouth was open most of the time because of a perpetual cold. 'A fist of Blackwood Guards stayed where you're sitting. Noisy brutes. That well-dressed lawful one with the cane took a room upstairs. Never taken to him. He's been in and out a lot recently. Always got an innocent tied up somewhere. I'd watch your back if I were you, Losley.'

Richard was not surprised that Daniel Blackwood had been in. He had seen the *Wanted* posters as soon as he'd arrived in the city.

'Oh, and a couple of peasants came in a hurry and left in a hurry, if you know what I mean.' Barry's eyes lit up for a brief second. 'Lovely lady, quite flushed, travelling with a young lad of the road. Full of hope.' Barry looked almost wistful.

'A lady, you say. She didn't have red hair by any chance?' Richard whispered, trying to sound casual.

'Now you mention it, she did, hair like Rudolph …'

The door flung open and hit Mitzy, who yelped and flew under the herald's table. A man in black strode in with a woman draped over his shoulder. Her buttery hair trailed across the floor and a silver tuning fork swung down from her neck, chiming against a chair leg. Barry frowned as he watched them cross the room.

'Great stoat!' the herald choked and dived under the table before Daniel Blackwood saw him. 'The kidnapping knave has got Amber,' he muttered to himself and Mitzy.

'I do not want to be disturbed.' Blackwood's cane scraped up the stairs. 'Is that clear, Barry?'

'Aye, crystal.' Barry sniffed and began to wipe down the bar. He waited for him to go and for the door upstairs to slam before saying, 'It's a sorry old business this kingdom now.'

'Mm.' Richard placed his recently purchased coffee on

the floor between his nose and Mitzy's teeth. The dog sniffed it and began to drink. He quickly put the remaining coffee in the leather pouch in his bag and crawled towards the door. 'Must dash.' The herald hurried out before Barry could involve him in any political conversations.

Outside, in a cloudy, oblivious afternoon, he noticed a familiar family crest painted on the side of a purple barouche waiting outside.

'Sir Toby Mole's barouche! That thieving lawyer.' The herald pedalled away quickly on what was left of his bicycle. 'This won't do at all.'

He creaked up the hill and with relief entered the maze of narrow alleys and passageways of the citadel. Something had gone very wrong indeed if Daniel Blackwood was in The Hog's Breath with Amber and Sir Toby's barouche. As for the two 'peasants' staying there recently, it was more than suspicious. *Could it have been Red Felian?* thought Richard. No one stayed at Barry's unless they had died or were desperate. Was either true of the princess? And what had happened to Will? If there was news to be had, The Cat's Back would know it. He hurried on.

When he turned into Dead End, there was a holy man knocking on the door of the great beamed house with a case of holy books.

'Excuse me, Father,' Richard asked, 'Are you lost?'

The holy man stopped knocking and looked down at the herald with merry brown eyes. He picked him up and kissed him on both cheeks. 'The herald returns! What happened? You look terrible! Thank goodness you escaped the son of a lawyer. Nasty piece of work; puts *teeth* on people, amongst other horrors. I tell you, the more I know of him, the more relieved I am Amber never ran into that rat in her youth.'

'Monsieur English!' The herald smiled. 'How marvellous you are safe.' His face fell. 'But I must tell you ...'

The holy man bowed. 'At your service, and of course God's.'

'... Oh, dear me. I think you should sit down.'

'You brought hot drinks,' cried Will, seeing the leather pouch in Richard's bag. 'Excellent, always so prepared, a herald to the end! Do you like my disguise? Been to see Tall Sal, and I'm about to surprise Amber with a nun's habit!' He was struggling with the case of holy books and a string of rosary beads. 'We are wanted criminals now, you understand, and must take precautions. There are posters up everywhere. But we did it! Foiled the lot of them, freed the giantess. It's time to leave this slum once and for all, Richard, and help the ...' he dropped his voice, 'you know who.'

Will frowned at the door, wondering why no one had answered.

'They must all be asleep.'

'I have some bad news ... Let's sit down a moment.' The herald looked nervously around him for guards.

'Sit? Where, my good friend? There isn't a bench left in this city, you know that! Or did you? I'd forgotten it's been a while since you left the palace. Well, it's now more than the cobbles that are going missing. The scrapers are selling everything they can get their hands on. All the best bits of this city are being broken down and taken away, even the stone pineapples. AND NO ONE KNOWS WHERE!'

Will leant against the door and took a breath.

'There's a bounty on our heads and the princess'. The Blackwood Guards have been but one step behind us the whole way, but she got out! We outfoxed the whole drumming lot of them. And then Amber and I went on a boat … Oh, Losley, it was a hoot. We met giants, lovely people, much misunderstood. I'm telling you; I haven't had this much fun since "Dressing Gowns and Daggers".'

The herald nodded. That had been a very good show – a farce, a lot of bed swapping – it had toured for a year. 'It's not over yet, my friend. There is something you must know …'

'The princess really is a decent sort,' Will continued, oblivious to the herald's fretful expression. 'A lot on her plate, that young Felian. At least the Man of the Road got shot of the voodoo for her, with a frying pan no less!' He stopped and looked sorry. 'Before he betrayed her for gold, the louse. She needs to let her hair down, though possibly not here with all the scrapers and spies. Hard times.' He gave his friend a political look and tried the door again. 'Don't worry, Sal fixed her up with another tremendous disguise … And she's back on her merry questing way.'

The herald stood on the case of holy books and slapped him. 'William!'

'Ouch! What was that for? You could have broken my beads.'

'Listen to me, man! It's Amber. Blackwood has kidnapped her.' Richard's hand turned white under Will's grip.

'What? Are you certain?'

'Unfortunately, yes. I just saw them. He has her locked upstairs at The Hog's Breath and asked Barry not to be disturbed.'

Will's face turned to thunder. 'Well, tough! He is about to be thoroughly disturbed. Don't sit down, Herald, this is no time for sitting. We must go to The Hog's Breath at once. We have to rescue Amber!'

There was a groan from the alleyway behind some bins. It was the sound of a man recently beaten and left to die alone, feeling the extent of his wounds. The two friends moved away from the smell of drains, and the murmur of, 'Helllmmp hmmelppp'.

'Another starving rag,' sighed Richard. Alba was not the shining city he loved and remembered.

'Quick, Losley, we need a horse, or an ass ... Are there no carriages for hire at this hour?' Will paced manically about Dead End.

'My bicycle won't take us any further.' The herald sighed. The final spoke made a sad twang as they both stared at it.

The groaning noise persisted. 'OVERRRRHRRRRREAR!'

It was insistent and faintly annoying. The herald lost all

patience and stormed down the alley.

'For Peter's sake, man, will you desist your moaning? Just get on and suffer like everyone else. We have important business to attend to here!'

'I think that was a little insensitive under the circumstances. Look at the poor man.' Will peered around the barrels. 'Great Stoat, it's the deceiver!'

'Who?' Richard was extremely tired and had not yet had his morning coffee. His usual herald's patience and gone to the place where all niceties stop.

'The last Man of the Road! Robert Wylde. I am supposed to hit this man very hard.' He lifted a holy book high above his head. 'Orders of Princess Felian. You led Daniel Blackwood here.' Will glared at Robbie.

'P-Please don't.' Robbie found the prospect of more pain enough to get his tongue working properly. 'I am uncomfortable enough as it is without the Word of God landing on my head.' He winced as he spoke, half propped up against a wall like a drunk. There was blood drying all over his shirt.

The herald had never seen the young man before. He did not look like a Man of the Road, even with a whisk, spatula, and a few potatoes littered around him. If you put him in a bath and gave him a sword, the man could have passed for something far more interesting. That is if you did away with the rat nibbling his little finger.

Robbie looked at the rat painfully and then at the herald. 'Do you think you could stop it?'

'Of course.' Richard shooed away the rat.

'Thank you. Blackwood has got Amber,' Robbie told them. 'I tried to stop him. He spiked me with his cane and some sort of opiate …'

Will crouched down and, looking apologetic, hit Robbie over the head with his case of holy books. Robbie reeled back against the wall with a groan.

'Was that necessary? The man is already down.' Richard tried to dab Robbie's bloody nose with a clean handkerchief and did what he could about the rest.

Robbie yelled at Will. 'What the hell did you do that for, you wazzack! I have already been drugged and paralysed. And I'm trying to tell you, Amber's in trouble.'

'I gave the princess my word. You are a bounty hunter!' Will yelled back.

Regret flashed across Robbie's face. 'I didn't. Let me explain …'

Richard could see that this was going to take some time and it did not really involve him, so he took a seat on the ground next to Robbie and opened one of the holy books. The book turned out to be a romance novel – there was nothing holy about it. Someone in the props department had repainted the cover and bound it well, although the original title and first page were still visible.

THE NUN AND THE PEDLAR
It was a hot day in June and Sister Ann was in prayers …

The herald made himself comfortable in the stinking alley while the holy man and the Man of the Road came to an agreement. Princess Felian had clearly escaped the city in a good disguise, and for that he was thankful.

A generous twenty minutes later, he heard Robbie exclaim, 'I'm telling you; I didn't take the bounty. Not one gold piece!'

'You were tempted, you accepted, and now he has Amber!' Will kicked the wall and winced.

'Fine! I agreed with one of the royal guards outside The Honest Sausage that I would follow the princess' tracks and bring her to Alba. I have no allegiance to the two deserters who wear the crown. I do not know the king personally. The queen seemed nice enough, but it's been seven years, and look around you. The whole kingdom could use a bounty.' Robbie tried to reposition himself on the ground. 'The royal family left the throne to a pair of vultures, and the princess has been left to pick her way through the bones.'

He continued. 'Outside the city, it's far worse; there're no more cobbles to sell and folk are hungry in every realm.' Robbie took a weary breath. 'I didn't take the gold. Not after I saw what they had done … with the voodoo … and the princess, she … was not what I expected.' During this speech, Robbie could only move his head and, rather uselessly, his middle finger to try to emphasise his point. Richard raised his eyebrow and smiled at his last words but said nothing.

'I never meant to lead Daniel Blackwood to The Cat's

Back. I intended to challenge him and send him far away from here.'

Will put his head in his hands. 'God only knows what he wants with Amber. You have lost the use of your legs and there's a reward on my head. If I walk into The Hog's Breath, the guards will hang me up by my cassock.'

Robbie was relieved to regain feeling in his elbow again, although his legs lay still like two very capable logs in front of him. He shifted into a more comfortable position. 'Let me help you now. It is Red Blackwood wants, no one else. He needs her to go fishing.'

'Fishing?' asked Will and Richard at the same time. 'What use would the princess possibly be for fishing?'

'I don't know, but it's what he said. There's a witch involved somewhere. Whatever it means, I have to warn her.'

'A witch,' the herald muttered quietly. 'Oh dear.'

'If he hurts Amber, I will cut off his earlobes and then ...' Will did not have an aggressive vocabulary; he was more usually the one being beaten to a pulp. '... hit him with this case of holy books. We're going to get her back. Come, Herald, to The Hog's Breath!'

The herald stopped reading. 'Do you mind if I have one small cup of coffee before we go? It's been a long week.'

'Certainly not, this is a matter of national security,' said Will. 'And true love.'

'Wait!' Robbie pointed with his elbow and middle finger at the leather pouch sticking out of the herald's bag.

'Where did you get that? That's *my* coffee.'

Richard raised his eyebrow and stood. 'Sir, I assure you it is mine. I bought it fair and square from The Hog's Breath only this morning. Some peasants left it behind.'

'Did you give it to anyone? Did you drink any?' Robbie could not believe it was the same pouch he saw Red use in Waterwood, the one he had watched her secretly fill up with slumbersap.

Richard had never known such fuss over an old pouch of coffee. On closer inspection, it looked more like mulch and smelt strangely sweet, like the woods. 'I did not drink a drop, but I would very much like to if you would give me a chance.'

'You saw no one else drink it?' pressed Robbie.

'No!' Richard's patience left. 'Apart from Barry's dog, Mitzy.'

Robbie began to laugh. 'You, my good little man, are a genius. This is not coffee, well, maybe a shot, but the rest is pure, single origin, one hundred percent slumbersap from Waterwood,' he said excitedly. Will stopped pacing and listened, and Robbie continued. 'I have a plan. As good a one as we can hope for under the circumstances. You will get Amber back and we will keep our tongues. I just need one thing.'

'What?' asked Richard.

'A Blackwood guard.'

'Why?'

'I need his drum, his boots, and his purple jodhpurs.'

Stanley Filch had been on patrol all night outside the great House of Gold, known more commonly as the Bank of Landfelian.

'Mark my words,' he spoke to the empty square as he marched up an impressive number of steps that led to the six-columned entrance. 'I will put this on my timesheet, and he will hear of it. No break, no supper, standing up all night – it's not right. This royal guard lark is codswallop.'

A holy man entered the square from the top of Peel Street. He carried a heavy-looking case and something that was steaming. Incense? No, it looked more like a thermos. The holy man stopped, rubbed his back with a weary sigh, and walked purposefully towards the House of Gold, where he sat down on the step next to a large sign.

NO SITTING, LOITERING, OR DRINKING OUT OF THERMOSES PERMITTED ON THESE STEPS

Stanley watched in disbelief as the holy man settled his robes around him, licked his lips, inhaled, and sighed. A waft of maple-y dark sweetness floated towards the relatively young guard and hit his saliva glands, which began to tingle. His feet ached to get out of his thigh-high boots and have a lie down. Stanley had never wanted to be a holy man more in his life. But his job was his job, and it was better than prison or living with his Aunt Maud, so he marched over.

'Father, did you not see the sign?'

'Hello, son. May the heavens bless this morning and a thousand virgin angels bathe you in your dreams.'

Stanley had never heard that blessing before. It must be new. 'The sign is very clear.'

The holy man raised his arms to the sky. 'There are signs everywhere. They are all around. You never know when one will sneak up and ask you to sit down and have some coffee.'

Stanley dribbled a bit and looked across the empty square. 'It is forbidden to drink on the job. I could lose my drum. Move along now, there is no sitting permitted here. It encourages thinking, you see, and there is strictly no thinking allowed around the House of Gold. New rules, Blackwood's. And no thermoses.' He gestured grumpily to the holy man's.

The holy man looked at the guard and blew a very long raspberry. 'What a load of heavenly tripe. An earthly law. You won't find such rules up the stairs in the heavens, dear man. You can drink from whatever you like up there. You can drink from an angel's breast if you're discreet about it!'

Stanley had never met a holy man like this one before.

Will delved into his robes, which were long, swishy, and belonged to someone called Thomas Finkermeyer. He withdrew a small paper bag full of fudge.

'Sit down before you fall down and have some fudge. There is no law that can possibly stop you or I from enjoying some of the finest butterscotch tablet all the way from the North Realm.' Will passed the guard the bag and whispered, 'Made by the purist of nuns.'

'Butterscotch fudge?' The guard began to sob and licked his lips. 'I have not sat down for two days.'

'Then it's high time you did. Dear man, what have you been waiting for? A sign? Do not worry, you will have your own cloud in the heavens. I'll put in a good word, get you a footstool as well. Have some coffee, for saint's sake, blow your nose, and… forgive me.' The holy man gave Stanley a sorry smile.

Young Stanley did not see it coming. He was expecting some coffee and a handkerchief, not a thwack from a frying pan to the back of his head. For a few seconds, he saw a bright light and heard the faint strums of an acoustic guitar. Twelve hours later, he woke in his underclothing, covered with a blanket, holding what seemed to be a holy book but which turned out to be the novel *The Bounty Hunter and the Heiress*. The holy man had the decency to leave bag of fudge next to him.

It was almost dusk by the time Will, Robbie, and the herald reached Viper Street. As soon as Will returned with the guard's clothes, they spent the remaining hours planning the rescue of Amber in the safety of The Cat's Back. The Dibbles were rid of the spiderlings; in a sudden violent movement, they'd swarmed out of the upstairs rooms. Robbie recovered from Blackwood's numbing opiate slowly with the help of more coffee and a good deal of toast.

'You ready, English? Off you go.' Robbie pushed him forward towards The Hog's Breath inn. It was full to brimming with Blackwood's guards.

Will was dressed in Stanley Filch's uniform. 'The place is crawling with Daniel's men.' He faltered when he saw a fist smash through one of the windows.

'Savage killers,' the herald added helpfully. 'All recruited from Hardplace Prison.'

'How do we even know Amber is inside?' Will looked up at the grimy windows.

'Look there.' The herald pointed towards the vast shadow of Sir Toby's barouche. 'Blackwood's stolen transport has not moved since this morning.'

'The only thing these guards are interested in comes in a barrel.' Robbie wore the holy man outfit. 'Just act like you've a sock for a brain and you'll fit right in.'

'Never been good at playing brigands.' Will's hand was shaking as he adjusted his drum. 'What if I get lost trying to find the right room?'

'If you get lost, I'll pray for you,' said Robbie. 'Barry said Blackwood always stays in the same one. Room Six.'

'I'll be waiting outside with the getaway carriage,' said Richard reassuringly. 'If there's any trouble, William, bang your drum.' The herald's smile was confident; it wasn't him going in there, after all. Richard wasn't sure what help he could offer even if he did hear a drum.

Will hadn't had time to warm up or get into character. He didn't feel confident dressed as a guard. He had never been much of a fighter. He was an actor and, if he was lucky, a lover. The boots made him walk like he had straddled a hawthorn.

The thought of a real fight terrified him.

The three men stood in the dark across the street from The Hog's Breath and waited for courage to find them. The herald sat on the holy case and started reading another holy book. Silence descended, the silence that an ill-equipped and very small army fall into when they are about to embark on a heroic act and are mere seconds away from getting the waste matter kicked out of them.

The windows of The Hog were smeared with large bodies and steam from Sarah's Tuesday pie, squirrel and fungus. One candle flickered in an upstairs window behind closed curtains.

'Right.' Will grasped his drum. 'I'm going in to rescue her.' He looked at the window, took a swig from a bottle that was being passed between them, and said, 'Tally ho.'

'Wait.' Robbie stopped him. 'This isn't going to work.'

'What?'

The herald was nodding profusely.

'You're right, you won't get past the guards.' He pulled Will gently back before he got to the door.

'I must save Amber.' Will looked desperate.

'You will, but not as guard. I'll be the guard. At least if I get punched, I can fight back. You are more convincing as a holy man. Do you still have those holy books?'

'A whole case.'

'Good. Take this coffee with you, give it to Blackwood the first chance you get, and go get your girl. I'll distract the rabble downstairs for as long as I can. And you, little man –'

'I prefer "Richard" or "herald".'

'Perhaps you could stop reading and find us a suitable getaway vehicle?'

'I will do my best in the time given.' Richard looked at Sir Toby's barouche, already close by, and smiled. 'Do not fear, gentlemen. It will be a victorious escape.'

Will looked pensive; last minute changes always threw him. 'But how will you …'

'The Man of the Road is right,' Richard assured him. 'You would be mauled in there. Two is always better than one in situations such as this.'

It is important to get it right when you are outnumbered forty-seven to three. Will and Robbie swapped disguises. The one good thing about the Alba slums was that you could get undressed on the street without raising too many alarm bells.

Robbie slimed back his hair and drew a ferrety moustache above his lip with soot. 'Follow me,' he said, 'and try not to speak.' Not knowing fully what they were going to do, they walked through the doors.

At first no one noticed them; such was the noise of vented aggression at the end of the working day amongst the guards in The Hog's Breath. Robbie swaggered in on a gammy leg, the last of his limbs to regain feeling after Daniel's cane. The poison had not done any more than paralyse him temporarily. Some men are not meant to die alone in alleyways, and Robbie was one such man. He headed straight to the bar, slapped his hand down, rested his drum on a stool, and, grabbing his crotch, shouted, 'A glass of your thickest, strongest, most stomach-dissolving spirit, Barry – and one for the holy dude.'

Barry stared at him, a long hard stare, as the order reached his brain. He grunted and passed over a tumbler of house brew with no look of recognition. The alcohol hit Robbie's nostrils immediately; it was the colour of a radioactive pond.

He lifted his glass and said, 'Grrrr!' A few guards joined in.

Will lifted his glass and said, 'Chin, chin.'

The room went quiet. Robbie stared at Will, who fiddled nervously with his holy beads.

The Hog's Breath was not a 'chin, chin' sort of establishment. It was not a 'To your good health' one either. Nor was it a 'Live long and prosper' or 'To absent friends' kind of bar. You said 'Grrrr' and you drank while your heart still beat.

Robbie mouthed, 'DON'T SPEAK' to Will and listened as the room gathered in its fists.

But the holy man could not help himself. He smiled desperately around the room and said, 'And peace be with you.'

Peace was a word spelt with an I and two Ss as far as the guards were concerned. Somewhere in the room a filling dropped out of a mouth. Robbie and Will heard it roll to a standstill. Robbie sighed and put his hand resignedly on Stan's sword, took a deep breath, and hoped next week would be easier.

Will hated violence. He did not understand it and he could not do it. He put his holy hand on Robbie's arm and mouthed, 'HANG ON A MINUTE,' before turning to the room.

'I come with gifts from the gods, oh worthy gentleman of the Blackwood Guard.'

Robbie groaned and watched Will fiddle with a buckle on the small trunk he'd brought in with him.

'Here in this holy case are treasures from the heavens, sent by the gods to heal your tired souls.'

The guards were not aware their souls were tired, but they were fairly certain they would like to beat the man or god who told them they were.

'Come take a book, no charge. Mend the error of your ways and believe again. You there, with the skull earring, start us off with chapter one.' Will handed a colossal man a book with a most promising title.

The guard whom everyone called Skull drew himself up slowly and leant over Will. With world-stopping breath, he said, 'I. Can't. Read', hurled the book to the floor, and stamped on it.

Robbie closed his eyes and continued to draw his sword. His leg wasn't going to help him in this fight; he still couldn't feel two thirds of it.

'No matter, dear heart. Stanley here has recently learnt to read,' continued Will, picking up the book and patting Robbie on the back. 'He will read to you, urm, Skull – may I call you Skull?'

Robbie looked at Will and tried to shout NO with his eyes.

'So modest!' Will blustered. 'A round of applause for Stanley ...'

There was no applause, round or not. At that moment, you could have heard a fly burp.

Will smiled manically at Robbie, who wanted more than anything to be that burping fly. He would kill Will if they got out of this alive. The holy man handed him the book and mouthed, 'READ IT.'

Robbie snatched it, opened to page one, and read with as much enthusiasm as he could muster. '*The Governess and the Piano Tuner.*'

'Ah yes.' The holy man drew his robes around him and encouraged the men standing to gather around, which they did not. 'This is a good one.'

'*Once upon a time, there was a governess. She was a stout woman with strong knees and firm breasts ...*'

The guards were hooked. After chapter one, Robbie was given a reading stool and Sarah came out from the kitchen with a pie for everybody to share. When he got to chapter three, Skull bought a round.

'*There was no doubt this lady knew how to work the pedals.*'

On the story skipped, and no one in the bar noticed the holy man was no longer amongst them. Stanley had a lovely reading voice, and Will knew the ending. He was sitting this one out and looking at what the rooms upstairs had to offer.

Will did not have long. Neither the piano tuner nor the governess played a lengthy courtship for more than a few chapters, and the attention span of the guards was shorter than a headline in the *Daily Miracle*. I will it say it again. Will did not have long.

The stairs creaked suspiciously. But no one heard, not even Sarah, who was sitting next to Robbie and fanning herself with a menu, Mitzy asleep in her lap.

Will stood outside a room wistfully labelled *THE BOUDOIR*, and, lo, there was a *DO NOT DISTURB* sign hanging from the door.

'Amber,' he whispered and reached for the knob.

Inside, the son of a lawyer was making terrible use of the room's only candle and dripping hot wax down Amber's defiant neck. His lips curled in concentration and his mouth was full of smoke as he stood behind her.

'Amber, my little dove, tell me where the princess is.'

He lowered the cheroot stub over her skin just as the door burst open. In walked an exuberant holy man.

'CONGRATULATIONS!' The holy man strode into the room. For a second, his brown eyes rested on the lady tied to the chair and faltered. Then he clapped his hands together and, with great joy and rapture, said, 'AND SALUTATIONS FROM THE GODS.'

'Who the hell are you?' Daniel picked up his cane.

'I heard the news.' The holy man glided closer. 'Newlyweds! I had to come right up and give you both my blessing.'

'We do not want to be disturbed.' Daniel gripped Amber's arm, which made her gasp. 'My wife and I are busy.'

Will nodded solemnly and narrowed his eyes. 'I see you are a man of tradition, principal, and moral standing.'

'Yes.' Daniel sneered. 'Kindly leave.'

'Teaching your young bride here her first lesson – discipline. Very good. Discipline is a rare practice these days. Things have become far too liberal for my holy tastes. Though we holy men prefer to whip ourselves with birch branches than tie each other up.' He laughed affably.

Will circled the room, his robes flying. He glanced considerately at Amber. She had been gagged. 'What a lucky man you are.' His voice broke a little. 'To find the one ...'

Amber wondered if she was dying. There was a holy man in the room. The angels must be too busy to come themselves ... It *was* Monday after all. They had sent this holy man to collect her instead. He didn't look like he knew what he was doing, though. Surely, he understood not to talk to the living. He smelt familiar. She stared up at him and tried to focus, but her head pounded from where Daniel's cane had struck her. The holy man had lovely eyebrows, Amber thought. So like Will's. A silent tear rolled down her cheek.

She closed her eyes and wished death would hurry up, but the holy man had taken a seat on the bed and offered

Daniel a book. She hoped it wasn't a bible. Angel or not, he was tempting fate consorting with Blackwood for this long. Amber felt sorry for him. Any minute now, he would be thrown clean out the window and they would both be sharing a seat on the way up to the heavens.

'Forgive the intrusion!' she heard him say. 'Lord knows you don't want a holy man stuck in the middle of your wedding night. I will leave you with this holy book and wish you every happiness. Be good, children.'

Will headed for the door.

Amber said goodbye to her life. Why was the holy man not taking her too? Amateur.

He stopped with his hand on the door. 'Soft! I almost forgot. Won't you indulge a celibate fool and join me in a quick toast?'

'A toast?' Daniel raised one eyebrow.

'Yes, to marriage, with some of my holy coffee. It will bring you luck, longevity, and caffeine – which you may want this evening, ho ho! I beseech you, accept a cup. It's from the foreign lands and very rare. There are few merchants stopping on our foggy shores these days. The palace took the last lot, I gather, for a rather large ball.'

The holy man had pulled various instruments out of his robes, including a thermos and a tainted chalice.

Daniel watched him closely. 'You look familiar.'

'We are all friends of God.' Will gave him a level look and poured some hot, brown liquid into the chalice. He made several holy gestures with his hands and uttered an incantation in an ancient language no one understood – or doubted, because he used the word *sanctity*. 'To you, sir, and your lovely bound bride. *J'espere que vu reviendrez a cette viee comme unne brossed trourriere.*'

Daniel eyed the coffee. 'Kindly leave now or my guards to throw you out of the highest window.'

'Yes, yes. Chin, chin …'

Amber's eyes shot open at these words. She looked up, and the holy man winked at her.

Daniel drank the contents of the chalice in one thirsty gulp. He coughed. It was sweet, it was warm, and as he swallowed, he knew it was not coffee. He sniffed the empty chalice. 'What is this?'

Will stepped back and removed the hood of his cowl. 'Retribution,' he said slowly and clearly. 'You foul plague sore.'

Daniel staggered forward, his expression incredulous, his eyes closing. Then came the sound of his cane hitting the floor.

Quickly, Will untied Amber and did his best to lift her, though she fought somewhat when he placed the wimple over her head. 'What are you doing?'

'It's a disguise, my sweet. Hold on.'

'Oh no.' She sighed. 'Not another one.' She looked down at Daniel. 'Whatever have you done to him?'

'A little present from the princess; first grade Waterwood slumbersap and a little drowsy powder from that chap on Eel

Street.' Will grinned. 'Daniel Blackwood will sleep like a hog while you and I leave this city for good.'

He carried her down the stairs, banging her feet against the wall. 'Ouch!'

'Sorry, my dove.'

Death was not what Amber had expected; it was not peaceful or painless. When she got up to the heavens, she would have words with the Guest Relations Manager there. Leaving the mortal coil should involve music and glasses of the cold, bubbly stuff from Fronze, not a stubbed toe and a nun's habit. What had happened to the halo and the fine, white cotton nightie? She was, however, exuberant to find her heart still beating.

Robbie heard something heavy fall in an upstairs room. He tried to break away from the guards, but they had formed an enraptured circle around him. They would not let him stop reading. The brute with the skull earring was now in tears, sitting at his feet. How long, in the name of love, could he do this for? How long would it take to read the whole book? He needed to leave Alba and track down the princess right away. She was alone, on a wild, improbable quest … thinking ill of him. He hated that. She would tell him to go straight to Thorne (a small locality in the West Realm somewhere, where they still put heads on spikes). But still, he had to explain.

The holy man swept back into the bar and mouthed, 'I'VE GOT HER,' rather unnecessarily, since Amber was obviously slumped in his arms. She looked dazed, angry, and was dressed as a nun.

Robbie nodded, stood up, and yawned. He handed Barry the book. 'Good men, it is time I left.'

There was an audible moan of disappointment.

'We shall have another story at the same time tomorrow. Now, I must escort this holy man and this nun home and beat them severely.'

The guards jeered approvingly as Robbie pushed Will roughly out the door. 'Good night and good luck. Grrrr.' He saluted, and they hurried out.

'GRRRRRR!'

There was a shower of appreciative shouts, belches, and farts as Robbie left. He banged his drum rather well as the door slammed behind them.

One of the guards, so inspired by the reading, began to sing a song about a milkmaid, and a barrage of drunken voices joined in as Will and Robbie left The Hog's Breath.

The herald was waiting for them, jumping up and down with excitement.

'I'm astounded you got out of there alive,' he said. 'Bravo!'

'I know. Not even a flesh wound.' Will smiled.

Robbie looked around for the barouche and then at the vehicle next to the herald. 'Please don't tell me this is it? Our getaway?'

'Quickly, get on,' the herald whispered.

'But it's a gewgaw,' said Robbie.

'It was going to be the Belair barouche, but there are a couple of frostbitten guards sleeping in it.' The herald blustered. 'I couldn't get them out.'

'A GEWGAW?' Robbie raised his voice.

'If I'd had more time and some breakfast, I would have done better.' Richard glared back.

Robbie stared at the contraption. A gewgaw was not a horse, an elk, or a turd-powered sky vehicle like Father Peter's Cloudbuster. It was a wooden platform on wheels with a seesaw on top, which, when pushed up and down by two passengers at great speed, propelled it forward. It was a most exhausting mode of transport, a lot like a pedalo on land, and mostly useless. The gewgaw was traditionally reserved for collecting the dead and almost dead and wheeling them elsewhere. 'I thought you were a herald! I thought you had connections everywhere and all that pap.' Robbie was tired and taking the news about their transport quite hard. He had, after all, only just regained the use of his major limbs.

'Young man.' Richard gave him a stern look. 'This city is not as accommodating as it used to be. My contacts have left Alba and taken their rent-a-carriage businesses with them. Either get on or walk!'

Will was already climbing on with Amber. 'It's marvellous, Losley.' He could now add gewgaw to his skillset of things he could ride, beneath 'asses' and 'swans'.

Robbie scowled. 'It will take us twice as long to get out

of here.' His shoulder ached, and his head spun from the last glass of Barry's finest. A manual drive was the last thing he needed.

As they were deliberating, a guard was thrown out of a window of The Hog's Breath.

Will looked anxious. 'The effect of the holy book must be coming to an end.'

'Quick,' said Robbie, climbing on. 'Let's go.'

Three strong cups of decent coffee and some more toast later, it was past midnight and edging into a pink dawn. They were gathered in the dark shadows cast by small clutch of trees on the edge of Alba, breathing heavily.

'I will never ride one of those things again.' Robbie confirmed.

Everyone nodded.

'What does Blackwood actually want from the princess?' Robbie asked, looking at Amber. 'Did he say anything?'

'I don't know, but he won't stop until he has her.'

'Why?' Will questioned. 'Must he be quite so unpleasant?'

'Daniel takes pleasure in capturing things denied to him,' Amber explained. 'Although in this, I don't think he's working alone. He seemed bewitched, not all himself, too bright and too cold. Worse than ever.' Amber shuddered.

'Maybe it's this witch he spoke of?' Robbie looked

anxiously at the moon and mounted his horse, who had waited patiently for him and was now a little fed up. 'He will wake from the slumbersap soon enough. Get out of the city fast, all of you,' he told the others. 'Head for the Lake of Stars – it's the safest place in Landfelian now. Lose yourself in the crowds. Few Blackwood guards will travel that far into lake country. They fear it is enchanted.'

'If you are going to try to find her,' said Amber searchingly. 'She thinks you betrayed her.'

'I know, but she needs help. Do you know which way went?'

Amber gave Robbie a curt look. 'That young princess is perfectly capable of surviving in this kingdom without anyone's help.'

'My guess is south towards the borderlands, although she never said,' replied Will. 'She's disguised as a merchant, a spice-seller from the islands.'

The herald smiled at this. Red Felian had always enjoyed a spot of cloak and dagger when she was a nipper. 'She has godmothers in the borderlands, if they are still there. Not far from Monkey Wood.' He looked at Robbie.

'Beyond that, we don't know. She loathes you to the core,' Will added.

'Thank you, Will.' Robbie smiled. 'I'm not going to ask for her hand, I just want to warn her. There's something bigger at play. You've all noticed it, ever since the Great Vanishing. The fog, the guards, the rumours. No one is safe from it now.'

He began to lead his horse away. 'Stay out of sight, all of you.' Robbie was still dressed as a guard, although he had his tattered travel bag, kitchenware, and spare hat.

'Wait,' said Amber, fumbling around in her pocket. 'The Dibbles found these at the inn.' She held out a handkerchief, inside of which lay one of the smaller spiderlings. It was still. 'They swarmed in when Daniel climbed into my room to kidnap me. I'm sure they are connected to the hunt for the princess.'

The spiderling was curled up like a winged tarantula, and a sprinkling of metallic dust surrounded it. As they peered at it, a leg twitched.

Everyone jumped. The herald shouted, 'ARGLE!'

Robbie went cold. 'Spiderlings.' He hastily wrapped it up and tucked it into his pocket. 'They are a swarm of couriers, sometimes used as spies,' he explained.

'How do you know?' Will had shared digs for a time with a swagman who kept earwigs. He had grown fond of the insects; they cleaned his ears for free. Although this creature did not look as small or amiable. 'I thought spaerits and spiderlings were nothing but the talk of witch folk.'

'I once had the misfortune of hiding out in the Forest of Thin Pines and stumbled upon the spiderlings' nest – and quite possibly their queen,' Robbie said. 'They are harmless enough unless controlled by a spaerit; a fractured soul, an earthbound and restless thing. Spaerits are nothing more than a dark smudge in the sky. Invisible to most, they have no power unless offered a living thing to possess, consume, and control. My mother knew a little about them. They have been woken and sent to Alba for a reason. To hunt down the princess.' A sense of urgency started to creep up on him. He didn't even have time to change out of his guard uniform. 'I have to go.'

'Who sent them? Daniel?' Amber whispered, looking nervously at the sky. 'In the years I knew him, he never involved himself in sorcery.'

'I doubt it. The South Realm has grown unearthly. It's covered in a strange fog. Even a man like Blackwood would think twice before entering the Forest of Thin Pines. I believe whoever brought the voodoo to the palace is behind the spiderlings entering Alba.' Robbie looked haunted. 'You must leave and so must I.'

'Go safely.' Amber held out her hand. In the nun's habit, she looked ready to lead a choir of virgins in 'All Things Light and Lustrous'. She smiled at him. 'Thank you for your help.'

Will drew her away. 'The swan boat awaits. Come, sister.'

Amber gave Will a look that put an abrupt end to their dalliance with the swan boat. 'We go by wagon or foot.'

'As you wish.' He shook Robbie's hand vigorously. 'So long, Wylde, and good luck.'

The herald bowed. 'I hope you find her.'

They parted under a sickly moon and left the city unseen (although no one is truly unseen. There is almost always a pigeon).

Inside The Hog's Breath, most of the guards had passed out; the rest were reliving their favourite bits of the holy book. One was practising spelling his favourite words. Lidia slipped through the front door unnoticed and glided quietly up the stairs, buzzing faintly until she came to a *DO NOT DISTURB* sign. Daniel was far away, kissed by the equivalent of eleven fully grown treetoads. It would take more than a shaft of sunlight to wake him now.

Lidia opened the window and whispered into the air. At her signal, the spiderlings dispersed immediately from hiding in the small, dark corners of the city and took flight across the Four Great Realms in search of the young heir. Lidia smiled; she would take great pleasure informing the witch of Blackwood's failure.

Robbie had never needed a map. His sense of direction was inbuilt. Every hill, stream, and spinney in all the realms of Landfelian was logged in his memory. It would be easy tracking a princess on a horse twice the size of anything else stamping across the countryside. Plus, he could always ask.

'Have you seen a nut-seller pass this way? Goes by the name of Mary Drew, big horse?' he asked as he left the city.

The frosty air of the borderlands cleared his head and helped him think. Robbie loved the land between the east and south realm; it was a beautiful part of the kingdom, the start of hill country. He had neglected his other work; Lord

Heydon at Mountfitchet had expected him a fortnight ago. There had been no time to send word. At least his family had enough potatoes for the month. It was good not to be making crumbles, repairing dry-stone walls, or listening to the sadness in the voices of the families left behind by the quest. He was on the open road again, free from the burdens of others, and following his own path. What surprised him most was that his own path was also the path of Red Felian. Time with her had not felt like a burden. Time with her felt different; light and promising. Robbie knew he had to find her, but for reasons not quite understood by his young mind.

For the remaining hours of the day, Robbie rode fast. The next night, he stopped, made a small camp, and had a supper of porridge, honey, and dried fruit, which he shared with his horse. Occasionally, he found the good kind of mushroom – the fat and juicy ones with gills the colour of malt. These he pan-fried with a little butter and garlic and ate with dense soda bread.

'Have you seen a nut-seller pass this way? Auburn hair, strong chin, big horse?'

'Why, yes. She went that way.'

Landfelians are good people, he thought. Even the destitute country dwellers stopped to give him directions and didn't try to rob him.

It took a further few hours for Robbie to realise they were sending him in circles. The destitute country dwellers were directing him back to Alba; they'd taken one look at his thigh-high boots and his drum and sent him right back to where he came from. Chasing an innocent merchant girl, the brute. The disguise may protect him from the scrutiny of other guards, but it made everybody else want him lost or dead in a gorge and partially eaten by snakes.

But Robbie soon found the valien's tracks; they continued towards Monkey Wood and the start of the South Realm. The further he rode, the more he noticed the cold and inconsistent shadows. How the paths and villages were eerily quiet and strange shards of fog lingered low over the ground. No one ventured far from their hearth on the borders between the East and South Realms now. The fog hovered above abandoned houses and consumed derelict farmsteads. It unsettled Robbie and awoke a memory from his past, buried deep in the places where we hide pain. The fog was not new to him, he had met it before, but this time, he would find out who was behind it. Here, the countryside felt afraid; there was little birdsong. Nature was somehow absent and no longer able to offer comfort from a new evil in the air. Robbie urged his horse on; he would not let the same fate of his mother happen to Red Felian.

5

THE STILL PLACES

Red intended to use Landfelian's network of Still Places as points of refuge on her journey. Just finding them on her map made her feel closer to her mother than all the years spent locked up in Paloma. She rode south, avoiding the main thoroughfares and keeping to the cover of forests. Tiny smudges in the sky made her look up more often than normal, little shadows flitted over the ground, and occasionally she thought she heard chittering. Her horse instinctively rode faster. 'Are they bats, Face?' Red murmured. 'Or some sort of hornet?'

Whatever they were, the valien did not linger, and he galloped to the first Still Place, near the wool village of Sheepe.

Queen Felian had created dwellings across the land, where houses were few and where nature ruled. The queen called them Still Places; in other lands, they were called churches, cathedrals, temples, and holy places. She created them for animals, people, and everyone in-between. Unlike other kingdoms, here in Landfelian, there was no dominant creed or communion to adhere to, only the belief in good gods, good things, good deeds and not evil ones. The holy men and holy women that peacefully dedicated their life's work to practising this were treated with respect in the same way a farmer or a man of medicine was. The Still Places were simple structures made from local stone – the pale chalky cliffs of north Landfelian, the darker woods and clays of the south. Some Still Places appeared quite suddenly in the middle of forests, while others perched on the sides of hills. Several floated, sure and safe, on islands upon the great lakes. Two were way out on the high plains, exposed to the sweeping winds of the Goby's wasteland. Still Places were intended for anyone far from home needing somewhere safe to collect their thoughts and rest. They were marked by small orange stars on Red's map, and each had a name.

In these houses of quiet, the doors were never locked. If they were, the key was somewhere obvious, hanging from a particular branch or under a mossy rock. The spaces inside smelt of the land, a touch of damp in the cushions, musty books, hay, and the dried sage that sometimes hung in the windows.

Depending on who was visiting, there was often an assortment of bird droppings, baskets of wrinkled apples, a couple of elderly men playing cards, and families on the road travelling between realms. The Still Places of Landfelian remained constant, and in return, they were loved and protected by their people and the stars that watched from above.

Blackwood's guards did not visit them. There was nothing to entice them. Neither the witch's gaze nor her fog was drawn to these unassuming places either. Selina Carnal hated the queen even more for wasting her time and power on such a pointless collection of rudimentary shacks. These places of community, with their good feeling and grace, repelled her fog and sickened her. And Daniel Blackwood was not a follower of anything good or still. To his mind, they were insignificant buildings filled with mumbling peasants, unadorned by riches, and a dog does not converse with his fleas. Little did he know the simple power behind what the queen of Landfelian had built. There was a bell in every Still Place in Landfelian to be rung in the event of a Long Wind, a wedding, or a significant threat.

It was in the queen's most treasured Still Place that the king had got down on one rather nervous knee and tried to ask a question (to which she had responded, 'Oh, did you drop your glasses?'). In this same building – a floating pagoda upon the Lake of Stars – the king had made his leaving speech. His heroes, their horses and maps, and one hundred able men and women had gathered around the banks, all thinking the same thing.

'Does anyone know where we're going?'

King Felian had spoken quietly – which was unusual for a man whose voice could carry out to sea.

A trusted friend standing behind him felt compelled to say, 'Speak up, Austin, they need to hear you.'

'My dear Landfelians, I find ...' The king had stumbled, and he never stumbled. The assembled crowd had waited, flags flapping in the biting wind. The heroes were worried he would not finish his sentence, and they willed him on silently. 'I find that ... at this time ... I am unfit to rule. Forgive me.'

There was a shudder and a murmur of 'Oh no's from the edges of the vast lake.

'You see, I have lost my wing, my heart, my world.' He coughed gruffly. 'And I believe something dark is at work here. I will not rest, I will not sleep, I will not blink, and I will not return until I have found her. My wife. Your queen.' His eyes were blind with tears. 'The quest will succeed, and I mean to return before the year is out.'

His daughter had stood next to him, a stoic little figure, although too young for what was to come. She held his hand, her mouth trembling. The king looked at her with such a burning pain it made her sway on her young feet. Father Peter reached out to steady her, his hand warm on her shoulder. They returned to Celador, and the king never finished his speech, but it was too cold to wait, and when the big rains came, the crowd left, quietly wondering.

'He didn't really say how long he was going for, did he, Hector?'

'No, Eunice, he didn't. Although an average quest takes somewhere between three to six months.'

'Oh right, well that's not so bad. We'll muddle along. He'll be back in time for the princess' next birthday. Poor grub. She will miss them something terrible.'

The heroes had said their goodbyes to their families. 'We won't be long,' they promised with confident smiles.

Standing next to her father was the last time much of Landfelian had seen the princess. Red never attended her step-aunt's balls for long enough to be noticed. Children know when a grown up makes a promise they are not sure of keeping, and she had clung to the king more and more as he led the quest south to Celador, where the rain kept them all castle-bound for a month. There was no leaving speech when he left and no flags, only fog.

Red reminded herself to look ahead at where she was going. If she got lost in the past, she would fall off Face or ride into a manure pile, and then where would they be? She blew her nose and wiped her eyes with her sleeve, cursing herself for not feeling very strong. 'I miss them,' she whispered. 'Where did they go, Face?' She held on tight to her horse. As he galloped on she thought how far away her mother and father seemed. Almost unreachable.

By the time she reached the Rookery, her feet and hands were numb. The Still Place was made from crude-looking wood faded by the sun. It had a leaning steeple with a copper roof and the engravings of sheep and hills on the barn-sized doors. Once inside, she settled down in a straw-strewn corner and moved closer to Face's warm, rising belly as he lay down to rest. In the centre of the Rookery was a vast fireplace built on a plinth of red stone. The stones of the great chimney, warmed from the fire, heated the Still Place up quickly. Surrounded by hay bales, there were five or so people sitting and preparing tea. Red tried to settle her mind as her horse whistled like a kettle and kicked gently in his sleep. She reached into her sack for her journal and scribbled down what she could remember of her last dream, and memories of her mother, before it dissolved in the morning. She also surreptitiously removed her tennis racket from her bag should one of the strangers by the fire turn out to be a guard.

'Oh hello, dear, you must be from the city.' An elderly woman wrapped in a plum shawl had smiled at Red from a stool by the fire. 'Don't worry if it's those undesirable guards you're worried about. Blackwood's lot don't come in here, unless you are a princess!' The woman gave a raspy little laugh. 'Apparently, she's on the loose. Notices everywhere. Isn't it fantastic? I hope she gives them numbskulls a run for their money! Sit down and have a slice of cherry cake. My cherry tree hasn't given up the ghost yet, despite this devil's weather. There's plenty of time for tennis later.' She winked at Red, who was soon folded into the small circle of people, and a blanket was thrown over her shoulders. 'Anonymity is fine, dear, but catching a cold is plain silly.'

Red's journal was a record of what leaked out of her brain in sleep. It was not a light read; there were nightmares and sketches of unnatural things standing over her in the dark. But the princess found if she wrote them down, they did not imprison her. Some nights the visions did not appear to be hers at all; whoever they belonged to; she did not want to meet them without her tennis racket. She had begun the journal the day she'd arrived at Paloma after her parents had disappeared. At the time, she'd intended to note down any clues she found during her time in the North Realm that may help the Quest. Being imprisoned by voodoo had hindered that somewhat. The content had become more frightening as the years wore on, although now, Red's dreams at least appeared to be hers again. The unsettling feeling of someone watching over her had gone. She was gaining strength and she was regaining her voice.

Red heard dawn arrive outside, and the nightmares that made her soul weary fled with the light, as always. She stretched inside Robbie's jumper and rubbed the feeling back into her toes. Early light shone through the windows. Wrapped up, she gathered kindling outside until she was warm again. It was peaceful, picking up sticks, listening to the birds and animals. She watched an owl quarter the meadow with feathers the colour of burnt cream. After this, she laid a fire and boiled water for tea as she had watched Robbie do. Sitting down, to stare at the flames, she sipped at the steaming cup of brew and smiled.

As Red made her away across her map she was thankful for the shelter of the Still Places. After each long day's ride through a kingdom she did not recognise, they were welcome, peaceful sanctuaries. Inside them, she felt closer to her mother and wished she could remember her with more clarity. Her parents, Red realised, were vast, mysterious lakes, and she only knew a small part of their depth. The countryside soothed her mind as she busied herself with the simple tasks of staying warm and feeding both herself and her horse. So far, Blackwood's Guards had not caught on to her trail, although she had seen several in the distance at one of the busier junctions intimidating a wagon trail full of harvest.

Red lived well on the road, without the bustle of a palace, the crackle of voodoo around her or the echo of Caroline's heels ringing through the rooms of Paloma. She did not miss the prattle of courtiers, the falsely gay songs of the minstrels, or Daniel Blackwood's cane stabbing the grounds in search of her, filling the air with his cheroot smoke. The princess began to wonder at her future. Before her parents left, Red had always enjoyed reading the stories of explorers like her godfather and studying the maps of foreign lands and skies. She was fascinated by tales of knights and spent most of her childhood either riding or in a den by the fire in the great library of Celador, wishing she were galloping across new lands and sleeping under the stars. Now, she did not know what she wanted, other than answers.

The Still Places were rarely empty, and Red found she was never completely alone. Many Landfelians wandered in for a cup of tea and a moment of quiet contemplation before making their way out again. She was wary of seemingly helpful strangers since Robbie's betrayal. Thinking of him made her chest ache quite unexpectedly as she sat down by the crackling fire and looked at her surroundings. It came as a surprise when the face that turned to greet her was that a of a large black sheep called Winifried.

'Oh, don't mind Winnie,' said a young man laughing at Red's expression as he scratched the sheep's uplifted chin. 'She can't abide the cold, and I don't want the fox to nab her.'

'Either the fox or the guards,' someone muttered, and everyone joined in with a healthy moan about the guards.

There was always a fire and a shepherd with a mouth organ in a Still Place. Children smudged over schoolwork on slates and sprawled out on rough blankets, elbowing each other before falling asleep in a soft heap after tea. She discovered some Landfelians hid things inside – sentimental trinkets and jewellery likely to be pilfered by guards were sewn into cushions. Thieving home-visits had become as frequent as fog under the new decree:

EVERY DWELLING WITH A DOOR
– EVERY FARM, HOVEL, STABLE, ESTATE, AND COTTAGE –
MUST DONATE ONE ITEM FROM THE ROYAL LIST
AND GIVE IT TO THE GUARDS WITHOUT ARGUMENT.
THESE COLLECTIONS WILL BE TAKEN TO THE PALACE
AND USED FOR GOOD WORKS.

Red listened as a tired-looking woman read out the four items on the last list recently found nailed to her door. Her three children danced around for her attention.

'*An ostrich feather boa, one chocolate fudge cake with butter icing, seven mid-length beards of distinguished grey* – oh, this is my favourite: *a small but tame spotty pig.*' She looked at Red. 'Who up at that palace would want a small, but tame, spotty pig? And as for the chocolate cake, we haven't had sugar in the village store for several years.'

'When did this arrive?' asked Red, knowing full well that her Step Aunt enjoyed wearing animal skin gloves of different patterns to go riding. 'How long have these lists been going on?'

'Since the Quest, they started gradually, one or two a year. We thought they were a joke at first.' The woman gave her children a handful of speckled, yellow plums from her pocket and told them to run along.

'The last one came through just before that ball. Hold the wool still, can you dearie?'

Red adjusted her hands and let the wool loop off them smoothly into the woman's knitting needles. 'I had no idea. Why …?'

'I know,' agreed the woman. 'What do them guards want with a pig? Before, it was a pair of black swans and a syrup pudding. Probably things for the half-queen's next ball and that gluttonous half-king's belly.'

The woman shared her cushion with Red. She had

moved on from Sheepe and was now sitting with other folk from the village of Tura and its surrounding homesteads. Red had found herself on the map as soon as she'd left the Rookery. It felt a small victory to finally see the map come in useful. She wished she could tell Robbie, who never believed in her ability to read it. After three days' travel, she was two days away from the South Realm, where she hoped Tikli Bottom, her godmothers smallholding, still stood. She warmed herself by another fire, thankful for her father's travel coat as an extra layer against the cold. After checking the dressing around her ankle, which now only showed a faint blue bruise, Red shared the little food she had left with those around her. They politely refused her stale bread and rancid almonds and offered her salt biscuits, handfuls of figs, and a well-travelled blue cheese that stank like a bishop but tasted like smoked cream and honey.

'That's kind, thank you.' She smiled, trying to not show how hungry she was.

The princess sat quietly by the glowing embers, her mind raging. The guards had been robbing these people. Where were they taking these items? Her guardians were careless, of that there was no doubt, but she did not remember any black swans arriving at Paloma – or, for that matter, any of Alba's cobbles. The voodoo had left the palace and been destroyed, which must have released her step aunt and uncle from the enchantment she was sure they were under. She doubted there was any gold left for Paloma to hold another ball. These tiny chips of her family's kingdom must be going elsewhere to the mysterious castle in the south that she had heard mentioned.

'Did anyone bring any chicken? I could murder a drumstick,' said a skinny man with only a few teeth.

'Aye,' replied another. 'I've got a small smoked fowl here, and Philip's on the way with the condiments.'

'Oh goodie.'

A man called Philip Bramble always brought condiments to the Tura Still Place, and he got very sensitive if anyone came with their own compote or relish. Despite hard times, Landfelians were a practical people, and when the chips were down, they rallied and shared what they had. Even if that meant barbecued stoat with pickled sprouts.

The following day was Wednesday, and the princess' nut-seller guise caused several furrowed brows as she rode further into the borderlands with her teasel. Tall Sal had been in the attic for too long. If she had put the romantic literature down and gone out to buy a real newspaper or listen to the rumours at the docks, she would have learnt that the merchant ships had stopped coming, due to the spreading fog around Landfelian's southern coast. The fog had become so thick, no trader's ship would risk the journey. Something did not sit right around the kingdom's waters, and even the most hard-bitten of pirates were frightened by its strength. The spice-sellers had not returned for years. As a result, Red was treated with a mixture of sympathy and suspicion. She stood out like a fox by some bins in broad daylight. Or a young lady who had not got the squirrelgram to say that the fancy dress party was cancelled.

Red slowed down past a cluster of deep-pink cottages and the high walls of a large, beautiful house of the same colour. Its tarnished copper gates were crawling with the letters *Windfall*. Inside, she could see the rolling grasslands of an estate. A little further along her path, next to a beautiful spinney of silver birch trees, she found a Still Place, thatched and warm. Here, she decided to stop and check her map. 'We're here! I found it, one of my mother's favourites. Face! They have a library here.' The thatched, dusky pink chapel was called Lapedra.

Red noticed the gentleman immediately. There was no one else inside. He prodded a dying fire with a nearly empty bottle of wine in his hand, making no attempt to rebuild it or split the generous pile of wood that lay next to it. He appeared to be waiting for someone and swayed disconcertedly in front of the flames.

'Good evening, milady,' he slurred, hearing Red enter.

'Hello,' Red answered cautiously. She tied up her horse next to a pretty brown cow. In Lapedra, the larger animals could enter, such was the size of the main hall. The gentleman smelt of stale wine, and she hoped he was not staying long. The sight of the wall of books behind him made her heart soar.

He squinted at Face, as if trying to focus. 'That's a very large horse.'

'Do you think so?' Red whispered fondly into her valien's twitching ears, poured water into a bucket, and brushed the mud from his legs and hooves. Face did not take his eyes off the gentleman by the fire.

He admired her tall, slender figure. From what he could see, the strange girl's legs were shaped the only way a leg can be when it has grown up in a castle and a palace with seven hundred and twenty-one steps between them. Her hair, although it was tied up and away from her neck, was the most unusual colour. The gentleman struggled to stand up straight as he approached her.

'You're not from this realm?' He made a dry, swallowing noise behind her.

'No.' Red gripped the hoof pick she was holding and hoped he would go away. 'I'm from the islands.'

'Really. Which one?' He squinted at her searchingly. 'I would have sworn you were from the south. What brings you to our Still Place, so far from home? There haven't been nut-sellers in these parts for many years.'

Red did not answer immediately. She turned to look at the gentleman. 'There haven't?'

'No, the fog.' He resembled both a mop and a spaniel, she thought, but not as nice. 'You must have arrived a long while ago. If at all.' He had a mean mouth and wore a crushed-velvet waistcoat and a black tailcoat, both stained with wrongdoing. The man's hair was curled with what smelt like goose fat, and one stray lock hung over his jowly face. His breath was heavy and his eyes were rheumy.

'Oh, I've been here for many months,' said Red, looking at the door. 'I'm on my way home.'

'Is that so? You'll have trouble finding a ship to take you.' His eyes narrowed.

The valien flattened both ears and shifted his weight, lifting his back hoof in warning.

'Yes, what an unusual horse.' The gentleman leered.

'I would stand a little further back.' Red smiled carefully and tried to move away. 'He doesn't trust strangers.' As she did so, the gentleman caught her upper arm and squeezed it. His fat fingers trailed inside her shirt.

'Come, dine with me.' He pulled her towards him. 'I may be able to help you with that ship.'

Red glanced around her to see if anyone had arrived. The few who had were all busy bartering their food and building up the fire. She was alone, apart from the animals, and would have to deal with the drunkard herself. She counted to three. 'No, thank you. I do not require your help.'

He stepped closer. She could see black dots in his gums. He tightened his grip around her arm.

'You look ...' He recognised something in Red then and his eyes widened. 'It can't be.'

'Let me go.' She looked him in the eye. 'Sir.'

The gentleman tried to steer her towards the door. 'I live close by. Come, there are several guards I know who would be most interested to know your whereabouts, Princess Felian.' He took a step closer and whispered, 'As for the bounty ...'

Red quickly removed his hand and twisted it back until the gentleman cried out. She forced him to turn around and face the pretty brown cow's rear end, then firmly kicked the back of his knees. With a pained grunt, he knelt. 'Stay away from me, do you understand?' Her grip was as firm as any man's. 'I prefer to dine alone.'

The gentleman whimpered, and Red let go and watched him stagger away, leaving quickly without saying another word.

A few men and women stared as she approached the fire, others whispered, 'Well, blow me to Paloma! Emily, did you see? That young nut-seller just sent Hugo Clamphands-Knox into one of Catherine's cowpats!'

Lady Emily, a woman of astonishing paleness, continued to read her book. As her maid bustled about, she spoke quietly: 'She is foolish. Clamphands-Knox is dangerous, and he will not take kindly to such humiliation. His allegiance is not with us. It is with Blackwood and his guards.'

Red took the seat farthest away from the lady and her maid and avoided their gaze. She pretended to peruse the books which took over one entire wall of the Still Place. She had drawn far too much attention to herself and felt scolded and not at all in the frame of mind to read. *They will be coming for me soon; I must leave,* she thought to herself. There was even a ladder on wheels, Red noticed, just like the one at Celador she used to race about on. She took a breath, closed her eyes, and tried to focus on the beautiful spines. Books normally calmed her down.

A matronly woman wandered over, smiled kindly, and handed Red a clay bowl of soup. 'It's parsnip.' She smiled.

'Don't mind Lady Em. She's a quest widow. Hasn't smiled for seven years. Have some of this soup, love. Got the bay leaves from Clive, the condiments man.'

'Thank you.' Red gratefully took the steaming bowl; it was salty and nourishing. Her hands, she noticed, were shaking. 'That horrible Mr. Clamphands-Knox is a real old leech. You did well to send him running.' The woman, whose name was in fact Janet, continued to chat away. She was the owner of the pretty cow and sometime housekeeper for Windfall Hall, home of Lady Emily Hamilton.

'I always wanted to go to the islands myself,' Janet said. 'See the queen's birthplace.' She looked behind Red at the books. 'We have her to thank for this beautiful Still Place and its library. Terrible that the ships have stopped coming to Landfelian. How on earth are you going to get back, my dear?'

'I will continue to wait.' Red smiled.

Janet nodded. As an afterthought, she added, 'Best not to mention the islands to Lady Hamilton; it'll only upset her. According to the rumours, it was the last place the king's quest was seen.'

Red looked over at the pale lady reading her book. She was very beautiful, she thought, like a fragile vase. 'I'm sure the king will do everything he can to keep his fleet safe,' she said.

'Poor thing. I wish she would eat properly. You can see right through her on a fine day,' Janet continued.

Unlike Maureen Maples – who was built for a squall, with her wiry frame and strong hands and feet – Lady

Hamilton was barely there. Although Red thought both women looked like they had a part missing; sadness pervaded them. The lady drank chamomile tea the same colour as her hair and turned the pages of a book, which appeared to be about the constellations.

'And what do you know of her husband?' whispered Red.

'He's a good man.' Janet looked sad. 'Edward Atticus Hamilton. More a man of the mind than the sword. Terribly bright.' She leant in and lowered her voice. 'The lady, too, an academic sort. She's often here reading rather than up at the big house. She's got a Man of the Road who comes to Windfall once a season; lays the fire and fixes things. It's a draughty old place.'

'Did you say a Man of the Road?' Red tried to keep her voice calm.

'Yes, young one, bit of a wanderer. Last one we've got, I should think. A fine cook.' Janet looked behind her before continuing, her voice low. 'That gentleman you met earlier, Clamphands-Knox, wants Windfall. He wants it with every ulcer in his rotten mouth. He wants the lady, too; hopes to wear her down and take over her estate. Lost all his money gambling. You sure put a turd in his mouth this evening, though! It will make the next newsletter.' She winked at Red.

'Newsletter?' asked Red. Oh no, what had she done? 'Please don't mention me in any newsletter.'

'It's harmless, really, a local rag, delivered to every

113

Still Place in the land. Keeps us in the know. The Blackwood Guards don't see it. Good way for us to check up on the rumours, pass messages between the valleys, warn one another of any unwanted visitors. The squirrelgrams aren't what they used to be, and I don't believe any of the newspapers that come out of the city or the palace.' She offered Red a warm bread roll.

'What rumours have there been?'

'Speak to our condiments man, Clive. He can tell you the latest.' Janet grinned. 'Now finish your soup.'

CONDIMENTS MEN

If you were to find yourself in an area of Landfelian you have never been to before, the condiments men would help you. They will know what time the toast-seller starts his round, who the nobleman's daughter favours, and if there is any work going at the nearest castle. After a conversation with the local condiments man, you won't feel like a stranger and your food won't be unseasoned. They travel door to door with a bureau on wheels pulled by one or two condiments goats. The many brightly painted drawers of their bureaux are filled with pickled, dried, smoked, salted, cured, and sugared things of deliciousness, including candy, jams, chutneys, and preserves. For the price of a caper and a bag of chocolate-covered cloves, the condiments men will tell you anything. Daniel Blackwood censored as much free thought as he could in and out of Paloma, but he could not censor these men or the rumours.

So Red bought a bag of marzipan-filled dates from Clive that evening and introduced herself. 'Can you tell me everything you have heard?'

'Good evening, milady.' Clive doffed his large felty cap, smiled, and gave a little bow. 'Rrrrummmour has it that ...' This was how a conversation with a condiments man always began. Clive was very good; he rolled his 'r's beautifully, and at the same time his ears wiggled.

'Yes?' Red waited patiently and popped a date in her mouth.

'... a mighty castle is being forged in the south.' His voice dropped and became terribly dramatic.

'Where in the south?' She nearly choked.

He looked vague. 'Down a bit from the South Realm and past some fog, apparently.'

Red frowned. 'There is nothing after the South Realm.'

Clive waved this off and gave her a serious look. 'There's always something beyond somewhere else. But rumour has it, no one will find this castle because no one wants to try.' His eyes widened.

'Well, I would try.' Red scribbled in her journal, doubting any mysterious castle existed if it wasn't on her map. 'Is that where the guards are taking all the cobbles?'

'Yesssss,' he hissed excitedly. 'They are being sold to that same kingdom in the south, along with some of the nicer statues, ornamental trees, and the stone pineapples.' Clive raised his brows at her. 'And rrrrummour has it ...'

'Yes?' Red tried to remain patient.

'... King Felian will fall.' He looked about the Still Place nervously.

'Don't be ridiculous, Clive.' Red was indignant.

'Nothing ridiculous about it. Man's been gone for seven years.'

'FALL?' Red shouted now. She gripped the condiment man's arm. 'Where will he fall?'

'Rumour has it, he will fall into a ...'

'What?' She gripped his other arm.

'... a net.' Clive squeaked. 'Would you mind terribly ...'

'A net?' She let go and stopped shouting. 'That's impossible.' For a start, her father was not a fish or a fisherman.

'Rrrrrrrrrrrrrrrrrrumour has it, the quest is stuck.'

She gave him a look. 'In a net?'

'That the king and his men are lost.'

Red sighed. 'Everyone knows they are lost, Clive.' *That's why I'm here*, she thought, *running madly across the kingdom trying to find them, while some thieving little cobble hawker dismantles my home!*

'They can't find their way back through the fog.' Clive stopped rolling his 'r's for a second and noticed the girl's chin. 'Do you know, you are the spitting image of ...' His ears wiggled again. '... the princess ...?'

'Utter nonsense. I'm nothing of the kind.' Red smiled and drew away quickly. 'Good night and thank you, Clive.'

The condiments man watched her pack up her things,

rouse her horse from his slumber, and walk quickly away from the small group by the fire. 'Looks very like Princess Felian. Don't you think, Beryl?'

Beryl was a crone and mostly deaf. 'MARBLES,' she replied.

'No, the princess is long gone from here – and as useful to this land as a feather in a hat.' Emily Hamilton looked up from her book, stared directly at Red, and said clearly, 'Take the path through Monkey Wood, find the Trees of Goonock. It's as quiet as a tomb that way; you won't be followed. The man you offended is one of Blackwood's spies. His guards will be here in less than a few hours.'

Red nodded and left quickly, the lady's words ringing in her ears. How could she have been so stupid? Blackwood must have spies everywhere hunting for her, and now she had involved innocent Landfelians.

The figures jostling around the fire looked at Lady Hamilton. 'Why did you send her straight into bandit territory?' asked Clive. 'The Trees of Goonock. No one comes out of that part of the wood without a part of them missing.'

'Safest place for her. I'd take my chances with the Branch Bandits over the Blackwood Guards any day,' Lady Hamilton replied, returning to her book.

'But no one goes that way.'

'Precisely.'

Emily's grey eyes were at times so intelligent it was best to change the subject and offer her something to chew on. Janet passed a bag of caramels around and whistled.

'Fancy Princess Felian stopping here?' She said, her eyes wide.

'Well, if it was her, she's got my vote. I've been wanting to push Hugo Clamphands-Knox in a cowpat for years.' Beryl sniffed.

'I worry for that young lady. She's travelling alone through the borderlands,' Clive muttered.

Lady Hamilton knew the sharp taps at the window later that night were not caused by twigs in the wind. She noticed how the red-headed visitor frequently touched her left ankle. She saw that the white scars on her skin there resembled teeth marks. The king's crest was stamped on the buttons of a coat she wore inside out, and her horse whistled in its sleep. A valien, no question, although not fully grown, and covered in patches of tea and clay. She smiled for the first time that evening. 'Don't worry, Clive, the young lady will be fine. I believe she's just starting to get into her stride.'

6

THE BRANCH BANDITS

Red rode quickly through the valley of Windfall and away from its deep pink houses. Her horse grunted in protest. He hadn't finished his oats or said goodbye to the nice cow, Catherine. They came over a hill and looked across at a vast, empty plain where the moon shone high and bright and everything below appeared silver. She had reached the South Realm.

'The Southern Plains.' Red caught her breath and slowed down to gaze at the purple heather and hazy mauve hills ahead. She was closer to her true home than ever before. It would be morning in a few hours. Three standing stones engraved with directions stood under the wide sky, buffeted smooth by the wind.

WELCOME TO THE SOUTH REALM
SPICE TRAIL – TO HALF MOON BAY FOR THE ISLANDS OF AQUILA
SWIFT HIGHWAY – TO THE CASTLE OF CELADOR
MONKEY WOOD AND THE AUTUMN HILLS (NOT
VIA THE TREES OF GOONOCK)
THE TREES OF GOONOCK
– NOT ADVISABLE WITHOUT A FAST HORSE

Red thundered straight on towards the Autumn Hills the most direct way, through the Trees of Goonock.

'As helpless as a feather in a hat … How dare she speak of me like that?' she told Face. Red let rip across empty the plain. 'As for that condiments man and his rrrrrrrumours! He can stick them where there's no chutney. Honestly all these rrrrrrumours are doing is frightening people.' The young valien was more concerned with the little dark shadows he had noticed again, flitting across the plains as he galloped. Wild ponies tried to join in, galloping together in a herd. Red smiled and made a noise like SHOO SHOO to chivvy the ponies on, and then she looked behind them and went cold. In the distance, on the hill, where she had stood only moments ago, was a figure on a horse. It looked like he possessed a drum and wore purple jodhpurs. 'Quick, Face, we're being followed.' She swallowed. 'It's a guard, they've found us.'

The giant Trees of Goonock rustled in the distance, and on either side of them stood Monkey Wood. When they reached the great towering Scots pines, Red grew quiet. She followed a path; it was not that clear, but it was the only one. She hoped it would take her straight through Goonock territory and out into her godmothers' valley.

'Another wood I do not know,' she whispered and urged her horse on, following a winding and leaf-strewn way. Pinecones the size of pineapples littered the way, dawn was approaching, and the low light was forking through the trees.

The branches moved slowly above them. There was no ominous scraping or garboling of treetoads, only the dry swish of leaves and snap of twigs, as if hundreds of tiny feet and hands climbed softly above them.

It was not long before the valien realised something was missing. He stopped to scratch a fly bite on his back and found Red had gone. Seconds ago, she had been right there, slapping the low branches and muttering to herself, 'Helpless, am I? Well, at least I'm doing something about the situation, Lady Hamilton of the supremely intelligent and pale clan! At least I'm trying to find the king. Impossible fathers keep disappearing, and as for mothers …' She had not quite finished her sentence when there was a quiet swoosh and Face found his back was princessless.

The valien checked beneath him and whinnied. He whistled their whistle. He studied the ground suspiciously and prodded it with his hoof. The ground didn't bounce; there were no desperately waving fingers holding matches up from a leafwell, which had been their last experience of a rarely visited wood.

Flicking his ears back, he listened to the trees. He then

snorted and lifted his nostrils up to the sky to sniff. Children. Unmistakable. Face smelt children. She must have gone bird-spotting or climbing with some local children. The valien sat huffily down under a large gum tree, whinnied loudly, and waited. It would have been good of the princess to tell him she was going. At least the children smelt good, not like the voodoo had smelt, full of dark, ungrounded things.

Red banged her head on a branch and was briefly knocked out until she was poked awake by a stick – a sharp stick in the small of her back.

'Ow.' *Prod, prod.* 'I said OW!'

Her vision was slow to return. A blurry figure shuffled closer. It smelt of jam and grass.

'She's awake. The grown-up's awake!' a young voice blurted out with a slight lisp.

Thieves, Red realised. She looked around, wondering what form of maggot these young criminals would take, and found she was stuck. They had tied her to a branch with her braces. Darn these disguises! She was in the bandits' lair now; at least the guards were unlikely to come into this wood. Poor Face would be very put out at being left alone, though. The agile monkeys had plucked her from her horse and strapped her to a U-shaped branch up a tree. If she wriggled loose, swung down via that rope ladder, and …

Hold on a second. Red stared through the branches of the gnarly, stooping pines. 'Is that a den!' she shouted forgetting herself for a moment.

What the princess had spotted, what threw her off the more relevant train of thought and stopped her planning her escape, was indeed a den. And the princess had a ready opinion on dens. How to make a good one was a subject dear to her heart. The one sprawling through the branches of the trees of Goonock around her was a highly accomplished tree den.

A tree den was very different from a ground den and not to be confused with a tree house. A tree *den* was purposefully hidden and concealed from prying eyes. This one was covered in bark and moss-stained rags and positioned in a cunning way. A tree den melted into its environment – at least, it did until it met the princess, who knew a den when she saw one.

'It *is* a den,' she yelled again causing Face to whinny up at her. 'It's remarkable!' She couldn't help herself. Even while tied up by bandits in the lap of a ginormous twisted pine, Princess Felian craned forward to see more.

Three grubby faces appeared in front of her, giving her quite a surprise.

'We know it's a den.'

'Children,' she whispered. 'You're children.' Repetition can help one feel less out of control, although it changes nothing.

'*Bandits*, miss, we're *bandits*.' They swung down and gave her an exasperated look. 'We, the Branch Bandits of the Trees of Goonock, Autumn Hills, the South Realm, Landfelian, hereby tell you that you are ...' There was a small discussion between them. '… from about five-and-three-quarter minutes ago … our prisoner, and we will shortly eat you.'

'You're children!' Red said again, rather pointlessly.

'I think she's deaf,' said the lisping bandit.

'Or dumb,' said the one with the glasses.

A bony little girl patted Red's head. 'Bump on her head must have knocked the brain out. It happened to my uncle.'

'Shall I go look for it? The brain?' asked the lisping child. 'Can't have gone far. Might still be on the big horse.'

'Face! He must be worried.' Red looked down at the ground below to see where he was waiting for her.

'It's no use, you won't find the brain,' said the girl. 'She's almost a grown up, so it will be a very small shrunken thing. Doubt it could help her much now, anyway.'

'But you're children?' Red didn't seem able to get over this point. 'I don't understand. You can't possibly live up here. Surely, you're not the *real* bandits.'

The most patient of the Branch Bandits was a thin boy with glasses. He lowered the book he was reading and tried to clarify the situation for Red. He did so with a weary sigh and a frown.

'We are Branch Bandits, miss, not children, and you are our hostage. This is our home, and you are trespassing. We are boiling up some water and sharpening our sticks and then we will put you in a pot and cook you with some potatoes and … do we have anything else, Kitty?' His glasses slipped down his nose as he waited for the bony girl wearing a handkerchief over her hair – in an early form of bandana – to answer.

'Parsley, I think, though it could be a weed. Oh, and I found an onion,' Kitty answered.

'Very good.' The bespectacled boy turned back to Red. 'We will cook you with some potatoes, parsley, or weed and onion until you stop talking. You will be left to rest before we carve you. We are extremely hungry bandits.'

'Yes.' The lisper was the largest of the three. He looked quite sorry and tried not to meet Red's eye. Instead, he stared solemnly at his feet. She saw he only had one boot on and no socks. 'We're ever so hungry, you see, Miss.'

'Do you have any last words?' the boy with glasses asked.

She thought for a moment and then smiled. 'I love your den.'

This time it was the Branch Bandits who were surprised. Kitty, Griff, and Dodge (who wore the glasses and whose real name was John Grub) grinned back.

'I know, isn't it great? The trick is to pick a good base branch,' Griff boomed out suddenly.

'And check first with the owls,' Kitty added with a sniff.

'Really, the owls?' asked Red. 'Do they have an opinion?'

'Of course. If anyone is going to know where best to build a tree den, it is the owls.' She was very matter of fact, was Kitty. 'There is a parliament of owls living here, and they were here before us,' she explained. 'It is only polite.' Kitty thought this hostage was an idiot and would probably make a very silly-tasting soup. They would have to season it well.

Red felt stupid for the second time that day. 'Can I see the rest of it? Your den. I would so love that. Then, by all means, put me in the pot and cook me.' She paused. 'I made a den once. It was shaped like a rhombus.'

The bandits stopped what they were doing and stared at her.

Griff seemed to be on her side. He was dribbling with excitement. 'A rhombus! No way. That is my favourite shape. You don't see many these days. We had to make ours a sleeping rectangle. Some of the smaller dens are triangles.'

'Griff!' Kitty nudged him with one sharp little elbow and glared at Red with such glaring that it became hard not to laugh. 'Don't make friends with the prisoner.' She turned back to Red. 'We'll trade you a look at the den for some nuts.'

'I'm sorry, I don't have any nuts.'

The bandits were visibly disappointed, and Griff's stomach gurgled loudly.

'Well, if you ask me, you're in the wrong line of work, miss,' she said, 'not having any nuts and being a nut-seller. How about marbles? You got any marbles?'

'Sadly, I left them at home.' This much was true; Red had a beautiful marble collection in her turret at Paloma. She missed them most when unable to sleep. 'I miss holding them very much.'

'At least you didn't lose them.' Dodge looked grave. 'If

126

you don't have something to trade, we can't let you see the tree den. Kitty, go chop the onion.'

'Why do *I* have to chop the onion?'

Dodge was an honest bandit. 'Because you know what an onion is.' True, although unfair; if Griff had been asked, he would have chopped something else, and it would have tasted horrible.

'Wait,' called Red. 'I do have something interesting I can show you. But you'll have to untie me first.'

It took the bandits a few minutes to consult on this before they untied her and stood back, their sticks held up ready to attack.

Red smiled. 'Are you ready?'

The branch bandits nodded.

She swung elegantly down from the U-branch. Through the lower branches, she flew like a trapeze act, and after a neat, if showy, airborne forward roll, she whistled for the valien. Face stood up in surprise, moved into position, and allowed her to land on his back with a light thud.

The bandits roared with excitement. It was better than anything they had seen at the circus, and it was happening right here in their wood!

Red winced slightly on landing and hoped they wouldn't ask her to do it again. 'I won't be long,' she whispered into her horse's curious, twitching ears and collected her hemp sack. She climbed back up to the dirty audience of children.

'Kitty! Hold the onion.' Dodge's glasses began to steam

up. 'Do you know what this means?'

The three grubby faces stared down from the trees. They looked like playful imps and nothing like dangerous cannibals.

Dodge pointed at Red with his stick and laughed. 'Why didn't you say you was a Branch Bandit?'

'I am?' Red blinked.

Kitty was not sure. 'She's very forgetful, Dodge. Are you sure she's a bandit?'

'She's built a rhombus den, hasn't she?' Griff beamed at Red like an old friend.

'And she can move through the trees like us.' Dodge cupped his hands around his mouth and made a noise like a gibbon. 'And she looks a bit like a knight on that horse,' he said truthfully.

There was a rush in the leaves, and a chorus of gibbon yowls answered him. The trees moved and creaked, and hundreds of grubby bandit faces swung down through rust-coloured branches to stare at the visitor.

'You are welcome to come up and see our den, princess.'

'You're mistaken,' said Red quickly. 'I'm not a princess.'

'You are – Princess Branch Bandit. You're too big to be a plain-sized one like us. You must be one of the elders.' Dodge pushed up his glasses. 'I'm Dodge. No one calls me John Grub anymore. If they do, I poke them with my stick. This is Kitty and Griff – they are brains like me, but not as brainy as me. I wear the glasses in this wood. Your horse must stay downstairs and keep watch. We don't have the space up here.'

The bandits looked down at the vast, muddy horse who was looking back at them with wise eyes. 'Is he one of them valien?' marvelled Griff.

Red didn't answer that. 'I'm afraid I can't stay long. I'm in rather a hurry.' She followed the bandits into their tree den. The sign on the outside of it said in smudged letters,

OFIS: KEP OWT.

'We used blackberry juice to make the ink,' Dodge said proudly and offered her a seat. It was a purple velvet pouffe with gold tassels.

'Where did you get this?' Red asked. It looked very familiar.

'A fancy barouche passed this way a while back. Very shrill woman inside. Had some pickled onions with her. We took those, although didn't like them much.'

A network of ropes and ladders fed out of the largest tree into the branches of neighbouring trees, which held a swaying village of smaller dens.

'Do you sleep up here?' asked Red.

'Mostly, but when the nights are too cold for the small bandits, we take them home. If we didn't have Griff and his warm hugs up here, the fog would get right through the leaves.' Kitty sneezed. Red thought she looked terribly tired for one so young. 'We try to light a fire some nights, but it can get awfully smoky.'

'Yes, probably best not to light a fire up here.' Red

noticed many of the bandits were underweight, their skin sallow and their patchy clothes threadbare. 'How many people have you taken from the road and eaten?'

Dodge wiped his glasses and pretended to count his fingers in a non-committal way. He sucked the last one. 'Around seven.'

'Mmm, really? What do they taste like?' Red settled herself on the pouffe and raised an eyebrow.

'Bit tough,' he said, looking at his feet.

'It's a pity you don't have any condiments or milk to wash them down with.'

Griff blurted out with a sob. 'We don't really eat them, princess! Kitty has made some lovely broths from the scraps in her mam's kitchen. One time we enjoyed some pork scratchings from the old wizard with the moustache and the owl. Another time, we stole a whole ham sandwich from a guard.' Twenty-seven little stomachs bubbled. 'Most of the time we just make noises to keep up the rumours.'

'Don't say "sandwich", Dodge, I'm starving,' sighed Kitty.

Red wished she had an apple crumble the size of the North Realm in her bag to give them. With custard. She pulled out some honey, a bag of sweet plums, a little bread, some leftover terrine, and a very stinky cheese from her sack. 'Here, take these. It's all I have left from the last Still Place.'

'Thank you!' They scrambled over and looked close to tears. 'We will make you a badge.'

'Where are your parents?' Red asked gently. 'The rest of

your families.'

Kitty scoffed. 'They don't get a badge. They are too hungry and sad. They can't climb, either. No brains.'

'They must be worried about you.'

The bandits looked at their feet.

'Doubt they've noticed we've gone. They're too busy trying to keep the crops alive and the cows fed.' Kitty sniffed. 'And then these notices appeared from the guards offering a good price for any unwanted children. They're taking them away as servants for some new kingdom in the south.' The children looked frightened. 'Our families thought it the safest place for us, these old Goonock trees, that's why we're here.'

Red turned cold as she listened. Not only were Alba's cobbles disappearing to some greedy miser's castle, but Landfelian's children were being taken too.

'We thought, if we made our own way in the trees, our folks wouldn't have to sell us and the guards might stop coming.'

'How do you survive here without food?'

'The two witches look out for us – they aren't sad or hungry,' said Griff. 'The two witches drop off hot food and blankets when they fly over.'

The others perked up at the mention of the witches. Some clapped and shouted, 'HAIL!'

'Witches?' To Red's knowledge, there were no official witches left in Landfelian; none without letters of reference. At least, none she trusted with these children. What unofficial hag had been feeding them? Unless it was the work of her godmothers; she smiled and very much hoped so. They were close to the Autumn Hills, after all, and they were more witch than anyone else.

'And these women, I mean witches, are they local to this area?'

'Oh yes, they live on the two hills shaped like ...' Griff blushed, 'A BOTTOM!' he blurted.

'Goodness,' Red said. 'Tell me everything.' She made herself comfortable and encouraged the bandits to do the same as she spread out a blanket for the food.

'Mad Aunt Mags and January the Cloud. They are witches through and through,' the children explained.

'Tikli Bottom.' Dodge turned pink. 'It's about a day from here. You can't miss the two hills and the witches' houses on top.'

Red tried not to laugh. 'How extraordinary.' It sounded like her godmothers were alive and well after all.

'They leave parcels of bread and moussaka in the branches,' said Dodge excitedly. 'It's like Christmas. Mad Mags flies a broom when she's delivering, although she hasn't been over this way for a long time. She's a very busy witch, always digging for signs, although not a great broom rider,' he added. 'Crashes a lot.'

Red's heart lifted. 'Well, Tikli Bottom, that's where I'm heading. I'll tell the two witches to return with more food ...' The day was drawing on and her horse was waiting, but then there was a noise that made her turn cold. 'Did you hear that?' She knelt down and peered through the branches at the path below.

The sound of whistling. Male, grown-up, out-of-tune whistling, and it was a whistle she knew.

The bandits crouched in the trees, and Dodge put his glasses back on to get a better look.

Red stood up. She had turned a little pink and seemed unsure. 'He's found me.'

'Princess, sit down, you're rocking the den. Bandits, man your posts!' Dodge whispered and began to climb gingerly down the largest tree to get a better view of the trespasser. 'I'll go and see who the whistler is and bark if I need help. Kitty, get ready with that onion!'

'Roger that, Dodge.' Kitty saluted.

Red followed down to a good vantage point and peered through the leaves. Her eyes narrowed and her stomach lurched when she saw him. 'The bounty-hunting gigolo,' she whispered. 'How dare he try to track me? And dressed as a guard! How telling.'

It was late in the afternoon and everything smelt green, of pine and fern. In other lands, families were sitting down to tea and enjoying thick slices of malt loaf spread with butter. To the bandits, stuffed whistling man with potato and onion would have to do.

'Oh no. It's a guard, and a hairy one at that,' said Griff.

'He'll taste horrible.' Kitty made a face. 'All gristle and fat.'

'A Blackwood Guard, too,' noted Dodge. 'The worst kind. Look, he's got some of those purple tights. And a drum.' This was good; the bandits did like a drum.

'He's bound to have a sausage or a roll on him.' Dodge had done a survey, and the average passing Blackwood Guard always carried a deliciously unhealthy snack.

'Look! He's got a whisk,' Kitty cried. 'If he's got that, he must have food. Let's nab him!'

'What do you think, princess?' asked Dodge. 'Shall we cook him?'

Red looked down at the Man of the Road's deceiving head and nodded slowly. 'Yes. We must absolutely cook him.'

In seconds, the Woods of Goonock were filled with the sound of high-pitched barking and scrabbling hands and feet.

Robbie was whistling. Not because he was feeling particularly footloose or fanciful (his feet were sucked into a pair of toe-hating boots and his fancies were nowhere close to free – they required gold, time, and a Cloudbuster). He was whistling because his horse, whose name was Legs, was petrified of something in this wood and whistling calmed her down. He was contemplating changing out of the uncomfortable, sweat-collecting guard's uniform when he heard a noise above.

Legs was not enjoying the Trees of Goonock. She looked up at the branches with quivering nostrils. She twitched at every suspicious leaf. She smelt trouble; she smelt children. Legs did not like children. As a foal, before Robbie had found her, she'd regularly been used as target practice by a gang of feral ones, and the smell of children and conkers had stayed with her to this day. The children in this wood smelt pleasant enough, but one bad oyster can put you off anything in a shell for life. The leggy mare side-stepped through the woods with great caution.

Robbie did not have a problem with children. He attracted them without even trying. It was something to do with his hair, merry eyes, and collection of appliances. To them, he looked like a pirate. At this point, he smelt only the trees, the afternoon, and the path. If he was honest, he was thinking of the princess' neck. He liked the back of her neck. It was clean. He had enjoyed riding behind it for their few days together on the road before she'd started hating him.

'But where are all the birds?' he asked his horse, looking up into the trees. 'I haven't heard a single tweet or seen a stray feather. It makes no sense. Birds like woods.'

Fantails, bobtits, kites, swifts, knobeaks … They had to land sooner or later. Robbie looked on the ground; there was not one dropping or nest. Unbeknownst to the Man of the Road, the birds of Landfelian were in fact flying north, moving fast in droves too high to be seen from the trees between Autumn Hills. They did not like the look of the fog creeping ever closer from the south or the sound of distant chittering.

Legs trotted on. It was very quiet, and then she realised the whistling had stopped. She looked behind her and saw the empty saddle. Robbie had gone. He had taken his bag with him and left no note as to when he would be back. She checked underneath her, walked around in a circle, and stamped. This wasn't good at all. He had left her in a wood and the air was thick with children. Worse still, she smelt raw onion and a very smelly cheese. The chestnut mare trotted further into the trees to find a safe place to wait ... and that was when the princess' valien strode out to whinny at her.

Robbie woke to the feeling of a sharp stick prodding the small of his back.

Oh wonderful, he thought. The Branch Bandits had found him. Now he would have to negotiate his way out of their lair, and this would delay everything. Robbie sighed and hoped next year would be easier. He would never have normally risked the Trees of Goonock, but if the princess had come this way, she must be at the mercy of these legendary bandits too.

He tried to check his pounding head but achieved little. His hands were tied to a U-shaped branch behind him, and, oh good, they had tied his feet as well.

It could be worse, he thought. He could be paralysed and left by some bins. He had survived this long on the road without ever bumping into the bandits of Goonock, but their reputation preceded them. Robbie readied himself for a beating and opened one eye cautiously.

A person in a slurry of trouble that may not have run its course should never think 'It could be worse'. Never.

It was then that Robbie remembered, for the second time, that he was dressed as a guard (though the bandits had

136

removed his boots, which was a relief for his toes). He could hear strange barking and hundreds of tiny feet running through the trees. Were there gibbons in these woods? Black squirrels possibly.

Suddenly, a grubby-faced boy in smudged glasses appeared in front of him, holding a stick.

'Hello,' he said.

'Hello,' replied Robbie, politely trying not to look surprised – the boy's father would be along shortly.

Two more dirty faces swam into focus and smiled. He felt a lump the size of a scotch egg forming on the side of his head. Soon, many children surrounded him.

'Does it hurt?' Dodge waved his stick a few inches from Robbie's nose and flicked it.

'Yes, it does.'

Kitty smiled. For a boy, he knew how to torture grown-ups well. Robbie wished they would leave his nose alone.

Griff lisped in the prisoner's face, 'PERMISSION TO SEARCH THE GUARD?'

'Permission granted, bandit,' Dodge said.

They tipped up Robbie's clanking bag first. 'I found a sandwich! I knew it!' He sniffed it. 'A real one!'

'Filling?' asked Kitty, still staring at Robbie.

'Ham and cheese.'

'Very good. Continue,' said Dodge.

'A whisk, a frying pan, erm ... some garlic,' Griff went on. 'This guard carries garlic! He's the dangerous sort, alright.'

'Rosemary and other herby bits.' Kitty sniffed a bundle of green things. 'There's ... chocolate! It's all powdered, but we could add milk.'

They hopped three times, waved their arms in the air, and barked twice at the mention of powdered chocolate.

Dodge silenced them with his stick and one hop. 'What sort of Blackwood Guard keeps condiments, doesn't cut their hair, and travels with chocolate? Must be new or a deserter.' He chewed on a twig thoughtfully and paced in front of Robbie. 'Good work, bandits. Report back to the princess. Take the prisoner to the pouffe!'

Robbie had no ready response to this. He sat open-mouthed and let the lisping boy and the little bony girl untie him. He could not quite believe it. The Branch Bandits were children? Hungry, thieving, mud-stained mites? He laughed out loud and got poked in return. How many months had the Branch Bandits been feared by the East and South Realms? Even he, a well-travelled Man of the Road, had never discovered their well-kept secret. Princess Branch Bandit, Robbie guessed, would be half his size and still waiting for her wisdom teeth to come through. *Children*, he thought, *HA HA!*

'So you're the Treacherous Tree-Dwellers of Goonock?' he asked, smiling. 'The Ghosts of the Mighty Pines? The cannibals of the ...'

'That's right.' Kitty knew a chump when she saw one. 'This one's got a small brain too, Dodge,' she tutted.

Robbie tried not to laugh.

'Poke him again,' was Griff's suggestion, which Kitty did.

'Well, he's a fully grown grown-up *and* a Blackwood Guard – what did you expect, Kit?'

Robbie decided to be quiet after that. He was soon wrapped in enough rope to open a modest rope shop and taken to the pouffe by four of the bigger bandits. A piece of purple jodhpur was used as a gag. He wasn't worried, though. He would simply explain to this princess that he was on their side and be on his way in no time. These children were hungry, and there was nothing worse than being hungry, apart from reading a romance novel to a room full of guards. If he could get hold of some eggs and milk, he could whip them up some pancakes.

They led him to an impressive tree den with a sign on the door. Robbie stepped inside and was introduced to the bandit's princess.

A young lady smiled at him. A smile that did not quite reach her eyes.

'Hello, traitor.' She said.

Robbie was not an easy man to surprise. Running a business called 'At Your Service Milady' and spending most of his time being politely homeless, he took life as it came. And it came in many guises and often involved encounters with those Landfelians that lived on the periphery of sane. But when the Princess of Landfelian said hello to him from a pouffe in the middle of a tree den, dressed as a nut-seller, it threw him. When he saw her surrounded by child bandits with a leaf badge stuck just above her breast saying *PRINTCEST BRASH*

BANTIT, wielding his whisk like a sceptre, he couldn't lie; it really trucking threw him.

He spat out the gag and stared at her. 'What the blazes …?'

'Silence and kneel,' she ordered in a voice that if persuaded could summon tsunamis and incite typhoons.

'I will do no such thing.' Robbie decided to gamble and threw her a defiant look.

Dodge kicked him in the shin, and Robbie knelt. 'What's all that purple stuff on your face?' he asked.

Red got up from the pouffe, stood before him and with a straight face replied, 'Blackberry juice, you deceiving pile of road scum.'

Robbie said nothing more after that. The tree den wobbled. The bandits stood still like statues at all four corners and watched the young princess and the young, hairy guard.

'Why are you following me?' She narrowed her eyes at him. 'Are there more guards on the way?'

'I sincerely hope not.' He looked up at her. 'Yes, I am following you and I'm pleased to find you looking so well.' She looked very well indeed, despite the blackberry juice. Fit as a fiddle.

'Liar!' Red shouted. 'You leather jerkin puke stocking.'

Robbie thought how best to continue. 'Ankle recovered fast, I see?' Nothing could dissolve the look she gave him. He looked at her feet. 'I like your boots.'

'You are a spy of the lowest order of slimy spy places.'

Red continued.

'Did you hit me on the head with your tennis racket?'

'Yes, and I desire nothing more than for us to be strangers.' Red stared at him and something dangerous began to shine in her eyes. Anger, it was anger. Robbie had not seen it before.

'I thought so. Glad it finally came in useful,' he said.

Red actually hissed then, like a cat. Griff leant in and asked her in a very conspiratorial manner, spitting a good deal, 'What would you like us to do with him, princess? Boil him whole or in chunks?'

Red wiped her ear and patted Griff gently on the back. 'Chunks. Before you cook the guard, I would like to ask him a question.' She pointed at her heart with his whisk. 'Was I on the list?'

'What list?'

'You know full well!' She shouted again, which, Robbie noticed, made her blush. 'The Blackwood Guards have been stealing things, looting the kingdom. Drawing up lists from the palace on the orders of Daniel Blackwood and taking them to a new kingdom in the south.'

'I have nothing to do with that.' He tried to shift closer to her on his knees. 'But I did know about the lists. Let me explain.'

Robbie got poked again by Dodge. 'You call her Princess Branch Bandit!'

'Were you sent here by Daniel Blackwood?' Red

demanded.

'No.'

'Which one of your burgeoning careers do you enjoy most – travelling gigolo, bounty hunter, thieving guard, or giant excrement of …?' Words failed her.

'Fox,' Kitty added helpfully.

'I'm not a guard,' Robbie thundered back, never one to remain calm for long. Everyone looked at his jodhpurs. 'Well, yes, apart from my current attire. If you'll untie me, I can explain.'

The princess was angry, there was no doubt; there was no room in that tone for even a small mewl of doubt. Her ankle seemed in pretty good shape, poised a few inches from his face in those long, soft boots.

'That's a nice disguise,' he said, very nearly earning himself a kick in the face.

The children were enjoying the electricity of the moment. Children are the keenest observers of human electricity. They can sense it gather in the air, like a breeze but with more magic. Grown-ups like to pretend human electricity is just make-believe and does not happen to them, which is codswallop. Grown-ups could learn a lot if they stopped and looked around them once in a while. At this moment, the whole wood was zinging with the stuff; it was coming off the princess and the guard in waves. And it was very exciting.

The princess was a bandit, right down to the tips of her flaming hair, and the Branch Bandits were right behind her in this interrogation. She knew some good words, she smelt nice, and she looked very royal on their pouffe. The bandits did not know what a gigolo was, but they took note because it sounded like an interesting word and was fun to say. Neither did they have the first idea what 'burgeoning' meant or how the whisk was involved. But they were all enjoying the electricity between the pair of almost grownups.

'I am not a Blackwood Guard, no more than I am a travelling gigolo, a bounty hunter, or a giant.'

There was a collective gasp from the bandits, who knew about giants. They were a people one should never try to cook and they liked yodelling and peanut butter.

'I'm a Man of the Road.' Robbie paused and tried to run his hand through his hair before remembering his arms were still tied behind his back. 'I run a small and mostly successful business cooking and fixing things, which has led me into the great houses of Landfelian. Nothing more. I help those families left behind, which is more than can be said for the king.'

He loaded guilt pretty thickly on that last word because his head hurt. And a new feeling upset him even further. He had missed her. He wanted to be part of this princess' quest and he wanted to make sure she ate enough. All this made him angry.

'You took a bribe,' said Red.

'I did. It was at a time when I was keeping my options open, gathering information.'

'Options?'

'The reward was enough to make a fresh start. I never meant for it to go so far.'

'In the alley ...'

'There's no avoiding that son of a lawyer, he runs half of Alba. So I met him as I'd agreed before his guards found me. He stabbed me with his cane – but I told him nothing.'

'Good. Where did he stab you?'

'My chest.' She moved his shirt aside with the whisk and saw the wound. Her green eyes blazed across his face, searching for the flicker of a lie or twitch of deceit. Robbie swallowed.

She stepped back and looked away from him at the gathered children. 'Bandits.'

'Yes, princess!' they bellowed.

'Do with him as you will. He is your prisoner. I must go.' She turned to leave.

The bandits did not have a pot big enough to boil a man, so they busied themselves collecting sticks and making ominous scraping sounds with Robbie's knives.

'Wait!' Robbie shouted after her.

Red did not stop. The light was fading, and to the west the sun was setting. She wanted to get to her godmothers, if they were there, and have some moussaka. Maybe even a goblet of wine, take a bath, and be in the company of those she knew well and trusted. She needed to hang this rubbish week onto something that smelt familiar.

Robbie could stay with the bandits and be blanched for all she cared. The 'cook' story was a particularly big pill for her to swallow, although she had a niggling suspicion it was the truth. It explained the implements, the spice pouches, the accomplished breakfasts, and the scars over his hands and wrists. That night at The Honest Sausage he had arrived wearing one of those white fold-down shirts that looked horribly like something the chefs in the palace kitchens wore. A part of her didn't want to leave the woods without him, and this made her nervous, what if he betrayed her again. Emotions are the devil's work sometimes.

Robbie tried to move towards her, which made the tree den wobble and Kitty frown. The bandits watched the princess gather up her hemp sack. To them she seemed sad.

'Dodge, Griff, Kitty, thank you for showing me your beautiful den.'

Griff turned the colour of a strawberry mousse when she kissed him gently on the cheek.

She shook Dodge by the hand, and he saluted, holding onto her hand. 'Can you tell the witches to drop off some more sandwiches?'

'Yes, Dodge. I will make sure you don't go hungry ever again.' She squeezed his little hand.

'Promise.' He looked forlorn.

Red looked at him and nodded. 'You have my word.' And she meant it.

She said goodbye to the bandits, ruffled their matted hair, and barked like a gibbon before climbing down to the path below.

The Branch Bandits gathered around Robbie. Although they would not question a young lady bigger than them who had a valien and very green eyes, they were not so sure this guard was all bad. He smelt of the land and looked like fun. Like a dragon, but hairier.

In fact, after Kitty received a pastry brush, Griff the spatula, and Dodge got the whisk, the Man of the Road was released from the bandits' lair. He left with the solemn promise to include them in any future battle or feast, whichever came first. He told them to be wary and stay high in the trees. Robbie hurried after the princess, slipping down the trunk of a tree and ripping his jodhpurs a bit in his haste.

She was almost out of the woods when he caught up with her and called out, stopping alongside the valien. 'Wait. There's something else you must know – spiderlings from the Forest of Thin Pines are tracking you. Spies.' Face grunted and looked up at the sky, his ears flat.

Red slowed down and stared at Robbie. 'Spies? Why should I believe you?'

'One of the heroes' wives at the Still Place, Lapedra. She sent me this way to warn you. The spiderlings have been awoken and they're looking for you.'

She stopped. The little smudges in the sky, the chittering. He had talked with Lady Hamilton and her maid.

'Daniel Blackwood has been delayed,' Robbie went on, 'but not for long.'

'How?' Red questioned.

'I gave him the slumbersap you collected in Waterwood.'

'You did?' She smiled.

'If you insist on going alone, take this.' He handed her a small dagger. 'Store in your boot and it will do more lasting damage than your tennis racket.' Robbie closed her hand around it. 'I hope you never have to use it.'

Red looked at the knife in her palm, unsure. 'Why do you want to help me?'

He looked into her eyes and smiled. 'You're quite important.'

'My father is.' She turned away.

'I know the land better than anyone. The spies are not looking for me but a lady travelling on her own. It won't take them long to find you. There is something bigger cooking in the pot if the swarm have been awoken, and ...' He paused and looked at the ground. 'I don't like seeing good people get hurt.'

Red gripped her bag tight. Her horse looked steadily at Robbie. It was true that he had not drowned her in the leafwell when he'd had the chance.

'I can't promise you fortune or glory,' she told him. 'Only certain injury and probable death.'

'Nothing new, then.' He pulled his hat on.

Red watched him for a moment before nudging her horse on and saying, 'I hope you like moussaka.'

7

THE WITCHES OF TIKLI BOTTOM

'Witches?' Robbie checked again. 'We're going to the home of two witches?' He was not sure how many voodoo-chanting jewellery designers he could take. 'They're not *really* witches, are they? Weren't they all banned? They don't fly or turn men into frogs?'

'Men, no.' Red looked at him. 'Bounty hunters, however; there's a spell for them.'

They slowed to a walk and let the horses drink from a brook running through a wide valley banked by heather-strewn hills. The evening was young and there was still time to get to Tikli Bottom before the night became dangerous. There was no sign of any guards or spies. The Trees of Goonock were now nothing but a dark blue smudge on the horizon behind them. The South Realm brought hills, gently at first, with neat piles of stones on top of each one. The further south you went, the bigger the hills became, until snow covered the mountains far ahead.

'Turning Men of the Road into slugs is a speciality of these two witches.' She smiled at the hills; she had missed them. 'Magatha Guiler and January Macloud. My parents trusted them enough to make them my godmothers. They will know if Father Peter has news of the quest from his travels over the other kingdoms.' She looked ahead. 'They are all I have now. I just hope they're home.' *And they remember me*, she thought.

'Where do they live?'

'On the two hills they call Tikli Bottom. The other side of this valley, a small holding. They are entirely self-sufficient.' Red hoped they had not changed like the rest of Landfelian.

Robbie didn't ask any more questions. He knew of the hills from her map, and it stirred a vague memory of his mother telling him a story about two well-regarded healers on the borderlands.

'When I was young, they used to come out of their houses at midnight on Halloween wearing pointed black hats and jump off the roof holding umbrellas.'

'Why?'

'Just to keep up the rumour that they were witches.' Red appeared calmer the closer they rode towards two hazy hills that appeared in the distance. 'People left them alone then.'

'They are sign-readers,' she added quietly, 'And my family now.'

'And Father Peter?'

'The wisest friend of my father's.'

'And the only one who flies a Cloudbuster.' Robbie grinned, and Red said nothing.

Robbie hoped they would make it to the hills before night fell thick and full around them. There were sheaths of fog hovering across the land, and they were in full view of anyone following.

A scream of birds flew over them, heading north. The horses spooked and moved a little quicker as the sky darkened. They did not pass another soul. It was quiet and eerie. Two hills shaped like a pair of cornice pears grew out of the dusk ahead. On top of one there appeared to be a windmill, its sails gently turning. On the other a tall, thin house, with a remarkably long chimney. In fact, both dwellings had chimneys as tall as the first floor and wide as doors.

'There!' cried Red, relieved.

Robbie followed close behind and stared at the strange hills. No turning back now.

Magatha Guiler rode a broom to clear her head and let the good winds get under her skirt, which she found very invigorating. Her broom was called Bernard and it was a Standard 777. You would only know this if you were from

Landfelian. There was only one model of household broom and that was the Standard 777. The ones that flew had been discontinued, so were rather rare nowadays. You needed a lot of faith to ride a domestic broom, and most witches that tried lost that faith as soon as it dawned on them that they were straddling a branch midair. When Father Peter had talked through the spell for flying the Standard 777, he'd warned her it would only work for short journeys on a fine day, but Maggie had no problem with flying. Maggie rarely lost her faith in the universe. She found the run-up before take-off quite exhilarating, provided she hadn't just eaten. Landing, however, was a different story ...

Maggie had mounted someone's shed recently, before tumbling off the roof and falling into their garden amongst the squash. On account of her being the only well-known witch in the area, no one came to issue a warning, save a few angry birds nesting in the shed at the time. Although a nice pathway patrol man had witnessed her most recent crash. Maggie had laughed affably with him and stood up with as much dignity as she could muster.

'Have you been drinking, miss?' he'd asked. 'Fraid it's my job to ask. I assume you have a permit for the ... broom.'

'You would need a drink if you tried to ride one of these,' she'd replied. 'No, the problem seems to be the fog. It has filled Landfelian's skies with doubts.' She grimaced at the sky and walked away with as much dignity as she could muster, waving her permit.

'All witches have been grounded you know. New law. Blackwood and his guards' orders.'

Maggie gritted her teeth. 'That man has no true authority over what a witch can or can't do.'

'I would tend to agree with you, ma'am, but the law's the law.' The pathway patrol man looked sorry.

Bernard was now in the fireplace because he refused to start. Maggie had tried everything, even running down her hill with wheels she'd fashioned out of doorknobs attached to her feet. She wondered if it was a sign. The birds were also fleeing, and the weather was worse, if that was even possible. Maggie gave the broom a hard look.

'Oh, come on, Bernard, it's not that bad.' The broom said nothing. 'Is it just that I'm too heavy?'

Either way, it was deeply frustrating. If she could not fly, she could not pinch the air and smell the waters. She could not easily visit the old folk who relied on her company, get her lowlights done in Dood, feed the Branch Bandits, or check on her goddaughter. Even more vexingly, it was impossible to look for signs further afield. There was always the public carriage which went to Alba once a week, but it was often stopped and raided by guards. Few travellers passed her way, and the old donkey that grazed over her hill was an obstinate mule who needed a rod of carrots dangled in front of his nose to carry Maggie further than a mile.

Madame Guiler was not a woman who liked to sit and wait for things to come to her. She was rarely still and being housebound had thrown her. As a result of her confinement, Magatha had become a dedicated grower and drinker of tea, and she was fiddling about with that process now. She kept her teas in a tall apothecary cabinet in her kitchen – which was also her work room, library, and snug. Flavours included mint, nettle, spearmint for indigestion, and sword grass and muscle pea for courage. She had recently been working on more obscure blends like Blush and Boost that made the cup omit pink steam, but today she was indulging in a bowl of Purple Zing and humming as Red and Robbie approached. She rarely hummed; it must be a sign, she realised. Animal, her long, black dog, who doubled up as a useful draft excluder, thumped his tail against her leg and rolled over.

No, she had not hummed since the brief Age of Romance when everyone was at it. No one had been caught humming with real gumption for seven years. She looked out her window – beyond the sill covered with herbs, shrunken knobs of soap, and a collection of crystals – and wondered what it could mean. Her left boot fell onto the mat by the door.

'Oh, goodie! Company's coming.' Maggie rubbed her hands together. 'It's about time. How many boots this time? Just the one?'

The other boot wobbled and then landed on the first. Her cat Julia slunk in and mewed.

'Julia! She has a companion. I will rustle up something hearty for them to eat.'

She laughed a husky little laugh, eyed the door

expectantly, and poured the rest of her tea into a wilting tomato plant, which duly shuddered. Her goddaughter had made a new friend – how wonderful. It explained the butterflies in her bedroom that morning. She'd hoped the signs were right, that Red Felian really was on her way.

The fair, graceful form of January Macloud loped past the window, singing, 'Visitors, Magatha!' in a high soprano. The scent of incense and the sound of small bells came with her. 'I have seen.' She had the soft breathless voice of a woman talking through a lot of scarves.

'Tea, darling. I'm making another Purple Zing.' Magatha liked making tea more than she liked drinking it. The ritual was so often better than the result.

'Oh lovely. Something soft and romantic, please.'

'Oh dear, you too? Humming?'

'Mmm hmm. Woke myself up. Can't seem to stop.'

The godmothers were soon sipping thoughtfully and gazing at Maggie's fireplace, where young flames crackled. The wide chimney had many uses besides burning logs: the broom lived there, and Father Peter's owl, Marmadou, came and went that way – when there wasn't a fire.

Jan finished her tea and looked at a small clock on a chain around her neck. 'I've got a pupil coming for harp therapy in three minutes. As soon as that red one arrives, tell her to come and see me. She's bound to climb up here first for your moussaka. The smell of it enchants anyone who passes below.'

'Melted cream and cheese, never fails.' Maggie put her apron on and began opening cupboards with purpose.

Jan clutched her hands together and did a little jump. 'Oh Maggie, do you think she's got out of Paloma? Do you think she's really on her way?'

Maggie reached for her friend's hands and beamed. 'I most certainly do. It was only a matter of time.'

A scarecrow dressed as a witch was staked at the bottom of the two hills directing visitors to the correct house and deterring everyone else from going any further.

THE BIRD HOUSE – PSYCHIC JAN, WITCH:
LEFT PATH AND STRAIGHT UP

THE SNUGGERY – MAD MAGATHA, WITCH:
RIGHT PATH AND STRAIGHT UP

BEWARE OF THE ANIMAL

As the fire licked and glowed, Maggie opened the door and inhaled the night air. A page from the last Still Place newsletter, *RUMOUR HAS IT*, blew in.

MYSTERY NUT-SELLER LANDS SIR CLAMPHANDS-KNOX, A GUARD SYMPATHISER, INTO COW PAT.

She chuckled and looked to the distance. A flock of red-footed nips flew up and curved into a five and a seven before shooting north. 'Fifty-seven minutes.' Maggie put a moussaka in the kiln before turning to her dog. 'Animal, I'll wager she is going to need a hot bath and a tight hug. Fetch me some lavender.'

The long black dog wriggled up from the rug by the fire and bounded into the garden, quickly coming back with a sprig of the mauve flowers in his mouth. 'Good boy, now drop. Go and find Julia.' The dog barked and trotted outside, his round tummy sweeping the floor to stalk the two hills for the slim, grey cat who had left the palace shortly after Red to return to her owner.

Maggie started fluffing up her ebony hair and dabbed rose oil on her wrists. Her mouth had once been declared 'enigmatic' and her brown eyes hailed 'very fine' by various suitors from all four realms. Although she was perfectly happy in her round house, living and working alone. Witches knew what was good for them. She straightened the watering can outside her front door. It was there for the express purpose of being kicked every time something bad happened. She called it the Can of Fear, and kicking it made her feel less jittery and considerably better about the lay of the land – as long as she wore boots. Any visitors to Maggie's hill were invited to kick the can before entering. Fear was not allowed inside a witches' house – it made the animals unhappy and her kiln go cold. These days, Maggie kicked that can more than ever. But not tonight. Tonight, she felt no need: Red Felian was on her way again.

The last time the princess had visited Tikli Bottom she had been nine. The king and queen had dropped her off during their last *And How is Everyone Doing?* tour of the kingdom, and she couldn't have been more excited. Staying with her godmothers was as good as staying in a rhombus den with a bag of custard tarts, another of sausage rolls, and a bowl of cherries. The stories Red heard spoken between the two women made the fire crackle and her eyes sparkle. While under the watch of Daniel Blackwood at Paloma, she had clung to those memories like a crab to its shell in a cross-current.

Maggie had made her goddaughter promise one thing before she'd left. 'When the cows sit down, come here.' Red had looked confused. Witches of Maggie's calibre had their own way of making sense, and it sometimes took others a week or two to understand them. She'd squeezed Red's hand and whispered, 'When you require directions, when you need a rest stop halfway through a long and difficult journey, when you would like to get out of one chapter and are not certain how to find the next, come and see me.' She'd held her close for a second. 'Promise.'

Red had breathed in her godmother's rose oil smell and promised. And both Maggie and Jan had waved her goodbye noticing with a frown unusual clouds gathering above the mountains.

The valien galloped towards the two smoking houses upon the hills. The princess turned to Robbie, pointing with the excitement of a small child. 'Look! Can you see the dragons? They've lit them for us – they know we're coming!'

Robbie was less than enthusiastic about the strange mounds ahead and the unusual shapes made by the smoke that came from the chimney. He imagined the bones of unfortunate men buried beneath these hills. Although these women obviously meant something to Red, he doubted they were able to offer her any protection or knowledge of the quest. He looked across at her open, hopeful face. Something had happened to her. There was a confidence in the way she held herself. When he glimpsed hidden feelings scud across her face like shadows, he wanted to understand, but when Red caught Robbie's eye, he turned away and did what many men do in delicate moments. He coughed.

The horses followed the faint lights that glowed at the bottom of each hill. Two enormous dragons moulded, hollowed out, and fired from red clay were filled with guttering candles that flickered through the carvings, lighting up shapes of sorcery and witchlore. They marked the start of the pathway up the hills; a winding elm handrail had been provided.

Red jumped off her horse and hurried up a trail barely visible between the wildflowers and tall grasses. Robbie looked up at the top of the hill. Shrubs, some almost tree-sized, sprouted out of the rooftops, looking like hag's hair and making both dwellings seem almost alive. He felt he was walking into a fairytale without being sure if the women who lived here were good or evil.

Maggie's windmill had two rooms – one up and one down, both surprisingly spacious – and several lean-tos that attached to the main like old barnacles. She had begun to feel the cold and knitted reluctantly when there was nothing else to do. She now wore colourful mittens most nights; they helped her see in the dark and kept the chill away. Her house was full of cracks and holes she had never noticed before. They had never bothered her until the fog began to stalk towards the hills.

'Friday Felian,' a warm voice called down. 'You've arrived! Who's for moussaka? It's made from real mousse and fresh saka.'

'Maggie!' Red ran up the hill to meet the witch with a husky laugh.

Magatha was the most colourful woman Robbie had ever seen. She emerged over the crest of her hill and trotted down to meet them wearing a long, soft coat of patchwork silks.

'Darling girl, what took you so long?' A slim grey cat sat around her shoulders like a stole. She mewed gaily at Red.

'I ... I got waylaid.' Red smiled bravely and then fell into her godmother's wide, open arms.

Both women toppled over into the heather.

Red held on very tight. She took a deep breath and swallowed. 'I knew when Julia arrived at Paloma that I should come here. It was just a ...'

'Difficult time.' Maggie blew her hair out of her mouth and searched her god-daughter's tearful face. 'Well, of course it was, oh my dear. Remember our promise? When the cows sit down, come straight here. January and I have been wishing it since your father left – none of our letters reached you.' She grew angry. 'And visiting that palace was impossible. These terrible brutes with drums asked me for a password. I did try, my darling girl. I'm so sorry you were alone. Now ...' She wiped her eyes and grasped around for her glasses, only to find them hanging from an old gold chain around her neck. 'Let me look at you.'

Maggie Guiler took a good look; a very thorough, searching, energy-boosting, orange-filled look. And what she saw furrowed her brow.

'Right, well.' She sniffed. 'There's been some bad business up at Paloma, but you're here now and that is all that matters. Come in. Get warm and bathe before you flatten the flowers and tell me everything.' She held gently onto Red's face. 'Oh, but you are beautiful – and you finally grew into this chin. It had me worried. Didn't want you walking through life with a third foot attached to your face.' Red rolled her eyes but she was smiling. 'Goodness me, and you're such a long, rangy creature.' She laughed. 'Like your father. We must feed you up immediately!'

She turned to look at the young horse standing behind Red and bowed her head respectfully. 'You are welcome here, brave Face of the valien. Rest and eat as much sweet grass as you can find on these hills. They will protect you.' This invitation was received with a long whinny.

Red squeezed Maggie's hand, and they climbed the rest of the way together, arm in arm. 'I've got so much I want to tell you. How is Jan? Can I see her? Shall I run up there now? Are you both still flying?'

'Now, now, all in good time.' Maggie laughed and held her close.

Robbie was only halfway up the hill. He never thought the time would come when he missed the actor William English, but right now he did. There were a lot of strange folk roaming about here and very few men. The current company all appeared a little on the conkers side of autumn. Robbie would have welcomed his new friend, who could at least be relied on to do all the talking and be a clown. Legs had taken one look at the ascent and stopped. He dragged her to the top of the hill, his thighs burning. The colourful godmother, the cat, and the princess were already at the door, chatting away in that way women do when there has been an absence of time. A long black dog waggled up to Robbie, sniffed his hand, and began to lick it. He stood shining with sweat and waited for someone to notice him. After a few moments, he coughed and said, 'Good evening, Madame ...'

Maggie jumped, turned straight towards his sweaty chest, and said, 'Saint Christopher!' She put her glasses on. 'My name is Maggie, not and hopefully never to be a Madame.'

Red smiled. 'This is Robbie Wylde, a Man of the Road.'

'I help with the navigation.' He held out his hand and added, 'In particular, woods.'

'Ah yes, Landfelian's woods are full of secrets.' The small woman kept hold of his hand and turned it over with searching fingers. 'Robbie. Wylde. Mmm, January knew it was something with a double B and a whisk.' She looked into his eyes and smiled. 'Well, well, welcome! Come in, there's more room in The Snuggery than you think. Appearances can be very deceiving where size is concerned.'

She gleamed at him, and Robbie wondered if there were any talking amphibians in the lavender.

Reading his mind, she said, 'I won't turn you into anything just yet, although that rumour did us proud for months. Goodness, you're broad.' Maggie could not stop patting his chest. 'And hairy.' She pulled on a hair. 'And yet still so young.'

Robbie rubbed his chest, deciding to ignore the fact that the witch was discreetly pocketing a few hairs. 'The horses, are they safe here?' He looked at the ramshackle number of sheds and lean-tos around the house, none of which looked big enough to house more than a goat. Red was already inside, gasping in delight at strangely shaped ornaments she clearly remembered from a time before.

Maggie continued to stare at him noticing the savage scar around his neck. 'The horses? Oh, yes. There is enough good grazing between these two hills to feed a family of valien. The fog will keep away this evening. Hope has returned.' She winked.

'There is a chance we're being followed by guards and spiderlings,' Robbie said, watching Maggie's face harden.

'Spiderlings, did you say?' She stepped closer and looked at Robbie.

'Yes, they were in Alba's skies the night the princess left.'

'Mmm.' Maggie sniffed, looking at the moon. 'I must speak to January about this. Don't worry, my land is protected for the time being by a respected spell, older than this new malice.'

When Robbie returned from checking the horses, breathing like a bull, the warmth of the day had gone. Lanterns glowed inside and the smell of melting cheese hit his mouth and made him forget all talk of witches and broomsticks.

'Time to get out of those horrible plum tights.' Red's godmother appeared at the door. 'Here, try these for size. I see you've brought your own frying pan, too. How well-equipped.' She handed him some clean clothes, directed him to a cold trough of water, and hovered with a toothy smile.

Robbie peeled off the jodhpurs, which was hard to do without falling over, and put them on the ground. He was unused to taking his clothes off before a witch, but there was a first time for everything. The dog picked the jodhpurs up and shook them vigorously.

'I hate them too.' He smiled and patted the wiggly mutt, going to sit by the fire in a combination of his and what looked like a pirate's clothes. If someone had asked him his name and his five-year plan at this point, he would have answered, 'To sleep and not be turned into a slug.'

Looking around, Robbie could see the house was well loved. There was a good fire and candles flickering in all the crevices. On a little round table were three plates piled high with moussaka. There was bread, butter, and spinach salad, and a wooden cup brimming with red wine was placed in his hand. Red had never looked happier, which pleased him. As the night drew on, Robbie drank and ate in thankful silence, listening to the two women talk. The elder barely drew breath. The princess gradually dropped her shoulders and stretched out her long legs. When she did speak, it was to tell Maggie what had happened during her years at Paloma up to their arrival at Tikli Bottom; she seemed wary to discuss it again and grew sad when describing the Half King and Queen's treatment of her.

Maggie's face became very still as Red spoke. When she finished, she took a grateful gulp of wine. 'Do you have any idea where this son of a lawyer found the voodoo charm?' Her voice was low.

'None at all. I remember very little about the day it was placed on me.' Red looked at her hands. 'I really don't understand what it was for. I was only small.' She swallowed down a lump that tightened her throat. Julia jumped onto her lap and started purring.

'January must know of this. She will be here at first light. She would have come sooner but knew I would do all the talking and that you would be tired.' Maggie looked sorry. 'It should never have happened at all. Your guardians must have been bewitched; I do not believe they were in their right mind as soon as that voodoo charm was allowed into Paloma.'

'Bewitched? Have you seen this kind of sorcery

before?' Robbie asked, keen to understand what lay behind it and how to avoid any more. The thought of the voodoo anklet made his fists clench.

'Possibly. A long time ago. Did you bring what was left of the teeth?'

Red shook her head. 'No, I fled Alba in a hurry. I did not care to look upon them any longer.'

'I can well believe it.' Maggie reached out for Red's hand. 'It's quite miraculous you overcame it.' Robbie noticed the curious look that passed over the older woman then.

Later, after everyone's appetites were satisfied, when time became full, drowsy, and not entirely responsible, Magatha said good night and left the travellers in a safe heap on the cushions. She wanted to go and talk to Jan about the voodoo without alarming the young ones. It was with some urgency that she trotted down the hill and up the next.

Robbie lay near to Red by the fire. They had both washed and smelled a lot fresher. He stroked Animal's upturned belly and swirled his remaining wine in lazy circles. Soothed by the quiet roar of the fire, Red's feet stretched closer to the heat as she lay upon a battered chaise longue.

'So, Princess Felian, what's your hook?'

'My hook?'

'What do these spiderlings, guards, and unpleasant men with canes and voodoo want with you?'

'I wish I knew.' She frowned, scratching Julia's upturned chin.

'What is it you have? A secret power? Gift? Hidden talent? Ancient wisdom? Are those rubies you carry around magic? Do you own an invisible cloak?' He smiled at her.

Red yawned and made a noise like a cat. 'No, but I'd like one.'

Robbie passed her the remaining wine.

'No more.' She said. 'I'm too sleepy.' It had gone to her head and caused her cheeks to go a rusty pink.

'There must be something ... The secret key to immortality? No, I've got it.' He shifted up and reached across to study a lock of her hair. 'It's your hair. It can perform miracles, control the weather? It can make a cup of tea.' In the light of the flickering den, her hair seemed to glow. He looked at it and said, 'It is ... astonishing.' Red laughed. 'I'm serious.' No one felt like being serious, least of all Robbie. 'It must be something big to wake up the spiderlings. They've been asleep for hundreds of years. Why does everyone want to catch you?'

She studied the fire, as if trying to find the answer in the embers. 'I don't have a hook or a secret key. I don't know why this is happening.' She pummelled a cushion into shape behind her and sunk down into it. 'I wish it wasn't.' She laughed through her nose. 'I'm left-handed, that's it. Not to be trusted, definite witch in the making. Have you heard what they were doing in Engerlande to those poor women?' She wanted to change the subject.

'Hold the whistle.' Robbie waved his left hand. 'We have something in common! I'm left-handed too! Who would have thought.'

When the clock slid past midnight, when anything could happen and often did, Robbie asked, 'Do you miss them?'

'My parents?' She opened her eyes and looked at him, stroking Julia's tail. 'I think of them every day.' He watched her mouth while she spoke. 'Sometimes I forget how it used to be. I remember once, I fell off my horse at Celador and my mother looked at me so fiercely it scared me more than the fall.' Red looked at the flames. 'I never understood why. I think I do now. She looked at me as a mother. She was frightened. She knew how fast a life can be taken – one fall and gone. I knew so little about her. I would love the chance to find out more.'

'I don't think we ever truly know anyone,' Robbie said quietly.

Red shivered and pulled a blanket over her. 'I miss them most in the dark.'

The candle by the window petered out and the cat flicked her tail, jumped to the floor, and started to knead Robbie's leg with her claws.

'And your mother, is she …?' Red asked.

'No. She died.' Robbie's voice closed down any further questions.

She watched his young face harden and considered how full of thoughts he was; thoughts she could only ever wonder at. 'I'm very sorry.'

Robbie rubbed his eyes and drained his glass. 'We

lived in the kitchens mostly, of an abbey called Nun's Drift. I remember the smell of apple crumble and her laugh. And many boots by the door. She was always feeding folk; such a feeder she was and listening to strangers' stories. We were never without company for long, and I was never hungry.' He smiled. 'My mother taught me how to survive on the road.'

'And your father?'

'Never met him.' His voice locked.

Red faltered. 'Why do you want to leave Landfelian so much?'

'Leave? This great kingdom?' He laughed. 'There is nothing for me here.' He started to get up. 'I'll check the horses. You should get some sleep.' He looked down at Red wrapped in his jumper and pulled the blanket over her feet. 'My mother would force me into that yook wool. It smelt of goats and was too big, but it was warmer than a bed of goose feathers in the winter.' He opened the door. Outside the moon was drawn over by clouds. 'It was my father's; the only thing he left behind and all I know of him. He travelled to cold places where the yooks roam.' Robbie noticed she was already asleep. 'I'm looking for a ghost,' he told her. 'Like you.'

The princess opened her eyes to gentle light the next morning and marvelled at the sound of bees hovering outside the window, where lavender and peach-coloured roses waved. She stretched and rubbed her feet together. Julia mewed in her face.

'Good morning,' the princess whispered in reply. She picked her up and smiled across at Robbie. He was on his back, next to the fire, his mouth wide open and one arm flung across his eyes, deep in sleep. She felt someone or something watching her and looked across the room to find the solemn, sloping eyes of a hare. It was hovering by the stairs, one paw pricked up, black nose twitching. 'Luna,' Red whispered, and she crept upstairs to find January Macloud sitting on Maggie's bed, smiling.

'Jan!' Red rushed forward, and the fair lady wrapped her silvery shawl and long arms around her. She said nothing but held her very tight. It was then that Red found her eyes full of tears. She stayed there in her godmothers' arms and wept until it was done. January said nothing, but she held on tight and did not let go. She was good at waiting.

'I've run you a bath, my darling, and here's some tea.'

'I've missed you.' Red clung on.

'And I you.' Jan gently let go and studied Red's face. 'You have been so very brave.'

'I don't feel very brave.' She sniffed.

'I don't think we ever do, but godmothers are here to remind you that you are.' Jan passed her a handkerchief.

'Where's Maggie?'

'I believe she's having a disagreement with the local condiments man about some relish.'

Red smiled.

'Come, bathe, it will make you feel better. You don't

have to talk. I will be just here.'

As Red sank into the steaming water, she watched Jan fold her shawl around herself and look out the little round window of Maggie's bedroom. While one godmother was always in perpetual motion like a breeze, January was calm and still as the moon.

'What do you remember about my mother?' Red asked suddenly.

'Well, let me see.' Jan looked entirely serious and then smiled. 'I remember that she still has my favourite shawl. And I'm not letting that go without a fight. Landfelian's fairest queen and her Still Places, Realm Feasts, the Lake of Stars, heroes and heroines, always allowing experts in their field to shine... Yes, quite a legacy she left behind.' She looked at her hands and said, 'I remember how her face changed when she looked at you.'

Red washed herself and tried not to cry again. 'Do you think she is still alive?'

'Yes.' Jan did not hesitate. 'Your mother had many talents, some she chose not to follow, but they will be with her now, keeping her strong, protected, and ready to return. Talents that you ...' She paused. 'I remember her as if she were here with us now. Most of all, I remember how much she loved you.'

'Why did they leave me behind?' Red's voice wobbled.

'My dear girl, you were the best thing they ever made,' said Jan gently. 'They would do anything to keep you safe.'

Jan looked at her goddaughter. 'I don't know why your

mother left. But you must know this. She is a very talented reader. Far more powerful than Maggie or I.'

'Reader? You mean my mother is a witch?'

'She could read people. She could See, understand subtle changes in the things around her and when necessary she could protect others.' Jan looked at the sky. 'I believe she saw something the night she vanished, something that took her away. Something she wanted to keep from you and your father. To keep you safe.' Jan looked out the window. 'Something she thought she could settle alone.'

'I never knew that about her. Have there been any signs?' Red wiped her face and swallowed.

'A lot of fog and one sign that makes no sense. No sense,' Jan said again. 'Like wigs.' She sighed. January believed that, unless you were bald and didn't want to be, choosing to wear someone else's hair on top of your own meant you had a peg missing.

'Tell me,' said Red.

Jan pulled a tiny goldfish hook, curved like a bass clef, out of her dress pocket. 'These hooks. I find them everywhere. In the bottom of my cup, the garden ... Magpies drop them at my feet. Maggie, too; even more so.'

Red turned the hook over in her puckered fingers. 'How queer. It's so cold.'

'My pockets are full of the things. Maggie started to make a wonderful collection of earrings from them but didn't feel herself when she wore them. So now we throw them in the fire.' Jan frowned. 'Where they refuse to burn.' She paused, deep in thought, then continued. 'They appeared the day my letters to you at Paloma were returned. I know they're important somehow.'

A while later, a soft wind came through the window and with-it Robbie's voice.

'I've just found a patch of strawberries!' he called up. 'Breakfast is ready, Your Highness.'

Red smiled. 'I'm coming,' she called back.

Jan watched her. 'As long as that young Man of the Road is near, you will be kept warm, safe, and well fed. 'This is important, Red, do you understand? Don't lose sight of each other. Don't lose sight of your friends. They are your army now.'

'I understand.' *Army*, Red thought, *why would I need an army*.

A few minutes later, downstairs and clean, Red accepted a cup of purple tea that tasted fiery and three thick cut pieces of hot buttered toast. She sipped quietly and fiddled with the tiny gold hook.

'So, who's the bait, princess?' Robbie asked without thinking any more about it.

Maggie dropped the bowl of strawberries when she heard his words. It smashed to the ground and the sound rang through a sickly silence in the snug house on the hill.

Jan turned pale and murmured, 'The hooks. That's it!'

Red remained very still. Her knuckles gripped the hook, and she looked across the kitchen at her godmothers.

Both women were ghostly white and did not meet her eye. The look they gave one another was full of only one thing – fear. 'It's me, isn't it? That's the sign you've been unable to read. I'm the bait. I'm the bait for somebody.'

Maggie nodded slowly.

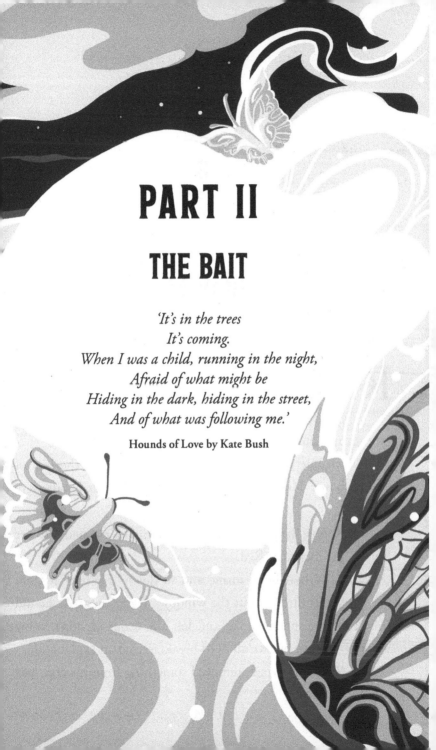

PART II

THE BAIT

*'It's in the trees
It's coming.
When I was a child, running in the night,
Afraid of what might be
Hiding in the dark, hiding in the street,
And of what was following me.'*

Hounds of Love by Kate Bush

8

HOOKED

R ed's voice was shrill. 'Jan?'

Robbie had never heard her sound so full of fire.

She held the gold hook up and demanded, 'Tell me everything you know.'

Maggie crumpled to the floor to pick up the bits of broken bowl. 'How could I have not seen it?' Her hands were bleeding.

Robbie helped her into a chair and cleaned up her fingers. He looked at Red.

'Give that hook to me and sit down.' He took it from her hand and threw it out the window. 'Right then.' As he did this, the atmosphere broke and left the room. 'I don't know what's going on, but we all need breakfast and an explanation.'

Robbie frowned, removed something from his cup, and

placed another tiny gold hook on the table. 'I will make some more tea.'

When this was done, Maggie took a thankful slurp, rested her hands on the table, sat forward, and looked at Red. 'The hooks are a sign. A warning. Jan and I believe you are part of a plot to ensnare the king. The bait that will bring about his downfall.'

'You got all that from a fishhook?' Robbie did not look convinced. Red said nothing.

'Yes, as unlikely as it sounds.' Maggie's answer was perfunctory. 'Why would someone go to such great lengths to track down Red after her escape? The arrival of the new guard, the unease in the city, the voodoo. It is far too dark and methodical for her guardians, Uncle Gerald and Aunt Caroline … Red's the only one who still stands with a true and rightful claim to the throne. If she is not controlled, this unseen force can't win. It needs her to draw the king back from his quest, out of hiding, alone, without his most trusted aides, and …' She stopped.

Maggie's slim grey cat wandered gracefully towards the group, leapt up, and landed lightly in Red's lap. Red stroked her soft head and looked at the goldfish hooks before her. 'But I have to continue my search. I must try to bring my father back and stop this dismantling of Landfelian going any further. I can't give up now. The kingdom needs him.' She thought of the rags and the cobbles in Alba and the frightened, hungry Branch Bandits.

Jan took her hand. 'My dear, that is exactly what they want, although I don't imagine they foresaw how hard you would fight the enchantment.'

'Who are they?' Red looked at her godmother's wise eyes.

Jan sighed and rubbed her head. 'A rogue witch, meddling in sorcery, forging this mysterious castle in the south with hired help. We have tried for seven years to see past the fog and find its maker and yet when we try, their identity conceals itself with a spell. A very powerful spell.'

Maggie reached for Red's hand. 'The only person who could bring your father back from his grief-stricken quest is you. If he heard you were in trouble, imprisoned, he would return immediately, walking straight into the witch's trap. It is the king they want to snare, and once they have him ...' She looked at Jan. 'We're finished.'

Red remained very still. 'Well, I'll just have to reach him before the witch, whoever she is, catches me.' She paused. 'And then we must fight.'

Robbie looked at her in surprise. 'Before we do that, I suggest we eat something.' He stood and rolled up his sleeves. 'Ladies, why don't you go and sit in the garden and get some fresh air?' He glanced at the princess. 'And take the bait with you. This won't take long.'

After a little more rummaging, Robbie found chives growing around the back of the mill, cheese, butter, and bread. He arrived outside with four odd plates and wearing an apron embroidered with smiling bumblebees. The godmothers were talking quietly; Maggie and Jan held Red's hands between their own. They looked anxiously up at him.

'I hope you're all hungry.' He put the plates down with the flourish of a man who never follows a recipe. 'Your Highness, Madame Guiler, and Madame Macloud, may I present ... cheese on toast.'

'Goodness,' Maggie said when she took a crispy, golden bite. Jan said nothing, but she sighed a sigh of great contentment once her plate was finished.

'There's something very grounding about bread and cheese,' Maggie said finally.

Red tried to re-find her appetite but felt a cold dread inside her stomach. Robbie sliced a further heap of very strong cheddar onto her plate with a small knife he kept in his boot. 'If there is going to be more voodoo and running, you need to keep your strength up.'

'You must have seen something,' she asked Jan. 'A clue as to who is behind all this. Did my father have a rival, a sworn enemy? What about the Englanders or those bearded rebels in Thorne? Has he banished anyone who might want to seek vengeance?'

'I ...' Jan's voice faltered.

'Eat up,' Maggie interrupted. 'I will speak to Father Peter. When he came here last, he had discovered a fortress beyond the South Realm shrouded in fog and was hoping to return with more news of this and the king. Our ability to see anything behind this fog has been hopeless.'

'Who lives in this fortress?' Red asked.

'The sorceress,' Jan whispered.

Maggie gave Jan a fierce look and she said no more. 'The king had enemies. Not many; nothing like the other kingdoms, although there is always someone who wants more.'

'The witch,' Robbie muttered to himself.

'What did you say?' Maggie snapped.

'I had forgotten until now - Daniel Blackwood mentioned something about a witch fishing when he caught me in Alba.' He rubbed his head. 'Yes, that's it. How strange, I had completely forgotten.' He rubbed his forehead again and looked confused.

Jan looked like she wanted to say more, but Maggie carried on in a brisk manner.

'It's probably best you remain here until we've had time to think.' She looked at Robbie. 'Help me make some coffee?' The time for tea had left for the hills.

Maggie disappeared inside, and Robbie followed with the plates.

She smiled at him. 'I'm glad you're here.'

Robbie searched her wise face and dropped his voice. 'You know who's behind this, don't you? Red needs to know. Why don't you tell her?'

A shadow passed across Maggie's kitchen, and she wrapped her long patchwork coat around her. 'I will not frighten her any more today. She has just escaped one curse. It's too soon to hear of its maker.' She looked at Robbie. 'Not until Jan and I are sure, and we are not. Until then, the princess has earned a moment's peace. We will all need her courage for the next fight, for things still to come.'

Outside, Red looked like someone had walked over her grave and invited three friends to play Twister on it. She held onto Julia to hide her shaking hands. Robbie could not imagine someone so young fighting for a kingdom, let alone running one.

In the furthest southern corner of the Island of Tum, where the ground looked as if it were continuously melting, ice thawed on the black stone of a vast castle; a castle called Mirador. A castle that took up most of the little island with its black, glistening walls. No plucky seabird mewed here, but a conversation was being conducted.

'She knows.'

A man who would be called handsome had it not been for one of his eyes being oddly pale, as if dipped in milk, spoke to the witch. He did not look at her but continued to stare out the window. A hovel waited there, perched upon a sea stack surrounded by tumultuous, grey waters. He was dressed in a dark padded garment, commonly worn by knights, with wool hosen and heavy boots. There were plans for the castle spread out on a long feasting table in the centre of a cavernous hall. Despite the roaring fire, the room was cold. Selina had travelled through the night over the hinterland from her fortress to meet with the self-exiled hero from Landfelian. A striking figure called Alec Thorne, known to his servants at Mirador as the Knight. This was the man she had formed an unlikely union with.

'How could she?' the witch laughed.

'The godmothers have worked it out.'

'Oh, those wretched women couldn't read a sign if it fell on them.'

The Knight reluctantly turned away from his stormy watch of the window and looked to his plans. 'The princess had help. There is someone with her. He is young but knows the land.'

Selina ground her teeth until her jaw cracked. 'Who? What have you seen?'

His voice was cold. 'The spiderlings see more than that son of a lawyer you hired. His mother was a healer, one of the White Ones.' The Knight looked out the window again. 'I met her once. She had a boy; a boy I scarred years ago, here.' He gestured to his neck and collarbone. 'He will protect the princess. He is I one I warned you of.'

Selina hissed, and a light flurry of snow began to fall outside the window of Mirador's great hall. 'I will have that Felian girl and her father in the well before the wolf moon.'

'There can be no more delays. The king must fall.' The Knight looked at her, and his good eye glinted. 'A new throne, a stronghold to Landfelian, begins here in Mirador.'

'Yes.' Selina paused. 'I have noticed, there is only one

throne.' She gestured at the empty cavern of a hall and the space next to Alec Thorne's seat. 'Where, may I ask, is mine?' she drawled.

The Knight smiled and his face transformed. 'Dear lady, I thought you would prefer to choose your own.'

Selina left the Knight of Mirador alone in a room that looked remarkably like the Great Mirrored Hall at Paloma, only without the life, the mirrors, or the beauty. She left without another word. Had she uttered another sound, it would have had the resonance of thunder and would have rhymed with 'muck'. Selina Carnal was seething.

The Knight stopped studying his plans and returned his attention to the window. Through it, he could see frothing great waves crashing into a bay of black sand strewn with tumbleweed, and about half a mile out shone a faint light through the mist. It shone from the hovel perched on the sea stack. The frail structure creaked in the wind – the Smoos called it the 'House in the Clouds'; it was here a woman waited to be set free. This woman had no way of reaching the mainland unless the tide was out and someone was good enough to provide a rope in which to lower herself down the steep limestone to shore. She waited not in chains but imprisoned nonetheless, by nature. She had waited in the same cloak and gown she'd left Landfelian in, refusing the countless other fine gowns the Knight had offered her, preferring to make her own clothes and broth than be kept by a traitor. In the seven years this lady had been held captive, nothing had changed, accept on this particular morning, her cloak, powder blue and covered in stars, had been taken from her. She had struggled to give it up but was eventually consumed by fog. It filled her prison in the clouds, after which the Queen of Landfelian could only stare out at the Castle Mirador in fear at what her captors intended to use her cloak for.

Once outside, Selina Carnal's smile withered as fast as a woman trying on corsets behind a changing screen in January. Why did the Knight persist in keeping the queen alive? It was never part of their plan. That wretched woman was turning him; Selina knew it as soon as she saw the way he gazed at the shack on the stack. Honestly, what was it about these Felian women that sabotaged all her carefully formulated plans? They seemed to cling onto the wreckage of their precious kingdom with surprisingly tenacious teeth. Selina screamed with frustration, and the noise echoed through a courtyard where only a few oily crows watched with beady eyes.

'A sorceress should always work alone,' she said to them.

A few Smoos working in the stables hurried away as she climbed on board her sleigh, dragging the Queen of Landfelian's powder blue, star-spangled cloak with her.

Here Selina waited, taking in the castle at the start of a long, frozen avenue. She was satisfied to see the trees the Knight had taken from Landfelian were dying. The imported cobbles had turned black and the fountains were frozen. The skreekes clawed at the ice, impatient to return to their squats beneath Tallfinger to feed. She howled again, and a window behind her shattered. He was trying to recreate the palaces of Landfelian, and it was not for Selina's benefit, of that she was certain; it was all for the queen he kept in the clouds.

'Well,' Selina muttered to the skreekes. 'I will end this obsession. He will surrender to me,' she crowed and threw the blue cloak in the sleigh next to her.

The Smoos harnessed the enormous scaly beasts with nervous hands. The witch cut a sinister figure trawling through the snow across Tum; animals buried themselves like worms until her shadow had passed. She whipped her beasts faster, cackling until she was hoarse and felt marginally better.

'I will finish those royals once and for all ...' Jealousy drove Selina on, although the start of a chesty cough stopped her from cackling any more. She always felt under the weather after seeing Alec Thorne; he brought out her human side, which was extremely vexing. For too long the exiled hero's attention had been directed elsewhere. 'It is time, my darlings,' Selina cawed at the skreekes, 'I take matters into my own hands.' The beasts grunted towards Tallfinger. 'First, we capture that despicable redhead. The king will follow. And then I will return here and take my place on the throne with or without the Knight.'

The godmothers of Tikli Bottom recognised that the hooks were not one of the good signs, although they could do very little to stop the princess from following her course. It was decided, without a lengthy discussion, that the princess and the Man of the Road would travel on the following morning after one more night in relative safety.

They both agreed that to stay would not bring them peace for long. The guards, the son of a lawyer, and all the unseen forces that appeared to be hunting Red would in time find their way to the godmother's hills and through the magic that protected them. The hills themselves were too exposed to offer a safe house for long. What they needed was a crowd; the good kind. They needed an army, but also lots of bunting. There was only one place and one time of year that offered such a cocktail: the Lake of Stars.

'Are they asleep?' asked Maggie.

'Yes,' said January. 'Red and I went for a long walk; we kept close to the trees. It calmed her. We noticed the birds and butterflies and tried to name them; that always helps. She's frightened, Maggie.'

'Do you have anything to drink?' Maggie asked, who never found flower pressing very calming.

'Talk to the fire; I've got just the thing.' Jan disappeared into her kitchen.

Maggie knelt to remove a bit of charred bread from the fireplace. She added logs, a few musty newspapers, and a match. Very soon the chimney was smoking nicely. The godmothers sat with two bowls of psychic hot chocolate (which is far more effective than stirring a cauldron). Jan's recipe had been handed down from her spiritualist mother. It involved cream, nutmeg, dark chocolate, rum, and vanilla sugar that had been sung to from an early age. It was thick like soup and very aura-affirming.

They stared into the flames.

After a while, Jan spoke. 'Good news first.'

'Oh, please.' Maggie took a slurp and smacked her lips.

January Macloud took a delicate sip and whispered, 'I have had a good sign. Clear for once. The king is safe. He is on his way back to Landfelian.'

Maggie's eyes narrowed. 'I could throttle him. King or no king, I have known that rangy man long enough to dump the title on him from a great height. Do you know where he is?'

'It's hard to see through the fog. By the sea, I think.' Jan twiddled with a strand of jade beads.

'What the hell is that hound doing on a beach? Topping up the royal tan? Collecting seashells?' Maggie tried to keep her voice down and failed. 'Neglecting his daughter like that – and the kingdom.'

Jan looked worried. 'He looks awfully sad, Maggie.'

'Well of course he's sad. He's been searching for seven years. Gone to where the queen was born, I'll bet my last marshmallow. To the Islands of Aquila, to swim in the arms of melancholy and walk in her footprints.' She sighed. 'The poor devil. But he still has a responsibility, a child; she's almost a woman now. What he did was cowardly.'

The godmothers stared at the fire and sighed.

'Well, he'd better return and say hello to his daughter before she becomes fish food.' Maggie blew her nose into a handkerchief.

January reached for her harp to play something

soothing. 'How did you uncover the riddle of the hooks?'

'The Man of the Road gave me a clue.' Maggie spoke softly and rubbed her temples. 'A trap waits for Red and the king. I know it,' she murmured. 'The voodoo, the hooks, the fog … They are all connected. It's strange, every time I'm close to uttering a name, the sorceress, I forget everything. She's not allowing me to see her.'

Jan took a deep breath and began to choke on a caramel she forgot she had been sucking. 'It is the same for me. There is a strong anti-revealment spell at work here.' She coughed.

Maggie thumped her on the back and said, 'SHOOO.'

She stood up and stared at the window. 'Did you open that?'

'Yes,' replied Jan. 'What is it?'

'Chittering,' Maggie said. 'There is too much darkness in the air tonight for my liking.' She shivered. 'And it's turned cold. The moon is covered in stains.'

'I will send Luna out to keep watch.' Jan stared at the flames for a moment. 'Can you remember if Red was holding the hook at the time Robbie's words were spoken?'

Maggie nodded.

'Oh dear, then it is a complete sign. No holes in the tights for misinterpretation.'

Both women looked grave.

Jan wrapped a blanket round her shoulders. 'A set of events has been set in motion, and all we can do is help Red as much as we are able. She is stronger than she knows.'

'We must find a safe route across the kingdom now, to Father Peter's folly,' Maggie said.

'At least she has the valien.' Jan smiled. 'He would follow her off a cliff.'

'Dear Face, he is a blessing,' Maggie agreed.

'Aren't all animals,' said Jan, stroking the long ears of an elegant hare who had woken up at the mention of her name and come to sit nearby.

'And, we must not forget, she's no longer travelling alone.' Maggie found herself smiling as she finished her hot chocolate.

'The young man of the road?' January looked unsure.

'She won't go hungry. And he knows Landfelian like no other.' Maggie smiled as she thought about Robbie's capable hands. 'He will see her to the West Realm.'

'He is something more. I saw it,' said Jan.

'What?'

'On his shoulders; a mark, a scar of the most distinctive shape.'

Maggie frowned. 'Yes, I had noticed, around his neck.'

'It is the sign of the ...' The wind howled like a banshee on cue around the two hills. '... the Ohoara.' Jan's eyes grew wide and bright.

The fire crackled and the flames grew tall.

Maggie was not sure what the Ohoara meant, truth be told. It was in her book of signs underneath an illustration bearing the legend, *THE WINGED MAN: divided, inconstant, torn between the fates.*

'I am sure the Man of the Road's shoulders are something to be praised, not feared.' She threw another log on the fire. The flames lit up her lined face. 'And he softens when he is with Red.'

Jan rubbed her toes. 'There is something not quite finished about him. He will have to decide his path.'

'You're too cautious.' Maggie nudged her. 'We all have to decide which path, on a daily basis.'

As Jan spoke, a shape appeared in the flames. 'There's a bit missing.' She gestured at the flames. 'His aura – one side is clear and sure like a comet. The side that has only known love.' The flames began to move. 'The other is hazy, burdened by his past. The part of his soul that has known neglect, abandonment.' The fire grew low, wary, and began to smoke.

'So, he is divided,' Maggie whispered, trying not to cough. 'It will make him.'

The walls of Bird House creaked.

The godmothers huddled closer.

'Which would you choose to be, Magatha – a queen or a hero?' Jan asked. 'The princess has barely come of age, but she may have to decide which she would sooner be.'

'Everyone has the right to let the wild thing that gallops within them remain free,' Maggie said quietly. 'Maybe another choice will find her. Red will find her people before anything else. As for me, I have never been one for sitting on a hard chair, waving things for long.'

'No, you haven't.' Jan gave a deep laugh. 'So, we will

travel to Father Peter's, following behind, passing the Lake of Stars.'

'Yes, it's the least dangerous way. The Man of the Road knows the safest paths to take. The lake is a sacred place and there will be a good crowd there for the festival. The spiderlings can't linger there; neither, from what I have seen, can the fog. Not yet at least. It is the one place in Landfelian that still repels the encroaching darkness. It holds the most powerful kind of magic.'

'What about Blackwood's guards?'

'It shouldn't appeal to them. Too much bunting for one. Nothing to attract the corrupted, only merriment and mead. No guard would risk showing their face.'

Jan looked wistful. 'I remember a time when there were festivals every month, flags flying in every part of the ...'

TAP

TAP

CHITTER

Luna scrambled up and loped to the door, her ears twitching. Magatha's mouth quivered.

'Spiderlings,' Jan whispered. 'Outside. They must have seen the horses. Don't say another word. We cannot let it get away.'

Maggie threw a blanket over Jan's harp and crawled behind it.

She passed Jan her broomstick, glared at the window, and mouthed, 'You have a better aim.'

Grasping the handle of the broom, Jan narrowed her eyes and threw it like a javelin threw the curtains and out the open window, stunning the spiderling flat. She quickly stood up, closed the window, and checked the others, drawing all the curtains.

'Maggie, the young ones. Is your house secure?'

Maggie nodded. 'Animal and Julia are guarding it. They will deter anything with more legs than them. It is time we left the borderlands. We can't hide up here any longer.'

'I will send word to Father Peter, let him know we are all coming, and give Mrs Tweed a wink – you know how she hates surprises.' Mrs Tweed was Father Peter's housekeeper, and unexpected visitors threw her linen cupboard out, along with her good demeanour.

Maggie put a small teapot and a clear quartz crystal into Jan's harp case. 'Now, we must get packing. I will visit the Branch Bandits before we leave and warn them that we'll be gone for some time.' She opened the door and looked up at the stars. 'Dawn is a few hours away yet. I'll make up a food parcel to take them.'

The godmothers did not sleep for the remainder of the night. Maggie packed for the long journey while Jan, who had a good rapport with the resident bats and moths, asked them politely to keep watch over Tikli Bottom. The night creatures' instructions were to attack any spiderlings that dared to approach their hills again. Luna, Jan's hare, was sent out in the night to alert Father Peter of their visit. She was faster than the other familiars. The princess and the Man of the Road slept on.

Father Peter was awake through the night as well, eating coffee beans and smoking a pipe in the company of his owl. The night was fine as he soared above the fog line, sailing slowly away from the Islands of Aquila. The Father hoped the faint chittering he could hear and beat of little wings were only his imagination. He prayed for rain and instructed his owl to fly high. The King of Landfelian was camping alone on the island he'd left behind. In the company of his wolfhound, Atlas, he stared out to sea and waited. In his eyes, a mad kind of hope shone. The rest of his fleet he'd instructed to sail towards home. The Quest had come to an end.

A yellow sun yawned over the Lake of Stars, turning the hills that surrounded it to gold. Maggie's dog scratched at the door to be let in. His night surveillance was over. Nothing to report.

In the windmill, Robbie rolled over with a sigh and little commitment to waking up. For the first time in a long career on the road, not one part of him was damp or cold.

Outside, Maggie was sewing and looking at the sunrise on the horizon. She had kept watch most of the night. *There must be some good advice she could give*, she thought – it was her duty. It was what the title 'godmother' was for. But it made no difference how hard she sewed; nothing came.

Sewing was what old wives did when discerning

suitable and worthy advice before a farewell. Those old wives had been advised by even older and wiser witches that if they kept sewing, the right advice would come eventually. Even for a temporary farewell such as this. Maggie had never been a wife and held no truck with age, but she was a good witch. She succeeded in sewing the arms of her cardigan together and hemming Julia into the tablecloth while upstairs Red woke slowly. The only advice that came to her when the cuckoo struck *TIME TO GO* made absolutely no sense.

'Don't follow the blue,' she muttered repeatedly and wrote it down. 'Whatever does it mean Julia, "don't follow the blue"?'

Upstairs, Red stretched until her bones clicked. Maggie's house smelt of garden and toast. She took a deep, comforting breath and waited for the nerves to find her. They always did, like nits in assembly, as soon as she was conscious.

'Did you sleep?' Her godmother appeared at the door, looking pensive. 'You were snoring like a hornets' nest. It's better than a leafwell, my bed; an elm frame, wonderful wood.' Maggie swept in, wearing her patchwork, floor-length coat over a peacock blue dress and sat down by the window. 'I stayed with January for the last quarter of the night, and lord does that woman talk in her sleep – something about an heiress and a bounty hunter.' She decided not to tell Red about the spiderlings they'd seen and shooed away. The girl had enough on her mind without adding flying spies outside her window.

The princess smiled. 'Does she still read the romantics?'

'Oh, she's insatiable for them.' Maggie grinned.

Downstairs, there was the sound of cooking accompanied by tuneless male whistling and the smell of rich coffee. Maggie rootled around her room, flinging dresses, boots, and hats onto the bed.

'Does your Mr Wylde have any brothers?'

'No.'

'Oh, what a shame.' Maggie sighed. 'I've always hankered for a manservant. Now, let me see. Hats, yes, you may need one.' She threw what looked like a cavalier's hat at Red, complete with ostrich feather, and smiled. 'That was always my favourite.'

Red tried it on and gave herself a vampish look in the mirror. 'He's not *my* Mr Wylde. I called him a gigolo and worse.'

'Do you remember Gigolo?' asked Maggie. 'Your father loved that dog. Little terror, always rogering the bolsters.' She prayed the next question wouldn't be about basket weaving.

(Basket weaving, for any young readers that may not have remembered, is the term used throughout this tale to refer to – ahem – lovemaking. It saves a lot of embarrassment for anyone being read to by a grownup. But I can assure that this is not a basket-weaving sort of book. You're safe on that score. Regarding kissing, however, I cannot be so certain.)

'Do you think I should trust him?'

Magatha rolled up her sleeves. 'Go with your gut. What

does your essence tell you?'

'I don't know what my essence is telling me.' Red tried not to snap. 'Are those the wise parting words of my godmother? The great sign-reader of the borderlands? You could have at least made something up ... Perhaps about the test of a true spirit or fear being my enemy; fate and the gates of decision ...' Red pretended to be serious. 'Anything along those lines would help.'

'I'll think of something.' Maggie sniffed and poured half a glass vial of a green liquid labelled *Muddle Tonic* into the bath. 'I like him. Good teeth, bright eyes – you can see the whites of them – and he's mostly clean. So many men on the road these days think it's alright not to wash.' She looked up.

Red dunked her ankle in the water, and it barely ached, although it still felt colder than the rest of her. 'I like him too.' She smiled.

'Did I ever tell you the story of how the king met your mother?' Maggie bounced about the little room.

'Countless times,' Red groaned, submerging herself in the water. 'At the lake.'

Magatha ignored her. 'Stripped to a slip, she was. She loved the water. Your father didn't see that fish coming, I can tell you; none of us did. He fell hook, line, and nearly sank her.' She smiled at the memory. 'She met a king and I met a pesky pirate.'

'He wasn't king then.'

'January and I knew he would be. He had the right

walk. Always walked well, your father.' Maggie stopped, and the light faded behind a cloud for a second. She gripped Red's hand suddenly. 'I must warn you, there is something enchanted about that lake.' Her eyes looked unsure. 'Watch your step and ...' She hesitated, sat up quite straight, and said in a strange voice not quite her own, 'Don't follow the blue.'

'The blue?' Red wavered. 'What is it, Maggie? Have you seen something?'

'No, no, nothing clear, just a hunch, that's all.' Maggie shook her head and put a folded bit of paper in Red's bag. 'Try to remember, don't follow the blue.'

'I will.' Red stared out of the window at the fine day and wished everything were as it was before the quest. 'From what I have seen of the North and East realms, people no longer trust their shadow. Things are being taken from them, from their homes. Animals, the cobbles of Alba. And those children hiding in the Trees of Goonock.'

Maggie agreed. 'Landfelian needs you.'

Red shook her head. 'The daughter of two deserters? It would be best if I disappeared.'

'No, you great sprout! You are many things to many people – goddaughter, valien rider, bandit, princess, friend. And you are one of the good things left from a time before ... A time when things were better.'

Red did not want such a burden. 'In time, everyone will forget.'

'You did not kick the can outside hard enough,' said

Maggie, standing up. 'It is time for you to see the mirror.'

Downstairs, Robbie heard raised voices. He finished preparing the horses, wondering what it was with women and baths and why they spent so long at it.

Maggie disappeared under her bed, still muttering about a mirror. She crawled out holding an oak jewellery box, wrapped in a piece of blue velvet. She pulled out something gnarled, grey, and mottled.

Red turned it over doubtfully; it was the size of her palm, not quite a perfect circle. 'What use is this old bit of shell?' There was a delicate silver chain attached to it to make it into a rather ugly necklace.

'It is a mirror,' Maggie explained. 'From the Sea Dwellers, given to your mother when she became queen. She gave it to me the last time I saw her, for safekeeping. I never understood why.'

Red failed to see how it was a mirror. She turned it over and held it up to the light. It still looked like an old bit of shell, the size of a saucer for a small coffee cup. On one side it was mother of pearl, a translucent cream and pink; the other side was rough and callused. It smelt of salt and the sea. 'Why did she leave it here?'

'The sea dwellers gifted it to her before all that trouble with illegal fishing and trading routes kicked off. Long before the weather began to turn and the fog arrived. It's yours; you are the closest thing Landfelian has to a queen. When you are ready, take a good hard look. Fear has made you as blind as an earthworm, Red Felian. Don't let those tiny, insignificant hooks shake you. Remember, there is a light in you that overcame the strongest voodoo charm.'

Maggie got up to leave.

'I don't want to be Queen,' Red said quietly. 'I don't know what I want.'

'Of course, but don't let fear stop you from taking up your space in this life.' Her smile was kind. 'I've left some clothes on the bed.'

Red looked scathingly at the so-called mirror when her godmother had gone. What could a piece of old shell tell her? There was nothing there but a steamed-up, milky reflection of her face – flushed and unsure. More hocus pocus.

She looked at all the bottles of tonics and crystals on the shelves and felt angry. None of this alchemy or sign-reading and listening to her essence business could help her now. Red looked at the shell again. There was nothing to see. 'It doesn't even work.'

Red closed her eyes and took a deep, slow breath. She thought of her journey to this very point. Holding the shell, she opened her eyes ... and this time, in the reflection, she saw herself – riding her valien like a bat out of the chamber of hell where they keep and torture bats. She watched them fly over the Bigeasy river, with a great storm gathering behind. The picture faded, and in the mother of pearl, she saw herself in a room she had been in before, Celador, and someone close by was making her laugh. Fireworks rained above; there was a crown of rubies and a sword on the throne next to her. Red swallowed. She put the shell to her ear and heard waves and then felt the hot trickle of water running out. The misty image disappeared.

'So, I have a choice to make. Is that it?' Red asked the shell. Quests, she thought, had a lot to answer for.

She got out of the bath, packing the shell safely away in her hemp sack, and drained the tub. She didn't notice the tiny goldfish hook at the bottom, glinting in the sunlight. Red was standing tall and, for the first time, considering her future.

There was a highly suspect pile of garments left on Maggie's bed, the least worrying of which was a dress, the colour of tulips. Red pulled it over her head; at least it was not like the crinoline monsters her step-aunt favoured and tried to encourage her to wear. The material was soft against her skin and hung like it knew her well. She put her riding boots on, rolled up her sleeves, and, holding the cavalier's hat and her bag, went downstairs to face the day.

As she entered the kitchen, Robbie looked up and the toast he was working on began to burn. He noticed her hair first. He had seen it before, but this morning it noticed him. The toast charred on quietly, held hostage over the fire. Red opened the door to let out the smoke.

'Your toast is ready.' She smiled.

'Oh. Did you ...' He floundered for the next words. '... sleep well?'

If a percussion instrument was chosen to play at this moment, it would be the triangle.

'Like a top, thank you. And you?'

'Fine. Very fine. I slept fine,' Robbie said gruffly as the princess politely took a piece of bread. 'You look different today.'

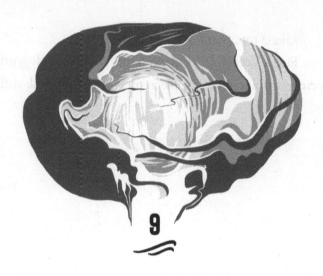

9

STAINS ON THE MOON

It took Selina some time to return to her fortress. The journey was a cold one as the wind began to howl and the snow did not abate. Hundreds of Smoos and guards were coming the other way, dragging carts of cobbles, parts of fountain, fine condiments, terrified Landfelians, and solemn-looking statues back towards the castle of Mirador from a landing post on the coast. The Knight's creation was almost complete. Selina was glad to be leaving.

The young trees from Landfelian kept trying to leave; the castle guards had to bind their roots and carry them down the avenue, whining in the wind. The saplings wouldn't survive one night and became petrified when they saw their bleak surroundings. For some inexplicable reason, the cobbles turned black on arrival, and the Knight's servants could not stop the silver from tarnishing nor the cherubs' stone faces turning into gargoyles. Still, it was taking shape – a twisted, doppelgänger, jabberwocky sort of shape, although Celador it would never be. Possessed by winning Queen Felian's heart the Knight was. Selina saw it all so clearly now. How foolish, she growled to herself. How foolish to believe he was different. Well, she smiled, his plan was not working, no matter how big he built his castle.

The skreekes grunted over the ice; the witch was no light load with all her furs and the addition of the Queen's cloak. When she finally swept through the door of Tallfinger, she was not in the best of moods. After several hours of lying in the dark on her bed of bones, she summoned Alfred.

'Has there been any word from Daniel Blackwood?'

'He was delayed in Alba, madame. He is on his way. The spiderlings sent word.' Alfred tried to take her cape, and a river of frozen animal skins dropped on him.

'Delayed? Fetch me something to gnaw!'

Returning to the pleasant discomfort of her rooms, she changed into a slippery black dress and put a different choker of teeth around her neck, some of which still moved, like worms on a hook. After a supper of ice and pickled herring, she felt marginally better and thankfully still not one hundred percent human. Selina stooped over a table supported by several antlers and gazed at a deck of black cards, laid face down on the petrified wood. She closed her eyes, grew very still, and took the top card.

'The Star,' Selina muttered. 'Inspiration and happiness.' She threw the card down, stamped on it, and picked another. 'The Moon; well, following one's instincts, is she? Let's muddy the waters a little.' She hissed and chose one more card. 'The Devil.' She smiled. 'Good.'

Something scratched at her though, and it was not the label of her dress. Selina stared south from her balcony as she fingered the sky-blue, star-spangled cloak on the chair with unveiled disgust. It was embroidered with stars made from the finest yellow sapphires and white topaz in the kingdom. It smelt unpleasantly of that woman, and even after seven years of isolation, it still brought an unwelcome light into the room, as if the love that the cloak had seen was absorbed into every fibre and could not be quelled. The fog that followed Selina everywhere like a pet would not go near it. 'Soon I shall bring the Knight a king and bend his mind to look only on me. The queen is no match for Selina Carnal.'

She brooded at the blot of blue night sky through her spyglass, hundreds of miles away over the mountains. The persistently pleasant kingdom of Landfelian.

Not for long, she thought. That stinking hole was flailing, and soon it would be weak enough to take. As fog embraced her fortress, she began to laugh.

It was a laugh of such evil and bitterness it made all the

other laughs run and hide. Her inky black hair blew around her crazed eyes. There would be no more distractions to draw the Knight away from her. She would control him like everything else. As soon as the spiderlings returned with news of the royal runaway, she would travel to Landfelian and deal with the girl herself. Selina looked down at the two dragon-like creatures at her feet, snuffling quietly.

'There shall be no more of this playing the adventuress.'

Daniel Blackwood was waiting outside The Hog's Breath. Sarah looked as if she were stifling dreadful wind in her efforts not to laugh at him as she dragged in the meat and beer barrels for the evening ahead. He was seated uncomfortably on a crate of half-plucked pigeons. His normally slicked back rat-coloured hair was ruffled like it had recently been in a fight with a cockerel in a strong wind. Daniel lit a cheroot and blew the smoke out in a thin, slow line.

Amber would never sing again; he would pluck out her vocal cords with tweezers and make braces from them. Let them laugh, let them have their fun now. In a week, neither the holy-man-impersonating actor nor that infernal singer would recognise their own eyeballs if it was offered to them on a stick. He would lock them up in Hardplace Prison with the rest of the circus and burn the place to the ground.

Barry had found him in the morning when he'd knocked on the door to see if the young lady wanted any breakfast.

'No, the young lady will not be wanting breakfast. The young lady will want to consider the dimensions of her coffin,' Daniel had mumbled through a gag.

'Right you are, boss. Things not going well with the missus, I take it?'

'Never marry them, Barry,' he said, looking almost pleasant for a moment. 'Now, be intelligent for a few seconds – break the door down and untie me.'

'You'll have to pay extra for that.' Barry was tempted to leave the door just as it was and go about his business.

'Do it or I will have you arrested.'

'Hold on, I'll get the dog.' Barry had stomped down the stairs begrudgingly.

Mitzy held the keys to the upstairs rooms around her collar, which meant Barry had never lost one; removing her collar meant losing a finger to anyone but him. In the case of Mitzy, everything they say about small dogs was true; she was terror.

Inside the room, he had found the son a lawyer tied to a chair. This surprised Barry, who had not realised the room had a chair. Daniel looked like he had spent the evening in a ring with some bad fairies. His pointy black boots had been placed on the wrong feet. Someone had written *DO NOT DISTURB* on his forehead and tied a dirty sock around his mouth as an afterthought, which he now mumbled through. Although his silver-topped cane was still by his side. *They should have taken it*, Barry thought. He thanked his stars that he and Sarah had never tied the marriage knot, if this was what came of it.

Lidia arrived at the Hog's Breath dressed in a gentleman's coat to hide her wings as Daniel emerged. 'Oh no.' He sighed, and had it been anyone else, one might feel quite sorry for him. 'It's you.'

'The witch is waiting for you.' Lidia spoke quickly and, with so many squeaks and hisses, it was like listening to a recently stood on python.

'Princess Felian now travels with the man you thought was a bounty hunter. He's acting as some sort of protector. The spiderlings tracked them as far as the two hills beyond the Trees of Goonock. They intend to travel towards the Lake of Stars. One of your guards was found outside the House of Gold, stripped and preaching from a holy book.'

Daniel closed his eyes and took a pained breath as this news sunk in. 'Don't tell me, the bounty hunter – does he have some interesting scars?'

Lidia twitched, visibly enjoying herself. 'Yessss,' she whispered. 'He is the one the witch warned you about. The winged man.'

'He's a peasant,' Daniel snapped back. 'You're mistaken. He must have got those scars by frying onions.' The thought of Red Felian with that young Man of the Road made Daniel stab his cane into the ground, where it became momentarily stuck. He stormed passed Lidia and into the waiting barouche.

She followed, smiling. 'It appears you have failed again.'

'Oh why don't you fly through a raincloud? I'm capable

of delivering myself to Tallfinger without a bug escort.'

'Don't keep the witch waiting.' Lidia slipped away up into the sky, kicking a plume of dust into Daniel's face as she took flight.

A grey dawn was breaking over Alba's wet streets and cold blew through the windows as the horses galloped towards the Petrified Tree. Daniel arrived all too quickly outside Tallfinger fortress, where daylight stopped and night prevailed.

'Where in the name of Hades have you been?' Selina pulled off her choker and whipped Daniel across the face with it. The sharp, squirming teeth cut through his skin like paper.

'It's lovely to be invited back so soon, milady.' He winced, shook out a silk handkerchief from his pocket, and blotted the blood from his cheek. It was back, that same gnawing hunger that always found him when in the presence of the witch. It drew him in despite himself.

'So, the young heir has escaped again. Tell me, how did she get out of Alba alone and why shouldn't I feed you to the skreekes?'

Daniel was tempted to say, 'Because you are oddly attracted to me.' But he didn't. Instead, he said, 'I know who is helping the princess.'

'One of your wives, I believe,' Selina spat. 'The circus girl and an ACTOR.' The last word was so drowned in sarcasm it wondered why it bothered.

'I will stop them.' It was colder than Daniel remembered in her chamber. His breath hung in front of him in an icy mist, making it very hard not to sneeze.

'With what, your charm?' Selina laughed. 'The last time you made such a claim, Lidia had to save you from a PUB.' She spat out the last word, scratched the skreeke growling at her feet, and studied the man before her. He could still be useful; she did need a driver, someone to do the heavy lifting and take her to Landfelian. 'When you have stopped bleeding over my wolf rug, escort me to the Lake of Stars. I've spent too long watching your attempts to catch that brat. I will do the job myself.'

'But she's mine,' Daniel's voice shook.

'That very much depends on you doing exactly what I tell you.' Selina strolled towards the door and whistled to the two hulking creatures lying either side of her bed. 'If he opens his failing little mouth again, my darlings, bite it off.'

'It won't be easy to lure her away from those travelling with her.' Daniel ignored the skreekes. 'The Lake of Stars is a difficult place to conduct a kidnapping. There will be people protecting her everywhere. It drips with good will and is protected by ancient magic.'

'Ancient magic, HA!' Selina glared at him. 'Dress a scorpion up as a faun and it can kill a lion. The only item I need is this.'

When Daniel saw the blue cloak embroidered with stars in her arms, he was silenced for a moment. 'Queen Felian's cloak ... She's alive? Have you kept her captive all these years?'

'Not by choice,' Selina said flatly. 'It's of no consequence to you. The queen will not exist for much longer. Come, we must hurry. The longer the redhead stays in Landfelian, the more people will fall in line with her.'

A day later, Daniel Blackwood and the witch stepped out from the Petrified Tree into Landfelian. Selina's eyes filled with liquid cold as she strode from the beaten-looking tree into the South Realm and looked into a misty morning. She made no comment climbing into the barouche or about the sign on the bumper that read, *HOOT IF YOU LOVE BEAGLES*.

'Why aren't you bringing the skreekes?' Daniel had been relieved that they were not travelling with them.

'The water in the lake is too pure for them, and they will not survive for long in Landfelian. They have a role to play later. Hurry. I don't want to linger in this petty little kingdom longer than I must. The lake encourages – devils cover your ears –' She grimaced. '*Love* ...' Selina narrowed her eyes. 'It breeds like bacteria in that godforsaken valley.' Selina's least favourite place, besides a maternity ward, was the Lake of Stars.

A blizzard silently buried the Petrified Tree as they waited to set off. The horses were hoping they would qualify for an early retirement after the week they'd just had.

'Hateful place.' She turned to Daniel and snapped. 'If you want her, I suggest you get this barouche moving.'

Daniel closed his eyes, he imagined Red's hair between his fingers and her long white throat. At least Lidia had left and returned to Mirador. Although he had never met the Knight, every time Daniel heard his name spoken, a small stream of blood would start to drip from his left nostril. Which even he did not deem a good sign. Whatever the relationship was between the witch and the self-exiled hero, it was clear that the decision to keep Queen Felian alive was not reconciled between them. Daniel made a note of this; it may be important should he have to negotiate between the two tyrants for his life. He was a lawyer after all. And a good lawyer never forgets the details. He wrapped himself in his cloak, climbed up to the driver's seat and whipped the struggling animals forward. They surged into the dawn faster than they had arrived, fuelled by the will of the witch they carried.

The light of a harvest moon lit the way. A family of badgers stopped and watched the bewitched barouche sail past, followed by a worm of fog. The badgers are still there now, frozen, wondering if the sound of violins and the clinking of glasses is meant for them.

10

LAKE COUNTRY

The journey up to the Lake of Stars was one that hundreds of Landfelians made year after year. Not only did it take them through an area of outstanding beauty, it was also the safest place to meet folk from the other realms. Here you could share food, news, and current fashion trends and not wage war. It was as neutral as the pH balance in the water, as it belonged to no one realm but gleamed at the heart of their kingdom. At the start of autumn, people from all over made the pilgrimage to the lake for the last of the summer sun. Even those from foreign kingdoms came; they liked the eccentricity of Landfelians and found the whole dressing up and camping thing a hoot. Along the way, Red and Robbie passed through the lake town of Dood; a place where one could buy every musical instrument thus far invented, the more obscure ingredients for love potions, ponchos, and hundreds of different designs of bunting. Maggie and Jan had bought all they needed from Dood in the days they'd been actively practising witches.

The Lake of Stars was where many young Landfelians came of age, and getting there without a chaperone was the start of the adventure. Gentlemen discussed poetry with peasants, ladies of stature with farmhands, horses with mules, and everyone removed several layers of clothing to swim in the lake. The lake was a leveller. It put the F in festival before the notion of swaying to music in a meadow had been truly discovered in other lands. It was a goosebump, a stomach flip, catch your breath, wipe a tear, marzipan dipped in chocolate, roll-over-and-call-me-Cassandra natural wonder. When people glimpsed it for the first, fifth, and even seventh time, it gave them a pleasant fluttery feeling below their diaphragm and their eyes watered a little bit. It was no wonder that the Lake Country was deemed magical.

Despite the creeping sense of unease throughout Landfelian, few missed the opportunity to dance under the harvest moon. It was the one night of the year when the kingdom felt as it once had: like a happy hippie ruled over by a good family with some half-decent realm custodians. On this night, friends, lovers, wives, husbands, and anyone you fancied and may not ever see again made a vast, happy camp together, floated a candle, flew a lantern, made merriment, and said to someone near them, 'Isn't this lovely.' It was an occasion for bare feet. Oddly, many came dressed as pirates; corsets were ditched and flowers worn everywhere.

The water in the lake was so content with being water, it had been known to make a *TRRRIIINNGG* sound when no one was looking. It didn't contain any nasty, toothy creatures that might grip toes and it invited no darkness. One area was home to lily pads so big you could float your baby on them; the flowers were yellow white with edges that looked as if they had been cut out carefully with scissors. And under the surface lived bright azure fish called heartskippers.

Day and night, tiny lights no bigger than fireflies appeared in the water, making the depth very difficult to judge. These bright lights gave the Lake of Stars its name. Some believed it was bottomless and that it led you around in a circle to the surface again. Others thought if you swam deep enough, you would end up in space and then possibly in some serious trouble. Logic declared it a reflection, a clever trick of the light and the purity of the water. Men of ecology concluded it a very rare type of bioluminescence. Bah-humbug to logic. Everyone believed that if the Lake of Stars carried on twinkling, the general run of things would be alright.

The water was believed to have healing qualities. It soothed a restlessness that, for some people, made sleep a distant shore. A deep internalised pain pondered upon by the lake would pipe down and be humbled. It was miraculous, and the people of Landfelian needed miraculous at this moment, so they travelled towards it in their hundreds.

The lake was wide enough to not easily see someone

dressed as a pineapple waving from the other side. If that person was holding a sparkler, they would be visible. If that person was on fire, you would see them no problem, though whether they would still be there by the time you got around to the other side was another matter.

The princess and Robbie left the borderlands of the south realm at a gallop, picking up a few interested folk at Dood. By the time the sun was making its way towards a well-deserved nightcap, they joined a merry trail of Landfelians hiking up to the lake. Wary at first, they slowed down and stayed back. The horses grazed in water meadows and drank from cold, clear springs. Red was offered pieces of fudge tablet that made her teeth ache. Sticky handfuls of loganberries were given to her by barefooted children running alongside the biggest horse they had ever seen.

On the way, Robbie said little. He could have picked a great many subjects – the flora and fauna of Lake Country, the nesting habits of the white egret, the grazing patterns of the water buffalo. But when words came to him, they quickly dropped off the ledge of his mouth before they were spoken. And so, he remained quiet. This, dear reader, we call 'shyness' in my land.

Robbie looked ahead at the princess. It was a nice view. He had not travelled with anyone for this long before, and for once in his young life, he could not think of anything to say. A wise wizard might have said the Man of the Road was befuddled, but there were no wise wizards around at the time to say so. Wizards were still finding their feet in Landfelian; it was not yet their time. A lot could have been avoided had they come to the party sooner.

Red spoke unguardedly to other Landfelians on their path, and everyone seemed happy to talk to her. She was currently admiring a collection of walking sticks made by James Treadworthy, an artisan from the western city of Kande.

'Are they all hazel, James?' She asked genuinely fascinated.

'I have a small arboretum with over twenty-seven species of tree. This here's Landfelian oak.' James smiled affably, enjoying the young lady's curious eyes and soft voice. 'The walking stick must choose the walker, you see, not the other way around. Not everyone is hazel. It wouldn't be right selling a hazel stick to an elm man – like giving someone the wrong boots.'

'How interesting.' Red picked up a walking stick of curved ash and swung it around. 'A little like choosing a horse.' She smiled, and her horse swished his tail and snorted. 'Or a sword.'

'Aye, you've got the idea. Try this one on for size. I think you're more of a beech or a rosewood.' He handed her a beautiful stick of a smooth pinkish wood. 'I'd wager your friend there is a green oak.'

'What is oak for?' Red turned and raised her eyebrows at Robbie, who was faraway in his thoughts.

'A strong heart, mostly. It's an honest, loyal wood; fairly stubborn, but resilient. My father made the king a walking stick, you know,' James Treadworthy said proudly.

'King Felian.' Red faltered. 'He did?'

'Aye, the king was an oak.' He smiled at Red.

Robbie the Quiet listened and rode on behind them. A few other riders tried to engage him in conversation, asking about the line-up for this year's entertainment, the rumours of the Mooncake Ladies' reappearance and what he'd had for breakfast. He only answered with Mmms and Ahhhs, until a young boy in a nearby wagon began to fling acorns at Robbie's head to see if he would notice. When he didn't, the boy's mother stopped him. The people on the road thought maybe he was a bit soft in the middlehead or from the foreign lands. One thing was certain: he would not take his eyes off the young grace in the red dress.

Quite an audience soon gathered to ride alongside Red Felian on the lanes through Lake Country. Her dress had a scooped back and she wore a feathered, fabulous hat. (If you have a back, it should be shown; just wear the dress the right way around, which Red did.) Face also looked rather magnificent. She had scrubbed her valien until the last spot of tea dye and mud had run free from his piebald coat, which now looked like it had been polished.

No one clasped her hand and wailed about the missing queen, which was a relief. Quite the opposite – whoever the green-eyed rider was, they wanted to be on her table, or at least next to her in the queue for a sausage. There was something exciting about her. She appeared full of new hope. She listened to what they had to say and looked remarkably like someone they once knew.

The son of an apple-presser told Red he thought her freckles to be the finest freckles he had ever seen.

'I would very much like your freckles to appear on the family scrumpy bottles.' He blushed. 'I keep telling Pa that a name like Fermented Core doesn't work up a thirst or encourage folk to drink from our barrel, but he won't listen. You remind me of an apple we grow called Speckled Red. Now, there's a much better name for a cider.'

The princess laughed and accepted an apple gratefully. She was thoroughly enjoying herself with all these lovely Landfelians. Gone was the cold, anxious feeling in the pit of a stomach that followed her every day spent at Paloma.

As the day wore on, the question of lunch approached and a moveable feast was passed around the travellers. Bread from the bread wagon was thrown into a cart, where it met a cheese maker, moved on to a tomato farmer, then next a family who cured ham, before finally ending up in the condiments cart. Warm bloomers filled to high with the best produce of the land that only a double-jointed mouth could bite into. It didn't stop eveyone trying.

The apple presser sat himself down next to Robbie and handed him a full jug of cider. They watched Red snort as she tried to fit one end of her cheese, tomato, lettuce, ham, and pickle sandwich into her mouth, to the encouraging shouts of children.

'BREATHE THROUGH YOUR NOSE!'

'IT'S NEARLY IN!'

He took off his cap and sighed. 'Wherever did you two meet?'

Robbie watched Red and smiled. 'On the road.'

'Does she have any sisters? I have six brothers and an orchard. There's not a bodice for a hundred straits.' He sighed.

Robbie looked at him. 'No sisters to my knowledge. We're just travelling together.'

'Two adventurers. I should have known. That is grand. I want to travel. Try some different apples, see Fronce and Engerlande, see an elephant.' He grinned and raised a tankard to his lips. 'Well, if you are ever west, look in and say hello. Sam Fellows' the name, Speckled Red Cider.' He winked at Robbie, and as a shadow scudded across their picnic, he said, 'Anything can happen at the lake.'

Something made Robbie look up then. He noticed clouds gathering to the south; they were not far from the lake, but nonetheless the hairs on his arms stood up. Chittering – a faint sound from high above caught his attention. No, it was just the wind.

Several trails merged into one where an ancient gate marked the entrance to the lake. The gate stood at the end of a dappled faery road that burrowed up through the hills. Faery roads were ancient ways where the trees had grown overhead until their branches embraced, making a hidden, leafy pass. From the sky, people passing along could not be seen. Robbie felt relief at being under the protection of these trees for the moment; he wondered how he would keep the princess in his sight when she was slowly becoming the most popular part of the festival. He moved quickly to join her.

No one could go through the gate without exchanging a kiss on the cheek, a peck on the hand, or a full-on teeth clank with the person behind them. If you were alone, you blew a kiss to the spirits of the lake, and if you had an animal with you, you gave it a pat. The kissing gate was bewitched with a charm, and anyone who tried to slip through without acknowledging the custom was thrown out. And I mean thrown on their backside in the mud. Mud would be found especially for them. The gatekeepers could not explain the engineering behind it. It was the way of the lake, and it had always been so.

Red had forgotten how beautiful the approach through the old trees was. The last time she was here had been with her father. The gate itself was carved with the shapes of roosting birds and stars. The sound of rustling leaves was all around them. It took several attempts to get through, however. A young family and a rabble of Branch Bandits all wanted to walk behind her. The princess was slobbered on by three babies and a deerhound and kissed on the hand by everyone else.

Then the valien got stuck in a patch of deep, sticky mud between two trees.

'Help!' She gently pushed him from behind.

Robbie laughed. 'He's too heavy. Allow me,' he said and slapped Face gently on the rump. The valien squelched through, snorting defiantly, and flattened his ears at Robbie.

'I'm surprised he let you do that,' said Red. 'You're not doing it to me.' She picked up her dress and strolled through the gate. She could smell the water and woodsmoke from many campfires. As she passed him, Robbie gently took her hand and brushed her cheek with his lips. It was the softest of kisses. Before she knew what had happened, he was walking briskly ahead towards the water.

'I'm going to see about getting a room at the boathouse – *two*, that is …' He coughed without looking back. 'Two rooms.'

Robbie's lips burned as he strode down the hill, dragging his bemused horse with him. He even slipped a bit in his hurry.

Red watched him go and put her hand to her cheek. She stroked her horse's nose. 'There's something about this place, Face – we must graze carefully.'

The boathouse stood on stilts with a long, wonky deck crawling out over the water at the north end of the lake. It was swathed in every-coloured bunting for the festival.

With only one look at the cool expanse of clear blue-green water, treading carefully was last in line of the things Red most wanted to do. The water beckoned her. It had been a long, hot journey. She leant into her horse's twitching ears. 'Come on, it's time for a swim.'

Pulling off her boots, Red began to lead her valien down the banks when a voice full of mischief whistled behind her.

'That's a hat.'

Red spun around.

'There's a trail of rumours about you and your big horse all the way from Alba to the Kissing Gate.' Amber grinned and curtseyed graciously before Face.

'Amber! Why are you dressed like a …?' A smiling nun stood before her.

'*My name is Maria*,' Amber hissed, though her blue eyes twinkled. 'Travelling nun. English and I are in disguise. Had a run in with Mr Blackwood and his cane.'

Red reached out to touch Amber's scarred wrist. 'What happened to you?'

She covered it quickly. 'It's nothing.'

'This is my doing.' Red frowned.

'Hardly. I married the swine.'

'Married?' Red's mouth dropped open.

'It was a long time ago.' Amber batted the thought away. 'And I need to strip out of this habit. It gets as hot as a baked Alaska under here. Oh, but it's good to see you are safe. Will and I were worried.'

At the mention of stripping, a holy man appeared on the crest of the hill.

'Princess!' he bellowed and then remembered himself. He ran towards them and whispered, 'Milady, may I say you look ravishing? Drop down dead in the radishes ravishing! Tulip is your colour.' He kissed her hand. 'And how is the jippy ankle?' He raised a concerned eyebrow.

'Much better, thank you, Will,' Red said, incredibly happy to see him.

'Ready to dance, I trust?'

An elderly monk passed by and looked at Amber, muttering, 'They don't make nuns like that anymore.'

'I think I'll just watch.' Red wasn't at all ready to dance. She had not attended a single one of the half-queen's waltz classes. Dancing had always gone hand-in-hand with balls and being shoved into a wig, so she had avoided it. 'Is it compulsory?' She faltered, thinking, *I have to stay focused*.

'Nonsense, I must have the first fandango with you!' boomed Will.

Red Felian had no idea what the fandango required, but the actor made it sound like something fun, like a helter-skelter. 'If you must.' She smiled at her friends and forgot about the quest for a moment. 'I'm a terrible dancer.'

Amber handed Will her holy book and led the princess towards the lake. 'We're going for a swim,' she called back. 'Go find the Man of the Road. I saw him striding towards the boathouse not long ago.'

'Robert of the Wylde! Is he here too? Excellent.' Will clapped. 'You should have seen the man act, milady! A true pretender. He silenced a brothel of brigands with a little book called, *The Governess and the Piano Tuner*. It was smashing. I could not have rescued Amber from that terrible son of a lawyer without him. Although I did hit him with my case of holy books first, just like you asked, for betraying you.' He looked dutiful and pleased.

'Thank you, William.' Red grinned.

He bowed exuberantly and flounced off, robes flying.

The two women were a dot in the distance when Will shouted after them, 'I'm not sure about you swimming alone. THE PLACE IS TEEMING WITH ROMANCERS.' At that moment, a stream of nearly naked Landfelians galloped past Will in the same direction as the lake. 'Are you sure you don't want a chaperone, ladies?'

'I know a lovely little spot by the lilies where it's nice and quiet. Even Will won't find us there,' Amber said. 'The circus troop used to come up here to rest between tours. We would hide bottles of ginger beer in the reed beds to keep them cool.'

Amber unpinned her hair, closed her eyes, and took a deep breath. She stared out over the water. She looked a little older and thinner than Red remembered. There was weariness about her eyes that had not been there before.

'I love it here,' Amber said with a sigh.

Red dipped a toe in. The water was cool and soft.

'I'm sorry you got involved in all this.'

'The whole kingdom is now.' Amber squeezed Red's hand. She removed her habit to reveal an early form of bathing dress. 'I wouldn't have missed it for the world. We'd been hiding too long – and then you jumped out the palace window and woke us all up.' She smiled and then looked behind her briefly to check there was no one close. They were concealed by the reeds. 'Mind your step when you leave here, princess; the wolves will descend fast. Blackwood's mind is bent on it.'

'I have been warned,' Red said with some defiance. 'I won't stop looking for my father.'

Amber smiled and said, 'I hope he's worthy of you.'

They let the lake envelop them, and the afternoon lulled away into a hazy pink evening. The sun began to sink, orange, behind the hills. Red listened to Amber, her eyes wide to tales of the Cornucopia circus and life on the road. Her own stories from Paloma after the Quest were rather different in tone and experience.

When Amber left to prepare for her performance that evening, Red swam further out to the middle of the lake where there were no other bathers. She was close to the south shore and floated on her back with the last of the sun's warmth on her face. Dragonflies hovered from lily to lily like lazy pilots after a good lunch. Her valien ambled around the lake, staying as close to the princess as he could without getting wet. He rubbed himself against the rough bark of a willow and grazed on the sweet grass, making satisfied grunting sounds. Valiens liked a good splash – but they were not Labradors.

'The open road. That's what I want, Face. To roam free with a whisk, like Robbie.' She smiled and went under –

kicking down deep, swimming until it got dark – until she ran out of breath before popping up to the surface, her lungs bursting.

'I'm not ready for a crown, I want to see other lands.' The water ran from Red's eyes. 'Maybe Father Peter would let me study with him if ...' She couldn't bring herself to say, 'They don't come back.' A horribly familiar smell hit the back of her throat. She coughed and swallowed some water in surprise.

Cheroot smoke.

It trailed towards the water like a serpent and crouched in a thin, putrid line over the surface.

Red's heart began to pound. A shadow that hadn't been there before now darkened the area next to the willow tree. When she looked again it was gone. Her horse reared up, but the smoke still hung above the shallows. The valien's ears were flat, and he was staring at the space next to the willow. There was no one there, though, only rushes whispering in the breeze. Her heart thumped and goosebumps raced down her skin. Her horse stepped closer to the water and whinnied very loudly like he was raising an alarm.

Red stayed where she was, frozen. Her imagination was playing tricks on her. 'There is nothing there,' she said out loud. She was alive and able to shout – these were both good things. 'There are no fishhooks in this lake,' she said more quietly, swimming fast towards her horse. Daniel couldn't have found her so soon, she reasoned. It was not possible. For now, she was safe, amongst good people.

In the distance, she could just make out children who splashed in the lake and clung to the necks of parents happy to be clumsily strangled. Small babies played in shallow pools. Boys shrieked, balled themselves up, and hurled into the water while portly men paddled about them.

Torches flickered around the banks. Colourful stalls were opening, selling melon slices and honeydew ale. Sam Fellows' cider stall was doing surprisingly well now that the cider was called Speckled Red. Hot, buttered cobs of corn and chickens, baked and crispy on spits, were relished in the balmy evening. The lake was alive and illuminated by lights. A small bandstand had been arranged on the reed island where the Still Place stood.

Red watched, listening to the faint sounds of merriment. Her eyes tingled at the sight. It was her mother's favourite place. She shook her head and took a shaky breath. It would be safer for all if she moved on and continued alone to find the king. No one else could get hurt that way.

'I'm not coming in to rescue you.' Robbie's voice found her. 'You had one shot at drowning in Waterwood and you blew it.' He smiled at her from the bank. 'What are you doing all the way out here? You nearly missed the Wylde Lake of Stars food tour. Step this way, please, Milady, because, frankly, you have not lived until you've tasted a mooncake.' He stepped into the shallows and held out his hand. Red looked cold and frightened.

'What happened?'

'I thought I saw a figure by the willow tree.' She gave him wary smile. She glanced at the tree and made no move to get out, although the feeling of dread inside her had vanished.

'Impossible,' Robbie frowned, walking around the tree and looking up at its branches. 'Everyone's down the good end of the lake, eating, which is what we should be doing. We must try something from every stall. And I mean *every* stall. An edible education if you will.' Red raised an eyebrow at him. 'It is your royal duty. You need to keep your strength up.' He smiled. 'And that actor is worried you will miss his performance. He won't leave me alone. Please help me.'

Red laughed, swimming toward him. 'I'm on my way.'

It was hard to look directly at her. Robbie made a point of studying the banks and the area just above the princess' head. Her under-dress was now wet. Part of it had slipped off her shoulder, where there was some milky skin that should be covered up fast. Robbie held out a blanket, struggling to maintain a neutral expression.

She was staring at the willow, beside which her valien stood pawing the ground. 'Come for a swim. It's lovely once you're in.' Her jaw trembled and she backed into the water again, looking unsure. Her lips were blue, but that smell of cheroot was there again.

'Swim, absolutely not. Exposure is very serious. Trust me. I prescribe staying on land for hot chocolate and roasted hog.' Robbie moved closer and said, 'Take my hand. Trust me.'

There are as many versions of 'take my hand' as there

are of 'trust me'. There is:

'Take my hand, this uncouth scrum might get a little rough.'

'Take my hand, the ice is breaking and you may die if you don't.'

'Take my hand, this road is full of potholes.'

And the common, 'Take my hand, it appears the horses got here first' to avoid a large manure pile in the middle of the road.

The Robbie version of 'take my hand' involved two hands, and the princess took both. She stood with her wet feet on his boots and dripped over his shirt.

And then she said, 'Sorry.' And Robbie forgot to breathe.

After living locked inside a palace for seven years, the princess had no experience of flirting or courtship. There were few books on it in the palace library - although whole shops were dedicated to it in the towns of Dood and Kande. This did not stop her from finding that it came naturally. The probable certainty of being hunted by a ruthless son of a lawyer and a heartless witch meant Red no longer cared what rules she broke from the princess handbook (which she had never read anyway). It was a heavy book filled with essays on conduct and royal etiquette, there we no illustrations, and Red had found it more useful as a doorstop.

'How did you get that scar?' Leaning closer, she gestured to his neck, moving his shirt aside to touch the white jagged line that wrapped around his neck and across his collar bone.

Robbie managed to say, 'Well,' as she traced it with her finger, a look of concern on her face. He swallowed, looked at her ear, and tried very hard to think of the first rule of trigonometry.

'A whip ran into me,' he said quietly.

'Whose whip?' she asked, standing on tiptoes to get a better look. Red Felian knew a lot more about injuries from horse-related accessories than she did about flirting and she was interested.

'A stranger on a valien.' He swallowed. Robbie wanted to tell her everything as she stood so close. But not tonight. He would not bring his own sadness to this beautiful place.

'A valien? When?' Red stood back and looked at him in doubt. 'All the valien are accounted for.'

'Not everything is accounted for.' Robbie looked into her eyes.

'But they are for the chosen. The valien finds its rider and there is a list.'

'Maybe the list is wrong.' Robbie smiled. 'It was a long time ago. I was a boy, but I know what I saw. Anyway, at the Lake of Stars, you forget the past and enjoy the food. Let's go.'

They could hear music, steel pans, fiddles, and something raspy tuning up by the boathouse. Red turned to look and could see that several people with lutes had started to fling themselves around in circles on the deck. The smell of sweet chestnuts and steaming dumplings floated out to them on the breeze.

'You must be hungry,' he said, relieved to change the subject.

'I'm starving.' Her stomach yowled, which made them both laugh.

11

BUTTERFLIES

Sir Toby was tired of travelling. He was in sheep country, or did they call it hill country by the way his poor horse was breathing? By the time he reached two remarkably pert hills, it was dark. A signpost told him he was somewhere called Tikli Bottom. It was very quiet and smelled of lavender, and faintly of melted cheese. Toby decided, if he was going to arrive anywhere exhausted, Tikli Bottom got his vote, his horse, and his boots.

From the morning after the half-queen's ball, Sir Toby had improved beyond recognition. Several days on the road had rumpled him up nicely. The sun had caught his sallow skin, his soft muscles had grown fit and saddle-sore from all the riding, and his eyes were now alert and shining from over a week of being sober. Sir Toby no longer woke up with the dull throb of a headache and no memory of where he had been. His days felt new, frightening, and liberating in equal measure. He had a purpose: as a loyal aid to the much-wronged and only available heir to the kingdom, Toby would help the princess find her family and overcome an evil that was seeping closer to the throne. He would sample the occasional pastry and peruse some nice art galleries along the way. He was just having a spot of trouble finding her.

Magatha Guiler was locking up her house. Her departure had been much delayed by a series of domestic disasters. If she had not grown distrustful of the signs, Maggie would say something was trying to stop her leaving. After finally finding her front door key, she locked it from the inside and climbed out the chimney with her broom. Jan must have been mistaken about her vision that a wandering artist would arrive and offer her a more comfortable lift. She was about to convince Bernard her broom to fly and face the fog when there was a loud crash. A deep voice whimpered and something heavy and soft slumped against her front door.

The voice said, 'Oh blast, my toe!'

The sun had faded below the horizon when Toby walked into a large watering can and fell into a bush. He now lay next to a round wooden door, his head spinning. There was nothing more to do than lie back and enjoy the view that this plump little windmill afforded. The Branch Bandits had sworn he would find help here, but it appeared to be abandoned. To the west, at the furthest point the eye could see, a full moon shone over the hills that surrounded the Lake of Stars. He was pondering whether to get out his sketchbook, the light was so beautiful, when a husky voice called to him from above ...

'And who the hell are you?'

He looked up at the sky and answered, 'I am Sir Toby Mole.'

'And what business do you have with my lavender bush?' the sky replied.

A blue-grey cat jumped lightly onto his chest and licked his nose with a sandpaper tongue. She looked terribly familiar.

'You are Princess Felian's cat.' Toby held the cat in amazement. 'Hello, Julia.'

'She was a loan. Although a cat is never truly anyone's,' the voice from above said curtly.

'I can assure you, madam, as the once fiancée of Princess Felian, I know a royal cat when I see one.'

'I beg your pardon?' The front door opened suddenly, and Sir Toby rolled through it. A colourfully-clad woman smiled down at him. 'My goddaughter didn't say anything about a fiancée.' Maggie took a long, interested look at Sir Toby and then said, 'Ah, it's you. You're late.'

'I'm sorry?'

'Why didn't you knock?' Maggie smiled.

Toby was not sure why this woman seemed to know him and how he was late. 'I'm rather lost and kicked your watering can over by mistake.'

'Jolly good. That's what it's for. There is time for a shot of tea before we go.'

'Go? I've only just arrived!' Sir Toby tried to regain control over the situation from the floor and found himself considering two bright hazel eyes as several scarves attached to a patchwork floor-length coat brushed over him. The woman winked, and Toby wondered if he was fully conscious.

'Are you a witch?' he asked. 'Apparently there's a couple about.'

'I was, but please call me a sign-reader or I'll be locked up. I am the princess' godmother, Maggie Guiler.'

'Why were you on the roof?' Sir Toby asked reasonably.

'It's the best place for taking off. Do you always ask this many questions?'

'Possibly.' Sir Toby held out his hand from the floor. 'I'm delighted to meet you. Goodness, this is marvellous! What luck. I've come to help the princess, you see. I believe there is some serious usurping business going on in the North Realm.' He tried to roll over elegantly and bow. 'And it must be quelled!'

'January said you would find your way here eventually.' Maggie laughed as she watched him. 'She's obviously getting her powers back. You've just missed her, she left first. I lost my key.'

'Powers?'

'Yes, her mojo, her juju, her second spring.'

He must have bumped his head too, unless a good part of his sense was lodged in his toe. Toby felt remarkably comfortable on top of this hill, with the sails of the windmill creaking gracefully past. Although he did question the sanity of the woman next to him. And who an earth was January? He felt very at home in her lavender, with no clear idea of how he got here, other than his horse getting a fright amongst the Trees of Goonock and some feral children telling him to head to a pair of round hills if he needed further assistance. Hadn't they yelled something about witches?

'Are you coming in? My dog may pee on you if you stay there. I hope you like moussaka.'

Sir Toby did not know if he liked moussaka as he had never eaten it before.

'Ah, the children in the woods mentioned this dish.'

He got up and followed the woman's colourful form inside, realising that he was in fact famished. For the first time in seven years, Sir Toby felt he had arrived exactly where he was supposed to, at precisely the right time, on the right hill, and outside the right door.

'I see you met the Branch Bandits,' Maggie said, pointing to where Sir Toby's face had been painted with two horizontal blackberry stripes.

'Yes, I was not expecting to find children.' He rubbed his cheek and chuckled. 'They released me when they found my sketchbook, though.' He looked sorry. 'They were terribly thin.'

'I know.' Maggie looked sorry. 'They won't be safe in the trees for much longer. The guards will be onto them in no time. I have sent a message, they are to head to the lake with their families. It is the safest place for everyone now.'

Sir Toby pulled the sketchbook from his coat to show her. The last drawing was of the princess looking surprised, halfway up a fig tree in the Paloma gardens.

'I understand they made her acquaintance a few days ago,' he continued. 'She made quite an impression. I gave them the last of my bread and they promised not to eat me.'

When Magatha Guiler laughed. She placed her hand gently on his arm, and Toby forgot about the recent muggings. 'So, you're an artist.' She smiled. He forgot about the incident at The Hog's Breath involving the pie of the day and the run-in with the robbers in other less welcoming woods and he put to the back of his mind the feeling that this woman was of witch descent.

It had been an eventful journey from Paloma. He had learnt a good deal about life. A drawing, it seemed, did not guarantee him a hot dinner. His countrymen from the North and East realms were not interested in art. They too were hungry and scared; a number were being recruited and taken to somewhere called Mirador. Sir Toby was about to relay all of this to Red Felian's godmother when she stopped dead and all the colour from her wise face dropped away.

'Dear lady, are you quite well?' She was staring at a page

of his sketchbook; the wind rustled the pages and settled on a drawing right at the beginning.

'Oh yes. The hag at the gates.' Toby shuddered. 'I never forgot her face. Haunts me to this day.'

Maggie sat down on the nearest chair. 'When did this woman visit the palace?' she asked, her voice sharp. She looked at Toby with such intensity, he swallowed nervously.

'Years ago now; just after the princess' fourteenth birthday.'

'Tell me everything you can.' Maggie gestured to a chair. 'It is of utmost importance.'

Toby decided it was not the time to enquire about tea. 'Yes, of course. It was a time when the princess and her step aunt did not get on. There was great tension between them and there were many balls. Considerable quantities of the king's gold was being spent on entertaining, and the princess began to run away from Paloma as often as she could. On the last occasion, she made it over the Bigeasy river, and then a gentleman arrived by the name of Daniel Blackwood.' Toby grimaced. 'He was the son of a lawyer in Alba. Jeremaih Blackwood. Notoriously bad sort.'

'I am familiar with this man. His reputation has made it to these hills.' Maggie's face was grave.

'Then you will know he is more corrupt and manipulative than the rumours say. Twice as deadly as his father. Well, he took the princess back to Paloma with several of his men. From that evening, he barely left the palace, and

I heard him tell the Half King and Queen that he was to make sure the princess was safe. Of course, they did not need persuading; he has the gift of making people do what he wants.' Sir Toby remembered his steely presence at the ball.

'But this woman,' Maggie urged, tapping at the drawing. 'When did she meet Red?'

'The next day at dawn. They woke her up. I'll never forget it.' Sir Toby swallowed and looked at his hands. 'I was in the gardens, still drunk from the ball before and hopeful of seeing the princess. I knew she had tried to run away. Unfortunately, by then, I had been rather to easily seduced by the opulence of Caroline's court and was rarely sober or sensible. But that morning, the princess was nowhere to be seen, which was unusual as she was always outside; it was the only way she could keep out of her step aunt's way.' Toby looked sorry. 'I believe Blackwood drugged her with some sort of sleeping opiate. The hag at the gates was allowed entry. The guards and the servants stepped aside when they saw her. I watched from behind one of the pillars as she met Blackwood at the door. He seemed to be under her spell too. Under the mottled, dirty rags was a face neither old nor young; it was unforgettable. She held out a box and said it was a gift for Princess Felian. I did not see any more. But when the princess woke the next day, she wore a voodoo anklet.' Toby turned the page of his sketchbook. 'Like this; it was made of teeth. Whatever dark magic it held stopped the princess from leaving the palace grounds. She was never the same after that. Some part of her youth died and the rest fought hard to stop the voodoo from taking the rest of her.' Toby clasped his hands together.

Maggie looked at him and said nothing. She closed the sketchbook and pushed it away, then she stood up very slowly and closed her eyes. In a voice full of feeling, she said, 'Selina Carnal, that meddling old witch.' There were a few other words that Magatha Guiler used which I cannot repeat. Although I can say they rhymed with wench and stench.

'The princess left this behind in the bandits' hideout. They were keen to get it out of their tree den.' He placed a handkerchief on the table. Inside it lay the broken teeth that had been bewitched and placed around her ankle. 'I am awfully glad she is free of it. A terrible business. The half-queen is mad, I tell you. Mad.'

'She was bewitched, poor woman.' Maggie looked at the dark shining objects. 'We have to leave immediately.'

'We do? Why?' Toby had been rather looking forward to some moussaka.

'The woman responsible for this.' She looked in dismay at the shattered teeth and quickly covered them up. 'I knew her well. She won't rest until she has what she wants. Dark magic. I wasn't sure before; Selina's been keeping herself hidden with very tenacious spells. WELL, now we have proof. Come, we must get to the lake!'

Maggie grabbed her broom and marched out, with a bemused Toby close behind her.

'Get on.'

'I beg your pardon?'

'The broom.'

There was no hesitation this time. Sir Toby knew not to argue with a woman straddling a branch. The Bernard 747 lifted steadily up into the sky above Tikli Bottom and, with one wild call from Magatha Guiler, whooshed off.

Toby was not very good at duels; a few unsuccessful attempts with Blackwood's Guards had not done his wrists any favours, though he had managed to send them off in the wrong direction and hide behind some bins in the citadel of Alba. He'd then lost his horse to a man claiming to be his brother and had to hitch rides the rest of the way.

Whatever this remarkable lady and her broom were going to do to him now couldn't be any worse, he thought as he closed his eyes and held on tight.

Amber was in lodgings above the boathouse, reserved every year for the entertainment, doing what she did best besides singing: she was talking.

'I'm telling you, lady, he's a goner. He's befuddled, titivated, smitten, drop-down, head over heels, over the moon, blow out the candles, fallen, and sunk a pirate's ship … for you.' She leant on the wall for support.

The princess was having a wash and only half listening. She had a small, quiet sort of smile on her lips. The sort of smile you get when you remember the night you met someone and stayed up till dawn talking to them while drinking wine from a bottle, eating flapjacks from a paper bag, and getting locked in a beautiful garden by the water. No one knows when their next bath will be their last, and the princess intended to enjoy every one. So, she was in the bath again, smiling quietly.

The two women, now unlikely friends, were sharing a room. It had a mattress stuffed with the feathery heads of reeds, a complimentary limoncello candle, and a large tin bath. Tonight, Amber's eyes shone the blue of a cherub's – a cherub, that is, who had done things a cherub should not do (and would do again in a heartbeat). A blue that said, *let us dance under these stars and be delighted with everything until the guards turn up and ruin everything.*

Red had caught it too. Her eyes glittered a sheen of Robin-Hood-come-into-my-forest green. A green that promised something you wanted to order but couldn't for the life of you find on the menu. No one was thinking of finding the king at this point. The Lake of Stars was working its magic.

There was a knock at the door, and Robbie Wylde made a noise outside. Amber made a face like a surprised apricot, and Red threw soap at her.

He coughed again and asked, 'Ready?'

'She's covered in bubbles.' Amber opened the door a chink and smiled sweetly. 'She'll be down in a wink.'

She shut it with the force of a matron protecting a girls' boarding house and applied the finishing touches to her glistening reflection using a hand-held mirror. Her hair was laced up with lily flowers, gold thread, and small bells. The whole effect was not for the faint-hearted; she looked like a pagan empress.

'You know, I never thought anyone would get under the young Man of the Road's hat,' commented Amber. 'He's not what you call a stayer, a stick-around let's-get-an-ass-and-two-matching-curtains sort of man. More of a wanderer.'

Red looked out the window. 'It is not my concern. I have to find –'

'The king – I know … still, there's no harm in having a little fun along the way.' Amber clapped her hands. 'Now, where's that red dress of yours?'

Will was outside their room and keen to make himself heard.

'Lady of the lake? The hour is late, the stage is set, the musicians are taking their seats, the night is –'

Amber hollered back, 'I'M COMING!'

Red carefully dried off her map and unpacked her bag. She had to stay focused, keep on her guard, and not get swept up in all this starry-eyed lake nonsense. She would eat something sensible, check on her horse, drink a glass of milk, go straight to bed, and set off for Father Peter's at dawn. Her godmothers would be arriving soon to travel there with her and Robbie. She smiled again.

'The problem is that you wander off more than he does, and it's thrown the boy.' Amber shook several dresses in front of her. 'Why don't you try on a few of my frocks and bejewel yourself a little?'

'I'm happy in my old clothes, thank you.' Red tried to pull her dress gently back from Amber, who paid no attention. She put down a pair of scissors and her sewing kit. 'We are all visual creatures. Let's give the crowds some fireworks!' She swept up the tulip-red dress and twirled around the room.

Minutes later, Red was looking in fear at a pile of sparkly things Amber had left on the bed. Something had happened to her red dress: the sleeves fell off her shoulders, and were those feather fronds? She didn't put up a fight, though. It was the least intimidating option, and she liked the colour. It kept her hair company, which was loose and drying in waves of scarlet. She tied in a bit of leftover gold thread to keep it out of her eyes and popped in a few wildflowers, because everyone else was doing it. And then she told herself to be vigilant and in bed by midnight.

Robbie and Will were outside, taking the air, walking up and down the deck. They had been doing this for some time.

Will stopped when he got a splinter and sat on the deck with his feet in the water. He began to sew the missing sequins back onto his bolero. One of the more surprising gifts of a true player was not stage fighting but being able to sew torn costumes whilst on the road. Many accuse the acting trade of being impractical, but those people are wrong. Tonight, Will was playing the fiddle. Amber had agreed to sing one song with him, something she had never done before because his range was limited.

'It is as obvious as the cows coming home and the saints marching in that she loves me,' sighed Will.

'Has she told you?' asked Robbie, who did not pay much attention to these things.

'We are beyond words.'

Robbie walked to the end of the deck again and stared at the water. He was not sure where to put his hands; they seemed big and alien to him. Who gave him these hands, for the love of God? He glanced at the windows above and resumed his pacing. Thankfully, it was a long deck.

Tables were dotted with flickering candles and covered in chequered cloths. The place was set up for a relaxed banquet. Outside, the moon appeared to be dipped in sherbet. Every now and again a fluorescent heartskipper broke the surface of the lake. People dried off, dressed, and settled down on the soft banks to open a bottle of something meady, enjoy busker's corner, and gaze goofily at the stars.

Never one to miss the festival, the king's herald arrived. He looked brighter after a cup of coffee with tall Sal and a good night's sleep. He checked the baton in his top pocket and adjusted his bow tie, skipping over the stepping stones to the island where the musicians were tuning up. He hoped the rumours he had heard on the road were true and the princess was here. Lake country was a sacred place – she would find no enemies here, not yet. Love for King Felian and the vanished queen still reverberated around the hills.

A kingfisher watched Robbie pace on the deck from its perch on the bunting. Will continued to sew up his costume. Poor man, Will thought. He hadn't seen a case as bad since he'd met Amber. When that had happened, he'd paced for two weeks, breaking only to drink a little water and eat some toast. It had been a very restless time.

'Here, try this. It will put hairs on your chest – not that you need any more,' he told Robbie, moving a bottle towards him. 'I wish I had more of a pelt. I have other qualities, though – fine eyebrows and needlework.' He gestured to his bolero.

Robbie was too busy pacing to drink anything. 'She's throwing herself out there.' He pointed to the crowds gathered along the shore and continued in a half whisper. 'With no disguise, no hat, no wig, nothing. Her horse has a queue of children asking for a ride. There are spiders with wings on her trail, guards, hooks, voodoo, and she is under the impression that her father, the king – who abandoned her for seven years – will be found near some mad old wizard's folly.

'If no one has discovered the whereabouts of the quest in seven years, I don't see how a wizened godfather could know,' Robbie continued. 'We should have stayed at Tikli Bottom and not stopped here.' He gazed at the water. 'This was a mistake. There are too many people I cannot account for. Any one of them could be one of Blackwood's spies or the rogue witch.'

'Tikli where?' Will's eyes widened.

'Bottom.'

'Remind me to ask you about that later. But why do you care?' asked Will, dropping his voice. 'Red Felian is not your burden. You are a free Man of the Road, are you not? There is no bind; you are not sworn to her. She has asked nothing of you. Celebrate! You have your wings back, my friend! Apart from a slight fever and a scar on her ankle, the young lady looks in pretty good shape to me ... You are beholden to no one. Many young adventurers would be thankful for that. You are able to leave here at any time.' He raised his eyebrows and smiled. 'This rogue witch sounds frightfully exciting.'

A lady had arrived on the deck. She was causing quite a stir. As she walked, people parted to allow her through and everyone stopped doing what they were doing to stare. A fair few were bowing. This was someone to sit up and take notice of. This person looked better than a mooncake, and she looked familiar and quite important.

'Ah.' Will smiled and said, 'She has arrived,' which seemed to sum up everything.

Everyone should make an entrance like Red Felian's if they get the chance. Go forth and quieten a room, and for goodness sake, don't worry about your hair; your hair will be fabulous.

In Landfelian history, there had been countless entrances of note. Will believed he'd made most of them on the stage. The herald had marked a modest number in his journal, although the king tended to upstage him shortly after. Amber made a solid gold entrance once a week and twice on Fridays everywhere she went. Queen Felian rendered everyone else's redundant when she found a door to a busy room and walked through it, although she loathed an audience and had to hum 'Edelweiss' under her breath to distract her from the fact that people would be looking at her.

The king became accomplished at entrances after several intense months of tutelage from his herald, his most famous occurring between the legs of two sparring giants after a scuffle over a lost game of tiddlywinks, which was apparently cause for war to be declared. He stepped between the two giants with no armour or army, walking over churned ground that had once been field, and said, 'Excuse me, honourable giant gentlemen, I have been informed that you are brilliant weavers. I wonder if you might embroider something for my wife? You see, we have this one very troublesome wall.' After a pin-dropping silence, war was postponed, and a very long tapestry arrived a week later with a reasonable invoice. It took King Felian some time to perfect his entrance, being a quiet man with a tendency to round his shoulders, as is the way with most tall men.

January Macloud and Magatha Guiler had made a notable *exit* from a WI meeting once in the nearby village of Loddon. There had been complaints that the two residents of Tikli Bottom mixed margaritas before six o'clock on Mondays, to which they had enquired, 'a.m. or p.m.?' There had also been complaints that inappropriate cakes were being contributed to the local cake sale, along with sightings of brooms on rooftops. So, both women had arrived sensibly dressed for the next meeting, and as it droned on, they began to take their clothes off until, at the close of business, they were mostly bare apart from their reading glasses. And thus had made quite the exit.

Red's entrance was different, mainly because she had no idea that she was making one. A group of children clapped without knowing why, someone whistled, several gentlemen offered their hand should she slip, and Landfelians hurried off to fetch her a cup of wine, even though drinks were free; it was a bartering situation at the lake and a generous one. These people had lost all sense and would have offered to buy Red Felian a unicorn if one was available.

When Robbie saw her, he stopped pacing. There was a sky-diving event going on between his chest and his stomach.

Will stood up and patted Robbie on the back. 'If there is one thing I know, my friend ...' He paused to look at the sky like a sage. 'Nobody knows anything about anything. It can only be felt.'

'She's a royal,' Robbie said under his breath.

'She's a young lady. And you are a very capable young man. This is not a fairytale – if it was, I would be a prince or a wise, young wizard and not a banished player. A lowly peasant like you can win the love of a princess – you just need to perform a few heroic acts and get a clean shirt.'

Robbie could have done without the 'lowly peasant' comment, but he appreciated Will's support and optimism.

Red felt flushed. The boathouse was crowded and the

attention overwhelming. She was having unpleasant déjà vu from attending step aunt Caroline's balls, although no one there had ever smiled with their eyes. There was little of that falsity in the faces around her; everyone appeared genuinely pleased to see her. And yet she desperately wanted to escape. She missed the roof of her turret. The people looked as if they expected her to say something important or amusing. Her mouth was dry, and she could not think of what to say. Why did she not stay in disguise? The weather. She could comment on that. 'What a big moon,' she said quietly at the next person to bow.

She attempted an interesting, non-committed, and wholly unpolitical smile and looked around for someone she knew.

A hand found hers. 'Come with me.' At that moment, the music started and people began drifting towards the shore to watch. Robbie led her quickly away, around the side of the boathouse, and up a ladder to a pitched roof where there was a large blanket, a few stolen candles, and a picnic in need of company, overlooking the water.

'You looked a bit clammy down there.'

She looked relieved. 'This is wonderful. I love roofs.'

(You'll say some dumb things in life, and you will keep saying them, so don't worry too much about it.)

Robbie handed her the small copper wing he had found in the mud when they'd first met. 'I've been meaning to give this back to you since the night of the ball.'

'My wing,' she whispered. 'I thought you might have kept it.'

'No, not much of an earring man.' He laughed. 'Although it looks important.'

'It must have fallen off straight after I jumped the river.' She touched her mother's earring and bit her lip. 'I only managed to pierce one at the palace,' Red smiled, taking the delicate wing and adorning her left ear. 'They were a pair. My mother has the other with her if she ...'

'Suits you.' He smiled. 'One is very debonair.'

'Her favourite bird was the Halcyon Kingfisher; she said it was a lucky omen if you saw one. It meant someone dear to you was keeping watch. The night before she disappeared, she left it on my pillow. As if she knew she may not ...' Red stopped and looked at the lake.

'It sounds like she saw magic.' Robbie wanted to reach out and hold her then.

'Magic?'

'My mother believed there was magic everywhere and finding it helped you survive things.' He spoke quietly. 'Like grief.'

Neither of them said anything else.

The blanket was covered in food from what looked like every stall. 'Look at all of this.'

'I hope you're hungry.' Robbie grinned.

They both sat down to eat and watch the festival come alive. Cherries, hot cheesy parcels seasoned delicately with sage, salt beef with horseradish, baked potatoes oozing butter ... I could go on, but I'm hungry so I won't. They drank a cooling cocktail called Lights On, made from oranges, lemons, honey, and rum. It was very good.

Although it was pretty boring for the Branch Bandits stealing glances at them from the ladder. 'I thought they had come up here to set off firecrackers or make a den.'

'What are they doing now?' yawned Dodge.

'*Talking*,' whispered Kitty.

Red told Robbie how she used to sit on her turret roof and storm gaze. How she found the royal court terrible and preferred being outside. How balls brought her out in a rash, which she duly showed him. He politely declined to look any further down her neck and made a well-meaning but obvious joke about how princesses were supposed to like balls. She explained that was not the case with all princesses. How she would try to merge into the walls so no one would see her unless they accidentally leant on her. Robbie said he did not need to see her become part of the roof; he could well believe she had a talent for disguise and agreed that life at the palace sounded stifling.

'It is not what I had imagined.' Red looked at the sky. 'My parents did not entertain unless it was for diplomatic purposes. They preferred books and sandwiches in front of the fire with the animals.

Robbie gave her his coat to wrap over her shoulders and told her an abridged version of how he had fallen into the business of serving the quest families of Landfelian. 'I've been trying to save up. It worked for a time.'

'Do you fall into everything?' asked Red.

He looked at her intently and said, 'No. Sometimes I walk willingly.'

Red swallowed a cherry stone and coughed.

Robbie skirted around the homeless, flea-bitten years of his life after his mother died. He told the princess about the remote valley in the north-west where he grew up and flew over a significant day by a river. He did not mention the scar on his shoulders or how he got it.

Red lay back with her head in her hands, looking at the night, and decided not to recite any of the poetry she thought she remembered about stars.

'Where are you going after this?' she asked.

'Far away.' He didn't look at her. 'I want to see the other kingdoms, maybe become an apprentice to those cathedral builders. I don't really know ...'

'Across the Sea of Trees?' She turned to look at him, thinking of her map, and noticed a flash of fear pass over his eyes. 'Or the White Ocean, perhaps?'

'I prefer to stay clear of water if I can,' he answered, turning away.

'How will you travel out of Landfelian without crossing it?' She studied his wary face.

'Why sail when you can fly?' he replied, gesturing to a constellation of bunched up stars that neither of them could remember the name of.

'I think it's Cassiopeia.' Red squinted. 'Of course, the

Cloudbuster? The only reason you offered to help me.' She had not forgotten. 'The sky is not mapped, you know,' she added seriously. 'Father Peter has not completed his cloud atlas.'

Robbie laughed. 'You like maps, don't you?'

'They're wonderful things,' she said.

'The fog around the kingdom hasn't given me much choice. Not many ships are leaving.'

'I know,' Red shook her head. 'We're isolated.'

She was about to say something about clouds and water being part of the same thing but was seeing three of him. 'I like it here.'

'So do I.' Robbie was enjoying the feeling of Red lying next to him, star gazing. There were freckles on her nose; not many, but he liked discovering the details.

'Father Peter collects clouds. Always lets them loose after he's studied them, though,' she said. 'He says that once we were all creatures of flight.' She turned to him, her eyes bright. 'That's the reason we sometimes get the urge to jump from high places, just for a second ...' She whistled and her hand dived to the ground. 'A small part of all of us still believes we can fly and desires to be that free again.'

'I think Father Peter has eaten too many spotty toadstools.' He smiled.

'No,' she turned over and whispered, looking at his mouth for some reason. It was definitely time for a glass of milk. 'It's true. Ask my horse – he will tell you. We both flew.'

'I know. I was there. Remember, I saw you on that

valien.' He smiled at her. 'Right over the Bigeasy river.'

'You did,' murmured Red.

'Yes. It was a leap of faith.'

'It felt like one.'

They lay close. It was unnecessary – they had the whole roof; they had the space.

'Would you like to dance?' Robbie asked.

'What?' answered Red.

12

MISSING MIDNIGHT

Around the Lake of Stars, Landfelians from every realm were beginning to sway. The herald could not keep control of Will, who was beating a merry hell out of some early form of drum next to a stout, bearded southerner on a fiddle. A double bass spun in and a hoot of brass instruments rasped out the throatiest chords they knew. It was folk and it was docey doh, and it got faster and faster until Amber's voice echoed around the valley where the lake shone. So pure and true was the sound, everyone slowed down and clapped. A few began to cry happy tears. It was an old song, from happier times.

A few stared up at the young lad and girl on the roof, giving them wistful looks that said, *We were young and soft once too* and *If he doesn't kiss her, I will!* and *She can't be – although you're right, Olivia, she does look a lot like the daughter of King Felian.*

Red reached out her hand, and Robbie took it. She began to twirl. He watched her and thought how he never wanted this night to end. The music changed after a deafening applause and things moved up a notch. While Robbie began to fling himself around with a couple of Branch Bandits, Red got shiny trying the medieval skip, a popular move of the time. Everyone else danced around them.

Sam Fellows had a go at an early form of breakdance that looked like he was trying to remove a ferret from his trouser leg, while the princess and the Man of the Road danced, their necks damp, hair flapping, arms raised, and feet stomping. The Branch Bandits stole on to the roof to polish off Robbie's well-selected picnic. The witches had promised them food and safety, and they were right. It was the best midnight feast they had ever had.

As it got close to twelve o' clock, the torches burnt low and Will stood next to Amber on a stage lit by lanterns. Together they sang a slow, sweet ballad, mostly about love and a little about summer ending.

Robbie led Red to the shore to be closer to their friends. And then something unexpected happened when they both turned to face each other. A large woman desperate for a paddle barged into the princess and ... Well, there are kisses and there are *kisses*. For those of you who don't like kissing, I am sorry about this next bit. When Robbie kissed Red, it took him by surprise as much as her and anyone standing nearby. He was about to tell her something about the moon but his mouth had other ideas. He had no recollection of how his lips fell on hers, not a caressing clue. But there were witnesses who told me this is how it happened.

During a pivotal moment in the seconds between the torches blowing out, a rogue firework going up, and Amber taking a bow, Red Felian was thrown closer to Robbie Wylde and someone behind her said, 'There were more fireworks last year. The half-queen must have nabbed them all for her last ball.' At that point, Robbie's hands found a waist. It was not his, and he did not want to let it go. Red felt a heart *thump, thump, thumping*. It all went a bit blurry and then Robbie said, 'You are standing on my feet.'

Red didn't know what to say next and neither did Robbie, so he kissed her. They both sank into each other and fizzed a little. They didn't know the time, the day, the year, or what they'd had for breakfast. To all practical purposes, these two were as useful to anyone as a couple of waterproof teabags. Robbie kissed her beautiful mouth, worried she might vanish into thin air. He tried his best not to black out. It was with such relief that Red kissed him back that for a moment every part of her felt at home. She smiled and held him tight.

There were witnesses who said the kiss shifted the lay of the land and those who said it made them kiss the person next to them. Face looked up from his field and stamped his approval, and the Branch Bandits made gibbon noises from the roof.

Selina Carnal waited on the quiet, dark side of the lake's shore. The ancient gate at the end of the faery road lay on the ground in splinters. Pools of fog hung around it. She remained in the barouche, hidden behind an old willow tree and tall reeds. She played idly with her pack of tarot cards and breathing through her mouth to avoid the sickening smell of woodsmoke and mooncakes. Daniel Blackwood returned; his face was a storm.

'She's here with that young Man of the Road.' His voice shook with rage.

'Well, we must find a way to separate them.' the witch sneered, considering him. 'What is it you want from the girl?'

Daniel kept his eyes trained on the area of light and music ahead. 'Purity.'

'That won't save you now,' Selina said bitterly.

When the music died down and paper boats filled with candles floated out over the water, the witch slipped the starry powder-blue cloak over her black gown and raised the hood over her head. 'Wait here with the barouche.' She smiled. 'This won't take long.'

Daniel watched as she stalked towards the boathouse. His thirst was unbearable.

People had started to jump in the water to cool off. There were minutes to midnight. There were still chocolates to enjoy and campfires to stoke. Red held on to Robbie's hand as she watched people paddling in the candlelit lake. 'Let's go for a swim,' she said with the excitement of a child.

Robbie did not want his hand to hold anyone else's, although he tried to change the subject from swimming. 'There is something we need to do first.' He looked at her lovely face and neck. He liked her neck; it smelt of melons and some sort of cream. It was not royal or heiressy at all.

'What is it?' She gave him a devastating look.

'Mooncakes,' he gulped. 'You have to try one. Wait here, don't move. You can't miss pudding. No one misses pudding here. I'll be right back. Stay here.' She smiled and nodded.

And then he let go of her hand. Red felt a chill in the breeze as she watched him disappear into the crowd, searching out the mooncake lady, whose little cart only made its appearance at midnight.

Two branch bandits on the roof watched Robbie leave.

'Where's he going?' asked Kitty, craning forward.

'I don't know.' Dodge pushed his glasses up his nose.

'She's on her own.' Kitty watched the princess, a frown on her young face.

'He'll be back. I bet he's gone to get her some mooncakes,' Griff said, his mouth full.

Kitty turned to him and said solemnly, 'He shouldn't have left her alone.'

Red moved aside for the tide of people starting a conga line. A happy trail of merrymakers, led by Will parping random notes on a small trumpet, high-kicked around the lake.

Between bellows of 'Sit Down, Bertie, You're Rocking the Swan Boat' and trying to kiss Amber, Will drew in people from their campfires, and he pulled the princess along with him to join the conga. 'Come, milady, you promised me a dance!'

Around the lake they laughed. After so many years in her own company, Red Felian was overwhelmed by the swell of people smiling and jumping into the water around her. She looked out for Robbie, but he was nowhere to be seen. The conga line was halfway around the lake now, not far from the old willow tree where she had swum earlier.

And then she saw it, a flash of blue. Something glimmered through the dark. It was a blue so familiar, it snatched Red's breath away, and she lost her balance and tripped. The revellers moved on without and suddenly she was alone in the reeds.

Red stood up and caught her breath. 'Wait.' It was the blue of her mother's star-spangled cloak. The memory of it choked her.

The flash of blue disappeared further into the reeds. It couldn't be her mother. She must be imagining things.

'Wait.' Despite herself, Red stumbled towards it – Will was too far ahead to notice that anyone had slipped behind. 'Wait!' she cried again, breaking into a run. She had to find out. She did not stop to think, she just kept running.

There was someone there, in the blue cloak her mother wore to go riding, the one she wore all the time. The cloak the queen was rarely without. It had been dyed from cornflowers, made especially, and given to her by the king. And it was the cloak she'd worn the morning she'd disappeared. Red sobbed as she ran. It was the cloak that had wrapped itself around her so often when she was frightened, like a magic den.

'WAIT!' Red screamed.

The woman did not hear her. Red saw her tall figure stop by the willow for a moment, then she disappeared into the long grasses.

'Mother ... is that you?' Red swallowed and ran towards her.

She stood in the dark. The reeds swayed in the wind. Red suddenly felt cold. Her face was wet with tears. No, something was wrong. She walked a little further – until she stepped on the hem of the cloak and knew at once it was time to turn and run.

But the cloak held her captive. Red found she could not move.

She faltered. 'Your cloak ... My mother had one so similar. I thought it was hers ... Where did you ...' The stranger did not move.

The music had grown faint. There was something in Red's mind, something she had promised Maggie before leaving. What was it?

Red whispered Maggie's words. 'Do not follow the blue.'

She turned cold and backed away quickly, stumbling over a pointed black boot. It was then that cheroot smoke engulfed her.

'Too late for running I'm afraid, my dear.'

The figure in the blue cloak turned around and smiled at her. Red stared into the yellow eyes of the witch, the old hag at the gates, the voodoo seller who had imprisoned her at Paloma. Her voice was riddled with sorcery. 'It is unwise to stand on the tail of a hedgehog after midnight. It's never what you expect.'

'You.' Red faltered, fog began to engulf her.

'Hello, Princess.' Daniel Blackwood's curling mouth smiled at her. Something soft wrapped around her mouth, and her arms were bound from behind.

They had come for her.

She tried to cry out. She leant against her captor kicking out hard.

The witch staggered back, falling to the ground, her face a mask of grotesque surprise.

Red struggled gallantly to free herself from Daniel's clutches. She lashed out with what she could and strained to get away. Robbie's knife was still in her boots, which were not with her.

Selina hissed, 'Keep her still!' She clawed her way up from the ground and approached Red with the silver-topped cane.

'Get away from me!' Red screamed.

'Silence, child.' Selina ordered. 'Hold out her arm.'

Daniel roughly grabbed Red's bare skin, and the woman stabbed the tip of his cane into the inside of her wrist.

Immediately, Red felt her arm filling up with a cold liquid. She was dimly aware that she'd felt the same numbness in her limbs when Daniel had placed her ankle in the vice of voodoo.

'What have you done?' she mumbled and then she fell softly into Daniel's waiting arms.

His voice was in her ear. 'Sleep well, princess.'

Sir Toby was alone.

He remembered holding a comely waist and having a conversation with a woman called Nin Potts about sausages. He'd lost his footing at some point after that and was now floating in the Lake of Stars. Tiny silver fish swam furtively around him as he flicked his toes happily and gazed at the moon. A foggy stain was creeping across it from the south.

'That doesn't look good,' he thought out loud. Magatha Guiler would say it was a sign – a stain on the moon, blood on the horizon; a virgin is lost. Something like that. He was here to find Princess Felian and he needed to get up and continue his search. She wasn't in the water; of that, he was sure.

The godmothers and he had split up after arriving at the lake to find the princess and warn her of the rogue witch.

Sir Toby swam towards the shore, feeling that his life had truly begun again. He was on an important quest and he had survived a broom ride. It was cold in this part of the lake and there appeared to be traces of fog hanging over the surface. He frowned at it and then heard movement in the rushes. A thin trail of smoke emerged above them like a spectre. He was about to call out when a gentleman's voice hit him like a head cold.

'Why must I ride outside?' Daniel's voice drawled.

'Do you see anyone else volunteering? Hurry, I have no wish to linger a moment longer in this ghastly place. Those sign readers will be here soon. I can smell them.'

The voice raising the objection was Daniel Blackwood's. A voice Toby had hoped never to hear again. He did not recognise the voice of the woman with him and he did not wish to meet her.

Toby held his breath and tried to crawl up the bank without making a sound. Now was his chance to do some good. To help the young heir beat this uncouth scum. To get a better look at what was going on behind the reeds. He sank a bit and swallowed a lot of water.

I will stop the swine once and for all, he swore to himself. *Hell, I left my sword at Tikli Bottom. But I will challenge him to a duel a week tomorrow and no mistake.* Toby's sword had not yet duelled successfully. It was good at flourishing heroically, and that was the sum of it. *But this time will be different*, he thought, and tried not to cough.

Sir Toby waded out of the water a determined man. He crawled towards the willow tree to set a date to trounce that worm-nat, that cane-wielding, princess-following scoundrel once and for all.

When he saw the willow tree, he gasped. His mother's barouche was standing beside it in a foggy clearing, and

Daniel Blackwood was putting something inside it. He tried to get a better look at the tall figure with him as she hissed instructions. A hood veiled her face, although he could see it had a bone structure that stabbed the air around it. She wore an unmistakable powder blue cloak.

'Soft!' Toby gasped again. 'That is the queen's cloak!'

Selina glared at the whispering reeds and raised a thin eyebrow. 'Hurry, Blackwood.' She flicked her eyes at the princess and sat down with a slight wince. Her behind was bruised where the girl had kicked her. Selina never bruised; she used sorcery to avoid most physical encounters. 'Spirited like your mother,' she muttered at Red slumped across the floor of the barouche. 'I hope you don't whimper. Nothing wrong with a good blood-curdling scream, but quiet snuffling I will not endure.'

The horses stamped and snorted, impatient to move.

Toby gasped yet again as Daniel took to the driver's seat and he was able to see who they had lowered inside. He crawled closer.

They were taking Red Felian away. *Dear God*, he thought, *her arm is bleeding*.

'TO THE WELL OF LONELINESS!' the witch inside cawed, and the air around the barouche thickened with cold, unpleasant fog.

Sir Toby tried to hold his breath as he watched his

mother's barouche leap several feet into the air and jolt away from the lake at an unnatural speed. It made light tracks, heading south, led by some bewitched animals and that twisted son of a lawyer. Toby was left in the shadow of kidnappers. His hopes that the bony woman and the princess were old friends were not high. A copper wing glinted at him from the mud. He picked it up and stared at it. 'The queen's crest. I must stop them. I must tell her godmothers.'

Toby scrambled along the lakeshore and ran towards the lights of the boathouse, jumping over smoking campfires and sleeping families. The Still Place on the reed island was empty, save one man with a viola who sat and played the same haunting notes over and over again.

Magatha Guiler was looking for Toby in the boathouse. She was relieved to see him hurrying towards her. 'Any sign?'

When he spoke, his voice sounded very far away and there were squeaks and rattles in it. 'We're too late.' Toby bowed his head. 'She's gone, dear lady. They've taken her.'

Maggie looked into his eyes. 'What do you mean she's gone? What did you see? You look cold.' She knew it was not going to be the good sort of gone. Toby's expression was like the moon over the lake – filled with dark shadows.

'They've taken the princess,' he said again.

'Who's taken her?'

'The witch. The voodoo maker. She wore the queen's cloak; it was a trap and ... fog everywhere.'

'The blue. Red followed it.' A light in Maggie's eyes left.

'So, it is as I thought.'

'And Daniel Blackwood was with her. They have mother's barouche.' The barouche had played a bigger part than anyone had seen coming. One day it would be in a museum and for many years admired as a vital cog in a very great adventure.

'Then it has begun,' Maggie whispered. Her eyes grew dark, and she looked for a minute like someone else, someone capable of summoning giant trolls from the ground.

'What has begun?' Toby faltered.

'The fight, Toby Mole. The battle. The one that will determine the fate of this kingdom.' She looked across the lake and gathered her coloured coat around her. 'I should have known Selina would return. How could we have been so blind? I must find Jan.'

Jan, who to all looked as if she had fallen asleep under some bunting, was in fact in a trance.

'Come back, Psychic! We've got a serious problem.'

Jan opened her eyes and said bleakly, 'Selina is back.'

'She's taken Red.'

'I thought we would have more time.'

The godmothers, with Toby not far behind, strode back into the boathouse and asked the housekeeping boy for three large cups of coffee and a quiet table. Amber and Will were with the herald, sitting outside and going over the options for a musical next year.

'What about, "Annie, Get Your Swan"?' suggested Will.

'No, I know, "Seven Princesses for Seven ..."'

The herald noticed Sir Toby first. He was surprised to see him, and the two women he was with looked familiar. It had been over seven years, but he knew them to be the princesses' godmothers. He stood, entered the boathouse, and, bowing beautifully, introduced himself. Toby's face was pale and his hands were shaking.

'Herald Losley?'

'Sir Toby, what has happened?'

After Toby told the herald what had passed on the far shore of the lake, he said, 'I must tell the others.'

'Who? What others must you tell?' Maggie stopped the herald going any further with the tone of her voice. She raised one finger at the door and it slammed shut of its own accord before he could leave.

The herald stared at it and his face turned pale. 'Madame, Amber Morningstar and William English. Without them, Red Felian would not have escaped the voodoo or Paloma. They are on the side of the king and they can be trusted. They risked the whole army of Blackwood Guards to help her.'

'Very well, quick, bring them in.'

Moments later, Will was the first to ask, 'Where's Robbie?' He stood up. 'He must know. He came here to safeguard the princess. We must tell him at once. If she's missing, he will find her. He's probably done so already.'

Maggie gripped his arm. 'Find him, William, quickly.'

'Try the horses,' Amber urged, and Will ran.

When Robbie had returned to the shore with a bag of mooncakes to find a long conga line dwindling in the distance, he had thought he would find Red with her valien. As unsure as she was in a crowd, it was the first place he would want to go. But she wasn't there. The valien pawed the ground, trying to free from where he was tied.

'What is it?' Robbie watched him, but it was Will who appeared behind them.

'Have you seen Red?' He laughed and slapped Will warmly on the back. 'I have to tell her something very important, should have told her weeks ago. You see, I can't swim. Silly, really …'

Will shook his head solemnly. 'Something's happened that might prevent that.'

'Can you believe she's never tried one of these?' Robbie offered Will a mooncake, not hearing his answer. 'It's grown cold, so I've brought her coat.' He smiled like a young boy.

'Robbie …' Will reached out and laid a shaky hand on his shoulder. The princess' horse reared up and made a deep, painful noise. 'She's gone.'

Something in the set of Will's shoulders and the crease on his brow made Robbie stop and drop the mooncakes. 'Where?'

'They found this.' He held up the copper wing. 'By the willow on the far side of the lake. He's taken her. Blackwood and some rogue witch known by her godmothers as Selina Carnal.'

The valien made the same noise, a distressed, mournful sound.

Robbie's jaw tightened as he looked at Face.

'I left her alone … I should never have done that. It was all they needed.'

'Who?'

'The ones who wait in the shadows,' he said.

Around the table in the boathouse, seven pale faces tried to form a plan. They tried to contain the problem and understand how it could have happened at the Lake of Stars. Of all places in Landfelian, this was the last place they thought evil would step so easily through the gates.

'It makes no sense. Red would have smelt a rat and run if Blackwood was close.' Amber fiddled with her ring finger.

'The witch.' Everyone looked at Sir Toby. 'She wore a blue cloak, embroidered with silver stars and yellow sapphires. I have seen it before, a long time ago. It was the queen's.'

Robbie noticed January's hands begin to shake violently.

'Yes,' said Maggie, putting her hand on Jan's. 'Red's mother wore it the day she disappeared. She wore it everywhere. It was a present from the king. He said he would never lose her in a crowd, but like the stars embroidered over it, he would never try to own her. The woman who wears it now is Selina Carnal.' The name did not bring warmth to the room. 'A woman we thought lost to Landfelian. She trapped Red with the cloak. Signature move. Very Selina.' Maggie sniffed.

January continued. 'The voodoo was her doing. She has been here all the time, waiting, planning, honing her powers. Casting out fog and veiling spells to make finding her impossible.'

'Before they left, she ordered Daniel Blackwood to take her to the Well of Loneliness,' Toby added.

Maggie fiddled with the broken voodoo.

'Who is this witch?' Robbie looked at the godmothers.

Maggie looked sorry. 'Dear boy.' She sighed. 'Selina is no longer a witch; a dark sorceress stands in her place. She has lost that grounded part of herself. Any part of her that was human has gone now.'

The housekeeping boy stopped stacking chairs and listened.

'For a short time, many years ago now, she was a gifted sign-reader, like Jan and me. We trained together in Kande, with Phoebe Bird, the woman who would be queen – before Selina turned to an alternative path and stopped attending her studies. She discovered the thirst of the restless dead, of fractured spirits. She uses it to exert her will over natural things; the weather, people, animals. She has returned to Landfelian disguised as the queen to lure the princess away.'

'What does she want with Red?' Robbie's voice was rough, and he stood, unable to stay seated, and gripped the back of a chair.

'To use her as bait to snare King Felian. Red in danger would be the only thing to draw the king home and into a

272

trap. The cloak gives us reason to believe that she knows the whereabouts of the queen and is involved in her disappearance.'

'If she wanted to use Red as king bait, why did she not do so years ago?' the herald asked. 'When the king first left the kingdom.'

Jan looked sorry. 'It takes years to gather and perfect the kind of sorcery Selina is practising now.'

Maggie added, 'Someone else is involved, the presence in the south where stolen parts of the kingdom are being sent.' She looked at the drawing. 'Perhaps there is a conflict of interest there. Whoever they are must have some sort of hold over Selina. She never liked Red's mother; Queen Felian was a nemesis to her. Whatever has made Selina wait this long to make her move will be a source of great frustration for her.'

The door of the boathouse swung open of its own accord. Jan's eyes opened and closed. When they opened again, they were looking somewhere else, rolled back to the whites.

'Company's coming,' she said in a low voice. 'We must leave now.'

'Guards?' Robbie asked.

'No, spiderlings. Their swarm is closing in.'

Robbie gathered up his bag. 'There's no time. I can follow the barouche's tracks. If I leave now and take the valien, I can trace them.'

Sir Toby shook his head and frowned. 'The valien is sworn to only one rider.'

'Why has he not broken free and followed the princess?'

the herald asked.

'Until he has heard from us, he will remain here and wait,' Jan answered.

Robbie looked out into the night, desperate. 'I have never heard of this Well of Loneliness and I'm a Man of the Road. But if anything can lead me there, it is Red's horse.'

Maggie's eyes softened at Robbie. 'We must be cautious. You will not be able to find her without Father Peter's help. He will know the Well – it is not a part of this land. His folly is the last turning off the road after Kande, over the border and into the West Realm. There is a sign on the gate for pick-your-own mushrooms. Head there, we will follow.' Robbie did not argue; there was something in the tone of her voice. 'You will be safe in the curtilage of Two Hoots Folly.'

'The valien will take you.' Jan looked at Robbie her voice tender. 'He is waiting. But you will have to ask for permission first.'

They could hear the princess' horse outside making a low and terrible noise on the banks of the lake.

'How?' Robbie asked.

Jan smiled. 'You and my goddaughter are of one heart now. Keep your head low and kneel; do not look at the valien until he gives you the sign. They are an ancient breed and require respect.'

Robbie walked without hesitation towards the princess' horse, and everyone watched nervously as he approached the animal and knelt down before him. He spoke softly and, whatever words were said, after a pause of due consideration, the great valien rested his head briefly on Robbie's own and breathed heavily into his hair. Sir Toby and Will had stood either side, waiting for Face to buck or bite, but to their complete surprise, the animal did not stir. He remained strangely still and then lowered himself to allow Robbie onto his back. Then, without hesitation, he reared up and galloped away from the crowd. 'Well, I'll be damned.' Sir Toby whistled. 'The strangest thing ...'

Maggie smiled. 'Red's horse has chosen to trust Robbie for he has felt his rider's heart trust him too.' She gathered her broom and put on her hat. 'Now, who's coming with me?' She looked at Sir Toby with a determined smile.

The housekeeping boy wiped the same bit of table until it began to squeak in protest. When the seven figures left, a chill descended over Lake Country. He shivered and closed the door. Whoever they were, they had the look of war about them. Not that the housekeeping boy had ever witnessed or been involved in anything close to war, but the word stayed with him as he cleared the boathouse of spluttering candles and wilting flowers.

War ... Landfelian had never fought one, not full scale, not W. A. R. Small skirmishes and realm disputes, a little pirate culling, and a few meaty discussions with the giants and sea dwellers over areas of mountain where territory was questioned. This was the sum of the kingdom's foreign policy. Most of

Landfelian's time was taken up with discovery, wonder, and honest work, but never war. With so little experience, how could Landfelian ever win?

13

TWO HOOTS FOLLY

The evening was not going all that well for Father Peter. His owl had recently returned from a solo exploration above the icy plains of Hinterland, where it had made an unpleasant discovery.

'Marmadou, are you sure that is what you saw?'

They were in the study of his folly, the owl perched on an open tome of a book.

The little owl raised its wings and flapped impatiently. He scratched a claw over the page where the illustration of a skreeke lay open. It was a well-worn book of Landfelian folklore – a collection of tall tales – most often used as a doorstop and taken with a trowel of salt. The tome was too heavy to hold in bed without a small lectern to support it. The tenth Father before Father Peter had put it together from years of research begun by the Fathers before him. Marmadou's claw made a fine graze across the thin paper.

'They are extinct! They are creatures of legend – of only the hairiest tales. They are not of this time, no. Impossible. Anyway, there is one blessing; they would not last long here. It is too pleasant and warm.'

Marmadou hooted.

'You're right, it has not been pleasant or warm of late.' Father Peter's garden had thankfully not yet yielded to the ghostly shards of fog that seemed to have encroached over much of the kingdom.

Two Hoots Folly was the smallest castle in Landfelian. Firemoths lit the way to the folly at night, alongside the tiny lights of glow bugs that shone from the hedgerows. The folly grew out of an ancient cedar tree, which the first Father had loved so much he said there was nowhere else he wished to sleep. Many had trouble finding the doorknob because the folly had moulded itself so well against the rust-coloured branches. A copper gate, covered most of the year in yellow leaves, led down to a mossy path where ramblers expected to find a great stately home of Jacobean beauty. Something sprawling, with a statue garden. Instead, they found Mrs Tweed, the housekeeper, and a solemn-looking owl coming towards them. In the distance, a wonky ruin wrapped itself around a tree.

Red adored it. The shape and angle of the folly, precariously balanced as it was amongst the wide tree, mystified the architects of the time. It had weathered well and stood so for hundreds of years. Visits to her godfather's folly had always involved a good deal of smoky tea, coffee cake, and bedtime stories from books that smelt of damp and adventure. It was remarkably spacious inside for a home built into a tree. There was little formality or strict rules about bedtime, or crumbs. It was where she'd wished to study before everything went belly up.

The folly could accommodate a party of five, but someone would have to sleep with Marmadou in the Branch Room at the top. It had been this way since Peter was a young Father, studying The Knowledge and making a start on his own books. He believed houses were kept alive by those inside. He'd once written an enlightening paper on the wellbeing of the Landfelian home, the importance of opening windows, of music, light, plants, and laughter. (In the years of the quest, many houses across the kingdom had begun to fold in – Father Peter had seen it from the Cloudbuster. Even his folly creaked anxiously in the night.) It was another unwelcome change to the kingdom.

The king had given Father Peter a heroship for his outstanding work in the business of discovery, which he accepted on the condition that he would not have to attend any meetings or go into battle. He did not want to be involved in the politics of running a kingdom. So Marmadou was sent in his place to listen and squawk at the most absurd suggestions when the heroes were called. The owl would bring a copy of the minutes back to the folly. Father Peter looked beyond the petty power struggles that occurred between men and women in positions of influence. Naturally, the king's heroes were not sure what to make of the man, his owl, or his cardigan, most notably Sir Toby's father, Christopher Mole, who scoffed loudly and referred to him as 'that outlandish wizard'. The others accepted the fact that Father Peter walked a different plane and would not be drawn by shows of heroism. It was Father Peter and the Queen who had encouraged the gifting of the heroships to be given to both accomplished men and women of the time. For their part, three of the Seven were women.

The Father took off his glasses and rubbed his eyes. The tired skin beneath remained puckered. He put them back on upside down and glared at his owl.

Marmadou blinked solemnly back, and they both sighed.

'Oh dear. Well, I haven't seen one for years, only that tail claw we found in the pumpkin patch. It was hundreds of years ago when the creatures roamed free.' He blew his nose on the tablecloth. 'The Fathers before me stuffed the last skreeke and put it on the wall as a warning. Although Mrs Tweed threw it out when it started to smell. There have been no attacks, no sightings since. I was right to assume they were extinct.'

He peered at the illustration and doubted anyone who spotted one now would have much time to pause and announce a formal sighting. The explorer who had entered the beast into the book had obviously done so with a shaky hand and in a great hurry.

The owl perched on the picture and squeaked.

'I know, I know. One can never assume. Turdit! I will say it again. TURDIT TO HELL! What kind of old Father am I? How could I miss such a creature's rebirth? But who in their right mind would entice them back from the brink of extinction? I blame my eyesight, Marmadou, it's gone downhill since the fog got at it.'

He stood back and looked out the window at the moon, patchy and pale. 'It could possibly be the work of a ... no, no impossible.' Marmadou made an odd little noise from the back of his throat.

'A revised edition of *Landfelian Folklore* must be penned immediately, with the revision, "Skreeke – a creature not quite dead, spotted in the hinterland beyond the Misty Mountains". And now spiderlings! That swarm has not been active for centuries, and we passed the whole ruddy lot of them in the Cloudbuster the other day. What on earth is going on?'

He walked around the Situation Table several times, muttering, and opened the window for a breath of fresh air before being sure to close it again firmly and draw the curtains. In the process, Father Peter showered himself in dust and fossilised moth wings.

'Blast and balls!'

There were no chairs around the Situation Table, as

chairs clogged up thought. Too much sitting was not good for the Father's circulation. The Situation Room was mostly all table – a beautiful roundish slab of oak. It was important, in a difficult situation, to have a piece of honest wood with no right angles.

There was a shout from the parlour.

'I'm still here, Peter Featherby! You can blaspheme all you want when I go. Until then, I like words with more than two syllables, thank you.'

The Father made a face. His daily, Mrs Tweed, insisted on good language while she was in the house cleaning. But if it couldn't be good, then it had to be long. 'Apologies, Mrs Tweed,' he called back. 'Crappingtonation!'

'That's much better.' She popped her head around the door. 'How about a nice rock bun?'

'Thank you, no.' He swallowed. 'I'm still trying to digest the last one.'

Mrs Tweed thought rock buns should do what they promised – be rocky and fill in the gaps of hunger with solidified cake.

'You've been in that Situation Room all day and half the night, with nothing but books and owl pellets to eat.' Mrs Tweed never normally stayed so late, but she was worried about the Father. Re-filling the oil lamp, she looked at him with concern. He was dressed in his usual mottled-green holey cardigan. He had aged in the last year and lost the sense of mischief that used to send her round the bend but made the job never dull. 'What about half a bun and a nice cup of smoky tea?' And the cold he had caught on his last expedition still had not shifted.

'Dear woman, I am quite full, thank you.' He thought he may never have a regular bowel movement again.

Father Peter lived in a very wild part of the West Realm, a land of few lanes and only the odd sign, where it rained a good deal and the land grew greener than anywhere else. The other realms left the west alone. They said it was filled with mischief and faerylore. A place people could not tame, where Fathers and other healers could work undisturbed. Mrs Tweed was a rare find for the west: she was right-handed and left brained. She lived a day's travel from Two Hoots Folly in the hamlet of Broome and she had not won the job due to her baking skills. The day she'd arrived for an interview, Father Peter was holding a meeting in his garden with the sign-readers, King Felian, two valien, Marmadou, and a giant they called Monroe (whose name was in fact Graham). Mrs Tweed told the king to wipe his boots if he planned on entering the folly. She offered the giant a cup of tea in a wheelbarrow and Father Peter hired her on the spot.

There was a curious tap on the window.

'Not again. *Tap, tap*, all week. Or that horrible chittering. Wherever is it coming from?' Mrs Tweed bustled in, slammed down the tray, and strode over to the window. 'If it's those pesky black squirrels again ...' She put her hand on the latch.

'Don't touch the windows if you please, Mrs Tweed!'

Father Peter gently barred her way with his walking stick. She was so surprised to hear him raise his voice that she trod on his slipper. 'I was only going to throw a bun at them.'

'In my experience, it is best to leave the things that chitter and tap outside. They are often a great deal larger than they seem. That is no squirrel, I'm afraid. If it would like to come in, I am a firm believer in a front door and a firm knock.'

She understood this much and was satisfied, although the Father's hands shook as he steered her away.

A minute later, a voice as warm as fresh milk called from outside. 'Peter, please may we come in?'

He threw open the curtains to see Magatha Guiler knocking on the window with her broom. She was wrapped up in her colourful coat, wore a black top hat with a plume, and she was smiling, although her eyes looked drawn.

Mrs Tweed hurried to the front door and spent the next minute unlocking it. In Father Peter's opinion, there could never be too many locks on one's front door. She opened it wide with an unimpressed frown.

'I do beg your pardon, Mrs Tweed, I hope you got my note. There are a few more of us now than originally anticipated. We are, in fact, seven.'

Susy Tweed grumbled under her breath and opened the front door. 'Luna never mentioned you were bringing an army.'

Father Peter, hot on Mrs Tweed's heels, looked relieved to see his old friend. 'My dear Magatha, come in quickly.

There are some unsavoury bugs flying around.' He looked up at the sky above the folly and then expectantly at the small group standing outside. 'Why do I not see my goddaughter amongst your party?'

Maggie handed him the bag of broken teeth and said, 'We have a situation.' She went to warm her hands by the fire.

'Is the queen still missing?' He laughed wearily, glimpsed in the bag, and sighed. 'I apologise. I have been wrestling with that situation for some time and I'm not going to beat around the birch, my friends – I have grown tired of it. Come, follow me.' He promptly led them to his Situation Room, which of course was the only appropriate place in which to discuss situations. The room was rich with books and lamps and seemed to have half a cedar tree growing through the middle of it.

Father Peter found things for a living. He found mushrooms, new lands, migratory tree patterns, interesting clouds, Magatha Guiler's house keys, and leafwells. As a Father, he was an experienced naturalist and explorer. This being so, he should not *lose* queens – especially good ones like Phoebe Felian. As the best and oldest of the king's advisors, losing such a lady had upset him. Father Peter loved the queen, in his way, and her only daughter as if she were his own. But looking for something for seven years will put wear and tear on any man, in that similar way jogging will eventually finish your knees.

'Selina Carnal has Red. She was taken from the Lake of Stars hours ago before she had a chance to reach you,' Jan told him as gently as she could.

The old man put his hand on the table for support and closed his eyes. 'Selina Carnal, eh? I never thought I would hear that woman's name mentioned again.' He took off his glasses and blinked. 'Although it's almost as if her name has been haunting me all along, but every time I ...'

'Try to pin it down, it fades into fog.' Maggie sighed. 'It has been the same for us.'

He counted the figures huddled around his fire, took his glasses off, and smiled.

'Well, seven is an excellent number in a situation such as this. Quickly, come in everyone, and welcome.'

'We can't fit any more in.' Mrs. Tweed bristled in the doorway.

'Thank you, Mrs Tweed. How right you are. Let me see.' The walls creaked and groaned as Father Peter took a deep, reassuring breath. 'There.' The room appeared to have expanded to accommodate the visitors. A light shower of plaster dust and several twigs fell from the ceiling in the process. 'Will you be so kind as to provide a little more tea and maybe some of your rock things for our friends?' The fire was now roaring nicely and seven more logs appeared to be burning fruitfully.

Mrs Tweed nodded. She did not feel in control, and it was not a place she liked to be out of for long. She held tightly onto her tray as a blonde woman who looked like Venus' less abiding sister wandered past in a nun's habit, followed by a tall man with merry brown eyes in a sequinned bolero. The king's herald approached, holding a baton and an apologetic smile, and a gentleman with an artistic quiff and smock shirt helped January Macloud to the table.

Mrs Tweed peered anxiously outside. 'If there is anyone else out there, then tough. We've not got the linen!' Her least favourite of the Father's regular visitors were the godmothers of Tikli Bottom, because of their complete lack of housekeeping standards. An elegant hare loped cautiously in and took a seat on the windowsill nearest Jan. 'Oh hello again, Luna,' Father Peter said before speaking up.

'Don't worry," Father Peter said. "Mrs Tweed. No one is staying long.'

A wild-haired stranger appeared out of the gloom before Mrs Tweed had a chance to close the door.

'Hello.' Robbie took off his hat and walked in, wiping his boots first on the mat. 'I've left the horses by the stream. Are you Father Peter?'

'Not today,' Mrs Tweed said, looking into the eyes of an impossibly distracted looking young man. He smelt of hay and horse and badly needed a comb. She blushed, which surprised her cheeks. 'Goodness, you must have had a long journey. I'm Susie Tweed, the Father's daily.'

'Of course, I'm sorry …' He held onto her hand and squeezed it before disappearing into the Situation Room. 'Thank you.'

He looked so agitated; she half expected him to keep

walking through the back wall of the folly. It was just as well she had prepared a fresh batch of rock buns; they'd been in the oven for five hours so should be cooked nicely through.

She loaded the tray with tea things and pottered about the folly's kitchen with purpose. Mrs Tweed did not understand what the Father involved himself in; she operated on a purely practical need-to-know basis, which suited them both. But when she heard the name Red Felian mentioned and saw the looks on everyone's faces, she stopped. Whatever situation that poor orphan was in must be serious. She whipped the cream and put out some raspberry jam; raspberries, in her opinion, were a gentle fruit in a crisis.

The wind whistled against the windows. No matter how many stuffed stockings Mrs Tweed brought with her, she could no longer cure the folly of the draught.

'I think a chair or two as well, Mrs T,' called Father Peter.

'Right you are.'

It must be bad news. Father Peter never moved furniture. Heaven only knew what she would find underneath the armchair in his study – cities of dust and Marmadou's ancestors, perhaps.

While the room was rearranged and the group seated, Robbie noticed the book on the lectern. It was open at a page bearing a description and drawing of a beast with two arms, four legs, a thick tail and claws the size of a bananas. Beneath the squatting beast, for scale, there was a drawing of two men lying head-to-head. The words, *No longer extinct?* had been scribbled next to the animal in new ink. Robbie hoped this creature was not to be found in the Well with the princess. His hands were still clenched from gripping onto the valien's mane as they had torn over lake country and into the West Realm. His horse had taken Amber and Will, the herald had travelled with January and Sir Toby with Magatha both by broom. Despite being the fastest horse, Face kept stopping and turning back towards the lake reluctant to leave the last place Red had been.

Magatha introduced Sir Toby to Father Peter.

'My new lodger, very talented with a brush.'

'I'm on sabbatical from my mother,' Sir Toby explained, and he shook the old man's hand vigorously.

'How sensible.'

'I am at your service, Father.' He put his sketchbook down on the table and bowed.

'I am glad of it. Artists are always welcome here. Try to remember everything you have seen, every detail. We will need it.'

While introductions were being made, Robbie continued to read the book at the open page.

SKREEKES

ALTHOUGH MOSTLY BLIND, THESE CREATURES CAN SMELL HUMAN FLESH FROM NEAR _ _ _ STRAITS AWAY. THEIR SNOUTS ARE COVERED WITH SMALL WARTY VALVES THROUGH WHICH THEY

BREATHE AND SMELL. THE SKREEKE CAN SURVIVE
INHOSPITABLE ENVIRONMENTS, LIVING ON FROZEN
AND DEAD TERRAIN. THEY DO NOT POSSESS
NOSES BUT HAVE HOLES IN THEIR PLACE AND
ARE THOUGHT TO BE RELATED TO THE DRAGON
_ _ _ OF MOSQUITO DENCH. THERE HAS NOT BEEN
A SIGHTING IN OVER ONE HUNDRED YEARS ...

He did not read any further. There were some gaps
in the writing, which made him worry for the man who had
penned it. Looking at a preserved claw on the mantelpiece,
Robbie noticed the tip was black and shiny as severed coal. He
picked it up and whistled to himself. 'That's a big claw.'

'Yes, the tail claw of a skreeke. Very nasty poisoned tip.
Take a seat – you are a Man of the Road, are you not?

'Yes, Robbie Wylde, how did you know?'

'Excellent. Years of travelling, dear boy; you start to
recognise the different makes of man. I can tell by your hands
and your restlessness that the life you have led has been an
active one. We are indeed lucky to have you with us. Take a
seat.' He smiled. 'Although I will not be offended if you do not.'

The kind, bespectacled man closed the book and gently
took Robbie's hand in both of his. His eyes were deep blue and
full of light. They were the eyes of a young explorer who has
lived long enough to see one of everything and does not worry
too much about dust or trifles. Robbie found looking at the
Father as calming as staring out at a wide horizon. 'There is

always something bigger out there than the situation you are battling.' For years he had dreamt about meeting the Father and his Cloudbuster, but now Robbie could only hope this was the man who would know how to find Red.

'Can you help her?' He wanted to hammer out a hole in the wall and get on the road. They were taking too long.

'I will, do not fear.' Father Peter patted his shoulder. 'It is far easier to avoid a rock bun while standing. Try to remember to fold your arms when you see the tray coming.' He smiled. 'This is Marmadou, my dear friend, and together we will tell you how to find the Well.'

Robbie nodded respectfully at the tawny owl that sat on Father Peter's shoulder. Marmadou looked at him with searching interest and a twitching head.

'She wanted so much to reach you,' Robbie told Father Peter. 'She had a map ...'

'I know, the dear girl, one of my most favourite people. And she will. She will.' He smiled. 'She always loved it here, you see – one very large tree to climb, places to read – and as you may already know, the princess is fond of climbing and maps. And dens.' He laughed. 'Although I must remember she's a young lady now.'

'She still likes dens.' Robbie smiled.

He walked to the window and looked into the folly's garden, where the two horses stood together. Legs rested her snout on the valien's back, which was a stretch for the mare. The valien would not stop calling for his owner. It was a low, forlorn noise. It had taken all of Robbie's strength to persuade him to stop circling the willow on the south shore of the lake where Red was last seen.

The Father coughed, and Robbie returned his attention to the room, where a strong fire lit up the contents on an oak table. Red's hemp sack.

Amber watched Father Peter study the broken voodoo teeth. She thought he must be a wizard, with his curling moustache and young eyes. His expression remained quite serene amidst the chaos of thoughts jostling around the table.

'How old do you think the Father is?' she whispered to Will.

Will looked across the table and whispered, 'Ninety-seven or thirty-three, it's hard to tell.'

'Actually, I'm both.' He twinkled at them and passed around the tea. 'Fathers are blessed with a long life; curiosity simply won't allow our brains to leave the coil early.'

Robbie gratefully took the tea being handed around. He stared at the fire and thought about Red, where she was now, and if she was hurt.

'Every hero needs a warm belly before a long, cold journey.'

'You are mistaken. I am no hero.'

Father Peter was not about to be mistaken twice in one day, and two eyebrows went up in question. 'Dear man, did you or did you not save my goddaughter from drowning in Waterwood?'

Robbie was flapped at by the tawny owl. 'How did you know about that?'

'Well, then? No qualms about it. Although I have never been convinced qualms have much to do with anything.' He smiled. 'Marmadou has many friends in many woods. And they see a great deal better than humans.'

The herald choked quietly on a rock bun. Mrs Tweed had placed three on his plate.

'Leave it to soak in the cream for as long as you can, Richard,' advised Father Peter discreetly.

The Father then rubbed his hands together and clapped. All tea tinkering fell silent.

'Welcome, everyone. It's time we began. Drink up, wriggle your toes, warm yourself by the fire. There is a situation to un-situate, and we are not leaving this room until it is done. A truly wonderful family has gone astray and they need our help. Marmadou, kindly light the candle.' The owl jumped from his shoulder and collected a taper between his claws, lighting a tall white candle in the centre of the table.

Robbie was the first to speak. He was barely audible. 'I never should have left her alone.'

Father Peter smiled gently. 'Thank you, Robert, but before you go any further, I must tell you the first rule of the Situation Room. There is a rock bun for anyone who says, 'I should have', 'I regret', or 'If only I had'. Guilt and shame have no place here.'

Will spoke next and realised he had not thought it

through. 'Tell me, Father, have you always had a Situation Room?'

The table looked at him.

'Yes, William, it came with the folly. Now, I find it helps to start with what we know and work backwards.'

Items from Red Felian's bag were passed around the table. It was a sorry sight. Her map, the old bit of shell Maggie had given her, the king's coat, her boots, the badge from the Branch Bandits, a journal she had kept whilst on the road, a signed copy of Father Peter's book, the broken voodoo, a flattened spiderling, fishhooks, and her mother's copper wing earring.

Amber stared at the objects and sipped her tea.

'January, would you be so kind as to provide the missing links?' Asked Father Peter.

January Macloud had put on a pair of glasses; they grew strangely tinted. Her eyes were partly open. It was easier to go into a trance without everyone staring at you uneasily. She had already begun to search. She had travelled past her own mind, gathered a warm shawl about her, and continued into the Nether Regions of consciousness. For a time, she slalomed across a dark sky where she saw broken bits of furniture, brass instruments, odd socks, keys, string, hats – people's memories, forgotten and floating about, no longer anchored to thought. She remained focused on Red, went through a door, and found Selina's ghastly fog. Here, things dragged and became difficult.

Jan was with friends, holding onto an oak table; she

knew where she had left her body, so she asked for protection and kept going.

There was something beyond the fog ... She felt it hiding there, a twisted shape climbing out of the white. She focused on the thing. Snow fell heavy and silent around her. God forbid the princess was trapped in a snow globe. There would be no getting to her then.

The twisted shape was barely a few feet away; she could see it clearly now. A tree. It was a tree. Petrified. Not living, not dead, but all alone. The shadow of Big Blue amongst the Misty Mountains rose up behind it. A noise came from deep within the tree's trunk. It was not a happy noise. She peered into the hollow of the Petrified Tree to listen closely and a fierce draught flew out, flinging her back.

Jan flew back in her seat, and everyone around the table gasped. It was as if a gale had been found personally for her. She opened her eyes fully, took off the glasses, blinked, and her hair fluttered back to normal. The rage from inside the tree rang on for some moments, far away in her mind. She had seen enough and was satisfied. She spoke clearly. 'There is a petrified tree in the South Realm. It has been bewitched. It stands in the fog, on the edge of Landfelian, on this side of the Big Blue, near the Forest of Thin Pines on the Frozen Straits.'

Amber poured more tea. She didn't know anything about Seeing, but she knew when someone looked like they needed a brew.

'It is a hollow tree, a portal.'

The Father frowned. 'Where does it lead?'

'To Selina Carnal.' The wind howled around the folly. 'To her fortress.'

'She was never one for company.' Father Peter pressed his fingers together in thought. 'I have seen this fortress.'

'She passed through the Petrified Tree only a few hours ago,' continued January. 'I could still hear her mind raging. And she has Red – her heart beats, strong and sure.'

'That poor tree, it must have been a spruce or oak.' Maggie signalled to Luna, who had been sitting quietly on the windowsill watching everything, and she approached, hopping gently onto Jan's lap.

Robbie had never seen such a tree. He tried to keep his voice calm and patient and failed most expertly. There was nothing logical behind this, nothing he could believe. 'Where does this tree lead?'

'Into the Hinterland. Selina has twisted a frozen path between our land and hers.' Maggie sounded weary.

Robbie shook his head. They were all mad. He would go alone, follow the barouches tracks south, and find his way.

The herald put his hand up. 'Excuse me, Father, there *is* no Hinterland. The king, to my knowledge, doesn't have a second kingdom. If he did, it would be on the map and I would know of it.'

'Astute and loyal as ever, Richard Losley. However, I must inform you ...' He picked up the map on the table, tore it in two, and tossed it in the fire. '... this map is wrong.

I have recently discovered the land of which Jan speaks – the Hinterland. Nothing more than a frozen stretch of sea.

'A recent trip over the mountains led me to it. A pointed place of ice; a little rock holding onto the southern tips of Landfelian like a scorpion. On it there is a great fortress, and beyond it a great expanse of white that I only wish I could have explored further. Due to a fuel shortage and poor visibility, Marmadou and I had to leave quickly.'

'How long has it been there?' asked the herald.

'I do not know. I would hazard as long as Selina Carnal has been absent from this kingdom. The king banished her not long after Red was born. It will take several more expeditions to map its full scale. I very much doubt she is alone in her work, though. She was never one for building anything. Something or someone is working with her.'

Jan spoke again. 'She is not alone. Mutual desire connects her to another, a man, or something that was once a man … His soul is consumed. I saw a knight's shadow.' Robbie looked up at the mention of a knight.

Father Peter leant over the table. 'The voodoo is Selina's work – the torture and separation of two souls … Very nasty stuff indeed. We must be prepared.'

Nobody said anything. There was a lot of tea stirring as they digested this news. The word 'crikey' floated to the top of the Scrabble pile in their minds.

Robbie walked towards the window. 'Tell me how to find this Well of Loneliness and I will leave now. Nothing else matters.'

'The Well of Loneliness.' Will rolled over the words and whistled. 'I have never performed there.'

'No, and be thankful,' mused Father Peter. 'Centuries ago, before water filled in all the gaps of the world, there was a volcano not far from our shores, surrounded by other mountains. Then the water came, and now it lies in the deepest part of the White Ocean – a place called the Ridge of Shadows. The well itself is the empty cavern inside an extinct volcano. The walls hold back the sea, the tips of which can only just be seen as jagged rocks above the surface. This surge of spinning water ensures no one can enter the Well. At least by ship.'

'How do you know this?'

'The eagles and the sea dwellers know of it. Ships must be careful to circumnavigate the area or they are dragged into the vortex that swirls around it and are dashed against its rocks. It has always been there.'

'Unfortunately, there are other winged creatures that will be keeping watch over the Well, and their eyes are directed at the folly right now. Miss Morningstar, we have you to thank for this neatly pressed example.' Father Peter pointed to the dead spiderling.

'Oh, it was nothing.' Amber shook her head.

'These spies await our next move and will inform Selina of it. Do not worry, this cedar will protect the folly from the spiderlings.' As he spoke, the scuffle of wings was heard above as a great number of owls swooped down to join a vast roost in the branches. 'I have asked some friends to keep watch.'

Robbie tried to imagine the desolate place miles out to sea and wondered how he would ever get there. 'Why has the witch taken Red there?'

'Selina has chosen the least hospitable place she knows to hold the king's daughter and wait.' He lit a pipe and puffed with a grimace. 'Once she has the royal family, she can take hold of the kingdom.'

'And the queen. Do you think the witch keeps *her* in the Well of Loneliness too?' Sir Toby asked.

'No.' Father Peter sighed. 'If the queen was under Selina's watch, she would never have returned to Landfelian and gone to the bother of disguising herself at the Lake of Stars. There would have been no need. Wherever Queen Felian is being kept, it is not a place fully under Selina's command.' He looked at Maggie and something passed between them. 'I do believe she was involved in her vanishing. They were never the greatest of friends.'

Just then, there were three firm knocks on the door.

PART III

THE HERO

'We'll never survive!'
'Nonsense. You're only saying that
because no one ever has.'

William Goldman – The Princess Bride

14

IN WALKS A TRAMP

'Hello, Mrs Tweed.'

'Well, good evening, Your Highness. Rock bun?'

'I won't just now, thank you.'

'The Father is waiting for you, and there is plenty of tea left in the pot.'

The man at the door gave a weary smile. 'I'm sorry, I am unforgivably late.'

'Late is better than never.' Mrs Tweed took the man's coat and hat and then she fainted. Everyone said years after the event that she did remarkably well to hold it together at all.

'Oh dear,' the voice said from the entrance hall.

The Situation Room fell very quiet. That voice … Where had they heard it before?

The fire crackled. Marmadou gave a merry hoot and

ruffled his feathers.

'Oh bother, I should have mentioned to Mrs Tweed that we will be eight.' Father Peter scratched his head and stood. 'She will be most upset.'

The herald knew it, without doubt. A herald never forgets who he has heralded. He rose from his chair and, with bright eyes, announced in a voice full of reverence, 'HE'S RETURNED!'

'Who?' Amber asked.

The door opened slowly. 'Sire.' The herald bowed low to a tall figure in the doorway.

'Dear herald.' A rangy man stooped through the door with an elegant wolfhound at his heels and clasped the herald's outstretched hand. 'I have missed you, my old friend. Stand, please, there is no need to bow. Poor Mrs Tweed has suffered a turn. I have made her comfortable but be so good and fetch something to revive her.'

The owner of the voice walked further into the room and smiled warily at everyone.

Robbie took one look at his infamous face, raised his arm, and punched the King of Landfelian squarely on the nose.

It was a beautiful punch, considering Robbie tried not to make a habit of punching anyone. The king went down, and a rather battered crown fell from his head and rolled under the table.

'Steady on there.' Will stood next to Robbie and took his arm. 'You've knocked out the king,' he spluttered. 'The chosen one. Lord of all FOUR –'

'Robbie, what were you thinking?' Amber hissed. She was fanning the great man with her wimple and picking up the crown from the floor. At least, she *thought* it was the king – his voice, before it was knocked out cold, was wise, full of lilt and charm – but the person on the floor looked more like an old Man of the Road, gone to seed. His clothes, once well-made and of regal cloth, were ragged and damp, his skin heavily lined, and there was a sizable beard showing months of travel sprouting from his chin.

'He's not moving! Did you have to hit him so hard?' The herald knelt at the king's side, placed the crown next to him, and dabbed his forehead with a cool cloth, while Amber blew gently on his face. No one could quite believe it. The King of Landfelian was here in the West Realm, strolling through the door after seven years elsewhere, only to be knocked out cold. Where were the trumpets and the roll of velvet carpet?

A small hope in Robbie's mind prayed it was a local impersonator – there had been a run of them lately, claiming to have divine right. But there was no denying that chin; it belonged to the princess, but with more hair. That chin *deserved* a punch for what it had put Red and the kingdom through. *Hang the consequences*, thought Robbie as he stared unsure at the man on the floor.

'He abandoned her – and left Landfelian with no one to protect it. I would do it again.'

Mrs Tweed recovered quickly. She bustled in and told

everyone quite firmly to move aside.

Father Peter quite unexpectedly started to laugh. 'I have wanted to do that for seven years, but the royal toad was never here for long enough!' He patted Robbie gently on the back and sighed. 'You got there first. Well done. I think I will light my pipe.'

They all looked aghast at the trampish-looking man flat-out under the table.

Sir Toby was terrified. If the king was back, did that mean the king's heroes were too? Was his father approaching the front door, ready to force him home to go hunting and feed the beagles?

Mrs Tweed splashed the king with cold water and put some strong-smelling essence of rosemary under his nose until they heard a gargle and that well-regarded voice again. 'Are you trying to drown me?'

The herald was horrified. He mopped up what he could of the royal robes. If he had known the king would return tonight, he would have brought him a clean shirt, a robe, and a shaving kit. There should have at least been trumpets sounding and a flag flying from somewhere. This was not the arrival of the great lost liege he had so long imagined. But then these were strange times. A rogue witch had the king's daughter and possibly a knight had his wife in a distant, sea-surrounded, extinct volcano. The herald sighed; he would have to adjust to the changing role as best he could.

'Does anyone have a trumpet?' he asked reasonably.

'I only have my ukulele,' offered Will.

The king reared up from the floor and glowered at Robbie, water dripping from his beard. Robbie glowered back. The room went quiet. A low growl could be heard coming from a large wolfhound at the king's side.

Amber nudged Will and mouthed, 'DO SOMETHING.'

They waited for the glowering to stop, which it did when someone's stomach rumbled and the herald dragged the nearest chair towards the fire and said, 'Please sit, Your Majesty. Would you like me to remove your boots? I'm afraid no trumpet could be found, but I have a song that I could sing,' he added.

'No, no, thank you, Richard.' The king blinked and then looked at Robbie. 'I suppose I deserved that.' He held out a weathered hand. 'Austin Felian. And who, may I ask, is the young fighter?'

The response was returned warily. 'Robbie Wylde.'

'A painful pleasure to meet you, Master Wylde.' The king clasped his hand hard. 'Would you be so kind as to help me up? That is before you punch me again.'

King Felian's smile was so like his daughter's that a bit of muscle near Robbie's heart ached. He looked away as he pulled the king up from the floor.

'Thank you.' The king stood tall and took a deep breath, which wheezed a little. 'Hello, everyone. Peter, I was held up by the weather. The crossing from Aquila is now completely covered by fog – impassable without an escort to

306

guide you around the rocks. If it had not been for this little owl ... Marmadou, you have not aged at all.' He held out his hand for the owl to nuzzle. 'Thank you for informing the sea eagles of our plight. They kept our ships on course.'

The king accepted a cup of tea from Mrs Tweed and drank it with a grateful gasp.

'The heroes wait for my signal; they are not far from Landfelian's south coast. I kept them at sea in case we need the fleet to move quickly to help ... my daughter.' His voice wavered. 'We were doing one final search of the islands when I got your message.' He poured a third cup. 'Good God, I have missed your tea, Mrs Tweed. I wonder if you might make a pot for my two companions. They are outside the folly seeing to the horses and would be grateful for the refreshment.'

The king was not prepared to be hit again. When a fist came flying at him for a second time, he reeled back and blood dripped from his nose onto his beard. He gripped hold of the table as his tea cup flew in the air and was caught by Mrs Tweed's retreating tray.

'Enough!' The herald yelped at Robbie. 'Do you wish to be banished?'

'The first was for me. But that was for all those left waiting – including your daughter.' Robbie's voice broke.

The king did not answer this. He closed his eyes and wiped the blood from his face, wincing as he did. His breathing grew more ragged. Amber thought she had never seen anyone look as sad as the king then.

After more cold water and several flannels were administered, the herald ushered the king towards the fire and hissed at Robbie.

'Walk in the man's boots before you try that again or you will feel the force of my herald training,' he whispered, removing his baton from his breast pocket and waving it in warning at Robbie.

The king rolled up his stained shirt sleeves. He wiped the straggles of dirty hair from his face and tied it behind him with an old bit of ribbon. 'Tell me everything, Peter. There may be little time.' With grave eyes, he looked at the table as Father Peter caught him up on what had passed, on Red's escape, the voodoo, and the recent abduction by Selina Carnal. He stared most intently at the queen's copper earring, his eyes drawn back to it again and again.

'Selina keeps your daughter in the Well of Loneliness and waits for you.' Father Peter gestured to a new map he unrolled on the table. 'I am terribly sorry she got this far.'

'Up to her old tricks again, I see. We never thought we would see her again, did we, Maggie? Although, she vowed never to forgive me for banishing her. This Well of Loneliness, Peter, is it the same black area of sea the ships have always avoided?' He pointed to the White Ocean. 'Not too far from the Sea Dweller's village.'

The Father nodded. 'I imagine Selina has shrouded it in her fog.'

'Then I will leave shortly.' The king gathered himself

up, seeming to struggle with the effort of moving from the warm chair. 'The fog will drain Red of her strength. I must hurry. The sea dwellers know a way in. I'll request an audience with Anook immediately.'

Father Peter put a hand lightly on the king's shoulder. 'Sit down, dear friend.'

'I must go. My daughter has waited long enough.'

January put her hand out and closed her eyes. 'Be still a moment and finish your tea.'

'This is no time for your hocus pocus, January.' He shook his head.

Maggie's voice found the rage of maidens. 'Drink your godforsaken tea! You took long enough to get here.'

There was a gasp, and the herald made a strangled noise. Will felt rather sorry for the king. He was covered in seven years of grime, he had been punched twice, and now all the women were shouting at him. He found it hard to connect the man in his memory, in fine robes, with the man who stood broken but beating before them now.

Maggie held the cup out to the king, who reluctantly took it.

'Very well.' He remained standing but drank the tea … and promptly began to choke. Robbie stepped forward to slap him on the back and earned himself another glower and possible banishment. But a small, shiny object flew out of the king's mouth and landed on his boot.

The king gazed at it in horror; he had always been on

309

the best terms with Mrs Tweed and now she was trying to choke him.

Maggie picked up a tiny fish hook and held it up to his nose. 'Now listen to me, you son of a king!'

'Steady on, Magatha.' He held up his hands, although his voice was deep and commanding.

'I will not! All this,' she waved at the table, 'is a trap, clear as day. A trap plotted, chopped, stirred, and simmered for years by the witch who fancies herself a kingdom. You are the fish, and she is waiting for you to swim right onto her hook! You cannot go down to the Well. Don't you see? You're the one she wants. If you go, you will not return – and neither will your daughter. That poor girl has waited too long to see you disappear again.'

The great man looked helplessly at the drawn faces around the table and sat back down.

'I'm no king,' he whispered. 'I am not worthy of the title, neglecting my people for all these years to look for my … a part of my heart was here all this time. I just could not bear returning to Red without her mother. I did not know how to look after her, and so I fled like a coward.' He took a shaky breath and began to cough. 'One morning there was a change. I knew she was running from something too dark to explain. It was then I turned the ships around and made for home, but the fog, the fog. It has got deep into my lungs.'

He gripped the hook in his fist.

'I must make amends.' He bowed his head. 'I will leave

now. Let me go and find my family. My men will help.'

'If you go, your ships will be dragged into the black water that surrounds the well, you will be caught, and Red will be lost.'

As Mrs Tweed returned with another pot of tea, Robbie looked at the tattered things on the table.

'Your majesty cannot go, but I can,' he said.

Everyone turned to look at him. 'Yes.' Father Peter nodded. 'There is another way into the well.'

Outside it was growing dark. No one said a word as the king picked up his riding coat, the one Red had worn since jumping out the window of Paloma. He brought it to his face and held it there a good while. Closing his eyes, he breathed softly and his shoulders shook. Marmadou sat close to his neck, and made soft clicking noises.

'Forgive me.' The king repeated these words over and over. 'My child, forgive me.'

It was a terrible, dreadful thing to watch.

Mrs Tweed scrapped the tea altogether and brought out the sloe gin and a vast chocolate cake she was keeping back for the Father's birthday (which he never remembered).

Robbie left the folly to prepare the valien for the journey ahead and get some air. He felt calm, dead calm ... 'Dead' being the word that most occupied his thoughts.

In the garden, he heard the owls and could see that the branches of the cedar were full of their solemn, slow blinking eyes. The air smelt of a frost; the first for autumn was settling. It was usually Robbie's favourite time. There was a bounty of fruit and nuts in the hedgerows and the countryside was still warm enough to sleep outside without feeling unwell in the morning. A horse he had never seen before snorted in front of him. She was a white, muscled beauty, several hands taller than Face. She towered above him and pricked her ears a figure approaching.

'She is one of the valien.' The king followed Robbie outside, watching the animals. 'She has lived through several lifetimes and kept me safe throughout all these years of searching. Her name is Beatrice.'

'She's magnificent. I've never met such intuitive animals before I met the princess' valien.'

Looking at Beatrice's hind legs, Robbie didn't doubt her strength. The king's valien stepped closer and nibbled the great man's hand with soft pink lips.

'She has a temper, much like her owner, but she's loyal to the end and the time after that.' Beatrice nudged the king's pockets and breathed heavily into his neck in a way that suggested a truly great bond.

She stood between the two men and eyed both suspiciously. One of these tramps was clearly going to cut her holiday short.

Face pawed the ground and looked unblinkingly at Robbie as he stroked his mane.

The king smiled and looked at the young valien. 'It is a wish from deep in Face's heart that you travel together until you find her.'

'How do I get to the Well of Loneliness?'

'The old volcano surrounded by sea,' said the king. 'It's not straight forward. Water rages around it, stirred up no doubt by Selina's will. The area is now surrounded by fog, but the sea dwellers and pirates know of it. In all my years of looking for my wife, I never imagined anything could live in such a place, let alone hide there.'

All Robbie heard was the bit about raging water in the deepest part of the ocean.

'The only way to get inside the old volcano – without being seen or drowned – is underground, through the sea trenches.'

Robbie put his hands in his pockets to stop them shaking. There certainly was a lot of water involved in this rescue.

'Trenches?'

'A network of caves that run through the underwater mountains. You could fly directly into the Well, but Selina will expect that and be prepared. Going through the tunnels that burrow inside the Ridge of Shadows, directly into the Well, will be much, much harder. But you will have the element of surprise.'

'I imagine swimming will be required, then ...' Robbie swallowed.

The king ignored this and carried on. 'The sea dwellers discovered the Well. They warned ships from straying too close to the black water and getting dashed against the rocks, which are barely visible from the surface. It has always been a dangerous place, but accountable and avoidable. Until recently, it held no menace. It was just nature reminding us we are at her mercy.'

'Mmm.' Robbie dry-swallowed.

'Over the years, it has grown hungry. It has been disturbed by unnatural forces. The whirlpool has got wider. The laughing gulls and the bearded pelicans do not fly over it anymore. The sea dwellers will not venture near the black water unless they are dragged there. On my quest, they warned me of this, keeping my ships safe.'

Robbie almost wished the king was not so thorough in his description. 'I see.'

He felt he was no longer in his body, and for that he was sincerely grateful. He was floating above it, watching it nod seriously, hands in pockets next to the King of Landfelian, from a high, safe place.

'Selina has taken my daughter to where life and time stop. Nothing can thrive there, and that is the main danger for Red. And she's waiting for me to rescue her and fall ...' King Felian did not continue. He gently patted his daughter's horse, who nibbled his beard.

It wasn't getting any better. 'Well, the witch is going to be disappointed to find *me* instead,' Robbie said. 'I'm assuming she will have a couple of those skreekes grazing nearby?' He tried to sound light and nonchalant, like he did this rescuing thing all the time.

'Highly likely. Marmadou spotted two of them travelling over her frozen sea recently. It would be wise to expect them.'

Robbie added nothing to this. Wherever Red was, he hoped to God she was delirious enough to make it all seem like a bad dream.

'You must jump off Great Scott Point at sundown and ask the sea dwellers to grant you safe passage to the start of the sea trenches.'

'Sundown,' was all Robbie could say to that.

'When the sea dwellers and Landfelians were on better terms, it was tradition for the two clans to meet below Great Scott point at sundown to share news, hold important conversations, that sort of thing. It is our best hope.'

Robbie took a deep breath and looked at the king. 'When did they last meet?' he asked.

'Around ten years ago.' The king looked cagey. 'There is something you must take with you.'

'Please don't say "courage".'

He smiled. The king had never met a Man of the Road like this one before. 'Courage won't kill a skreeke, my friend.' He looked grim. 'You need a weapon. But first let us return to the others; they too have a part to play in this rescue. You will not be alone; I can promise you that, Robbie Wylde.' With the briefest of smiles, he strode back towards the folly. The two men accompanying the king with were now guarding the door bowed as they entered. They were dressed in the signature kingfisher blue tunics with the Felian crest emblazoned across the front: a valien rearing up from a crown. They stepped aside to allow Robbie through, their worn, sallow faces lighting up at the sight of a tray filled with cake and tea.

Inside, Mrs Tweed piled on more logs to keep the fire burning. The king lifted everyone's spirits when he walked back in and announced, 'We have a plan.'

Will clapped. 'Thank the crown! Is it cunning, clever, and covered in make-up?'

'Certainly not,' said the king after looking at the actor in a way that stopped him saying anything more about makeup. 'It is almost impossible and not at all sensible. For it to work, Father, I need to borrow your Cloudbuster. Can it be ready to fly before daybreak?'

Father Peter removed his pipe and said, 'She will fly.'

The king began to dance around the table, his eyes bright and his beard wafting about. 'Miss Morningstar.'

'Yes, my lord?' Or was it "Your Highness"? Amber wasn't sure. It was hard to think past the crown. The king could really turn it on when he needed to. He looked one step away from kissing her hand and saying, 'Call me Austin.'

'I will need your voice.' He smiled before her. 'And a disguise.'

'You shall have them.' She curtseyed. Will watched the king closely and narrowed his eyes.

'Richard, are the True family still safekeeping Paloma's grounds?'

'Yes, Sire.'

'With their young boy, Billy?'

'I believe so.'

'Good! I declare that this plan has wings, music, an explosive surprise, and Robbie here. It is coming together nicely.' The king wolfed down a piece of Mrs Tweed's chocolate cake and resumed his circling of the table.

Father Peter had not seen him look this possessed since he'd begun preparing for the quest. It worried him in the same way you would worry about a carriage with no one holding the reins.

Maggie was also anxious. She fiddled with her beads, hoping she was wrong. Hoping that the king wasn't about to sacrifice himself.

'William English, Sir Toby Mole – I need you to accompany Miss Morningstar to the Frozen Straits in the South Realm,' the king added. 'You will disguise yourself as the king and my royal aids. My men outside can provide you with the uniform. Your role is to distract the spiderlings.' The king hopped up and down on one foot, waving away their questioning looks. 'Peter, kindly explain the other two ways to the Well.'

Father Peter nodded. 'The first is via the Petrified Tree. It is the path Selina has taken, I imagine – a series of tunnels and steps under the Mistys. There will be a marked drop in temperature when you cross into her Hinterland and emerge from the second tree to make the unpleasant walk to her fortress, Tallfinger, where she does most of her plotting. In the cellars there is likely a labyrinth of caves that will take you through the trenches and under the sea.'

The king slapped the table. 'And into the Well!'

'Bearing in mind the hero traps, freezing temperatures, and the fact that the witch will have it watched.' Peter paused. 'She will have made it almost impossible to follow her that way. I may be theorising, but I know a little of how that woman's mind works, and it won't have improved with age.'

'Indeed. So, the second way if you will, Peter.' The king grinned like a tour guide.

'We fly. Take the Cloudbuster, head out west – not south across Selina's patch. The Cloudbuster's sails will not last long in her fog, and I must check we have enough fuel. There is also the risk of a swarm attack from the spiderlings if we fly too low.'

Austin smiled fondly at the watchful owl and clapped his hands. 'Marmadou can persuade all manner of bird to fly with us.' He looked at Amber, Will, and Sir Toby. 'And we now have our decoy!'

The godmothers exchanged worried glances.

'And there is a third way,' cried the king. 'Allow me to enlighten you all. Our Man of the Road …' He gripped Robbie's shoulder. '… approaches from Great Scott Point, swims, and enters the well through the Ridge of Shadows, the Sea Dwellers providing him with a guide to the right cave.'

Robbie tried not to black out. Why did it all have to

come down to him swimming? In deep, black water – water deep enough for there to be mountains; a whole range of them covered in ocean. Somewhere along the line, whichever way he looked at it, he was going to have to get wet. His out-of-body self floated down and patted him on the back before retreating through the wall, humming a funeral march.

Jan spotted it and passed Robbie a white feather; it was one of Marmadou's. 'For the jump.' She smiled and squeezed his hand.

'Thank you.' He smiled back weakly and put the feather in his pocket. At least it wouldn't weigh him down, although he needed a full set of wings to do any real lifting.

Will gave him a thumbs up and mouthed THE KING SAYS IT WILL BE FINE.

Maggie had spotted a problem with the plan. 'Unless we stop the spiderlings, they will follow Robbie and inform Selina. Any element of surprise will be lost.'

'Not if we send out a few white rabbits to distract them.' The sovereign looked meaningfully at the gathered, his eyes bright and certain. 'Spiderlings are not intelligent things. They only inform, they do not attack. They will be bewitched by Amber's voice and confused by the disguises which Will and Sir Toby will be wearing. Father Peter, I am certain you have a spare crown in this folly somewhere. I left it here last time we tried one of those spotty mushrooms.'

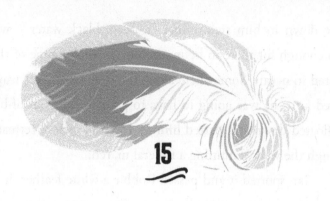

15

SWIMMING PROBLEM

Undiluted, undressed, stark-buttock-naked fear. Robbie couldn't escape it. Why he had failed to mention to anyone that he could not swim was unclear to him. A force he could not explain propelled him forward. He assumed, like a true optimist, that it would all work out in the end. That there would be time to learn, when the only other option was drowning. There was nothing any of the party could do about it; he was the only one who could go into the Well. Everyone else had their part to play, and the young valien trusted him. Will kept looking at him and raising his eyebrows in a way that said *Maybe NOW is the time to inquire into some swimming tutelage?*

He followed the king out of the folly, ignoring Will. They stood in silence with the horses for a moment, before the leafy gates. The king stroked his daughter's horse, who nuzzled his armpits and made knowing noises.

'You can't swim, can you, Robbie?' His hands scratched Face's handsome head with great tenderness. He had seen the young man's face fall, and the actors too, at the mention of deep water, and he did not make it to King without the gift of observation.

'How did you know?'

'An unlucky guess,' the king answered.

On good days, at low tide, Robbie could float for a bit. But actual full-on swimming? 'No. No, I can't.' Why lie when death was as unavoidable as the morning?

'And why, if you don't mind me asking, are you fearful of the water?' asked the king gently.

'My mother drowned when I was young. Ever since then ...'

'I see.' The king folded his arms and his face softened. 'You were too young for such a loss. I am sorry. And did you swim before that?'

'Yes.' He had been a strong swimmer. He'd liked collecting flat pebbles from the bottom of the river, saving his mother the white ones she liked.

'There you go.' As far as the king was concerned, the problem was solved and that was that. 'If you *can* swim, then it is a completely different type of fear. Not a permanent dye. It will come flooding back to you in no time. Trust me, when the only other option is drowning, you'll swim like a dolphin,

Robert Wylde.'

Robbie swallowed down the imminent threat of bile. 'You don't understand ...'

'Red is strong – and a good swimmer. I seem to remember ...' The king's voice broke. 'But her young heart can only fight in the well for so long. She needs a hero like you to help her get out, away from the fog and Selina.'

Heroes, Robbie knew, had swords. They had medals embroidered onto expensive silk shirts, signet rings, and hair that had seen a soft brush. Heroes passed through five years of training with the infamous hero trainer, Hamish of Kande. They travelled, used decanters, and had more than one middle name. Their teeth stood to attention, and they had the right socks.

'I'm no hero.'

'You don't need a diploma and a tassel if you've already saved a life. Save a life and it's a free pass – a scholarship, fees all paid. You are a hero, Robbie, and you are who she needs. Do not question a king or a valien.' Face stared at Robbie solemnly.

'I'm a cook. A Man of the Road. In the leafwell, I just used my whip.'

'I know who you are.' The king looked at the dawn sky. 'I knew your mother,' he said quietly.

'You can't have.' Of that Robbie was sure.

'No, not well. I knew *of* her. There were few white witches of note practising in Landfelian. She was one of them. A truly gifted lady, a bright soul, and a natural healer.'

'My mother, a witch?' She had simply helped folk with

crushed-up flowers and nice stews.

'Wonderful lady – cornflower eyes, smelt of cinnamon.'

'She made a lot of crumble,' Robbie explained. It did make sense though. There was always something magical about her. At the time, he had just assumed it was because she was his mother and he loved her.

'People inherit the good things, Robbie. They also inherit noses, unfortunately.' The king smiled, rubbing his. 'Your mother helped my wife once; she may not have told you. The queen had trouble sleeping. It is too complex a maze to go into now. But you have been sent to save my daughter. You are her friend. I will be right above you, with Father Peter, and when you most need help, all you have to do is look up.'

Robbie could not remember much of the years before his mother had drowned. The time immediately after had passed in a ragged blur of hungry, cold nights in fields and foraging to stay alive.

'It is going to be alright tonight, if we hold tight.' The king put his hand on Robbie's shoulder.

Robbie thought it was time the king had a lie down.

'You think me mad. Well, we have run out of options, dear man. I need you to take my word for it.' He patted him on the back. 'Now, it is time you made the journey to the point. Selina's scheming waits for us to make the next move.'

In the peaceful garden, with the sound of horses and owls, Robbie forgot about swimming for a moment. If the *king* said he was a hero, then he was, though it would have been easier to believe if he was not wearing a colourful waistcoat with a white feather.

'I have only been to Great Scott Point once. I'm not sure …'

'Face knows the way. He is the fastest horse since Windburn.' (Windburn was the fastest of the valien and the most painful to ride.) 'He will save you valuable time looking at maps.'

'When you arrive, find the pirate Patrick Dickie – he knows the seas like the front of his foot. Lives on an old ship in a small cove beside the point. He used to be the lover of Anook, empress of the sea dwellers. These two are your guides into the well. All you have to do is jump.'

'Jump?'

'Yes. Off the point.' The king unbuttoned his coat to give to Will and prepared Beatrice for a journey. She looked fierce and ready.

'Where are you going?'

'I have to collect some explosives from Paloma. The Cloudbuster will collect me there,' the king explained. 'The point stretches out to sea. Jumping off the end will land you in exactly the right spot to find a Sea Dweller. They are an elusive people, so we're going to make sure you land outside their front door.'

'I see.' Robbie decided to ask no further questions.

The king looked up at the sky and frowned. 'It is nearly dawn. Look to the skies when you need us the most and we will be there.'

The first rays of sun shone upon the leaves curling around the folly gates.

'It is very important that you don't jump until sundown. Do you understand, Robbie? Sundown. I will come for you both before the end. Good luck and Godspeed!' He muttered something into Face's twitching ear.

The king rode his valien north, flattening a circle of toadstools. He left Robbie his coat and all the royal aspects of his clothes to pass to Will. The two guards at the door were now dressed in the clothes of an out of work actor and a gentleman of the court.

Dawn arrived over the folly. It was a new day, and Robbie felt two hundred years old. Father Peter strolled out to find him.

'I've brought you some coffee. It's Eyerish.'

In a crisis, it's the little things that lift one from the swamp.

'What can you tell me about Selina Carnal?' Robbie needed to know what kind of bad he was about to interrupt. 'What is it about her that brings such fear to the godmothers?'

Father Peter took a deep breath. 'Dear man, I'm afraid there is not enough time to open that jar of demons. Although I can tell you she was a talented witch before she turned to the dark arts. Unfortunately, when one dabbles for too long in such things, it takes away their humanness, the part of their soul that can be reasoned with.' He leant against a vast beech tree. 'That is what Maggie and Jan fear most. There is not enough good left to appeal to, and that makes her unpredictable.

'When I knew her, Selina was young and restless, always wanting to push her talents and her studies further than was wise. We researched together for a short time, under the tutelage of January's mother, the renowned astrology professor Angela Macloud. Selina became well known for manipulating nature. Then she discovered books on sorcery, and she increased her power by utilising the energy that collected around the recently dead.' Father Peter gave Robbie a sorry smile. 'It's a funny old world. Selina chose her path, and it has consumed her.'

Robbie was not finding the world very funny.

'Her mind is a maze of twisted fantasies. Landfelian was a continuous source of frustration for her – most especially, Red's mother, who is talented, loved by many, and always a cause of jealousy.'

Father Peter looked wholly confident.

'You needn't worry. Red Felian is stronger than everyone here – even Mrs Tweed's rock buns.' His eyes shone. 'You will see – as long as she holds onto hope. Her time will come. For this part in the witch's game, she must play the pawn, although her shadow is shaped for so much more.' His eyes shone. 'And it's catching up with her. Try to remember, Selina's power derives from the dead. But the dead are dead, they are not living and never will be. No matter how powerful Selina thinks she is, she can't bring the dead back to life, and to promise this is a dangerous game.'

Robbie tried to imagine Red as queen. He couldn't. She had barely left the grounds of Paloma. She had not even tried a mooncake ... What powers could she be hiding?

'Now, you need a weapon. Come with me.'

Robbie followed the Father to a small hermitage at the far end of the garden. He rummaged about in an old leather trunk of walking sticks and hoes. 'Where is the blasted thing?'

He passed Robbie a willow wand and a butterfly net until he finally found the thing he was looking for.

'It's ... an umbrella?' Robbie shook the heavy object and a graveyard of dried-up spiders fell out of the canvas.

'Not quite,' Father Peter answered.

'I was hoping for a sword.'

'Very few swords have the right owner and therefore the right sense of direction.' Father Peter sniffed. He had never liked swords. He took hold of the umbrella as if it were a diamond dagger. 'Give the wrong man a sword and there is no knowing what will happen. You see, every blade needs a clear mind to show it the way. Giving the wrong mind a sword is like giving them an unbroken horse to ride.'

To say Robbie was disappointed was an understatement. There was no secret blade. No third eye to see the enemy approach before the enemy knew they were approaching. No spring mechanism that released a stream of dragon's fire.

Father Peter beamed at the dusty umbrella. 'This will protect you.'

'From what, the weather?' Robbie muttered.

'Precisely! And revive the princess for long enough to get you both out of that hole before the fog begins to –'

'The fog is not my main concern.' It was the skreekes, the witch, and the drowning that worried him most. He prodded the umbrella-y object into the ground. 'How does it work?'

'The fog should be your *only* concern. It eats hope. Without it, Selina is weak.' Father Peter took it briskly off him. 'Come, man, it is not a spade. You just open it. I loathe complicated gadgets,' he muttered. (Father Peter was once bitterly disappointed by an egg poacher.) 'The sunbrella will only work when opened in a truly dark place. It is my greatest defence against evil – besides Marmadou, of course. Never underestimate the simple power of light, Robbie. It will see you through the fog.'

Robbie was dubious. He did not believe most of what he had been told so far. The canvas of the sunbrella looked dirty and dull. 'It's certainly very heavy.'

'The handle is made of cold stone. If you fitted a sunbrella with a wooden handle, you would set fire to yourself. And then where would you be?'

Robbie made one last attempt at gaining a sharp weapon. At least he had his whip. 'No swords in that trunk?'

'You'll get one of those later.'

'From whom?'

'The king.'

Father Peter didn't quite meet Robbie's eye. He stroked

his owl's wing for a moment, looking up at the lightening sky. Robbie did not think much of the king's returning record.

'Why didn't he come back sooner? Look at what has happened while he was on a futile quest.'

'Don't be quick to judge what you do not know.' Father Peter's voice was sharp. 'Where there is hope, there isn't defeat. Galivanting is far from true of the quest. All those involved have suffered.'

Robbie tied the sunbrella around his shoulder. 'For seven years he sent no word.'

Father Peter held Robbie back. 'Dear man, have you ever woken up one morning to find your heart missing, with no note to say when it might be back?'

'No, I have never loved anything that much.'

'One day you will, and then you may understand the king's grief. It was given no clear ending.' Father Peter looked grave. 'That man knows full well his mistakes, but he is here now, trying. He may not have returned soon enough, but he asked his closest confidents to keep watch over his daughter. We were just stopped from doing so ...'

The others had gathered at the gates to see the Man of the Road off. Magatha handed him the old bit of shell, tying it round his neck.

'I don't think I'm going to need a shell, Maggie.'

'You don't know what you will need. Now, let me look at you.' She stood on tiptoes and gave him an eyeballing. 'Do an old nag a favour and look into the shell when you doubt yourself. Promise? Just a quick look if things turn in around you.'

Robbie gave her a nod.

Will strode over next and gave him a back-breaking hug. 'In the water, act like a wave. Do not try to fight and the sea will accept you as one of her own. I played the sea once, and it's important to not struggle …'

'Thank you, Will.' Robbie smiled at the actor, now dressed up as King Felian, spare crown in his bag.

Will leant in and whispered, 'I've added a very useful utensil to your bag. You can thank me later.'

Amber kissed Robbie on the cheek, held his face close, and said simply, 'Don't die.'

The herald offered his lucky baton because he had nothing else. 'When you return, I shall have you fitted with a decent doublet, shirt, and a pair of new boots. Clothes maketh the man. And you, Robert Wylde, are a man.'

'Thank you.' Robbie put the baton in his shirt pocket. It was the closest thing to a sharp weapon he had, and he was so grateful for it, he hugged the herald.

Sir Toby came forward with an apology. 'I would offer you my sword, but I left it at Tikli Bottom. Is there anything else I can do?' Robbie could not carry any more; the sunbrella was going to drown him as it was.

'Will you take care of my horse while I'm gone?' Robbie asked. He'd noticed that horses seemed to like Sir Toby, and unlike Will, he knew how to ride them. 'She won't understand why I have left without her.'

'It would be an honour,' said Sir Toby. 'We will need her in the Frozen Straits. She will be waiting for your return.'

Robbie gave his mare an ear rub, he kissed her noise, and, looking in to her eyes, said, 'Back soon, milady.' And then he walked towards Red's valien. Face stamped the ground impatiently with mighty hooves.

Father Peter walked him to the end of the path that met the drovers' route to the coast.

'The last test of any hero, the work for which all other work is but preparation, is this – never, ever despair.'

'I can't swim, Father.' Robbie looked at him.

'You will know what to do when the time is upon you and when you are wet. Remember your whip. It saved my goddaughter once.'

He smiled with such warmth and wisdom that a tiny chip of fear melted away from Robbie's toe.

'Don't forget me.' Robbie held on tight to the reins to stop his hands shaking.

'Impossible.' Father Peter squeezed his shoulder. 'We have much to discuss when you return.'

Robbie did not dally. One firm nudge with his heels and the princess' horse was off like the clappers.

Father Peter watched them, deep in thought before returning inside to pack up a small leather satchel.

'We must hurry, there is work to do,' he said to the

others inside the folly. 'We have gone beyond the realms of sanity, my young friends. By Georgina, we have. Mrs Tweed, power up the Cloudbuster! Mr English, go to the bottom of the garden – inside the stone badger there is a bottle. Would you fetch it, please? I will take it for our heroes; they will need it for the journey home.'

Will expected to find a potion of griffin-summoning, muscle rebuilding powers.

'What are you going to do with it?' he asked, his eyes wide, handing a slender green bottle with dark crimson liquid within it to the Father with the label *Brandak*.

'Drink it! What a question!'

'You don't have any long tapestries do you, Mrs Tweed?' asked Will importantly as they prepared the horse and carriage. 'I found one very useful on my last rescue mission.'

Robbie and Face galloped through the West Realm. Robbie didn't stop because he couldn't. He didn't have the faintest idea how to slow the valien down. 'Woah' didn't work, neither did 'Easy does it' nor 'Please slow down, I may fall off'. He barely noticed the land through which they passed. Face had a deadline. He had to get this young Man of the Road to the old pirate before sunset. Together, they had to get the princess back.

Anyone on the road got quickly out of the way. Some peasants went home, swearing they had seen one of the valien and a worried-looking chap in a colourful waistcoat riding it.

16

SKREEKES

Deep inside the Well of Loneliness, Red was holding on. But only barely was she holding. Her wrists were bound by locked chains attached to two creatures, and her wrists were slightly bleeding as a result. She thought this was a good sign, though – bleeding meant she was alive. Bled was not so good.

She had heard Daniel Blackwood refer to these animals as skreekes. They looked like descendants from a dragon family. Whatever opiate he had given her had worn off, and Red felt conscious again although weak. It was the same feeling she'd had when the voodoo wore away on her ankle as she ran further away from Paloma, heaviness in her limbs and a coldness seeping into her thoughts. The witch, Red saw with relief, was nowhere to be seen.

Red ignored the chains and looked around at her

surroundings. The area was vast, not a well by any standards. There were no properly constructed walls or nice sturdy buckets on long ropes to lift her out. She appeared to be in a desolate wasteland encircled by towers of crumbling, volcanic rock. With the sound of the sea around her, it all felt at risk of collapsing. There was something unnatural about the way the area had been hollowed out. The base of the Well was as big as the Lake of Stars. It narrowed up to a funnel where the sky could not be seen, only fog. The light was dim but torches had been lit either side of her.

Selina Carnal was, unfortunately, not far away. She was having a wonderful time in the Well of Loneliness. It was a holiday down there, the perfect atmospheric conditions for a sorceress as accomplished as herself. Compared to the last seven years, battling alone in her fortress and sparring with the Knight and his secretive insistence on keeping her wretched sister, the needle in her foot, Queen Felian, alive.

'This is how to seize a kingdom, Daniel.' She gasped in delight at the gentleman next to her.

'The queen is still alive.'

'Insignificant detail,' she spat.

'And the king,' he muttered.

'He'll be here soon.' Selina smiled.

The dead volcano revived her spirit; it was a wonderfully dramatic setting. The ground looked like the folds of a vast black beast, where the molten lava had dried. Every now and then, parts of the volcano wall cracked and fell into the well from the pressure of the sea that raged around it. She had lit a few torches, which set off some suitably eerie shadows over the princess' hanging body. The girl made good bait. She looked suitably breathtaking held captive below with her red hair and dress. It was going to be a wonderful show of Salina's power and skill. To manipulate the fog in such a way that it did not consume the prisoner but left enough of her to fight.

'This is theatre,' she crowed at Daniel.

And then Selina sent the black squirrel, squirming in her hand, with the following message to Mirador.

THE BAIT IS ON THE HOOK IF YOU WISH TO ATTEND THE KING'S CULLING.

The witch looked out at the desolate space with glee and watched Red Felian pull on one of her chains.

'My dear, if you so much as flinch, the skreekes will take a foot from you,' Selina called down. 'I say, she is doing awfully well,' she drawled. 'Let's hope she fights; I do want some drama.'

'For whom?'

'The king of course, and the Knight,' she said through gritted teeth. 'If he ever leaves his castle and precious queen behind.'

Selina had been disappointed when the princess did not faint or yell in horror on their arrival. She watched from an enclave in the rocks, like a box in the dress circle of a theatre, hidden and above the ground. Red had kept quiet and still, deciding early on to conserve her energy. Something told her she would need every ounce to escape such a dead place. She used her time to study the fog and the skreekes beside her.

The witch's fog pawed the ground and licked up to where she was chained. Cold had crept into her feet and her fingers. The skreekes appeared unable to see her, but when she moved, they lifted their snouts and sniffed in her direction. *That's interesting.* She thought. *They're blind.*

Red's heart remained warm with two thoughts. If she was ever going to hold Robbie Wylde's hand again, she had to keep breathing. And if she was going to find her parents, she had to hold on. This witch knew where they were. The fog was dead, she tried to remember this; it was not formed the normal way, from light and living molecules, but from something dark and disturbed. Sunlight burns through fog, Red thought. She focused her mind on her own light and began to practise …

But the well was a sad, draining place, and Selina's fog had all the time in oblivion to grind her spirit down. It wanted nothing more; it yearned for the brightness of Red Felian's soul, it hungered for all that youth and strength. *I have to find a way of shielding myself,* she thought.

As Father Peter summarised what lay ahead, silence descended over Two Hoots Folly. It was the sort of silence that comes before running a marathon when you feel you have never truly lain down and didn't truly appreciate it when you did.

'It's a shame Robbie couldn't borrow the swan pedalo,' Will said.

'The current around the Well of Loneliness could snap a boulder-whale in two,' said Father Peter succinctly. 'A pedalo, William, is out of the question.'

'I see.' Will looked at his hands and sighed.

'He must trust the sea and its people.'

Maggie pursed her lips and muttered something about the sea dwellers. 'I dearly hope they help him now. They're a fickle lot. There's no reason for them to come to Landfelian's aid.'

Sir Toby grew excited. 'Have you seen a Mermaiden?'

Amber was wary of the sea dwellers; she had seen the crazed, twitching eyes of Alba's fishermen lurch into The Cat's Back after months away at sea. They would drink themselves into a puddle, their minds eaten up with longing and their mouths leaking with desire for the watery folk they'd glimpsed in the water.

'Turned mad, poor souls,' she said. 'Most returned to the sea to drown, singing, "Take Me Home". At least, that's what happened to old Finn Collins.'

Father Peter ushered the worried party out the door with yook wool-lined snow boots and gloves. 'You will need these. The temperature in the south has dropped considerably.'

Will was still worrying about the Sea Dwellers. 'Do you think Robbie will be able to win the mermaidens' trust? They're notoriously hard to find. No one has seen a soul aboard their floating villages for years.' He got all this from Marlene's Soup Kitchen and the Still Place Newsletters.

'I have great faith in the young man,' assured Father Peter. 'The Sea Dwellers are there. They haven't turned their back on Landfelian, not yet.'

'How is he going to do it, though, if he is busy drowning?'

'The people of the sea have a good sense of humour; it is dark but abundant,' replied the Father. 'And do not forget, they too are suffering from Selina's fog.'

Will frowned; Robbie was not a natural comic. If he had known a sense of humour was important, he would have shown him his wet-kipper routine. 'Won't he run out of air before there is time to tell them a joke?'

'That's the idea. They are an extremely secretive people. But running out of air will give him the best shot at it. They have spies everywhere.'

Father Peter put his glasses on to search for a reference book, scanning the pile of frayed books climbing up one branch-like wall. 'Mermaidens rarely come to the surface now. They take refuge in a great wreck where the empress resides. The men spend more time on the boats, fixing their floating villages, selling sea minerals and pearls, although they are less approachable and more volatile. Aha! Here it is.'

The illustration in the book *Sea Dwellers – Beauty or Beast?* was covered in damp and smelt of the sea. It showed an aerial map of the waters around Landfelian. 'Most are located around the Sea of Trees.' Father Peter pointed to the waters to the west of Great Scott Point. 'Once they discover Robbie, they will hopefully provide him with a rare ocean plant known as airgrass. It will allow him to breathe while in their company.'

'Is it true what they say about their beauty?' Sir Toby gazed at images of raven hair, strange-coloured eyes, and wicked smiles.

The Father took his glasses off and said sensibly, 'They possess a grace that we land dwellers do not.'

'They've as much curve as an eel.' Mrs Tweed had a staunch opinion of water folk. She removed a pair of rubber yook-turd handling gloves and what looked like a welding mask. 'The Cloudbuster is ready, Father.' Through the window of the Situation Room a vast balloon the colour of red clay attached to a basket was floating inches above the ground.

Yook turd was a messy, highly toxic business. Unfortunately, it was the only current way to power a Cloudbuster. The stench could stay on the skin for years if you didn't wear protection. Any residue also made you highly combustible, due to the high levels of nut and clover in the animals' diet. Travelling all the way up to Giant Country and collecting the stuff left Father Peter's cardigan smelling of ripe drains for months.

'It's time.' Father Peter looked at the gathered, worried faces. 'Go carefully and don't catch cold. Remember, we need the spiderlings' eyes to be trained on you – not our young Man of the Road or the king. Head to the Petrified Tree – and,

Amber, make as much noise as you can. They will be drawn in by your voice and confused by Will's appearance and the king's men with you. The owls have kept the folly safe for the time being, but the swarm will be on the hunt again as soon as you leave the curtilage of my house. It is you who resemble the royal party heading for the bait.'

Will adjusted his robes and practised a royal wave.

Father Peter put on a pair of goggles and a leather skull cap.

'I will collect the king from Paloma and then head straight for the Well. Our best hope is that the spiderlings are confused for long enough to give this air rescue a window to collect Red and Robbie from that dark place. Maggie, January – you must go to Celador, open the castle, light the fires, and prepare it.'

'Of course,' said Maggie. 'For what?' She gathered her coat around her and collected her broom from the door.

'For casualties,' Jan answered.

'Even more reason to lay a good fire in the family wing and bake some bread,' Father Peter replied. 'Our heroes will need to thaw out when they return. It's the closest place for the Cloudbuster to land, and it will be a comfort for Red when she wakes in her true home. Although I fear it will take more than a warm bed and a pot of tea to revive our friends.' He remembered his encounter with Selina's fog; even such a short exposure could sit on the nervous system and bite for weeks afterwards.

The herald looked quite desperate. 'But I don't have the key.' He searched through every pocket of his herald coat. 'It's all locked up for fear of looters.'

Father Peter frowned. He was right. It had been a brittle, grieving night when they'd shut Celador's gates for the last time, and the keys to the portcullis had somehow been forgotten over time. The departure from the castle had been a rushed, chaotic affair; everyone was so focused on getting the young princess away from the fog and safe. Where the keys had ended up was anybody's guess …

'Who wants the last rock bun?' Mrs Tweed asked.

'Thank you, Mrs T,' volunteered Father Peter nobly. 'I wonder if you might recall the whereabouts …'

Maggie flew towards Mrs Tweed, snatched the rock bun from Father Peter's hand, put it on the floor, and stamped down on it hard with her boot. Amongst the currants, a worn bronze key glinted like a charm with the Felian crest engraved through its bow.

'There it is.' Maggie clapped. 'Oh, I do love a good sign.' She picked up the key, which glowed in the candlelight, and put it in her pocket. 'Come on, Macloud, let's go!'

By midday, the folly was quiet. Mrs Tweed was wiping down the Situation Table with a soft cloth while seabirds called outside. They had come further inland from the coast, where the fog had now closed in around Landfelian. She decided to have a good spring clean; it calmed her nerves. For even Mrs

Tweed knew the fate of the kingdom now lay in the hands of a very small, unlikely group of rebels.

There was a dry, choking noise below the window.

She picked up her swatter, put on her glasses, and walked outside. Amidst a pile of rock-bun crumbs, surreptitiously hurled out the window, several spiderlings lay slowly dying with indigestion.

'That'll teach you.' She smiled and returned inside, feeling hopeful once more.

17

THE PIRATE

The female sea dwellers were gifted with an intuition not matched by any land dweller. Males were brawny, calloused, anti-social, and not blessed with such ethereal grace. Athletically, they were gladiatorial; even the waves got out of the way when a sea gypsy approached doing butterfly at full pelt. They were talented salvagers, boat builders, repairers of wrecks, and masters of fishing. However, the majority of mermaidens (the term coined for the female sea dweller) thought them crude and aggressive. The seaweed was often greener, in their opinion, closer to land, which caused a certain amount of jealousy between the territories.

The sea dwellers' talent was free diving, seeking out the jewels of the seabed: pearls, sea diamonds, minerals, and turquoise. They traded these precious stones with pirates, foreign merchants, and Landfelians; cultured folk who could tell a joke about a squirrel, hoist a sail, recite poetry, and talk about wine. Hundreds of years ago, the sea dwellers had originally come from the Spice Islands and as their business grew from the sea, and soon, so did their home.

The previous king and queen of Landfelian, Max and Matilda Felian, were responsible for negotiating a peace treaty with the empress of the Mermaidens, a woman called Aquinnah Porites, and the leader of the sea gypsies, Soni Reef. Years passed of peace, and their two kingdoms rubbed happily alongside each other.

But this peace cracked when the sea became rather busy. Trading routes opened between other foreign lands, the most troublesome being Fronce and Engerlande. Fleets of discovery ships trawled through the sea dwellers' blue kingdom. Rumours of sudden drownings and unexplained shipwrecks spread, and some Landfelians began to fear the sea and its murdering, mysterious, tattooed people. The floating villages pulled further away from the coast and there they stayed.

Relations took a turn for the worse when the sea empress' daughter, Anook, fell in love with the most notorious pirate of the time, a man called Patrick Dickie. She acted against her people and broke the golden rule: *Thou shalt not cohabitate with a land dweller or walk his plank.*

The sea empress became enraged with everything. The sea gypsies were riotous – the most bewitching of the young mermaidens claimed to be in love with a pirate from Landfelian. Anook was forced to give up her pirate and the pirate was forced to remain anchored or face exile orders of the king. The fragile bond between land and sea was lost. The time when the two kingdoms used to send messages in green bottles to one another and meet for Sundown Sundays was gone.

The Pirate King, Patrick Dickie, had been five when Pirate Blueshank found him floating on a raft of driftwood, off the pink sands of Aromane, naked save a tattoo of a dragon fish curled around his tiny, tanned arm. They took him in and brought him up as one of their own. The little orphan became the most notorious plunderer of the seas.

Now in his late middle age, he had salt and pepper hair and highly changeable – and at times plain dirty – brown eyes, accompanied by a crooked smile. He called everyone "darlin", although he had only loved once.

Anook came from a different land, with different rules. She had lungs equipped to live below the surface for long stretches of time, exceptionally strong thighs, and pearly skin. Anook was a mermaiden and Patrick was a pirate. It was forbidden. On the day Patrick was exiled and banned from pirating, he gave up the ocean. It was hard to forget his lost love when his office roamed over the rooftops of her home. So, he dropped anchor and became a recluse; it was easier. Known as the hermit of Crabbie, he became a bad-tempered middle-aged man with a fondness for a dark, cloudy ale called Peaty. Without the mermaiden or the sea, his heart shrivelled to a winkle and so did his capacity for kindness. The shell-pickers who camped around small fires in remote settlements near his cove quite liked the hermit. He was a legend, after all, and so were his stories. Despite being a grumpy arse, he made good paella and kept Blackwood's Guards at bay by setting off the odd cannon.

Patrick's ship was known to the locals as *that piece of junk*. Like him, she had once been rather beautiful and extremely hard to say no to. The oars were engraved with pearls and curved like a wave. For twenty-seven years, she sliced and stroked through the most storm-spurned waters, her hull studded with turquoise and fool's gold. The pirate called her the *Flying Cloud*, or *Kon Tiki* in the island tongue. Now, she was wretched.

The *Flying Cloud* needed some serious wood feed, elbow grease, shoeshine, saddle soap, and, most of all, a swashbuckling adventure. She was made for sailing, not reclusing.

At this very moment, the Pirate King was reading the *Shipping News*, stolen each week by Alberta, his albatross. Although he had not left the small stretch of coast for over a decade, he still liked to know what kind of mess the kingdom was in. He lived off sardines and drank Peaty bought by the barrel from the nearest inn, The Cockle's Toes. It would take a miracle to make him stand up and say, 'ARGGHGHHH!' like a true pirate. On his decaying ship, he swept the deck of gull poo and walked the gangplank every day to check his lobster cages. On Sundays, he looked through his telescope and watched the floating villages of the Sea Dwellers as they held their weekly market of salt, ocean minerals, and pearls. Patrick was always hopeful of glimpsing his true love. Although he never did. The sum of his days had shrunk to merely existing.

The *Flying Cloud* idled in the shallows of the small cove, and, apart from Alberta, the pirate lived alone. An experienced pirate did not go in for parrotry. Parrots were conspicuous, nagging birds, digging their claws into a man's shoulder and causing one to walk around like a one-legged clown. He was occasionally visited by a tailless water-vixen who he'd named Victoria after the Queen of Engerlande, who Patrick thought was a hoot. He had found the fox trying to cross the Bigeasy estuary as he returned from one of his regular visits to Jabba Cave under Great Scott Point, where he hoarded what was left of his bounty.

It was both these animals, Alberta and Victoria, who tried to alert the pirate of a valien rider who was approaching his ship at a barnacle-startling pace. These attempts were ignored with Patrick Dickie's usual grace.

'Victoria!' he yelled above the insistent yelping of his vixen. 'Scratch the door one more time and I'll use your teeth to clean the mussels off the hull.'

The pirate was chopping up seven bulbs of garlic when he heard a firm knock on his cabin door.

Robbie waited outside, breathing hard. He had not opened both eyes at the same time since dawn. Face had not changed his pace or his stride all day. Robbie noticed the sea lay wide and far-reaching beside them. He stared down over the cliffs ahead and saw a swathe of torn skull and crossbones flags hanging from a worn-looking ship. They flapped forlornly in the breeze. The ship was half concealed by rocks. It looked derelict.

He walked gingerly over a number of rotten timbers on the deck. There was no answer on the cabin door. The knocker was a copper octopus; this had to be the right boat and the right hermit, although it smelt damp and, frankly, depressing. But there were no other boats in the cove.

'Hello.' Robbie knocked harder and called out, 'I'm looking for Patrick Dickie.'

'No,' came a voice back through the door. 'Not in.'

Robbie asked the closed door, 'Are you sure?' and frowned.

'Yup. Bugger 'off,' came a gruff reply.

'I was told the pirate Patrick Dickie lived here.' Robbie tried to keep the impatience out of his voice and failed. 'It's urgent!'

'You were told wrong, mate. He just left.'

'No, he didn't.' Robbie shouted through a spyhole in the door. From what he could see inside, there was a man of fifty years or so standing there in an apron and a pair of rolled up, torn, linen trousers. He did not have an eye patch or a parrot.

'How do you know?' Until now, Patrick had done well stopping sales calls by flying the pirate flag. It gave people what they wanted to see, pleased the children, and kept everyone else out. 'Go away.'

'No!' Robbie leant against the door and took a ragged breath. 'I must see the pirate.' He wiped the dust and road from his face, turning his sleeve brown, and slid down to the floor. 'I can't do this without him.' He rested his head in his hands and closed his eyes for a moment. 'I'll start singing and I won't stop until you open this door.'

The princess' valien whinnied impatiently from the shore.

Robbie began, 'There were thirty-one bottles of beer on the wall, thirty-one bottles of beer ...' And so, the song went on.

The sun was low in the afternoon sky and the ledge of Great Scott Point jutted out several hundred feet above the sea. Robbie didn't have long. His legs and arms burned from the journey. He could do with something to eat and drink before being pushed off a cliff. But beggars can't be choosers and all that tripe ... He carried on singing, and when he reached one bottle, he started again; somewhere in the distance, a cat began to yowl.

A water-vixen crawled out from under a piece of crudely patched sail and sat quietly next to Robbie. She licked his hand. He looked at her coat; it reminded him of Red's hair at sunset. He stroked the animal's ears and leant against the door of the cabin. It remained firmly shut.

Inside, the pirate watched the valien rider through the spyhole. It was not just any old valien, it was a royal one; Patrick knew it. He knew King Felian's horse well; it had paid him a visit every other year of the quest, desperate for clues of the missing Queen. He chewed on a piece of raw garlic and took the paella off the heat. This horse looked like a younger version.

'What's your business here, son?' he called out.

'I've come from Father Peter's, the explorer.' Robbie turned around and willed the door to open. 'On a rescue mission for King Felian.'

Patrick sat down heavily on a stool and opened a bottle of wine. 'Oh dear, I hope you haven't signed up for a Quest.' His laughter was gruff but not unkind.

'He said you could help,' Robbie went on. He took a breath, ran his fingers through his dust-ridden hair, and thought how implausible this all was. He was sitting on a rotting pirate ship, speaking to a squatter, claiming to be on a king's errand.

'What care I of kings, man? Their business is their own and their business is often a load of tripe.' Patrick's voice could be as rough as a wreck. 'Why are you really here?'

He was there for a princess called Red, who he'd bumped into several weeks ago and now could not stop thinking about. Robbie banged on the door with his head and his voice cracked. 'For … love.'

'That's more like it! For a horrible second, I thought you were one of those bureaucratic, diplomatic, sock-flashing, feather-wearing heroes.' Patrick dragged his stool closer to the cabin door. 'What line of work you in, son?'

'I cook, mostly,' admitted Robbie. 'Fix things, live on the road.'

'Good stuff. Now, tell me about this young fish in need of rescuing?'

Robbie told him. 'She's being held captive in the Well of Loneliness.'

There was a pause. 'The Well, eh? That extinct volcano still causing problems? Sounds simple enough. You've just got to understand the currents. What's the problem?'

'I can't swim,' Robbie said.

The pirate spat out the garlic.

'Ah. That may be tricky. How do you know the lady wants rescuing?' Patrick snorted into a rag. 'Is it true love?'

'I've only known her for thirteen days.'

'Well, do you think there's some good odds there? Do you think it's got legs?'

'Of course she's got legs!' Robbie tried not to shout.

Patrick stared squarely at the door and grunted. Whoever this cook was, he was an idiot. 'Ye lily-livered … rapscallion!'

There was a smash inside and a torrent of the best class of pirate swearing. Robbie hoped it would stop soon. He was tired and hoarse, and he still had to learn to swim. 'You're nothing but a bounty hunter!' the pirate growled through the spyhole.

'No, you've got it all wrong.' Robbie closed his eyes at the memory. 'I've held her hand and kissed her once.' Robbie whispered to himself and the water vixen. If he got out of this alive, he would tell Red how annoying it was having someone to think about and be willing to die for. It really got in the way of breakfast.

At that, the door swung open. Robbie fell through and landed on a dirty brown foot.

'That will have to do.' The pirate bore down on him, grinning. 'Drink this.' He heaved Robbie inside and handed him a jug, glowering out at the sinking sun before slamming the cabin door shut. 'We haven't long.'

'Is it rum?' Robbie sniffed it.

'No, you prat, it's water. You're dehydrated. Victoria! Fetch my flippers and the sea goggles.' The pirate held Robbie's face firmly in one hand and squeezed. 'Look at the state of you. And where did you get that waistcoat?'

Robbie forgot he was wearing half of Maggie's old clothes. 'Magatha Guiler.'

'THAT was my favourite waistcoat.' The pirate laughed like a bell. 'The witch.'

The water vixen slunk away, and Robbie stood before a brawny, sea-weathered face, with crinkly muscovado eyes and a sideways smile. 'Get off my foot, man, and tell me why.'

'Why what?' Robbie moved aside.

'Why you can't swim.'

'How can I be sure you're the pirate king?' Robbie hedged. The cabin was filthy.

'I'm the only one here, aren't I?' The pirate bowed elegantly. 'Patrick Dickie, Pirate King, at your service. Now sit down and tell us your story.'

18

WATER CHESTNUTS

Robbie's memories of the days before his mother drowned were like an abandoned house. She had drowned when he was young, not far off ten years old. The trauma of that day had caused his mind to shut down and block most of what had come before, in the same way a layer of cobwebs will stop one climbing into the attic despite there being some wonderful toys up there.

'Tell us, then. You haven't got long before the sun sets. It's the pirate way, I'm afraid lad. You live longer if you can tell us a story. And I'll throw in a free swimming lesson.'

Robbie drank some water, wiped his face with a rag, and tried to recall the memory to the pirate, a water vixen, and an albatross on the deck of an old ship as the sun began to fall. Only days ago, Red had asked about his mother, and he'd clammed up and shut down as always. With the very possible approach of his own drowning, however, he began to remember the day the water overcame her. Robbie closed his eyes and took a slow breath. With the first word, he felt a surge of pure, white relief.

"She was a cook to an abbey of nuns. They lived in a crumbling place called Nun's Drift. We lived in a gatehouse on the edge of the abbey's land, with our dog, a goat, and a pony and had the run of the place. My mother and I tended the kitchen gardens.'

Patrick filled up his glass. 'What was the dog's name?'

'Goose.' Robbie wondered why this was relevant.

'Arrr, a fine name.' The pirate seemed pleased with this detail.

'The abbey was in the far west of the North Realm, known for its abundance of apple trees and healing folk. It was remote, at the base of Mount Felian, and difficult to get to, divided by a number of rivers and hills. Such was the locals' delight that anyone should take the trouble to venture so far, flowers were thrown at their feet, jars of sweet quince jam handed out, and doors opened in welcome. The nuns gave up their beds up for travellers.

'One day, a stranger came by the abbey. He had been on the road for many months. There was no room for him, but my mother offered him her floor. She said the man was in search of something, looking to cure some inner turmoil. Over this time, my mother fell in love. He stayed with her until the leaves turned, and then she never saw him again.

This was all she told me and it is all I know. I was born nine months later. I believe this man to be my father.' Robbie frowned. 'I never met him.'

'Name?'

'Alec. That was all my mother told me.' Robbie paused. 'He rode a valien.'

'A valien, eh?' The pirate stopped and a surprised look passed across his eyes for a second. 'I've done plenty of wrong in my time, but I've never willingly walked away from a baby. Carry on, son.'

Robbie continued. The sun was low and cast long shadows over the ship's cabin. 'We often collected water chestnuts from the banks of the river that passed along the edge of the abbey's estate. The water was cold and clear, running straight off the mountain. Everyone knew the current could be unpredictable – the river could grow high and fast in minutes – but the water chestnuts were a delicacy. My mother used them to treat anxious folk. I liked them roasted and dipped in honey. The nuns loved them too and they loved my mother.

'There were many white witches and apothecaries travelling around Landfelian at the time. It was before some witches went rogue and the rumours began. The nuns and villagers believed one of the good ones had strayed and moved to the bottom of their garden. Until recently, I never thought my mother anything more than kind.' Robbie stopped to drink. 'I was nearly ten the day I followed her down to the river. It was a sultry afternoon and looked ripe for a storm. She put her hand on her hips and said the river was running like a devil, that I was to stay in the shallows and not lose sight of her.'

Robbie rubbed his hands on his knees and closed his eyes as he spoke.

'I didn't listen. I ran ahead, jumped in the water, and swam against the current. As the afternoon wore on, a mist started to crawl downstream and the air became still. I was too occupied to notice right away, until I grew cold and aware that I had lost sight of my mother. I searched that stretch of river and saw her head bobbing up and down as she bent to gather the sweet nuts. Her sleeves were rolled up over her tanned arms and she was humming to herself.

'The mist changed and a dense, cold fog rolled in fast like a wave. Like the one you can see spreading over the kingdom. I waded out of the water. Goose, our dog, stopped digging his hole and began to bark at something I couldn't see. I imagined monsters coming out of the fog and grew afraid, so I whistled for her.'

Robbie smiled. 'The nuns had taught me to whistle a jig around the bonfire when they celebrated spring by taking their habits off and dancing.

'My mother answered. The sound cut through the fog like a hero's blade. She called back to me; told me to stay out of the water and head for the trees. She sounded afraid. Our dog ran into the river and began to growl. I called him back and waited until my feet turned white with cold. A biting wind started up then, racing through the valley.' Robbie paused. 'I didn't know she was struggling ... I didn't want to wait, alone.'

'So, I started to walk along the shallows, calling for her, thinking maybe she was stuck on the other side. She never answered. I called and called and then tripped over Goose. He was petrified. He lay stiff and unnatural in the water. He wouldn't get up. I tried to lift him ... he was cold and heavy. His eyes were open but he didn't blink. He stared, fixed to a point in the river, and I knew there was something happening in the fog. I waded back into the water. Everything had turned so quiet.'

Robbie remembered how he had felt then, as if every frog, bird, and fish were held hostage to the ghostly cloud. He remembered calling out, crying as if he already knew his mother was drowning.

'I swam into the shadow of a horse, a valien.' Robbie stopped.

'A valien, you say,' prompted the pirate. 'Only the king's chosen ride, the valien.'

'I will never forget how it grunted and shifted in the current, shackled by a great many buckles and chains. I had never seen a horse like it, bigger than the king's own, jet black. I heard a whip lash out; it wrapped tight around my shoulders, and the rider lifted me from the water.'

Robbie rubbed his old scars as he remembered the feeling of hanging above the water at the mercy of a man dressed in a leather tunic and a vast fur coat made from what looked like the skins of wolves. He wore a helmet, like a knight, and the visor revealed his eyes.

'I can still see them as clearly as if he was in front of me. He had strange eyes, one like bracken and the other a dim, milky colour. He wore clothes made for the cold.' Robbie remembered his voice; it was restless and full of metal and night. 'He let me hang there, the whip cutting my skin, and he said, "So, you're the one." There was something familiar about him, but I'd never seen him before. And I haven't since.'

'What happened to your mother?' Patrick held his breath.

'I heard her cry out my name, somewhere behind the valien. There were chestnuts floating in the water around me. I struggled against the whip, and it cut deep into my skin. I cried out and the black rider said the strangest thing – he said, "You will never be king.' Robbie paused and whispered to himself, "Just the scarred son of a peasant."

Robbie had forgotten, but as he sat on the old ship, those last words came back to him vividly.

'I pulled hard and the whip cut my hands.'

'Did he fall?'

'I pulled once more and he fell from the valien. We both fell. My arm hurt as I struggled to my feet. I tried to look for my mother. I wanted her to tell me it was time to go home.' Robbie stopped. 'I wanted to hold her. I turned away from the monstrous horse to search for her, and then I went under and it all went black.'

'What happened?'

'My arm had been broken by the whip, where it held me. The nuns found me on the banks.'

Robbie swallowed.

'I was holding my mother's hand. The fog had gone and the river looked calm, as if nothing had happened. I could hear the birds. The nuns were crying. There was a small crowd gathered. My mother was covered in reeds and bindweed. She looked different – her eyes were closed and her body was empty. But she'd found me, pulled me to shore, and she was still holding my hand.'

Robbie stopped talking. He looked out the window and up at Great Scott Point and blinked hard, his face wet with tears.

'She was right next to me.' His voice grew hard and he stopped stroking Victoria's ears. 'Whoever that rider was, he drowned my mother.' Robbie wiped his eyes. 'All these years I've been running from the memory of that day. But the fog is back; it's everywhere I go. That's why I can't leave Landfelian now. The fog and the black rider are linked; they're close. I mean to find him and ...'

'Avenge your mother,' offered the pirate.

'Yes,' Robbie said, looking at him with fierce eyes.

'And your swimming problem?' Patrick stood up and squinted at the sun, then began to gather a few things.

'I have not gone in the water since.'

19

GREAT SCOTT POINT

'Well, we'll soon see about that, laddie!' Patrick took hold of both Robbie's shoulders and pulled him close. 'I'm sorry for what happened to your Ma. Tragic business that. Thank you for telling me your story.' He smiled sincerely, blew his nose into a spotty handkerchief and had a good scratch of his left eye.

. 'I will help, for what it's worth. But beware of revenge, son. Highly overrated and the best way to waste a life.'

'I have been a Man of the Road all my life and never found him. Somewhere in these cold new lands to the south of Landfelian, that's where he hides. Where the fog comes from.'

'You'll have trouble avoiding it, my friend. Darn stuff's everywhere now. I've seen ships full of guards heading south. Looks like they're pilfering bits of the kingdom and a fair few Landfelians, too. Here, have some paella – seven bulbs of garlic in that – it'll do you the world of good, clear the pores.'

Robbie accepted a steaming bowl gratefully. 'Thank you.'

Patrick Dickie rubbed his hands together, took off his apron, and opened the cabin door to let in the early evening light. After they had eaten, he clapped his hands together.

'So, that sad tale is why you can't swim? Well, I'm sorry, son, you'll have to do better than that.'

Robbie carefully put his bowl down before Patrick could say anymore and took a swing at his crooked pirate mouth. Although, after the week he'd had, it was more of a nudge.

Patrick laughed. 'Forgive me.' He held up his hands. 'I don't have the manners to be anything other than blunt.' He returned to his stool and laughed. 'You're headstrong. That's good. Although that was a rubbish punch. Made *you* fall over. No risk of that eye patch now.' The pirate's voice softened. 'Not one muscle of what I've heard is good. It is a terrible thing. You lost your mother, too young, to a shifty knight with a funny eye, a fur coat, and a big horse. But ...' He paused to point at the ocean. 'All that has nothing to do with the water.' He waved dramatically at the view. 'You're blaming the wrong side, son! It's time to dive back into the glorious stuff. You *can* swim.

Life threw you into a pit and you had a nasty shock. The best way to get over a shock is to shock the shock back to where it came from and give it a pirate shout like this, "Arghhhh!".'

The seagulls outside began to yell above the ship. The sun was low in the sky. Robbie stared at the pirate and realised this would be the sum of his help.

'It's time to go swimming.' Patrick Dickie grinned.

Robbie wanted a boat, a paddle, and a sail, not some old rookie's advice. He looked around the squalor. 'You're a pirate king?'

'Fraid so, mate. I've just been on a very long sabbatical from the swash and buckle business. No crusade has drawn me back into the fight until today, when you, a young, grubby Man of the Road turned up with his tale of grief, love, pale-eyed valien riders, and some pain in the backside rogue witch.' Patrick looked around for his belt and cutlass. 'She's been messing up the weather for too long now. Come on, laddie, there's not a moment to lose. It's time to get wet. We leave in three minutes.' He lifted the lid of an ornate lacquer chest and started throwing its contents out. 'I will need my cigars for this journey.'

At the base of the pirate's nut-brown back was a large tattoo. It looked like a map of the coast of Landfelian and the islands and lands beyond. In between two moles were the words, *The Many Plundered Paths of Patrick Dickie, Pirate King.*

If Robbie had wanted proof that this man was the right one, it had just bent over and flashed him.

'What about the …?'

'Swimming lessons?' Patrick pulled his boots on.

'Yes.'

'Well, you're cured.' Patrick threw on his hat, a crimson velvet affair with several greasy orange feathers, and gave Robbie a mad stare. 'Now, quick – eat up!'

Robbie looked at the paella and wondered how he was cured. 'You and Father Peter seem unlikely friends.'

'Old FP and I go way back. He once saved me from being cursed by an ex-girlfriend. A spirited young witch.' He gave Robbie a sly smile. 'Good moussaka, fine eyes, lovely laugh. Too good for the likes of me!' He looked regretful. 'But I shouldn't have hurt her like I did. Luckily, she didn't turn me into a shrimp. Didn't stop her giving away my best waistcoat though, did it?' He laughed and looked meaningfully at Robbie's front.

The pirate began to make his way gingerly over the ship's gangway to the shore. He bowed respectfully to Face, whilst holding his flippers and goggles, and whistled to Robbie to follow him. Great Scott Point and the cliffs blotted out much of the sky above the cove. It was a long way up to the top, along its jutting edge, only to jump off.

'Come, cook! Time waits for no man.' The pirate looked less steady on land. Robbie followed behind and reached out his hand to Face. The great horse snorted softly into it.

'Thank you,' Robbie said, looking into the horse's young, dark eyes. 'I'll do my best, I promise.'

He approached a crag in the cliffs where a spring trickled down. 'This is our path,' the pirate called, pointing to a watery death slide covered in scree.

The two men did not speak much on the climb up, mainly because it was steep and treacherous – and the closer they got to the top of the cliffs, the more scree they encountered. Both of them had other things on their minds.

'Pathway Maintenance don't come up here much. Those brigands should have had this trail marked as hazardous years ago!' Patrick bellowed when he was half way up. 'Slippery as hell. Shepherds have lost many sheep over the edge.'

Robbie climbed on; while his legs fought with the ascent, his mind was elsewhere. More than once he skidded down several feet and had to cling onto rocks with his fingertips, carefully inching his way back up. He was imagining the Well of Loneliness in impressive detail, his thoughts consumed by fog and deep water. Part of his mind tried to crawl away and return to the North Realm, where, only a few weeks ago, he had been happily roasting a bird and re-thatching a barn roof for the nuns. Now look, barely out of the first quarter of his life and he was about to dive off a cliff for a princess. Someone should write a book about this.

The two men continued to climb, pausing every so often to catch their breath. Gulls surfed in the thermals alongside them.

Patrick Dickie glanced back at the young Man of the Road. Nerves flew off the lad like sparks from a damp fire. He would either fly or belly flop into the waiting abyss of fear. Poor sod. Though he looked capable enough. But why he had agreed to involve himself in this mad-cap, half-witted knob of a plan – even if it was for a lady – was a mystery. He must have a death wish – love will do that to you. Not so long ago, Patrick had had a powerful feeling, an itch, a pirate's belief that there was more to come. That something was going to happen – something exciting, something that would unite both land and sea, wake everybody up like a full orchestra playing the finale of Stravinsky's *Firebird*. Something that would pose an even bigger challenge to Landfelians and Sea Dwellers than ever before. Although this hunch had said nothing about a non-swimming Man of the Road jumping to his death for some princess.

The pirate king decided to light a cigar when they reached Great Scott Point, sweating from the exertion. Alberta flew above both men like a nagging wife, squawking when they slowed down to catch their breath.

'Go and wag your feathers at someone else, you old crow! Check the tide and wait for us at the end of the point.' The pirate looked down at the tiny cove, his ship, the jagged coastline, and the horizon beyond. The valien was still there, watching the boy. 'Ah, it's turning into a beautiful evening for you, Robbie Wylde.'

Robbie didn't answer.

'A pink evening. All we need is a couple of steaks, a good fire, and someone else's treasure …' He laughed huskily.

'It's a crying shame you're in a hurry to jump. We could have shared a smoke and some of the finest peaty.'

'I thought a pirate's drink was rum?' Robbie would have been grateful for some at that moment.

'Can't stand the stuff,' Patrick spat.

Robbie was close behind and not much fitter. He had the right muscles, they were just hidden under a soft surface of good living. He crawled over the edge and lay upon the sheep-nibbled smooth expanse of grass for a moment to relieve his lungs. The sun had not yet fallen into the sea, and he intended to make the most of every last second of his time on Landfelian.

Deciding to ignore Father Peter's advice, he asked, 'When did you last see the mermaiden Empress Anook Elkhorn?' He thought it was the pirate's turn to tell a story.

'That's not your business, son.' Patrick looked sharply at Robbie for a long moment and said nothing more. Alberta returned and squawked loudly at him. 'Alright, you bossy old bird.' Then he sighed. 'I suppose it is my turn to tell a story.' He smiled painfully at the horizon and began.

'Anook. That comet. Lovely she was, and for a fleeting season, we watched the same sunrise. We parted after a game of cards and a lovely fondue, seven years, nine days, three hours, and one high tide ago.' He gave Robbie a faint smile and shrugged. 'Or thereabouts. I'll tell you the rest before you hit the deck.' Patrick Dickie knew every second of every day he had spent with and without the mermaiden. He looked ahead at the narrow strip of land that pointed over the water like an outstretched finger. 'There it is! Great Scott Point. Ready for a short walk, you mad son of a nun?'

He turned around to find Robbie on his hands and knees retching.

Patrick sat down next to him and patted his back gently. 'No rush.' He took a puff on his cigar and admired the view. 'Whenever you're ready.' He took out his spyglass and looked through it at the area of water where their villages floated. 'Let me tell you something of the Sea Dwellers.'

Jutting out from the mainland into the sky was a thin slice of stone. It was suspended over the sea like a very large, rocky nail file, or pirate's plank. Whichever way you looked at it, it was not inviting. It was not wide enough for two men to walk comfortably to the end without feeling insecure about the strength of their friendship. It was almost the length of a pier and not at all as entertaining. Supporting it were a series of magnificent arches formed from chalky cliffs hollowed and shaped by the wind and sea.

Robbie heard the sea crashing against them hundreds of feet below. He purposefully did not look down. But if he had he would have seen Red's valien watching him and waiting with bright eyes. Beyond the point, there was a breathtaking, blowsy sky. Playful clouds jumped over their heads in a race north. Any fog seemed to be mostly focused on the south, over the Well of Loneliness.

He was leaving Landfelian. He had dreamt of this moment since he was orphaned, though in his dream, Robbie did not swim away. He flew in comfort in a Cloudbuster or sailed on a great ship, bound to seek his fortune, escaping the fog and the nightmares, having avenged his mother.

The pirate's voice drew him back to the present. 'You just walk to the end and jump. It's quite a ride.' He whistled. 'Wake up those sea dwellers, young Robbie!'

'Is there no other way?' Robbie looked around him. Only a desperate person asks such a question now.

'If you were to enter their blue kingdom by boat, the sea gypsies would most likely capsize you and feed you feet-first to Big Squid. This way, you arrive on a more level playing field. It's tradition for Landfelians and people of the sea to meet here at this time on a Sunday.' Patrick began to walk towards the point. 'I do it every so often to keep me on my points, sweat the liquor out. Keep the muscles firm and the balls in place. You end up quite a way out. But don't panic. Let the current take you. It will spit you out topside soon enough. Between the Sea of Trees and the White Ocean is where you will find their kingdom. That's when you have to start ...'

'Swimming.' Robbie gulped back a lump that could well have been his stomach.

'You've got it, my man. Those watery nymphs will find you soon enough!' Patrick puffed on his cigar and blew the smoke into the wind. 'It's good to be alive, isn't it?'

A gust nudged the men from behind. The pirate could see Robbie was faltering, and who could blame him? If he got through the shock of the fall, the wedgie he'd get on impact could change his ability to sing bass forever.

'Best get on with it. Too much thinking opens the portholes to doubt.' Patrick held out his hand to pull him up. 'Don't want to keep the lady waiting.'

The sun had only half set, and Robbie intended to cling to the extra minutes like a child clings to Christmas. 'I still have some time.'

It was horribly windy, and the ridge they were walking along began to narrow. Robbie looked down and froze.

'If it's all the same to you, I'm going to crawl.' He got down on his hands and knees and began to inch further along the point like an animal. Robbie trusted crawling. If it was good enough for the bearded mountain goat, it was good enough for him.

A deep orange sun began to sink in to the calm, oblivious horizon.

'Will you look at that?' Patrick whistled. He appeared unaffected by the yawning height, walking with a swagger along the nail file of cliff. 'Never get tired of a sunset, best part of the job.' He sat down, swinging his legs over the ledge of Great Scott Point, and waited for Robbie to catch up.

Robbie stared at the blot of fog miles away and south from where they stood. 'That's where she is, under there, in that black water. That's where I've got to go.'

'You've got that right, mate. Some bad business being transacted over that patch – not a pirate's doing, though. Greedy swaggers we are, granted, but we don't upset the balance

370

of nature. Weather's been tampered with by a witch that's got too big for her prow is my guess. Been going on a while.'

'Her name is Selina Carnal.'

'Thought as much.' Patrick wrinkled his eyes. 'Now fancies herself a sorceress. King Felian banished her, you know, long ago. Got to hand it to the broad, she's nothing but dedicated to this grudge.'

Alberta landed on the pirate's head and picked at a few stray bits of food stuck there. Robbie watched the pirate swing his legs either side of the plank as it if were a seesaw, unfazed by the drop below and the buffeting winds.

'Relax, boyo, and have a smoke with me.' He passed the cigar across. 'Remember, you are alive and beating. No witch's magic is a match for that.'

Robbie closed his eyes and dangling his legs off the point like the pirate, he tried to imagine he was sitting on his horse and failed. 'I think I'll keep my hands on the ground,' he said, gripping the rough ledge rather than taking the cigar.

'Fair enough, lad. You do whatever makes you feel comfortable. Not got a head for heights, I see.'

'Not this height, no.' Robbie looked across at Patrick and swallowed. 'I could do with a distraction.'

'A mermaiden story?' The pirate flinched ever so slightly. 'That's what you're after, isn't it?'

'Yes.'

'You've got minutes left on this rock. Why do you want to hear about my wrecked heart?'

'I'm pain-delaying, isn't it o-o-o-obvious?' Robbie stuttered. 'And if you won't tell me how to s-s-swim ...'

Perhaps because the odds of Robbie flopping on his mission were high, and perhaps because he may not have another visitor for months, Patrick Dickie did something he had not done since his exile. He told the story of his lost love.

'Alright. Here we go, the potted crab version.' The pirate looked at what was left of the sun. 'The White Ocean was bewitched. Waves were reaching halfway up this cliff. Felt like the ground below was shifting. The *Kon Tiki* was in trouble – big trouble. The force of the waves bullied my ship's vulnerable parts until they began to snap off. We were stuck in the middle of a superstorm like a cork in a privy, going around and around, pulled into the start of that well you'll be seeing later. She was trapped in the spinning water, close to sinking, minutes away from being sucked onto the rocks piercing the surface.

'I decided to ask the sea dwellers for help. My crew were as much use to me then as a plate of linguine, throwing up over everything and bellowing that the sea was full of man-eating sirens. But as soon as I'd dived off the portside, I knew I had made a mistake, that I had royally screwed up.'

'How?'

'Because I still had my boots on and my scabbard.'

Robbie quickly began to untie his boots. He laced them together and tied them to his bag. The bag was tied around his neck and waist.

'I was also holding a bottle of wine. Been in the middle

of dinner, a few goblets down, right before the storm hit. I decided it would be a good idea to arrive with a shiny gift before pleading with the mermaidens. So I was wearing a few jazzy trinkets as I sank all the way to the bottom. Buggered up my hearing a bit.' Patrick stuck a finger in one ear and waggled it about. 'I'm sure there's still a small crab in there somewhere.'

'Did they help you?'

'Of course not! A young fool with a sword and his boots on, in one of the most dangerous parts of the ocean? Except, I was lucky. There was one mermaiden too curious for her own kind swimming away from her floating home that night, and she smelt me; I stank of garlic and wine. Bless that young woman's sixth sense. She swam towards me, putting herself at risk, and looked ready to unleash hell. So, I apologised, and the slippery fox found it funny. I was drowning, barely a breath left in me, and yet I was saying sorry to some coral, a few sea slugs, and a langoustine for disturbing their peace. She watched me with the most astonishing pair of eyes I've ever seen. Violet they were. They looked straight at the heart of me. I said the first thing that came to mind; not the most intelligent, but I was a delirious, dying pirate by then.'

'What did you say?'

'"Dance with me." Then I realised you can't ask a question underwater and that I was a drunken idiot. A woman will do that to you.' He gave Robbie a pointed look.

'What happened?'

'I blacked out for a few minutes. Got kissed by the

mermaiden and lived a little longer. She gave me airgrass. It creates a bubble inside your throat and nose, round your blowholes so that you can breathe as easily as them.' His eyes shone. 'The *Kon Tiki* was saved, the storm eased, and the rest is a lot of very enjoyable backstroking. I'll tell you about it when you return. We'll barbecue some bass and get properly ruined.'

'What's it like, below the surface?' Robbie stole a look at the foamy blue swell hundreds of feet below.

'Beautiful. You'll see ... quiet.' His eyes shone. 'So quiet and full of grace, life, and colour ... There are mountains bigger than Landfelian and great valleys of rainbow coral, herds of sea horses, luminescent plankton.'

The sky darkened over them. Robbie tried to smile and managed half a nervous grin as he looked at where the sun was. It was time.

'Put these sea goggles on when you get down there. No point until then; they'll snap off and make your eyeballs explode if you jump with them on. The Sea Dwellers love treasure. You got anything gold and twinkly?' Robbie only had Maggie's bit of shell, Father Peter's sunbrella, and the Herald's baton. He now wished he had a crown of diamonds.

'After I jump, w-w-waa-wh-at do I d-d-do then?' The stutter had flown back and kindly landed on the Man of the Road. 'I don't have anything t-t-twinkly!'

'Swim until you can't see land. Look through here, see. The village, the rafts, this is their home, where they trade.' Patrick handed Robbie his spyglass. 'They'll find you, don't worry about that. Mermaidens can't resist the smell of a land dweller.' Patrick gestured to Father Peter's sunbrella. 'And this is gold to them. All you have to do is open it.'

Alberta was hovering near Robbie's head. He had never wanted to be an albatross more.

'Pirate Dickie –'

'Call me Patrick or Dick or I'll be arrested.'

'H-h-how did you know th-hat you weren't g-g-going to die?'

'When I saw that watery lady, I didn't want to.' He smiled sadly. 'Not without a second date.'

Robbie was A-grade, fifth gear, double honours, full-throttle panicking now. 'How can I be sure the m-mermaidens will find me?'

'You can't. But they like dusk and a little intrigue. And you have that in spades, my man.' Patrick smiled kindly at Robbie, who was standing up on shaking legs and reaching out for a hand to steady him, his eyes terrified. 'Now listen to me. No one knows anything about anything, so you might as well jump.'

'Mmm ...' Robbie faltered and forced himself to look ahead at the blue horizon.

Patrick pointed straight up suddenly. 'WHAT IN THE WORLD CAN THAT BE?'

'What?'

Robbie looked up, felt a firm hand push him forward, and then he saw the sea below him. He tipped towards it and glimpsed a forgiving smile as he fell off the end of Great Scott Point.

'I wasn't ready!' Closing his eyes, Robbie felt his stomach lurch towards deep water. 'Ohhh blowww!'

'I never asked you her name,' the pirate shouted back. 'The girl!'

'Re-e-e-e-h-h-d Feliaaaaaaaaaan. Yooooooou fish loving …!' Robbie yelled.

'Point your toes, man!'

It was not a pretty dive. It was all wrong. It was a flurry of arms and legs. Robbie did not have time to finish insulting the pirate or get in a good dart-like position, if we're talking pilates.

Alberta squawked. Face whinnied in delight. Patrick closed his eyes and groaned, but then Robbie straightened out like a surprised arrow, just in time. Gravity helped.

He shot into the foaming swell below and surprised the barnacles clean off their callused perches. It was more of a *SHHLOPP* than a *SPLASH,* but at least it wasn't a *SLAP.*

He remembered to take a breath and hold on tight to everything he had, even his boots.

Once, you too had wings.

Who had told him that? Whoever it was had been mistaken. The water hit every part of him hard.

He heard Patrick shouting excitedly hundreds of feet above, just before the sea swallowed him like a pip. Underwater, all was quiet and dark, and he began to sink.

There was nothing to grasp. Robbie began to panic. What was the golden rule about swimming? He opened his eyes and felt his breath run out if his nose. Kick! That was it. He began to kick, kick, kick and wave his arms frantically until the surface grew close again and he heard someone yelling.

Far above him, the pirate took a puff of his cigar, punched the air, and shouted, 'You didn't tell me you were rescuing THE princess! I met that young sprite once – too good to lose. Only one left. You go and get her back!'

Robbie came spluttering into the evening. He felt the cool air on his face. 'YOU PUSHED ME!'

'I CAN'T HEAR YOU.'

Robbie flailed around in the water. Sea water. Not small water, not like a mountain spring, but big, limitless, far-reaching water. He began to talk to himself; there was no one else and he was frightened.

'How did this happen? The last time I got wet like this there was a black horse, fog, and drowning. Oh God. WHAT IS THAT ON MY TOE?'

He had to swim, he remembered. He had to try.

Robbie tried. But there was that problem of having nothing to grip again, so he gripped the water and ended up paddling upright.

Patrick Dickie watched with his head in his hands. 'What's he doing, Alberta? He looks like a constipated duck down there. Go help him' Alberta squawked softly and flew down towards the surface to jolly Robbie along a bit.

Robbie splashed along. 'South, I have to head south.'

South. He spun elegantly around in a circle.

Which way was south? How could he tell when he was too busy drowning? He turned towards Landfelian, kicking madly, and remembered how the pirate's cove hugged the south-west coast. The faraway summits of the Mistys rose ahead of him to his left – that was south; he would swim towards them. That was where the fog was. Alberta appeared in front of him again and mewed gently until Robbie began to swim in her direction. 'I'm coming.'

He struggled to put the sea goggles on and stay above the bullish waves. The land he'd left behind was shrinking. His home was shrinking. What did that mean? The current had him. The sea was cold – not warm or refreshing.

'This is hell,' he told Alberta. He was in hell.

'The pushing, deceiving, garlic-chewing –' Robbie ranted. 'That pirate ...'

It was not long at all before he was taken into the arms of a big swell.

Robbie was sucked down by the undertow in one guttering breath. He never got to finish his tirade against the pirate, which the gods and goddesses watching were most upset about. Never had an evening been so entertaining – they were on the edge of their clouds, passing around the olives, watching every ball-busting, hero-in-the-making, romantic second. They were placing bets – how long would this young Man of the Road last?

The sea pulled him under. The goggles pressed into his eyelids. One of his lungs ached and the other was beginning to burn.

The wave released Robbie, and he shot up to the surface like a sponge, along with two clicking dolphins. Several small fish were spat into the air too, where they became food to Alberta, who was staying close. These small fish cursed their fate as the young Man of the Road cursed his.

'HELPPPPP MEEEEEEEEE!' he whimpered and began to struggle again with the swimming problem. The albatross mewed at him, but without rope or a boat, she was not helping. Although it was a comfort to hear and see her above him.

The pirate's voice carried faintly out to him on the wind. 'KICK, LAD, KICK! WHAT ARE YOU WAITING FOR?'

A wave smacked him in the face, and he swallowed a mouthful of sea. Robbie shouted, 'ARGHHHHHH!' like a pirate.

'That's the spirit!'

It was then, finally, he showed everyone swimming. It wasn't doggy paddle, and it certainly wasn't crawl; it was closer to butterfly, but with more violence and splashing. It was hard going with a sunbrella and a whip and an old bit of shell tied in an awkward bundle against him. Robbie also had a lot of hair, and he was dressed for a hike. Anyone who has fallen in a swimming pool fully clothed will understand how heavy this made his legs feel.

But the Man of the Road kept going until he could not feel his legs. His shoulder ached, and his hands had frozen into claws. The fish felt sorry for him; he was a real beginner. His technique needed a lot of work, but he was strong and seemed determined enough. He followed Alberta, who glided quietly in front of him and swam towards the dark, foggy patch in the White Ocean; the part that looked terrifying.

Close to an hour later, Robbie was still at it, and he was thinking, *If she doesn't look pleased to see me, she can forget about the mooncakes and all future rescues are off.*

Robbie thought only of Red while he tried to swim towards the black water. Except when he got cramp – then he thought about what he could push Patrick Dickie off, should he return alive. What exactly did the pirate mean by, 'swim until you can't see land'? Go out of sight of shore? Or did it mean the land was going to disappear because very soon it was going to get dark? Were the sea dwellers going to escort him under? Where in hell's name were they?

Then it all happened at once. It got very dark – so dark Robbie could no longer see Landfelian. Night fell and he sank with no warning, without a fuss or a big scene. Shock and adrenalin had buoyed him so far, but then the sea took him. His kicking slowed to a standstill. Taking one ragged breath of night air, Robbie disappeared from sight. As he sank, he caught the glimmer of lanterns ahead where the sea dwellers' floating village lay.

It was dark and moonless in the watery kingdom below,

although infinite and strangely calm. It could have been the beginning or the end, Robbie thought as he began to run out of breath.

Father Peter was travelling over the Plain of Jars when Marmadou informed the passengers in the Cloudbuster with several squeaks and some frantic flapping, which were translated to, 'He's gone under. He's in the lap of the sea dwellers now.'

'We must hope he fights.' The king's eyes were bright under the light of their lantern. 'He will fight.'

Father Peter closed his eyes and said, 'They must find him first.'

Billy True was sitting in the Cloudbuster's basket, wrapped in a yook wool blanket that the king had given him for the journey. He watched the two men pass a spyglass between them, muttering seriously and looking out to sea. He unpacked his bag to find a vast tomato and cheese sandwich, warm gingerbread, and a note.

> *If you fall out of that turd-powered basket, I will*
> *put that king on a spit and roast him. Finish your*
> *tea and don't climb up anything without a rope.*
> *I love you, my boy. Come back to us.*
> *Mam.*

Billy swallowed and looked at the sky. He felt on his way to greatness. This was a true adventure. By special request of the king, his skills had been summoned, to help rescue his friend, the princess, from somewhere dark and foggy. He looked below as the Cloudbuster sailed over a snow-covered castle.

'Celador,' he whispered.

He had never imagined a place more majestic; even choked by fog it stood out like a cavalier in a room of cardinals, tall, pale, and true before the great range of South Realm mountains. Billy had never thought he would see the mighty castle of the south from such a height. Inside, someone had begun to light the fires. Orange flickers illuminated the windows and smoke plumed out from the biggest chimney. *The castle is alive again*, he thought.

'Do we have enough fuel?' asked the king.

'There isn't time to collect any more from Giant Country,' answered Father Peter.

'Then we need to find a good southerly wind,' the king answered.

The sky was still as snow. 'We have enough to keep us sailing until morning.'

The king nodded, and his hands gripped the edge of the basket. 'That's all we need.'

Billy looked up at the king and his voice faltered as he asked, 'We will be coming back, won't we, Your Highness?'

He smiled. 'Oh, I expect so Billy. I expect so.'

Father Peter said nothing and directed his sails into the fog. They sailed silently south.

20

THE SEA DWELLERS

Robbie sank slowly – so slowly that if he had not been one hundred per cent drowning, he would have been embarrassed. The water held him in its grasp and took a good look before letting him continue. Through the goggles he saw small bubbles of air leaving his body – bubbles of life.

So long, he thought.

It was a curious thing, probably dying. Robbie did not panic; he was too exhausted. He felt his heartbeat slow down, his muscles relax, and his fists unclench – and that was when the sunbrella dropped out of his bag. *Oh crabs,* he thought. *I might need that later.*

He closed his eyes, held between life and oblivion in the space where Death and the soul decide. They were currently having a heated discussion in a nice white space. If there was a good time to hear the voice of one of the more inspiring gods, it was now.

Robbie heard Father Peter instead. *'The last test of any hero, the work for which all other work is but preparation, is this: never, ever despair.'*

Whether the sunbrella had meant to land on Winona's head, we will never know. But it shot through the dark water and prodded the mermaiden's inky hair before landing in the seabed beside her. Upright and ready for use.

'Ouch!' She rubbed her head and looked around her.

Winona had been quietly reading a copy of King Felian's banned basket-weaving book when the sunbrella landed on her head.

She sighed and shouted, 'Thorr, leave me alone!'

Thorr was a young sea gypsy who would not take no for an answer. When he wasn't wrestling with squids, he was pulling bits of prow and hull out from their sunken graves and parading around Winona bare-chested, grunting heavily. *Typical Sea Gypsy behaviour*, she thought, always interrupting her meditation time.

But as she looked around, Winona saw that it was not Thorr. It was an umbrella. An umbrella a very, very long way from Landfelian. The mermaiden looked at it in wonder. She had just finished reading a chapter in which several parasols were used during a picnic, to great effect. She blushed and looked up towards the surface cautiously. It would not be long before the corpse followed. They always sank slower than their treasures.

Sure enough, Robbie landed quietly next to her on a rock, and she screamed, 'Great scallop!'

This corpse was quicker than most. Winona stared at the body of a young Landfelian man. He had a lot of hair. At fourteen, the opposite sex held a morbid fascination to Winona – especially those from Landfelian, because they were banned. Although that did not stop her coming every Sunday, to this rock, at dusk, where land dwellers and her people used to meet in case one arrived. She swam around him and looked at the boots tied around his neck with interest. Winona loved land dweller shoes. She kept a collection on her raft. She had a brogue, an oxford, and seven others, although there was not one matching pair. Disappointed there was nothing shiny attached to this land-lover, she spoke to him. 'How dull you are.'

She noted his bag. Maybe there was something interesting in there? He did not look like a pirate; too sober. He did not look like a sailor, either, although he had a sun-stroked face. The corpse did not move, although there was the look of a fight on his face. He was almost handsome compared to the usual wrecks that fell from their ships reeking of rum, scurvy, and desperation.

She felt his heart for any flick of movement, book in her other hand, ready to knock the man into the next life if he became the bad side of alive. You never knew with land dwellers.

His heart boomed faintly. She thought he must be a deep-sea fisherman, looking at the scars on his hands, although those tuna seekers had not been spotted in these parts for years.

Winona looked at the man's mouth, swam closer, and sniffed. Garlic. She sniffed again. Lots of garlic, seven bulbs. By the smell of him, this man had dined with pirates only a few hours ago. There was only one that made paella that strong. 'The Pirate King,' she whispered, and a smile lit up her impish face.

The old bit of shell around Robbie's neck chose that moment to float out, and the young mermaiden whistled.

'Mother's mirror,' she looked at his face. 'What's your story then, sailor?' Winona glanced around her before saying, 'Don't move,' loudly into Robbie's ear. She put her head next to his heart for a moment. 'And you will live a while longer.'

The mermaiden could rest assured that Robbie had no plans to go anywhere. But his heart was slowing down, wondering where all the oxygen had gone. Winona searched around her. There was a small, acid-green tuft of airgrass growing a few feet away between some coral. It would be just enough.

She picked it carefully and swam back to the Landfelian. Winona had always hoped that one day someone vaguely interesting would nearly drown on her watch. Not long before the Great Vanishing, when the queen of Landfelian had disappeared, the Sea of Trees had always been a busy thoroughfare of merchants and travellers. Now she was lucky if she saw so much as a piece of driftwood. She gave Robbie a searching look, opened his mouth, and quickly popped in the airgrass, shouting in his ear as delicately as she could, 'Airgrass.

Chew it or you'll die.'

The mermaiden left him there, and with a swish of inky hair and a kick of supple legs, she sped through the water. Winona had inherited her mother's speed and her father's mouth, and she could swim as fast as a valien could gallop at full pelt. It was fun that way, creating a wave behind her through the darkness.

Speeding was not permitted after sunset, although no one cared too much about the rules of the sea anymore. The elders were not watching their young, they were monitoring the creeping black water in the south and the crumbling coral beds. Above the surface, shards of strange fog kept Landfelian and its surrounding waters under a hopeless spell. Many sea dwellers were busy repairing their floating villages so that they could leave the bewitched sea and escape the fog.

When Winona reached the wreck, her mother was trying to placate a group of nervous, war-mongering sea gypsies. They were arguing. Winona watched the empress surrounded by the embittered faces of the men gathered around a great map. Her mother was looking pensive. Several clan leaders kept returning to the surface to check their rafts, their families, and to take in more air.

'It's spread even further,' the sea gypsy known to all as Huron gestured impatiently to the map, slowly chewing on airgrass.

'We must leave this place, Empress, head further out, far from Landfelian. Or return to the Spice Islands.'

'We will do no such thing.' Her mother's voice remained firm. 'This is our home. We must stand up to this sorcery and find its source. I will not abandon Landfelian. We will fight with them.'

'With whom? Where is their king now?'

'Mother?'

'Not now, Winona. We will stand our ground. Before we leave anywhere, I will seek an audience with King Felian and his heroes. They too are suffering.'

'Goodluck finding them,' Huron muttered and swam slowly back up to the surface aided by a thick, taut rope. 'We leave tomorrow.'

The other Sea Dwellers looked dissatisfied. 'When has Landfelian ever done anything to help us? Nothing can live under the fog for long. Our rafts are almost ready. We will be moving away as soon as the housing vessels are complete.'

'Mother?' Winona repeated, swimming closer to the group.

The empress held up her hand to silence her daughter. 'Gaeon, we must fight, not run.'

'King Felian and his men are lost,' the sea gypsy called Gaeon spoke with bitterness.

Winona took a deep breath and swam into the centre of the group. 'Someone has come. A young Man of the Road, and he has your mirror,' she said clearly. There was a stunned silence.

The empress dropped the bit of sponge she had been

fiddling with and looked at her daughter with wide eyes. 'Take me to him.'

Robbie was dreaming. In his dream, he was chewing some old bit of grass and Red was there, telling him not to stop. 'Keep chewing,' she was saying. 'Whatever you do, don't stop.'

Something brushed over his knees and touched his back. He felt fingers trace over the scar on his neck. Then his thigh was roughly squeezed. He opened his eyes.

'I could smell that pirate's paella all the way from Great Scott Point. What have you got to say for yourself, land dweller?' A bright, strong voice demanded his attention. 'And where did you get this?' The sea empress held the shell up to Robbie's confused face. 'My mirror.'

Within it he saw a man in sea goggles tied to a mast, chewing. Chewing? What was he chewing for? Whatever it was, it gave off a gas and there was a pale bubble shifting and shimmering in front of him.

Through it there was a woman, looking fiercely at him.

Some are silenced by great beauty – a stand-up-and-listen beauty, the sort that makes everything water a little bit.

The woman who floated before him was a silencer. A commander of attention. With one indigo look, she took Robbie's tongue and its ability to do anything useful. She was a mermaiden, of that there was no doubt. This was the woman Patrick had nearly drowned for. He was certain this was the Sea Empress, Anook. An impressive pendant of giant black pearls hung around her neck.

A young girl swam next to her, staying close. She had a very familiar mouth and whispered kindly, 'Keep chewing, land dweller.'

Robbie nodded and continued to with the strange, rubbery substance in his mouth. The delicate bubble around his head remained; it seemed to be keeping him from drowning.

'If you want to live, pirate, you will answer me. You have no rights here.' The sea empress raised her hand, and in it Robbie saw a small spear made from a sea-horn shell. The area around her was lit up by a cloud of tiny glowing blue plankton.

She was outstandingly beautiful when angry. In full warrior mode, Anook was devastating. For a woman in her middle age, the sea empress could turn the head clean off a man. Although this was part of their power, the mesmerising spell of the water folk.

Robbie tried to find some words and gather himself. He was surprised, despite all rumours to the contrary, that there were no fins or gills attached to her. The mermaiden had legs, feet, and everything else beneath some sort of slippery garment. Was it seaweed? It was the colour of autumn. Threads of misshapen gems shone like tears around her wrists.

Robbie looked again at the younger mermaiden. She had the same blue-black hair, mouth, and brown eyes of Patrick Dickie.

The empress demanded his answer again and impatiently batted away a hovering seahorse.

Robbie was worried about answering. He was worried about opening his mouth. His life appeared to be protected by gas expelled from the grassy stuff he was chewing that tasted of the sea.

He looked apologetically at the empress. Her deep fox-coloured hair swirled around an oval face. Her flashing eyes were framed by arched, dark eyebrows. She had a curling mouth and nostrils that flared from a noble nose.

Then she slapped him, and Robbie suddenly remembered something sweeter. It was a sound. Red laughing next to him on the roof of the boathouse. He began to choke.

Sea gypsies gathered around him with wary eyes. Some held spears.

'Take this man for some electric shock therapy,' ordered the empress. 'A few hours with the eels will loosen his tongue.'

The empress' daughter stood between Robbie and the sea gypsies approaching him. 'No, Mother. He has the shell,' said Winona. 'I think he has come here for our help.'

The empress turned to her daughter and narrowed her eyes. 'Do as I say.'

Robbie had to say something. He had heard about electric eels. You don't put them into a seafood bisque – one tentacle will light you up like a flare and stop your heart.

'Wait!' He could speak! His ears popped. The substance in his mouth acted like a wall, keeping the water out and the air in. 'What is this grass I'm chewing?'

A small crowd now surrounded Robbie and the

empress. They looked quite surprised by this opening question.

'Airgrass. It's keeping you alive. It will run out soon.' Anook held her daughter back. 'If you answer our questions, we will consider giving you more. What do you want with us? Who are you? Why have you come?'

Robbie faltered, 'I'm a cook.' A frying pan Will must have packed floated out of his bag and sunk in the space between them. His stomach rumbled loudly.

There was an uncomfortable pause. A few mermaidens near the empress gasped. They too had read the king's book and found almost anything from Landfelian exciting.

Robbie realised how threatening he might sound, so quickly added: 'I have never cooked anything that didn't look ready to die.' Water began to trickle into his left nostril. 'Mostly potatoes and eggs. Very little fish.' The protective bubble was getting smaller, and he coughed.

Someone was laughing. If he was dying, he didn't want to be laughed at.

It was the empress.

He stared at the mermaiden in amazement, and so did everyone else. She leaned against the mast to which Robbie was tied to support herself and sighed. 'A cook! Oh, that's good!' She wiped her eyes, which seemed a bit pointless to Robbie, being underwater and all. 'Have you come to whip us up a little clam risotto?'

Anook glided closer until she was level with his face and near enough to hold it between her long, soft hands. Her skin

392

looked blue under the bright lights of the plankton. A smile of unexpected kindness spread to her eyes.

'So, you're the one. I wondered if you would come.' She held out her hand and offered Robbie a tuft of bright green fronds.

'How do you know?' Robbie spluttered as water seeped into his mouth and down to his lungs.

'We heard the witch had taken the young heir into the Well of Loneliness. She's after the king of Landfelian, not a cook.'

'Here.' The grassy substance was pushed into this mouth.

'We hoped they would send someone to defeat her. I was not expecting a Man of the Road.' Anook had a deep laugh. 'Still, you have a strong flame inside you. Welcome to the kingdom of the sea dwellers. What is your name?'

'Robbie Wylde.'

'A cook, indeed? You are a faith leaper, a hero, and something that has not quite settled.' She looked at his scar, tucked her hair behind her ears, and it floated slowly out again. Brandishing the frying pan, she said, 'Although I'm sure you are very talented with this ... weapon, your modesty nearly got you killed. You have the scars of the winged across your shoulders.'

Robbie looked confused. The only scars he had were from the whip when he was a boy and burns from cooking. 'How do you know about the witch?'

Anook looked afraid for a fraction of a second. 'There are many creatures that live in this kingdom. You'd have to be blind not to notice the changes.' She smiled. 'Patrick must have liked you. He never used to share his paella with anyone but me.'

Robbie tried speaking again. 'I have to reach the princess.'

'And you will,' replied the empress. She sounded sure.

Winona gazed at the young Landfelian and then at her mother. She wanted to know what he did with the frying pan, but there would be no asking now. He had come for the Landfelian girl and nothing else. Being fourteen was so dull. She longed for her own adventure.

Robbie was untied and guided to a place that resembled a shipwreck graveyard. He took a moment to look at his surroundings. Anook took his hand and swam next to him. The shadow of a beautiful clipper lay ahead, sunk into the seabed, and a collection of ladders, ropes, and structures attached to its mast lead up to the surface. Tuba and trumpet flowers grew around the ruined hull.

The empress watched him. 'Do you like our hidden kingdom? I was thinking of getting a new tapestry for the captain's table, extending the poop deck.' She smiled. 'It needs modernising. The last ship to sink was seven years ago, and there has been nothing to build with since.'

She gave him a dry smile. He could see a pirate's glint in those astonishing eyes.

'You live here.' Robbie looked around.

'We spend more time below since the fog descended, although if you follow the ropes to the surface, there is a floating city of woven houseboats maintained by the sea gypsies – our armada should we need to fight or move quickly.'

'It's remarkable,' Robbie told her honestly. 'I had no idea, such craftsmanship. There are so many of you.' He looked around at the curious figures watching them.

'Over the years, our place here grew.' Anook gestured around her. 'We all came from the water, in the beginning.'

In every shadow, something glinted and sparked off another – gold and crystal, goblets and chandeliers. These reflections lit up the wreck. A secret kingdom on the seabed, forged from sunken ships taken apart and reclaimed by coral and the sea dwellers' carpentry skills. The whole area was as big as the old citadel of Alba, stretching above and below the surface of the sea.

'Translucent fish, plankton, and coral provide us with lights at night,' she explained.

A little shoal of white and silver fish moved between them and hovered above a large table.

'You have no sun.'

'That depends.' The empress held up Father Peter's sunbrella. 'Many treasures find their way here. There is still plenty of sunshine to be found on the surface, as long as we navigate the fog with care.' Anook looked grave. 'We have lost a few young ones too curious to see what hides in the dark waters.' She looked haunted.

'How far are we from the Well of Loneliness?'

The lights faltered around them at the mention of the

Well, and several mermaidens darted away in a fright.

'Please do not talk of such places here,' the empress whispered.

'I need your help reaching the trenches that tunnel through the Ridge of Shadows to the Well. We think it is the only passage the witch won't have guarded.'

'Could you leave me and the Landfelian for a moment?' Anook looked at the small group that had gathered around them. When they were alone, she said nervously. 'Come, I must show you something.'

She took him inside the largest wreck, where a large wax-paper map was nailed to the wall.

'You will have trouble finding a guide.' Her hands trembled as she showed him. 'See this water here? It is bewitched, all around the Ridge of Shadows. It has grown cold and black. All that surrounds that Well is dead to us, and the black water is spreading. We have lost young there – swept away by the water's force. It circles the Ridge of Shadows like a storm. Only the strongest of swimmers can get through and return alive. I will not risk any more lives.'

'I will take him.' Winona appeared out of the gloom. 'Please, Mother, I'm one of the fastest …'

'You will do no such thing.' Anook gave her daughter a firm look, and the young mermaiden grew quiet. 'You are needed here. Return to the village with this message for Lord Huron.' She looked at Robbie. 'Secure the boats for a storm and be ready to fight. We will not flee our home, we stand by Landfelian.'

Winona nodded and said nothing. She swam slowly towards the surface, aided by one of the many linking ropes.

'Too curious, like her father.' The empress smiled. 'She'll be floating around for days when you leave. It's been very slow down here. No ships to spy on or merchants to haggle with, just a lot of foggy days. Your arrival will have fuelled her imagination for months to come. Do you have children?'

Robbie watched her leave. 'No, I don't have a family.'

'You're young.' The empress shook her head. 'I was young once. It's the fog, it's getting to us all. Nothing is growing as it should, everything feels brittle, the vibrancy of the seabed is dying.'

Time was marching on, and Robbie was aware of a melancholy that surrounded this place. He wanted to find dry land, even if it was bewitched. He wanted to stop chewing grass and to feel one step closer to Red Felian. 'I don't have long.'

'I know.' She sounded sad. 'The good ones always leave.' She studied him and raised an eyebrow. 'Do you love this girl?'

Robbie looked at his hands. 'She's the Princess of Landfelian.'

Anook smiled. 'That is not what I asked.' She made a good meal out of fastening a dagger to her leg and doing something severe with her hair. 'Is that why you have come all this way and risked your life, to save the heir?'

Robbie looked at the faint traces of underwater

mountains on the wax map. 'No,' he said quietly. 'She's ... a friend. And she's all I think about.'

The empress took his hand. 'Come, I will show you the way.'

They left the cabin unseen and swam away from the wreck. Robbie held on tight to the empress' hand as a current travelling south carried them over the faint lights and shadows of the underwater kingdom. The empress led him in silence. She told no one where they were going and avoided other sea dwellers moving in the water near them.

Robbie swam over the sleeping plains and did his best not to think too hard about his current position. As long as he didn't swallow the airgrass, the deep ocean pressure and the prospect of his lungs flooding was not a problem.

After a time, the empress spoke. 'You could work on your swimming technique.'

'I'm not that bad,' he smiled at her. 'This morning I couldn't swim.'

She let go of his hand, and he fell quickly behind.

'I have heavier clothes.'

The empress gave a deep laugh and said nothing.

The landscape silenced Robbie. The border between the Sea of Trees and the White Ocean was humbling; he felt like a speck of plankton. The further they swam, the darker it became, and few fish followed, save the glowfish. He was glad of the empress' hand and the sound of her voice.

Anook's eyes stayed bright through the gloom. They

passed water meadows, ravines, and a reef as high as a castle wall.

When the Ridge of Shadows finally came into view, it was terrifying. Robbie dealt with it by imagining it was all a dream; the scope was too infinite to process without feeling sick. He concentrated on kicking his legs and breathing. They swam high between the peaks of mountains. He prayed they would not wake anything sleeping in the deep below – dragons or octopi with great swallowing mouths that would come winding out of the dark. In all his years on the road, the Sea Dwellers' kingdom was a reminder of how very little Robbie had seen of the wider world.

After what felt like hours, the empress pointed ahead at something. 'The Ridge of Shadows.' She watched his eyes widen.

First, a roaring sound of water came from the dark water ahead of them. 'What is that?'

'That is the black torrent around the well. It is starting to draw us in. What you hear is the sound of the water screaming.'

Robbie was sorry he had asked. Red was there. He wondered if she was afraid, if she still had his dagger.

Anook frowned. 'We are being taken into a tortured sea. From this point, the water is no longer that of the Sea Dwellers. This is the work of the witch.'

He wondered why he bothered trying to swim. There wasn't a chance in Engerlande he was strong enough to push through the torrent to the entrance of the trenches.

'I can't take you any further.' She was struggling to

stay on course. 'You are going to need the help of the turtles to reach the cave.'

'Turtles?'

'Yes, the saddlebacks. Hold on tight.' The empress squeezed his hand and dived low. A spinning wall of cold water found him, pulling Robbie away, and his grip was torn from the mermaiden. He quickly lost sight of Anook in the dark water. The shoal of small translucent fish that had accompanied them and lit the way disappeared in a flash. Robbie kicked hard and reached out to grab anything. He waited for what felt like enough time to reevaluate his life choices and fought to grip onto the rock without the torrent taking him into an endless spin around the Well.

The empress found him clinging to the side of a mountain. She was holding onto the shell of an enormous creature, several more paddling gracefully behind her.

'I thought I'd lost you. I began to miss the garlic.' She found his hand and pulled him towards her. 'Hold on.'

'To what?' he asked.

'To Roddy.'

Robbie gazed at a turtle the size of a pony. The creature had the face of a wise old man and seemed not to struggle as much with the force of the water. There were two others like him either side of the empress.

The turtle had a shell the same curve and comfort of a saddle, enormous and wide and mottled like the feathers of wild birds.

Robbie grasped onto the rough rim of the turtle, and the creature began to paddle through the torrent of water towards the base of the biggest mountain, further ahead and cathedral in size.

'There it is,' called the empress. 'The volcano.' She began to swim away, back against the current, towards the healthier, blue space they had come from. 'I can't go any further. Roddy will lead you to the cave's entrance.'

They were shouting at each other to be heard over the wailing sea.

'You're leaving?' yelled Robbie, looking frantically behind him at her graceful figure.

She smiled. 'I am not strong enough to get you to the mouth of the trenches. This turtle is my valien – he will look after you.'

'But –' Robbie did not want to be left with a turtle.

The empress swam close, held his face between her fingers, and looked into his eyes. 'Your heart and the princess' are your most powerful weapon. Together, they are mightier than the loneliness of the Well. Mightier even than the witch's fog and the dead souls she has disturbed to fuel it. Your life belongs up where the sun rises, but for now, it is sewn into this sunbrella. Don't forget to open it, Robbie.' She let go and kicked hard back towards the lighter waters. 'Good luck, and remember.' She placed both hands on her heart for a moment and smiled with pure joy before reaching out with what was left of her strength to return to her daughter and her kind.

He gazed for a second into the indigo eyes of the empress, and then she was gone. Robbie opened his mouth to say something, but the turtle was stoically moving forward.

The swirling black water burst the protective bubble that the airgrass had provided him. Robbie filled his lungs with one last breath and closed his eyes as the turtle swam closer to the witch's volcano. The other two turtles swam close in a V formation to counteract the force of the water and give this human the best chance to access the cave.

Maggie was fetching water from the well in the courtyard of Celador. She was wrapped up against the freezing cold, pleased to find that the well was full, the water clear and not yet frozen. She lowered the bucket and rubbed her arms, stamping her feet to stay warm. Pulling up the bucket, she felt movement. Maggie peered in with a lantern. A small indigo fish darted about in the dark water. Maggie smiled. 'Well, well, hello there ...'

She hurried back inside, releasing the fish back into the lake first.

'It's alright, Jan! Robbie's found her. He's found the empress.'

'Quick, Maggie, we must build a bonfire. We need to try to lift this fog.'

Jan emerged from the castle wearing three floor-length coats, followed by Luna, her hare. She was holding a wand. 'And look what I found.'

'Finally! Where was it?' Maggie's eyes lit up.

'In the airing cupboard.' She smiled. 'It's time to send that fog back to where it came from.'

Robbie tried to open his eyes; he could just make out that the mouth of the cave was shaped like a scream. A mouth gasping out 'O', as in, 'O, why am I the mouth of this cave?' He closed them again and stayed low as cold pummelled against him.

Selina had been busy, and yet she had not accounted for the tenacious strength of mother nature. To her mind, no creature was powerful enough to swim through the mad vortex of black water that concealed the caves. In her arrogance, she was confident the well was protected from anything living. But Selina had never encountered a saddle-backed turtle called Roddy or his two sisters.

The creature sliced through the water like a blade. When you've lived for one hundred and fifty years, a rogue witch's lofty notions of domination don't make much of a dent. The mouth of this cave was the least likely entrance through the mountains. And it was the one Robbie found himself dropped through with the force of a determined reptile. After a scrabble to find his feet, he kicked hard and broke the surface of a deep pool of water. Gasping for air, he looked around. It was dark and he was alone again.

21

THE WELL OF LONELINESS

Robbie's fingers searched unconsciously for the turtle's shell. They grasped at nothing, and he reached up and emerged blinking in a small, bitter-tasting pool.

'Air!' he gasped, as he reached for something to hold on to. 'Land.'

He was on land. It was not a pleasant land. It was a narrow tunnel below the surface of the ocean, next to a volcano. After swimming, Robbie's least favourite thing to do was caving and potholing. The pool he was in tasted of earwax. His ears popped as he emerged and warm water trickled reassuringly out of them.

'Argh puht!' He spluttered out the airgrass, relieved to hear his voice again.

Robbie had missed fresh air. He had missed being able to rant like a delusional man in the breeze. His hands shook as he took Patrick's sea goggles off and climbed weakly out of the water. He took a deep, hopeful breath and regretted it instantly. The still air smelt of nearly dead things hoping they would soon be completely dead.

He crawled away from the water and looked about him. 'Hello?' he spoke cautiously into the dark, damp space. 'Is anyone there?' Robbie tried out loud. He had an urge to speak, even if there was someone else in the cave with him. Or some*thing*. He shivered from cold. 'There appears to be no risk of this volcano being active,' he said. 'That's good.'

He hoped there was nothing else in that cave, unless it was a friendly, capable, and loyal dragon. A dragon who could provide Robbie with fire for tea before continuing his journey. A morale-boosting talk with oneself would have to do, although he didn't want to be laughed at, or eaten. Robbie took a deep breath. He would soon warm up. He had got this far, after all. 'If there is anyone in this cave, I do not want any more advice. If I'm going to do this, I'm going to do it my way. If only I had a flare or a lantern,' he muttered to himself, squinting around in the dark.

Something fell off the wall and made an unpleasant splat next to him. He fumbled to put his boots on with numb fingers and walked quickly away from the splatting thing, further into the cave. He could barely see his own hands in the darkness, although the sunbrella tied around his shoulder had begun to glow. A dull light came through the folded-up canvas, which felt warm against his skin. Robbie stared at it and smiled. 'So, you do work?' He did not want to open it fully in case it drew attention to anything unpleasant. While the heat slowly dried his shirt, Robbie silently thanked Father Peter.

'What is this place?' he asked out loud as he crept cautiously forward, using the dim light to guide him. There was a slight trail of bones and fish scales. Shards of fog floated past him along the tunnel as if possessed, heading in one direction at the same steady speed and, for the time being, it seemed, uninterested in him.

No one had elaborated on this part of the journey, but there was a good reason for that: NO ONE had been here, not these caves; not even the sea dwellers. Robbie convinced himself it was just a normal cave littered with normal cave stuff and stepped gingerly on. Maybe there would be some interesting stalactites or fossils to distract him from being terrified. The slime that covered the lower walls could well have been excrement from a creature that drank crude oil, for all he knew – it was hard to tell without a torch. Whatever beast had been here before him had left droppings. It was not a unicorn, that was for sure. Robbie was thankful for Father Peter's sunbrella; it was immensely reassuring being warm again.

After he slipped and scraped a fair-sized graze on his knee, Robbie decided to fully open the sunbrella. Now was as good a time as any, he reasoned. But as he did so, nothing spectacular happened, as is the way after any great expectation.

Maybe it is too wet to work properly? he thought.

And then it started. Thousands of tiny pricks of sunlight pierced through the dull fabric, and flecks of light illuminated the way. Narrow beams shone down on him in the dark cave. As they did, Robbie's heart and soul grew strong. He smiled and closed his eyes at the Father's invention. The ambience of the place was improved tenfold as he stood under this glorious, yellow-white light. The cave could still do with a wall hanging, a candle, a pillow, and maybe a ladder to a soft, green meadow, yet despite his arm shaking under the weight of the sunbrella after all the swimming, Robbie felt stronger.

'As long as there is no more water, this should be a relatively easy rescue,' he said to himself, swaggering on for a few more moments, truly believing it would soon be over without a big sweat, song, or dance. The sunbrella's power was great; it was a positivity inducer. Every child should take one to their first day of school.

The Well of Loneliness, Robbie thought, *PAH!* The sound of water physically screaming in agony around him … *PISHT!* This rescue was as simple as a cheese omelette. He was more than halfway there and he hadn't even died. He was incredible at this.

Robbie tripped over a shattered bone and carried on with a whistle. He tried not to touch the walls or the spongy crawling things that grew there.

Did something just bleat? No, it was just his stomach.

His last meal with the pirate had been many hours

ago. He was hungry and could murder some toast, a banana, and a pail of hot, sweet tea. But this cave posed no problem for him. He was a HERO, gosh darn it. And as for those skreeke creatures, he doubted they were even real.

The skreekes were also hungry. Their stomach sacs pulsed as they growled and squatted either side of Red. Their combined drool had left a layer of slime over the plinth, which smelt of putrid fish. The male skreeke was as broad as a canoe, and his tail was studded all over with sharp scales that moved of their own accord. He pawed the ground with two short front arms and raised his thick snout in the air.

Its skin was thick, calloused, and the colour of ash. Its eyes were small, black, and oily. Think twice before you call a warthog ugly because the skreekes would give a deep-sea blobfish nightmares. It would make the star-nosed mole and the naked elbow-rat feel a lot better about themselves physically. There was little to differentiate the male from the female: neither could be called beautiful and both killed without a conscience, although the female skreeke made a little humming noise when she ate and had orange spots on her belly.

Once they got their teeth into you and their jaws locked in a holding position, that was it. Call the florist. Skreekes didn't let go until the gobbling began, but first, you were brutally shaken dead. Unlike snakes that considerately swallow and digest you whole, squeezing hard in apology, skreekes take their time, saving the glands until last.

'What is it, Nip Nips?' Selina cawed down to the foul beast from an enclave in the volcanic wall that surrounded the basin of the well.

He scratched the ground and sniffed the air. His brute of a head turned slowly towards her voice. Being mostly blind, he missed, staring to the left of the witch, like a vicar with a wandering eye.

'Right a bit, darling, I'm here. Is someone finally coming?' Selina clapped with glee. 'Oh goodie.'

The last hour had dragged, and she was impatient for the royal liege. Although, something was off.

'What's happened to the spiderlings?' She sniffed. 'I was expecting a warning before the king's arrival.'

Daniel's voice was next to hers, his eyes fixed on the princess. 'You promised she would live. I'm going to unchain her.'

'You will remain here until I say,' Selina drawled.

Daniel felt the cold fog rise up and press against him and said nothing more.

The stage was set. The well was shrouded in Selina's terrible murk. She looked down at the princess and could see her spirit ebbing away. Landfelian would be hers before breakfast. How marvellous. She crunched her way through a roasted bat wing and waited.

Red was standing outside the gates of a big sleep. She could hear the witch, although her sharp voice sounded faint and far away. She was swaying in front of tall, white gates, waiting to be let in. They were beautiful gates; they reminded her of Celador. Whoever lived behind the gates was taking their time to answer her call.

Mother, are you there? Please, she thought, *I've had enough, let me in.* She wondered what she had to do to make these glimmering gates open. Red had never been anywhere like the Well of Loneliness.

The fog sucked scraps of hope from her exhausted soul.

She sank to the ground in front of the gates and waited.

It would not be long. But then Red had an image, back at the Lake of Stars, of her friends, of Robbie's hand holding hers. She closed her eyes, held herself still, and fought back. *I am alive,* she thought, *you have no power over me.* As she did this, the fog appeared to billow away.

Daniel Blackwood raised a thin eyebrow. Selina said nothing, but she saw it. *The wind,* she thought, *it must have been the wind. The girl had no true power, not like her mother.* Unless … No, it was always a gamble working with nature and the souls of the dead. If anything, Selina was a little afraid of her fogs growing in strength. *In time,* she thought, *I will send it away.*

Selina watched the princess above the haze and frowned. She had a clear view across the desolate space from her cave, the sound of screaming water outside providing a soothing accompaniment. She ignored the niggling fact that Red Felian had managed to endure her voodoo for years and emerge unscathed.

'Not long now. Be sure to whistle when Daddy arrives.' She took a few sips from a vial of blue liquid, which made her eyes twitch. 'We have so much to catch up on.' She paused and said slowly, 'No one banishes Selina Carnal.'

'How can you be sure the king will come? He hasn't been seen for seven years,' Daniel asked, standing next to her. Behind him, for some mysterious reason, there was a small, bright blue bird perched and still in a crude, rusty cage.

'The old fool with the owl will have informed Felian of his daughter's capture.' Selina turned around and scraped her nails slowly over Daniel's cheek. 'He will come. A part of his soul never left her. That meddling godfather has been getting messages to the crown one way or another.'

Daniel looked out at the fog circling around Red. 'It's going to kill her.'

Selina smiled. 'Now, now, dear man, have some faith in your little prize or I will send you down to join her.' She ground her teeth.

The son of a lawyer did not argue the point. But he did not take his eyes off the princess on the plinth. She was out of his reach, for now, but the barouche waited by the Petrified Tree. Tonight he would take her away. And finally, she would be his and he would be free of Selina Carnal.

A flicker of light on the other side of the Well caught his attention.

'There's something there,' Daniel whispered, searching for it again with darting eyes.

'Whatever it is won't be alive for long.' Selina narrowed her eyes at Red's hanging head. 'I must say, she's doing awfully well. Most wouldn't last a day before going through the gates.'

The princess hadn't moved for some time. The colour of her hair was changing and growing dull.

Daniel looked agitated. 'Something's wrong. I'm going down there.'

'You will do no such thing,' Selina growled. 'If you do, the fog will have you.' She began to laugh horribly, her eyes shining yellow. 'It will have all of us eventually.'

Red stood outside the gates and called. There were no violins, no white lights, clinking of glasses, or choirs of angels. Nothing but an empty avenue of rustling poplars, like those on Paloma's main approach. She wanted her mother to come, to tell her how to keep the fog away. She could, for brief glimmers, create a shield around herself, although it never lasted. Red did not fully understand how she did this but it felt instinctive and pure.

She focused on grounding herself, breathing, and her toes. If she lost sight of them, she knew she'd be in trouble. Her father had always told her a hero was only in real danger when his or her feet began to grow cold. This explained why all heroes received not just a sword but seven pairs of fine yook silk socks. If only she had her valien; he would have kept her feet warm. Oh, Face, how she missed him. Red pushed back the tears and held herself close.

Robbie crept out of the cave and whistled quietly.

'This must be the Well of Loneliness.'

He gazed ahead. 'Wherever are you, Red Felian?' His voice echoed around him. 'I'm coming.'

No wildflowers grew. The ground felt soft like ash. The place had a shadowy quality, and he struggled to see the other side. For something named the 'well', it appeared disconcertingly wide. Robbie looked up and strained to find the night sky, only a faint and murky light. There was no sign of Red or the witch. He had the distinct feeling that he was standing at the bottom of a vast funnel, which he was. The walls of the cavern were high, rough, and the colour of pummy stone. Desolation quickly crept over him.

Then he saw it, fog moving towards him at a terrifying pace. He held his breath and braced himself for its cold grasp. Despite this, Robbie stepped bravely forward, holding the sunbrella high. The witch's fog obscured the way ahead. He could not see his legs or what lay beneath them, which was probably for the best. He tried not to imagine independently moving teeth or roving scorpions. There was not a single earthly sound as the darkness loomed over him. Robbie felt he was trespassing in a land where nothing living had ever been invited. Where death had been disturbed and was most put out.

He began to choke; the air around him tasted empty. It seemed to take the breath from inside him.

He walked on, searching the barren space. It could not be much further until he found *something* living. As long as the sunbrella shone down upon him, the fog crawled out of his way and did not encroach too near. He hoped he was walking in a straight line towards the princess. He closed his eyes and tried to use his heart like Anook had told him.

'Where are you?' he whispered, holding the shell around his neck.

And then, after a few more minutes, he saw the hazy shape of a figure and a slight shift in colour from the gloom straight ahead. He began to run; she was there, he could see her long hair, but something looked wrong. She was stooping. He gritted his teeth and ran faster; as he got closer, Robbie could see Red's arms were extended with chains. They had been fastened around her wrists. Above him, she knelt on a plinth, a great piece of volcanic rock, crudely carved and shrouded in fog. The witch's substance swam around her like stalking sharks. She had built a sacrificial altar. 'It's a stage,' he said quietly.

Robbie could not see Red's face; her head lolled between her strung-up arms, the chains attached to two grotesque statues – these vast, grey forms squatted either side of her. The girl he had laughed next to.

Seeing Red released something inside Robbie that he'd not felt since the day by the river. Rage. White and pure. He had to stop himself from calling out.

No one else was visible.

It's too easy, he thought. *There must be more.* The witch, for a start – where was she? Looking up again, there was no telling where the volcano ended and the sky began. If there were stars, they were veiled.

To avoid drawing unwanted attention, Robbie closed the sunbrella. He took a deep breath and then crouched down, crawling across the ground towards the plinth. By keeping low he would not be seen in the gloom. He moved on his hands and knees, using the fog as cover. He knew it was likely suicide, but this was *his* rescue; he was damn well going to do it his way.

For a few minutes, it exceeded all expectations. His progress was slow, but he kept his head, hope, and direction.

Then the fog crept around his arms and encircled his boots. Slowly, an invisible heaviness found him, and he realised this was a mistake.

Fog swirled around him. It fed off every movement to get closer to Red. Robbie needed the sunbrella, although its light would give him away.

His knees trembled; his hands shook.

It will pass, he told himself again and again and pressed on. He could not give in to the power of the witch's fog; it wasn't real, just sorcery. Nothing living, only dead.

But it felt so hopeless. The lap of the Well felt like a fast of five hundred days. Selina's creation sat heavy on him.

This is what they want. Fight, he told himself. He had to fight. 'I am alive,' he said out loud.

On and on he crawled, closer to the plinth where Red waited alone. Thoughts of his mother, the drowning, and the pale-eyed rider taunted him relentlessly, slowing down his movements. The circumference of the Well felt unnaturally wide; it pushed the Ridge of Shadows out as if in fright.

This is what the fog does, he thought. He tried to remember good things: his horse, scrambled eggs, butter cake; he tried not to let the dark magic consume him. He tried to hold on to hope.

The scars around his shoulders began to sting. The old wound burned. The horror of that day – when his mother was struggling in the water and he could do nothing to save her – hung like a spider from a thread across his tired mind. His face grazed the ground and he fell.

'No.' *This is part of the spell.* He lifted himself up and dragged his body on in protest.

It was a heroic, cheer-inducing sight. It was a gold-medal performance. Robbie forced himself to stand up, grasping Father Peter's sunbrella in one hand and his whip in the other. To hell with who saw. He needed to feel the sun on his face to reach Red.

Gold rays splintered out of the cloth, although their strength was weakened. 'Oh no.' He shook it. 'Don't break on me now ...'

He could see Red's bruised face above him, so close. All he had to do was climb up a set of steep rocks to where she was chained.

'Hold on.' Robbie began to climb.

'There!' Daniel craned forward. 'He's come for her.' A

faint glow appeared again, slow and steady. It was not far from the princess – *his* princess. It was a man holding what looked like a shining umbrella just below the plinth of rock.

'The king!' Selina stepped forward to study the hero through the fog. She grew very still and scowled. 'That is not Austin Blue Felian. Who in hell's name is it?' she said icily.

Daniel stared hard at the figure, unable to see as clearly through the fog. There was something familiar about the man. The hair. It couldn't be that same peasant he'd left in the alley. He was nobody, a cook. He was nothing. How could he be the scarred man Selina had warned him about? Although, as he got closer, Daniel recognised the young Man of the Road he had left for dead in Alba.

'It's the one ...'

'So, this is the scarred man.' Selina's yellow eyes narrowed to thin black lines as she stared at Robbie. 'Stop him.'

Daniel gripped his cane. 'But the fog ...'

'If you want her, you will do as I say ...' She returned to her seat, hidden in the caves of the old volcano, to watch. 'Leave the fog to me.'

Daniel quickly disappeared down a passage that led into the Well. He smiled and fondled the top of his cane. Scarred or not, this peasant would regret coming back for more.

Robbie reached out and touched the base of the plinth with a wheezing breath. He could see now that the statues Red was chained to were not statues at all. They were skreekes and a good deal bigger than the drawing in Father Peter's book. Their tail claws were large and with black tips.

The beast nearest to him tasted the air with its long snout and grunted.

Robbie could see Red's wrists were red and sore. She made a pained noise as the creatures pulled at her chains, smelling another human.

The skreekes turned his way, their jaws drooling. They sniffed a frightened young man and reared up to gulp down more.

Robbie swallowed as quietly as possible as he moved closer, slowly uncoiling his whip. *They are blind*, he told himself, remembering the book in the Father's library. *They can't see me as long as I stay under the light.*

'Princess!' he whispered. 'Can you hear me?'

She didn't stir.

'Psst!' He stepped towards her and knelt. 'I'm here to rescue you. I know you don't need help; you've clearly got this part of the plan covered. I just need ...' He needed to break her chains, kill both skreekes, and carry her dead weight back through the fog. '... a moment to catch my breath and wake you so you can get us out of here. It shouldn't be too hard.' He coughed and a little blood came out on his hand, which was a worry. The fog had got to his lungs. His whip was all he had; a sword would have been nice. At least there was Will's frying pan.

'I thought you might need a light snack.' Robbie looked

at Red again and wanted nothing more than to stay near until she was strong again. But she would tell him that she wasn't that kind of princess and had not needed rescuing. 'I'm glad to see you, although you have looked better.' He carried on talking to her and hoped she would answer. She didn't stir. 'I don't think this is a very nice place. Shall we go?'

She swayed between the chains. The skreekes shifted towards the smell of man and sounds of faint whispering. The noise that came from deep inside them sounded like bones dissolving. Red's eyes were closed. Her hair fell either side of her face, shining even in this underworld. She appeared to be in a trance, breathing softly in and out.

Robbie knelt down before her and held the sunbrella above her pale face. Forgetting everything, with his free arm, he lifted her so she could lean gently against him. 'I'm here,' he said quietly. 'Sorry it's not someone else. Tricky to find this well. Not many takers.'

He kept an eye on the skreekes either side, snorting into the air. 'If we get out of here with all our digits, I'll cook us breakfast.'

Red felt something envelop her. It was immediate, a warmth, the beat of another heart close to her own, and a familiar smell; hay, the sea, garlic. It began to draw her away from the gates. She hurried back down the avenue of gently rustling poplars towards a yellow, faltering light.

'If you can hear me, come back. I can't come to where you are, it would take too long.' Robbie studied the chains while he spoke. 'I bet this place wasn't on your map.' He tried to smile.

Someone was speaking to her, Red realised. Where had she heard his voice before?

Robbie watched the beasts approach him slowly. 'Please open your eyes. It's been a long day and I'm afraid we haven't got long before these large lizards get peckish.'

She was so cold. Robbie wondered how to approach the chains. And then Red looked up at him, and said, 'You're here.'

The skreekes crawled closer, moving like reptiles with swaying heads towards the sweet-smelling aroma of flesh.

Her eyes closed again and he squeezed her cold hand. The sunbrella seemed to be helping.

'Yes, and I'm not leaving without you.' Robbie took a deep breath and noted that the skreekes were getting closer. 'There are no leafwells on the way home, just a lot of swimming I'm afraid. You will be fine. I, on the other hand, may not be.'

Red felt a warm light over her. The gates were moving away. 'Open your eyes. Let's go,' he said.

And for once, Red Tulip Friday Felian did exactly as she was told.

When she did, she found Robbie Wylde's face creased with worry gazing down at her, his dark hair brushing her cheeks and two shining bracken-coloured eyes blinking back at her. They looked surprised and then relieved.

'Hello,' she croaked.

'Hello.' Robbie smiled. 'You came back.'

She smiled. And then the light puttered and went out. They were no longer shielded by the sunbrella. The skreekes could smell them as clear as a guillotine in the dark. They could taste the fear that came from the humans as darkness enveloped them. What Father Peter's book had failed to mention was that the beast's blindness was exaggerated in daylight, but in the dark, everything was fair game.

Red smelt the cheroot smoke first. She cried out in warning as a thin shadow loomed on to the plinth. Blackwood.

'It *is* you.' Daniel snarled at Robbie. 'How disappointing. We were expecting a royal.'

Daniel stood before them, dressed in black and swinging a key on a chain. His silver-topped cane was in the other hand. The rat's head glinted and a sharp spike flicked out from its end. He smiled unpleasantly at Robbie.

'I should have killed you in the alley while I had the chance,' he drawled. 'This time, the princess gets to watch.'

Red tried to speak, to cause a distraction, but her voice came out as a rasp. She could not rouse herself to fight. The same hopelessness she had felt from the voodoo washed over her again.

Robbie felt her take a shuddering breath, close her eyes, and fall against him. He didn't have a sword, a cane with a spike, or even a small butter knife. He had nothing save his whip, the Herald's baton, a frying pan, and the sunbrella. If there was anything else, he could not remember it.

He looked down at Red and wondered if she had

anything useful with her. Blackwood began to circle around him with a sneer. Robbie couldn't fence without a weapon. It would be air fencing – both unfair and stupid. He couldn't fence, anyway, although neither could Daniel, if he was honest, which he wasn't. The son of a lawyer just stabbed in the right direction and had mercilessness on his side.

'Do you still have that tennis racket?' Robbie looked at Red's quiet face. 'Never mind.' He let go of her as gently as possible. 'I'll be back in a minute.'

He stood to face Daniel. 'Could I have one of those canes? I don't have a sword.'

'Stand aside.' Daniel lunged forward and stabbed at Robbie, slicing his hand from thumb round to the thin skin of his wrist.

'Ouch!' Robbie's sleeve seeped crimson. It had been dirty when he'd started out, but now it was ruined. He firmly told Red to hold on and then he shouted, 'That REALLY does it!'

The two men sidestepped around the plinth. The skreekes watched with interest on their hind legs, wondering which would be their next meal.

Robbie felt his right arm get stabbed again by the spike of Daniel's cane. It flicked towards him out of the dark. Somewhere from the edge of the Well, he heard the sound of ecstatic clapping. It was the witch; she was watching them. 'I wish you would stop doing that,' Robbie said, looking at his bleeding arm and then at Daniel. He swung his whip out but missed.

Red tried to lift herself up.

'Were you aiming for someone else?' Daniel smiled.

'No,' Robbie answered, throwing his whip out again before Daniel had time to think of another pithy comment. Lifting the cane from his gloved hand, it hurled towards Red.

Daniel hissed in frustration and began to back away, swinging the key idly in front of Robbie. 'You still need the key to free her.'

Robbie picked up the cane and, focusing on the nearest of Red's chains, held the sharp point above it like an axe. She nodded at him and closed her eyes as he lifted it and swung down hard.

'I wouldn't do that if I were you.' Daniel glanced at the skreeke attached to the chain. 'They're very hungry.'

Robbie ignored the son of a lawyer and swung again. The chain broke on the third go, and Red cried out in warning as the skreeke pulled at her other chain.

'Hold on,' Robbie said. 'One more. It might hurt.'

HURT? she thought. Hurt was only the beginning of it. The pain in her wrists was white and burning. She growled in Daniel Blackwood's direction and tried to stand. Something good was flooding back to her. Red was unchained. Hope was flooding back into the Well, and for a moment, Selina's fog seemed to back away from the princess as if in fear.

The freed skreeke looked at Robbie's bleeding arm hungrily. Robbie then realised what he had done. He had released both beasts and Daniel had disappeared. Where was he? The fog began to billow around him. A dark figure leapt out and knocked Robbie over. It snatched the cane back and raised it above him. 'So long, Man of the Road,' Daniel sneered.

Red hurled her loose chain towards Daniel. It lashed against his legs but did not stop him bearing down on Robbie. From the ground, Robbie had very little time to think. He felt the round rim of a solid cooking utensil pressing into the small of his back. And that was when he remembered the FRYING PAN. The voodoo-breaking weapon that had saved the princess once before. It was his only hope. Quickly, he reached out behind him with his good arm and drew it out like a sword, silently thanking William English as he did. Robbie swung the pan forward, and it blocked the cane with a loud clang. He pushed himself against it with everything he had, and Daniel fell back into the waiting shadow of a skreeke.

Robbie delivered the final blow, standing over the son of a lawyer and knocking him out cold. Everything was quiet, as the larger skreeke shuffled forward, grasped Daniel's narrow, black boot, and dragged his body away. 'Robbie, the key!' Red urged, and he reached forward, clasping at the key still clutched in Daniel's hand.

'I've got it!' Robbie smiled and then liquid cold flooded through his shoulder from the wound in his arm and he collapsed. 'Oh no.' He looked at the cane.

Red saw the pain etched across Robbie's face. 'He poisoned you.'

The fog surrounded Robbie as if preparing to feed. Red

watched it, horrified. She wasted no time, closing her eyes and focusing on the life he had yet to live. Her heart beat fierce and strong. She imagined two white wings of light coming from her and surrounding Robbie. And then something extraordinary happened. They appeared. Red held the thought and directed the light at the fog. In that moment, she felt its hunger and sadness. She opened her eyes, looked at it, and said quietly with grace, 'Go.'

It slunk away from them like smoke. She turned to Robbie, who was staring at her.

'How did you …'

'I'm not sure.' She took hold of his arm. 'If we can stop the poison going any further …' He nodded. She ripped a part of her sleeve off. Together, they tied it tight above the wound. 'The key,' Red whispered. It took no time to unlock the binds left around her wrists.

The second skreeke barked. It was not far away, and they watched it swing its wide neck towards them. They could hear its tail claw clacking.

'Can you walk?' she asked him.

The skreeke was up on its hind legs, swinging ominously from side to side. It reared up and lunged towards Robbie and Red, throwing its tail out violently, trying to catch a limb to drag into its waiting jaws.

The king's words came back to Robbie. 'Look up, we will be there.' *Where?* he wondered. He couldn't hear the sails of the Cloudbuster or the wings of eagles.

'I've seen enough of this old volcano.' Robbie looked at Red, who had grown pale. He tried to stand. 'It's not the natural wonder I was hoping for ...' He looked up and, for the first time, prayed. 'Your father is coming. And if I don't get you to the throne on time, he will have me exiled.'

'My father.' Repelling the fog had taken her strength. 'You've seen him?' she asked, pale and quiet.

He carefully wiped the hair from her face. Her green eyes looked at him. 'Yes,' Robbie said.

'It hurts,' she said softly. 'Keeping the fog away.' The white light around them faltered.

'I know,' he said. 'Can you stand?'

She looked pained, and then the corner of her mouth smiled. 'Can you not carry me?'

'Not this time.' Robbie winced as she leant back against his recently stabbed hand. 'Sorry to disappoint you, milady. I'm afraid there were no heroes available. I cut off your chains, though. That has got to count for something.'

She tried to laugh and closed her eyes in pain. Her feet were bare and there were some pretty raw-looking cuts on them. Robbie was the best-looking thing in the Well, and even he looked a bit maimed and sweaty.

The skreeke danced around them like a cobra drawing out time before the final lunge. The sound of something big lashed through the air before Robbie could question its source, and Red pulled him out of the way.

The tail claw cuffed his leg and cut a small chunk out

of his calf. He cried out, glowered at the beast, and watched it swallow its prize. The skreeke licked her claw dry and began to pant.

'These animals are not properly trained.' Robbie narrowed his eyes and stood. 'They need to sit, heel, and STOP EATING MY LEG!' he yelled.

The skreeke lurched closer and began circling her tail again, its scales clicking back and forth ominously.

She was breathing heavily, her mouth open, as Robbie tried to recall the Father's book. Had it mentioned that a skreeke did not have a nose like most other creatures? They could only breathe through their mouths.

'Your whip,' Red urged.

Robbie yelled at the beast in what he hoped was a warrior-like way, of which the Branch Bandits would have been proud. He swung his whip above his head, faster and faster, and then aimed it at the skreeke. It wound tight around the beast's snout and he pulled hard, locking its jaws together.

'I may not have claws, but I've still got my lasso!' Robbie yelled.

The skreeke fell hard onto her front, writhing like a terrier attacking a sock. Red was right; she couldn't breathe if she could not open her mouth.

An agonised scream rang out across the Well. It sounded close. The witch was no longer in her seat.

Red turned white and whispered, 'It's her.'

Robbie held on tight and blocked out everything else.

The pain in his leg, the slice on his hand, his burning scars – it all hurt.

The skreeke flailed like a fish on a hook. It felt like his arm would be torn off. But he would not let go until the creature was still. The old bit of shell twisted at his neck as Robbie strained to hold everything together.

Look at the mirror, Robbie. Magatha had told him that, hadn't she? It was coming back him to now, a memory of her bright eyes as he was leaving the folly, pressing this old bit of shell onto him. Red was murmuring to him too, reaching for the shell around his neck.

He stared at her desperately, the faded mother of pearl reflecting nothing but his ragged face. 'There's no time. We have to get out of here.'

Red's long fingers pressed the shell up towards him and held it there. He stared deeper, harder, and angrier at it.

The surface grew hazy and another image emerged. He saw himself as a boy. Robbie saw Robbie. Had he ever brushed his hair or worn a clean shirt? He was in the river, and he was fighting for his life. He pulled at a whip wrapped around his shoulders and yelled so hard that the banks of the river quaked. He watched a pale-eyed rider on a black valien fall into the water.

Had he really pulled the man from his horse?

Robbie saw himself lift Red from the leafwell, drag them through a Long Wind, and break the voodoo attached to her ankle with a frying pan. He watched himself read to a crowd of murdering guards in the Hog's Breath, punch the king, reverse park a valien, and get pushed off Great Scott Point by a Pirate King, where for a second it looked like HE FLEW.

Gosh. He had packed a lot into the last few weeks.

Robbie looked down at Red.

'I have something to tell you.'

Her eyes were closed again in concentration. The fog had not returned, but it billowed behind them, like a great wave, waiting.

'I can't swim.' He felt better as soon as he said it. 'I'm hopeless at it, truly. Until I met you, I was a total drowner. I'm getting better. You have changed everything.'

Red opened her eyes. For that second, it felt like she looked right into his soul. 'Let's go, Robbie.'

The skreeke was so close, they could hear its digestive system at work and the sound of its breath, tail claw poised.

Robbie closed his eyes, held on tight, and waited for a miracle. And then he heard a dog bark. And Red said, 'Atlas!'

22

FIREWORKS

Out of the dark, a huge dog sprang towards the skreeke, pinning it to the ground, and the Well was lit up by an explosion of neon.

CRACK
KABOOM
BANG
WHIZZLE

Sherbet colours rained down on them. The incandescent light of rockets and flares broke the air of that deathly place and shouted, 'WELL HELLO!' in hell's ear.

Robbie looked up, unable to believe the heavens would make such an effort for him. It must be for the princess next to him. The fog was retreating further. He could see glimpses of an inky night sky and stars. Fireworks? He wondered how fireworks were going to help. An enormous wolfhound stood between them and the skreeke. Red called, 'Atlas!' again and the beast wagged his tail briefly at her, eyes twinkling before snarling at the attacker.

The king craned out of the Cloudbuster with the spyglass. He hung out like a wild man, yelling instructions.

'Quickly, Billy! Set them all off, every one!'

Billy had never been allowed to do that before. He saluted the king, put his goggles back on, adjusted his ear protectors, and got to work. Marmadou held a fuse steady while he organised a large sack of explosives suspended carefully on a platform so as not to accidentally set fire to one of the Cloudbuster's sails.

'And make sure you're secure! Marmadou, is his rope tight? Your mother will put me on a spit if you fall.'

'Don't worry – I climb the roof of your palace all the time, Your Highness.'

'Jolly good!'

If Billy's mother had seen this moment, she would have prepared the spit of all spits for the king. Her son was tied to a ladder, surrounded by explosives, thousands of feet up in the air. But Billy had never looked happier as the Cloudbuster hovered over the funnel of an old volcano swirling with witch's fog far out to sea. He watched as the king flew down the ladder into the black hole, where, only minutes before, his wolfhound Atlas had leapt, swiftly followed by the pirate king.

The remaining skreeke did not like fireworks. To its ears and eyes, the bright bangs were like strobes. The creature swung its tail around, disoriented by the smoke, lights, and noise. It missed Robbie's head by three and a half inches and tripped over its own front leg. The king's wolfhound barred it from going anywhere near the princess.

Selina Carnal screamed at the fog as it swirled around her, out of control. Her cloak flew out behind and her hair was loose and wild. She swept down through the cave tunnel and emerged in the well, parting the fog like a sea. Walking towards the plinth, she saw Daniel on the ground, unconscious next to the lifeless skreeke, and she saw the Man of the Road and the princess limp down the last step. Selina composed herself, closed her eyes, and lifted her hands above the ground. She began to mutter the words of a spell, indecipherable and fast, and something began to happen. The Well began to shake.

King Felian wasn't king because he looked good seated, but because he gazed outside the box. When other kings declared war, he brought *sparklers* and his dog to the front line. And he was very clever because: what in the universe gives off more hope than a sky full of fireworks and a loyal wolfhound?

The distraction was Red and Robbie's chance. The fog had formed a tornado around the witch now, her terrible figure standing below them like the eye of the storm as it enveloped her. Then Robbie heard the noise as the ground beneath them moved, cracking, and a part of the volcano's wall fell and landed with a rumble not far away.

'She's going to bury us all!' Robbie limped on. 'We have to hurry.'

The last skreeke could not see or smell the two humans limping away – its head was filled with gunpowder fumes. It stood on its sister's lifeless foot and barked in grief like a banshee, piercing the air around it in panic.

Atlas barred his teeth and growled at Daniel, who tried to lift himself, roused by the noise, giving Red and Robbie a chance to run.

Robbie's left leg was numb, and his right arm was cold and extremely fed up. He hoped they were heading to something good – the way to two first-class seats on a sky ride home and a nice pot of tea. He could not see a ladder. He aimed for the clear sky, and then he heard Atlas whimper behind him.

'Atlas!' Red called. A leather glove wrapped itself around Red's wrist and pulled, and she cried out in pain. Daniel's face appeared through the gloom. The man looked possessed, sallow, and not at all sane. There was another rumble as the well shook.

Robbie did not have his whip or sunbrella to hand. He fumbled for them. The son of a lawyer smiled like a sadist.

Somewhere in that hellish place, they heard the dog whimper again. 'Dinner time for the skreeke,' Daniel sneered. 'Come with me, Princess Felian.' He smiled.

With a clear voice that rang through the murderous

air, Red looked at Daniel and said, 'I'd rather not,' kicking him hard with all the strength she had left. Her left foot sent him reeling back. The kick was mighty, and it was worthy, but it took everything in her, and Red fell. The wolfhound howled at her side and Red smiled. 'He's here.'

Robbie stared at her open-mouthed. 'Who?'

'The king,' she said. Another tremor came from the ground and more of the well crumbled, burying the plinth behind them.

The fog came in a wave and then the witch appeared, her yellow eyes burning through the dark. She stood calmly on the hem of Red's torn dress.

Robbie stood frozen. 'Selina Carnal.'

The witch bowed before him as Atlas growled, standing in front of Robbie and Red. The witch silenced him with one stare. The poor dog's leg was bleeding. Selina looked at Robbie with a snarl. 'It's an unfortunate pleasure to meet you, Man of the Road. You have your father's good eye.'

Robbie was speechless. At her words, the scars across his shoulders and neck burned like fury.

'M-my father?' he stammered.

'Oh yes.' Selina smiled. 'You are much alike.'

And then a voice spoke through the fog that carried the hope of Landfelian and resonated with the lofty nuance of a cello concerto in A Major. It said, 'Selina Carnal! I thought I'd banished you.'

'Your Highness,' she bowed beautifully. 'I just couldn't wait to come back.' The witch raised her hands, and as she did, the fog grew in height, waiting for an order.

Water. There was water pouring in from somewhere. Robbie could hear it and prayed that swimming would not be involved again.

'Step away from my daughter and this young man.' The king stood a few feet away.

'Aye, you bony-arsed, shape-shifter of a turncoat.' The pirate was next to Robbie.

'Patrick.' Robbie smiled.

'Hello, boy.' He winked and Alberta squawked loudly at Selina, landing lightly on the pirate kings arm.

Atlas limped to the king's side, and the remaining skreeke squatted next to Selina and made a slow clicking noise from the back of its throat. For a moment, all fell silent in the Well as the two parties gathered each other.

Selina began to laugh. 'I must say, Your Highness, you've brought quite the army.' Her hands rose slowly up towards the sky, and the fog mirrored their shape behind her, forming long, pointed fingers, and with a sudden flick of her wrists, Selina directed the full force of her creation on the king and his daughter.

'No!' Red cried out. As she created that light again, white and pure light shone before her like a force field. But it was not enough to shield them all. It wavered, uncertain.

The king whispered, 'You have your mother's light.'

'Go!' Patrick yelled to them, his face a grimace of anguish, the fog surrounding them. 'Both of you.'

The skreeke at Selina's side moved forward towards the group. Alberta squawked again and took a dive towards it, pecking at its head with beak and claws. Atlas barred the way as the king helped lead Red towards the ladder.

'Leave?' Selina's screech filled the air. 'No one leaves this Well.' At her words, another deep rumble from the ground filled the air.

'Robbie,' whispered Red as fog barraged through the light to find the souls behind.

'I'm right behind you. Go quickly.' He nodded at her, his face strained.

As the king reached the ladder. Daniel Blackwood reared up from the ground like a spectre before him.

'Silence!' The king pierced the fog behind them with his voice, and, drawing his sword (for he was the one man that did get a sword), he cut off Daniel's arm below the elbow. It hardly made a sound as it rolled across the ground.

'You dare to disobey your king?' King Felian bellowed.

Daniel took one look at Red and shrank back, his mouth making a wide 'O', and the son of a lawyer's body crumpled away into the darkness.

The king looked at his daughter. 'If that man survives the fog, he will emerge the better for it.'

She did not look well; the light had gone from her eyes and her skin was grey. Holding her close, he quickly carried her to the ladder. She was heavier than he remembered – seven years will do that – but she was his child, and he had missed her with a pain that took the breath from him. 'My Red one,' he said softly over and over again. 'I'm getting you home.' He coughed as fog swirled around him.

The king with his daughter began to climb the ladder, which hung from the sky.

'No!' the witch screeched, watching the king fade away from her sight, and she sent a barrage of her infernal fog up towards him while screaming, 'Get them!' at her remaining skreeke.

Robbie looked up. The sky was back and the silhouette of a mighty Cloudbuster hovered there, waiting for them. She was saved. She had found her father at last. The sight made him soar.

'Come on lad,' Patrick said. 'Stay close to me.' He reached the ladder and kept it still for the king's ascent. Alberta and Atlas surrounded the skreeke, distracting it with tooth and claw, nips and barks, but Selina's fog sat heavy on Robbie, his limbs refusing to move him on. As the king disappeared, along with Red's extraordinary light, Robbie collapsed.

Red clung to the king. He smelt like somewhere that was once home.

Father Peter was high above them, struggling to maintain control of the Cloudbuster. The fog had moved between the sails and upset the balance of the contraption.

Marmadou swooped up and down the length of the ladder, encouraging the climbers to *Hurry the truck up* in urgent owl hoots.

'I *am* trying to keep it still!' Father Peter swore as the balloon lurched violently. 'Where are they? Marmadou, we need the eagles.'

He felt a tug on the rope ladder. At last.

'Billy, help me pull the ladder up. Patrick, can you hear me?'

'Of course I ruddy heard you!' the pirate called up. 'We've got the royals.'

Father Peter had not planned on bringing the Pirate King along, but his albatross had threatened to puncture the sails if they didn't throw down the ladder over Great Scott Point to collect him. 'I'm not letting you balls up this rescue, Felian,' the pirate had hollered at the king. 'You need an extra pair of hands up there.'

'Marmadou! Keep a look out for spiderlings. I don't know if our friends have been successful in distracting them. We don't need a swarm attack now.'

Billy pulled with the Father, his hair sparking a little at the ends from the last of the fireworks. The rope burnt his hands; the king was no light load. 'Is the princess alright?' he asked, his voice sounding young and small.

'I don't know,' Father Peter replied. 'But I saw her light.'

The Cloudbuster bounced up and down. It had never carried more than two men and an owl before. The stove's steady flame faltered in the icy conditions created by the witch. It was like trying to keep a candle alight while riding a squirrel.

The Father began to talk to his ship like some men talk to their horse when it refuses to move in a forest of wolves.

'Don't stop now – in fifteen minutes, by all means, but not here.' He prodded what was left of the fuel with a fork and closed his eyes for a brief but potent second, muttering some words under his breath. It fired up for a spell. 'We really need to pull!'

Billy wondered if there was anything at the end of the ladder. What if it was just a horrible practical joke and nothing but a great lump of rock?

The king's head, followed by Red's brilliant hair, appeared through the swirling mists below the basket.

Billy yelled, 'He's got her!' and then he said, 'She doesn't look good.'

Patrick followed and grabbed the spyglass at the same time. 'What about Robbie, the Man of the Road? He was behind me with the hound. Can you see him?' He shouted for Alberta. She had not returned either. 'Why isn't he on the ladder?'

Father Peter scowled at the sails. 'We haven't long. We need to go – now.'

'We are not leaving without the young cook,' argued the pirate. 'He risked everything!'

'We are sinking, Patrick.'

'He's got my sea goggles and more pluck than a prize cockerel. And more heart ...' The pirate thought about hitting the Father and taking over the controls of the Cloudbuster, but there was a law against attacking Fathers midair. 'Fine, you selfish royal ... I'm going down to get him!' He threw the ladder back down into the foggy abyss.

Robbie had indeed fallen. The skreeke's wound had damaged his leg so that it hung from his hip like a spare trouser. The arm stabbed by Daniel's cane was lifeless, and he lay curled over himself. The fireworks had stopped, he realised. In a burning rage, Selina sent another finger of her fog towards him as he tried to reach for the ladder. Alberta and Atlas held the skreeke back but they couldn't stop the witch's wrath.

This is the part where a man dies, Robbie thought. He'd just never thought it would be him. He hoped Red was somewhere warm and had a blanket. He imagined he was there too and not alone in this dark place. There was seawater pooling around him.

A sharp voice peered at his slumped form, casting a thin shadow over his face.

'So, they left the scarred one.' Her voice was bitter. 'That's royalty for you.' Her mouth lifted into a small, sinister smile. 'He'll return. Your princess will die of a broken heart if you do not. The king knows this as much as I do. When it comes to affairs of the heart, mere mortals are powerless.'

Robbie closed his eyes, partly conscious of the witch's words. He sank deeper towards death; it wasn't so bad, really. Apart from the bleeding, sore bits.

But Death was not far away, considering his soul and thinking, *This one doesn't look ready.*

In the Cloudbuster, everyone was in hysterics.

The pirate was now yelling at the king. 'LET ME PASS, YOU SON OF A –'

The monarch was roaring back, 'ALLOW ME ONE MOMENT WITH MY DAUGHTER, FOR THE LOVE OF GOLD, PIRATE!'

They lay Red down, covered in Father Peter's blanket and the king's old riding coat. They took stock of her wounds. She was not a healthy colour – somewhere between Hospital-Bed Beige and Terminal White. 'You've grown up,' the king said quietly. 'I wasn't there.'

Marmadou was making a lot of noise about something down in the Well, but no one listened.

'Peter,' asked the king urgently, 'will she live?'

The Father gently touched Red's temple and lifted the sole of her foot against his ear, listening intently. 'She needs hot water, her godmothers, and a roaring fire in no more than seven hours.' For the first time, he did not look certain. 'But there's something else ...'

'I know.' The king's face fell in tenderness, and he kneeled and stroked his daughter's cold cheek. 'Can she hear me?'

'Yes,' Father Peter answered. 'Always.'

The great man began to weep. Tears dropped from his nose and landed on Red, as if she hadn't had enough. Patrick stopped shouting and passed the king a spotted handkerchief. Marmadou watched as the king held onto his daughter's hand. He tried to warm it as tears coursed down his weathered face.

'Forgive me.' His voice barely made a sound. 'I should not have left you.' He smiled and took a deep breath. 'Now hear me, Red Felian. You must keep living. It may look bad now, but it will get better. The weather will improve, and you are loved, you must remember that, so extraordinarily loved. Whatever it looks like now ...' He paused and then he said, 'You must come back.'

The king held her tight. He tried to replace seven lost years of being her father into her flickering spirit. He looked up at the sorry faces of Billy, Patrick, and Father Peter. No one spoke. There are sometimes no words. A hug from a king is a powerful thing. Far better than a kiss from a handsome prince, which have been highly overrated over the centuries, in my opinion.

Red opened her eyes andsqueezed her father's hand. The Cloudbuster lurched unsteadily. Was she flying? There were stars and a cool wind.

'Robbie?' she asked and then coughed painfully.

No one answered.

The king's smile did not reach the corners. 'He fell.'

Red's colour left and the cold crept back into her soul. 'No,' she said.

The pirate, never quiet for long, spoke up, although he kept his voice low. 'Your Highness, with all due respect, the

Man of the Road and your daughter, whether they know it or not - their hearts are tied. Now, are you going to go and get that poor sod or am I?'

The king gently let her go of her hand. 'Peter, hold the ship steady. I'm going back down.' He kissed Red's forehead and considered her fading green eyes. 'I'll bring him back. Patrick, you remain here. The Father needs to attend to my daughter and you must fly this ship, do you hear me?'

'Aye, as you wish.' Patrick tilted his hat.

Austin Felian took off his crown. The crown wasn't a grand bejewelled affair, but it could be cumbersome. He put it next to Red, stood up, and clutched the first rung of the ladder. Father Peter's face fell as he watched the king do this. The two men exchanged one more look.

'Don't wait for me to climb aboard – start moving at the first tug, do you understand? She must get back to Landfelian. She needs the sun.' He blinked back. 'So like her mother.'

The passengers in the Cloudbuster nodded silently and watched him go.

Below, Selina Carnal waited, as if expecting a prize at a school Speech Day. She knew the king would return. The scarred boy and his daughter were tied now, and one could not survive her fog without the other.

She stood a few feet from Robbie and the swaying ladder. In her cold hands, she held a tiny bird, which chirruped in panic. A hurricane of hate blew through her mind and out of her two flaring nostrils as she stood next to the floundering hero, the fog concealing her, sea water lapping against her legs.

This is what comes of banishing me, she seethed. The king would soon live to regret ever crossing her. For reasons only known to Selina Carnal at that time, she did not further Robbie's death but left the fates to decide. *He may yet be useful,* she thought. The wolfhound and the albatross guarded him as the water closed in.

The king of Landfelian flew down the ladder like a comet, calling out for the Man of the Road. He called again until he heard a faint groan and the sound of Atlas.

'NOOOOOO. ARGHHHHHHH! NOOOOT HEERRRREEEE.' This was followed by several spouts of bloody coughing. (Robbie was not actually answering the king's call; he was telling himself not to die in his current position.)

The king took a cautious step forward, careful not to lose sight of the ladder. All the worst bits of the Well's fog had begun to swirl around Robbie, eating away at his life and hope. He tried to fight back, but the fog sank heavier onto him. Atlas sat near him, keeping guard.

'You don't look well, dear man,' said the king. He was grey. 'The ladder is a few feet away. Can you walk?' He looked at the bloody pulp of Robbie's calf. 'Possibly not.'

'Mmmnnn ...'

'I'm going to get you out of here. Hold on, it's not your time to go.' He pulled Robbie up from his watery grave and dragged him towards the ladder. But something stopped the king short; he saw a colour through fog, a glimpse of powder blue.

'The witch,' Robbie said. 'My leg, I can't ...'

The king did not comment. He could see the man's calf was not all there. 'Don't worry, it'll grow back. You will be fine.' He stopped and slowly drew his sword. Atlas began to growl. The water was up to his neck.

'You're not going to cut it off, are you?' Robbie tried to smile.

'We're being watched,' the king said quietly.

They were, and the ladder kept drifting away. The king was not as strong in the fog, and Robbie was no waif. 'You are considerably heavier than my daughter.'

He gritted his teeth and hurled them on another step.

'I'm sorry I p-punched ew.'

'Twice. Punched me twice.'

'Yes.'

'Do not worry.' the king added with a grunt, grasping hold of the ladder. 'I would have done the same.'

There was a problem. Robbie could not hold it. His hand had no grip, little blood, and few nerves.

'Hold tight,' commanded the king as Robbie's hand fell off a rung.

'I can't.'

The king frowned. 'No, you're right. You can't. I'm going to tie you to the ladder.'

Robbie didn't like that idea, but he was not exactly

inundated with choice. There was something in the water, a dark shape, and it was approaching with confidence. Robbie muttered, 'Oh no, it can swim.'

'What?' the king asked.

'The skreeke!' Robbie yelled. 'Behind you!'

The king turned around just in time to see a great pair of jaws break through the surface of the water and lunge at his side. Atlas tried to jump but was held back by the water, Alberta swooped down, scratching at the skreeke's eyes. The king grimaced in pain as teeth found his flesh, and he bore his sword down true and firm into the creatures skull.

Removing his sword slowly, the skreeke floated away, motionless. Wincing a little, the king removed his coat and tore it to pieces. Quickly, he tied Robbie's feet to the rungs of the ladder, then his waist and arms. He was good at knots, thank God; he had a whole section in the library of books dedicated to knot making, and he trussed Robbie up well. 'I'm going to give you my sword,' said the king, gritting his teeth against the pain in his side and looking at him with a sense of duty. He strapped the sword to Robbie's side.

'Why?' Robbie asked. It was a little late in the game for a sword. 'You're hurt.' There was blood in the water.

But the king did not answer; he had his reasons, and they were mostly ancient and superstitious.

THE ANCIENT AND SUPERSTITIOUS REASONS FOR A KING OR QUEEN GIVING AWAY THEIR SWORD AND/OR CROWN:

If at any point a king or queen senses that they are on the brink of losing a battle, if they find themselves in true peril, if there is a chance that they may not make it out before closing, it is their duty to pass on the royal valuables to the most capable man or woman near them.

Fog drove over them then, covering their skin in goosebumps. 'Leaving so soon, Your Highness? Without a little tête-a-tête?'

Selina Carnal stood before them, swathed head to foot in the queen's cloak.

The king wasn't prepared for the jolt in his chest that the powder-blue cloak gave him. And he was not equipped for the aftertaste of the witch's voice behind it. He hid his shock well, cool as a kitten, although it disoriented him, filling his head with thoughts of his lost wife. 'Wherever did you find my wife's cloak?' His voice remained calm.

'The darling let me borrow it. So accommodating. Although blue isn't really my colour.'

The king faltered.

'It's a trick,' Robbie tried to warn him. 'She used the cloak to draw Red away.'

The ladder started to move. It lifted several feet off the ground and continued to climb steadily. The pirate was putting his back into it. 'Wait!' Robbie looked down at the swirling water slowly filling the well. It had reached the king's waist and the king was still not on the ladder. 'Quick! Get on!'

He stared down at the shrinking figure of Selina Carnal. The astonishing cloak covered in stars and sapphires seemed to power through the gloom. He remembered it from long ago, a happier time. The witch's face was a storm. She held her hands low, palms facing down, and the sea water seemed to ripple away from where she stood. The fog goaded the king. He stood transfixed, frozen, and picked up his dog, who could no longer stand in the water. 'Atlas, you must leave me now, my old friend,' he said softly.

King Felian glared at a woman everyone had forgotten. She was almost unrecognisable from the day he had banished her from Landfelilan; hunger had preserved her like a lemon but squeezed the human out. Now there stood a figure eaten away by the dark. 'What have you done with my wife?' he said.

'If you insist on leaving, you will never know.' Selina looked at the King of Landfelian's torn expression and smiled. 'Come, we have much to discuss.' She gestured with her hand and a worm of fog trailed towards the king's neck, pulling him towards her like a dog. Atlas howled and the fog hesitated.

Robbie was conscious of the wind on his face. Clean air blew through his lungs, and his head began to clear. The witch was saying something about the queen.

'Don't listen!' Robbie called down helplessly. 'It's a trap!' He gave a hoarse cry, but it came out a whisper. He couldn't move as he watched the king retreat further away into the fog, who looked desperate with indecision, anguish, and hope, and then, quite suddenly, he changed his mind and ran. The king ran like a burning man. The jump he made, holding Atlas in his arms, got him a handle on the last rung of the ladder, and he looked at Robbie and nodded.

The witch let go of the tiny bird in her hands, and a shot of azure feathers wavered in the air; a halcyon kingfisher. Robbie watched it with dread. The creature was disoriented and frightened. It beat its blazing wings and made for the sky, passing close to the king. The wings his queen had worn as her signature, her familiar, the bird that she loved the most.

Selina chose her props with precision, and this final trick turned the tables irreversibly. The halcyon kingfisher was native to the Islands of Aquila, the lost queen's birthplace.

As it flew level with Robbie, something tugged on the creature's leg, and it struggled against a thread tied there. The witch pulled hard, and the creature faltered back into the Well, chirruping with distress.

The king searched blindly for the tiny creature and cried out his wife's name.

'No!' Robbie shouted with all that was left in him. It was too late. The king leapt back into the well. He watched the great man, his eyes shining with hope. Atlas fell with him to the end. And then he heard the roaring swell of black water below him as the Cloudbuster lifted the ladder out into a clear starry sky. The White Ocean was crashing against the volcano walls. The sea was pouring in from several weakened places, and that was the last Robbie saw of King Felian, his wolfhound, and Selina Carnal.

He was untied and lowered carefully into the Cloudbuster.

Patrick Dickie took one look at Robbie. 'Son of a bucket! You look like fish food.' He wasted no time. He took the bloodless hand and motionless leg and bandaged him up fast. 'Haul the king up! Help the kid,' Patrick shouted quickly, opening a bottle of Brandak.

Billy tugged Father Peter's sleeve.

'Not now, Billy. I'm trying to find north!'

'But father, it's the king.'

'He's caused enough trouble as it is. Austin Felian – get up here and help me find your land!'

'But he's not on the ladder,' said Billy with tears in his young eyes. 'There's nobody on the ladder.' He sobbed. The ladder swung loose and light below them.

There was a long silence. Father Peter closed his eyes and slumped forward. Patrick put his arm around Billy and held him close. He'd suspected it all along and hoped for a change in the fates. But, like Magatha used to say, some fates don't change.

'He stayed to find the queen, didn't he?' asked the pirate. Robbie nodded. 'The fool,' he whispered. 'The poor, crazy fool.'

'Patrick, unless you have something useful to say, please refrain and concentrate on keeping that Man of the Road alive. I'm not losing anyone else this evening.'

The pirate obediently shut up. He had never seen Father Peter lose his temper. He bent over Robbie's leg, trying to stop the blood.

The Cloudbuster found north, and the sun appeared. It looked deathly pale, and cold clung to the sun like a mourning veil. The sky began to warm up the closer they got to Landfelian.

It was a sombre party that landed on the right side of the Misty Mountains before Celador. The Cloudbuster made a silent swoop into the courtyard of the castle, where the godmothers and the herald were waiting to meet them; small figures wrapped in colourful scarves and holding burning torches. They looked anxiously at the passengers.

'Are you all alive? I think someone may have lost a limb – my toenail fell off. Oh, thank God it wasn't you, Billy.' She petered out after a quick head count. 'And the king?'

A silent shake of Father Peter's head confirmed it.

'Oh no.' Maggie's eyes filled with tears. The herald bowed his head and closed his eyes. There was no time to discuss how it had happened. She watched two young, still bodies be carefully lifted out.

'Hello, Mags.'

'Patrick.' She smiled, surprised to see her old pirate love. 'Quickly, take them inside.'

The herald helped by summoning several footmen.

Jan clutched the Father's hand. 'Everyone, upstairs – the fires are lit. Peter, you look four hundred years old. We must warm you up.'

'Selina,' he mumbled, 'she's back, worse than ever.'

Maggie shook her head. 'First things first: we must get these young warriors beating again.' She squeezed his hand. 'In time you will tell us what came to pass.'

'Yes, yes, of course.' He ran a weary hand over his eyes.

'I need a wooden spoon, porridge, honey, lavender, and holy basil. Do we have any St John's wort and a sweet voice? Is Amber back yet?'

'They are not far away,' the herald confirmed. 'They sent a squirrelgram from the first village they passed. The spiderlings stopped following them not far from the Forest of Thin Pines.'

'Oh, thank goodness.'

Neither of the godmothers were trained nurses, but they picked up the most practical utensils and used them to great effect.

'Billy, fill both their rooms with plants from the garden – nothing dried or pressed, only living and green things. A young birch tree if possible. And when the horses return, send them in. Both our heroes need to hear and smell life around them. No sad thoughts, please.'

She clapped her hands and disappeared into the kitchen to begin.

It took seven days. Seven days for Red and Robbie to wake up. The plants breathed in the trauma and puffed it out the open windows, through which the smell of leaves and rain blew in. The horses snorted and padded about outside their windows, filling the air with comforting, earthly sounds. The beds were soft, the fires young and crackling, and the tea sweet. Their wounds were cleaned and bandaged and ointments from the godmothers had been dropped on the muslins. The two witches worked hard to keep any lingering fog away. They kept bonfires alight, played music, and did some thorough sweeping of the courtyard. The fog seemed to disperse like steam, leaving the castle in the South Realm vivid and free once more.

Red woke first and asked quietly, 'Is it over?'

This was followed by a second, much deeper sleep in which she was too exhausted for the clatter of dreams or the scrape of nightmares.

Magatha closed the door to find Father Peter. 'She doesn't know.'

'We'll tell her when she's healed.'

Red listened to them leave her chamber. She knew. She'd known in the Cloudbuster. Her father was lost to her. They had been reunited for a few minutes in the sky. In that fleeting moment, she knew he loved her and always would. It burned bright and white between them and was constant like an invisible thread.

On the eighth day, she sat up. Was it night? It was hard to tell. The birds were singing, it was dawn; she could hear them through the window. The birds had come back to Celador.

Amber Morningstar was asleep in a chair next to her bed. The room was lit with tall, yellow candles. She could see an early apricot sky outside.

'I know this place.' She looked around her. 'Celador.'

She was upstairs in her parents' room. Gingerly, she tried one foot, then the other, and slowly wobbled to the window. Apart from the ache of her bones, she felt well. The room was covered with trailing green leaves, ferns, and potted heathers. Her wrist was in a sling, and she stared at it sympathetically. Her stomach yowled and her throat was dry.

Red walked silently out of the room into a dimly lit landing. She was only half awake, the rest of her somewhere very quiet and peaceful. She stood outside a door for a moment and listened. Afraid of what she might find, she pushed it open and held her breath.

Robbie lay there, bandaged up and unable to move – and therefore unable to escape Will. The actor had thankfully stopped reciting from his book of poetry and fallen asleep on a pile of blankets. Although he snored like a warthog. The sun was beginning to rise and a warm red light cast a glowing beam over the floor and bed.

Robbie heard the door creak open and watched two long, pale feet hobble towards the bed. A soft shawl of deep auburn hair grazed his eyelashes and brushed across his face. Two anxious green eyes studied his face and his bruised limbs.

'Hello.' She spoke quietly. 'Can you hear me?'

'Hello,' he croaked. 'Yes.'

'How are you?' She looked at him full of hope.

'I am a bandage.'

Red smiled with relief. 'It's not that bad.' A tear dripped off her nose and fell onto the pillow. His eyes were dragon-coloured again.

'You're crying on me. That can't be good.'

'I'm getting on,' she warned him.

'What?'

'The bed.'

'Oh.'

She climbed up with difficulty and lay very still beside him. Her heart beat through his bandages and her presence warmed up one side of him. Robbie couldn't even pinch himself, let alone hold her hand. He could be imagining it, although dreams didn't normally hobble or smell of lavender, fields, and princess. He looked at her bandaged wrist and the pale blue marks on her neck. Her stomach gurgled.

'Are you hungry?' he asked. 'I'm afraid now is not the best time to ask for an omelette.' He could not hold a whisk unless it was put into his mouth. 'Give me a few days.'

Red laughed next to him. She frowned at his bandaged arm and leg. 'Does it hurt?'

'Not as much as Will's poetry reading.'

'Thank you for coming for me.'

Robbie looked at her. 'Your father …'

Red swallowed back the sadness. 'I know. He had to see if my mother was there, in the darkness. I would have done the same.' She would have done if it was Robbie's life the witch taunted her with. She would have returned to fight.

They listened to Will snore. Will had not left Robbie's side since he'd returned to Celador. He had announced that they were practically brothers and it was his role to nurse him and fill the room with verse.

Someone was awake downstairs – they heard feet thudding about and preparations for tea. Red shifted when she heard noises outside.

'Please don't leave.' Pain shot up and down Robbie's damaged leg. He tried to sit up.

Red lay next to him until he settled. She unclenched his fraught fists, splayed out his fingers, and gently held his good hand.

They remained like this for the rest of the day and the next night. Robbie floated in and out of consciousness. In his dreams, he fought the witch, the skreekes, and the fog.

Red didn't leave. She was home. She waited until Death got bored, accepted defeat, stood up from his perch, and vanished from the room. She listened to Robbie breathe and closed her eyes. For now, that was all that mattered.

LANDFELIAN
STILL PLACES NEWSLETTER
DECEMBER EDITION

Daniel Blackwood is missing a hand. He aches for the one that got away and searches for her in the darkness of his mind. The king should have taken his head. The fog has him, nothing human remains.

We do not know where the king is. Even the eagles cannot find him as they fly over the Ridge of Shadows. The Well of Loneliness has been reclaimed by the sea. Nothing remains.

The questing heroes are on their way back. Fireworks lit up the sky, as the king promised, guiding them home and marking their return to Landfelian.

The Blackwood Guards have disappeared. Abandoned drums and boots have been found in dykes and ditches across the land. It is rumoured that they have all fled south over the mountains into the Hinterland, heading towards the new kingdom in the south, Mirador, where the Knight rules over a growing land.

Hardplace Prison is unmanned, and a bearded lady has just opened the gates.

The fog has retreated from the South Realm while the rogue witch gathers herself for the final battle. It still lingers over the pockets of the kingdom. But where hope has been restored, it has no hold.

The last princess was left a crown, the young Man of the Road a sword. For the moment, the herald puts both objects in the airing cupboard until their time.

*Join Red's journey in Book 3
of the series, coming soon*

ACKNOWLEDGEMENTS

- CC Book Design – Cherie Chapman for designing the most beautiful cover.

- Sally Parker – map illustrator extraordinaire. Thank you, Sally!

- For Maddy, Carl, and the Softwood Self-Publishing team for finally making it happen.

- Philippa Donovan at Smart Quill Editorial for reading the first draft of this monster and believing in it.

- Melissa Hyder and Tilda Johnson at the Golden Egg Academy for all the editing, bolstering, and brilliance.

- To my family and friends for the inspiration.

- To the Tripod.

- To Fred and Bridget for choosing me.

- To Ben, my husband, for everything else.

10% of every book bought for the first 2 years will be going to Ormiston Families, a charitable trust devoted to helping children and families in need in the East of England where I live.

Previous works by Rebeca Fox:

Leaping Beauty
The 1st book in the Landefelian
Adventure series.

Find out more at:
www.tinytruths.co.uk